St Helens Libraries

P

The Gessami Residence

The Gessami Residence

JANE L GIBSON

Matador
9 Priory Business Park,
Wistow Road, Kibworth Beauchamp,
Leicestershire. LE8 0RX
Tel: 0116 279 2299
Email: books@troubador.co.uk
Web: www.troubador.co.uk/matador
Twitter: @matadorbooks

ISBN 978 1784625 030

British Library Cataloguing in Publication Data.
A catalogue record for this book is available from the British Library.

Printed and bound by CPI Group (UK) Ltd, Croydon, CR0 4YY
Typeset in 11pt AldineBT401 by Troubador Publishing Ltd, Leicester, UK

This book is dedicated to my girlfriends.

*Those girls who are there for me no matter what. Helping me
to laugh, have fun and drink a little too much on occasion.
You're both my shopping companions and my inspiration. More
importantly you are my best friends and always listen to me
when I need to talk. You are with me through good times or bad
and have entertained me so many times that I have lost count.
Life would be far less colourful without you.*

Thank you for being you.

Chapter 1

Chapter 1

I t had been three long years since my husband Paul had passed away suddenly. James and Mark, my two sons, had left home and gone to university and had a life of their own. At only forty-three I was starting to feel my age, although my three best friends Amanda, Elizabeth and Rose were always there to encourage me into seeing the brighter side of life.

Elizabeth, or 'Beth', being the oldest of all four of us had just divorced her very selfish and irritating husband and was definitely ready for some 'me' time. Amanda had long since thought that her husband was actually a cardboard cut-out, as his input into their relationship had resulted in a very non-existent role. She had often wondered if he was having an affair, but then decided that he was too lazy to even be bothered with that malarkey! Rose was the youngest of the four of us; she had at one point dated and been engaged to my husband's friend Robert, but she decided that she didn't want children and wanted to pursue her career. It ended amicably and she has remained one of our best friends for the last fifteen years.

So it transpired after a very heavy drinking session one night in town, that we all needed to get away for a couple of weeks; after all there were three of us that were single and Amanda was just ready to have a change of scenery. It hadn't really occurred to me that the getting away was going to be an issue, until both Amanda and Beth decided they had missed out on their youth and wanted to *'live it up'* and get a good look at some *'younger men'* or in fact any *'eye candy'* would suffice, and of course drink plenty during the process. Probably a bad idea then that we let Rose decide where we were going and when, and then let her do all of the arranging of hotels, flights and payments and so on. She did have her own exclusive travel business and so it seemed the right thing to do, but as I dragged my suitcase down to the taxi that was waiting outside, to say that I was nervous was a complete understatement.

The early morning flight from Manchester Airport meant I felt half asleep – make-up was not my forte and at this time even worse. Rose had given us strict instructions to be at the airport for 6am sharp, to meet by the information desk in the terminal. We had been told what we would need to bring for the two-week duration, but we were still none the wiser as to where we were going. It all seemed very cloak-and-dagger, a little exciting I suppose but quite honestly I had got used to just being by myself of late, and so I wasn't sure how this whole 'girls getting away' weekend was going to pan out. My boys had told me the holiday would do me good, and as I am always stating that I feel old, perhaps this girls' holiday is just what I need.

Remarkably, as I exited the taxi at the terminal Amanda was just arriving and so I quickly rushed over to her. She seemed glad to see me too.

"Have you any idea where we are going?" I asked her hopefully.

"Not the slightest, but as some of us are on a budget I'm presuming not somewhere particularly five-star or exclusive, although Barbados would have been nice, or Mexico, or perhaps Miami would have been fun?" she chirped happily. She seemed much more relaxed about this than I was.

We strolled to the information desk inside; Rose was hopping around as if on hot coals as we walked toward her, her excitement all too obvious. She threw her arms around Amanda firstly and then myself. "I cannot tell you how excited I am about this trip," she confessed.

"Really? We wouldn't have guessed!" Amanda sarcastically replied as she turned and looked for Beth. Rose gave her a very sarcastic look in response. "Are we the first ones here? I thought Beth would have been raring to go."

"Yep, first ones here. It's going to be great; some time together has been long overdue, away from all of our miserable distractions," Rose stated. "What did Gerry have to say about you coming?" she then asked Amanda sincerely. Amanda stood her case up on its end and rested her arm on the extended handle.

"Really? Do you honestly think that he's even noticed that I've gone? God it's like living with a robot: same routine every day; same expression, same responses. I will be extremely surprised if he even notices any difference for at least a week and then he will probably get fed up of having to cook, so that will be the only reason he misses me." She sounded honest in her comments, but we all knew that whatever she said about Gerry, it was obvious that he cared a lot about her. They had been married for twenty-five years and that in itself was enough to make any relationship a little stale.

"Oh come on, Amanda," I said. "At least you have him to moan about, eh?" I reminded her, trying to imply that it is better than my situation. She promptly stood and looked at me and then reached out and rubbed my arm.

"Yes, you're right. I'm so sorry, Jenny, I wasn't thinking," she grimaced. Luckily without having to dwell we were interrupted by the sound of Beth and when we turned it took us all a second to respond.

There she was, doing her best impression of a celebrity of some sort; big sunglasses, fake tan, wide brim hat and a very bright pink pair of cropped jeans along with a white linen top. We stared, she reached us took off her sunglasses and then in her own unique way simply said, "Tah dah!" and did us all a quick spin.

"Bloody hell, I don't know whether that puts the rest of us to shame or makes us look more mature?" Amanda was first to say.

"What? Oh come on – I was not going to pass up spending some of my divorce money on new outfits and hats and a tan, et cetera. It's a girls' holiday and I feel like being girly," Beth replied smiling as she popped her sunglasses back on.

"Well I think you look great," I said before trying not to smile too much. In fairness it wasn't the outfit that was a problem, it was more the fact that I would expect someone half her age to be wearing it. But good on her for having the confidence to do so I thought, I wish that I were that brave.

"I think you look good too actually, Beth, not quite sure what you were aiming for but I would probably say it's along the lines of Samantha from *Sex and the City*," Rose diplomatically said. Beth lowered her sunglasses for a moment and then shrugged her shoulders.

"I can live with that," she replied smugly.

We all quickly greeted each other properly and then made our way to the check-in desk following Rose like well-behaved school children. She stopped before we joined the queue and then faced us all. Oh God, this was the big reveal – I could feel it brewing and I hoped for something more than camping in France!

"Alright ladies, I think that I have held you in suspense for long enough. Due to the fact that a couple of us were on tighter budgets, I have had to bear that in mind with all other factors including food, drinking, the hotel and of course the eye candy." She stopped a moment as we all stood there eyebrows raised waiting to find out. "We are going to... Ibiza!" she excitedly expressed. With her hands clapping along in excitement, she obviously knew that was definitely not what we were expecting as no one spoke for a long while we just stood and looked at her.

"I'm sorry, run that by me again," Amanda said shaking her head.

"Ibiza, we're going to Ibiza," she confirmed again.

"That's what I thought you said," Amanda replied before rubbing her head. "Are you nuts? Have you seen

5

how old we are? Ibiza is full of twenty-one-year-olds trying to drink themselves to death, while partying in foam until about five in the morning," she finished.

"And your point being?" Rose then asked. "It is what you wanted. It's not all like that honestly, you're wrong, and it was one of the only places that ticked all of the boxes. Hey guys, don't get mad at me now, I spent ages on this." Rose sounded sad at our response and I felt sorry for her.

"Rose, I'm sure that you have spent an inordinate amount of time on planning, so thank you for that," I said trying to calm the others. I then turned to Amanda and Beth. "Come on, girls, it wasn't really about where we were going anyway, it was more about the fact that we went together. God it could have been a caravan in Scarborough for all I care, it will simply be good to be in each other's company." I tried to convince them, but I really don't know why because I was thinking exactly the same as Amanda.

Just as I finished speaking a group of around eight young men (we're probably talking early-to mid-twenties), arrived and walked past us and started queuing at the same desk. We all stopped and stared as they were overexcited and noisy and then I tried to carry on, but Beth had other ideas. "Well I don't care where we're going as long as you get me on the same plane as them," she remarked as she joined the queue behind them. We all watched her and then looked at each other and joined her and became mesmerised as she started flirting, then we started laughing, something that I hoped we would be doing a lot of!

Once we checked in and after trying to get Beth to stop following the poor men she seemed convinced that she was now somehow attached to, Rose insisted that we had a glass of champagne. Slightly early in the morning for me, but never the less I had decided to 'go with the flow' and so we perched ourselves on the stools at the bar and asked the waiter for a bottle – far more cost effective. Needless to say that giggling like teenagers became our main priority as we relived previous trips, which had not happened for at least three years due to different commitments from everyone. After the second glass, Amanda said that she was already relaxed just to be away from her mundane life, and she in particular said quite honestly she didn't care now where we were going. Rose was ecstatic that we were simply actually at the airport, and I think that she revelled in the knowledge that she had organised the whole thing. Beth moaned about the fact we had stopped her from tailing the poor guys from earlier, but we reassured her she would have the chance to do plenty of that when we got there. For me, I simply thanked them for being my friends, and in particular for their support over the last three years; it made me extremely proud to have friends like them, and I knew that a large part of our not going away was due to how they felt about my situation.

"Ah, thanks, Jenny," Beth replied as she rubbed my arm.

"Well, that just changed the mood slightly." Amanda grimaced. "Yeah, we love you too, but let's move on from this sombre confirmation," she finished as she winked at me to show that she was jesting. I wiped my slightly damp eyes and then Rose raised her glass.

"To us, the best friends we could ever possibly have," she toasted. We all smiled and then clinked glasses. "To us."

We decided to do some duty free shopping, stocking up on make-up and perfume mainly and I purchased a new pair of sunglasses. Gucci, none the less; the ones that I had Paul had bought me about ten years ago and they were a little old and scratched. It was apparent that we were noisier than we should have been; everyone kept looking at us as they walked through, and with the help of the staff in there I think that we all had at least two different types of perfume sprayed on us. The other passengers had no idea what they had let themselves in for. Breakfast consisted of a quick bacon sandwich and then before we knew it, boarding was starting.

"We're in business class," Rose suddenly informed us.

"Excellent," Beth and Amanda chirped.

"How on earth did we afford that?" I asked.

"I know someone who has the power," Rose laughed. "Luxury is what I aimed for, so more drinks on board."

"Actually, Rose, I take everything back I said before. This is panning out nicely," Amanda concluded.

Rose dragged us to the front of the queue once business class had been confirmed to board first. For some reason it felt somewhat embarrassing, but not for Beth however who made it her sole duty to deliberately squeeze past the young guys from earlier, winking at them as she went while they chided her about being in the 'posh' section.

Beth was lapping it up; Amanda grabbed her elbow and told her to leave them alone as they were young enough to be her sons. Probably not the best thing to say at this point, Beth was not happy and asked her if she was going to ruin all her chances at getting laid while we were away.

"For God's sake, is that all you think about?" Amanda retorted.

Beth laughed; "Yes, actually, right now it is."

Take-off was not my favourite part of the flight; Paul used to always hold my hand as I wasn't the best flier. The seats helped as I wasn't crammed in too tightly to Amanda at the side of me, she saw the look on my face and remembered and without thinking squeezed my hand. The cabin crew brought around some pre-flight drinks for us and that helped. Amanda leant over and whispered, "It won't take long, and then we will be at the 'Adventure Island'. Think about that for a while, you may even hook up with a tanned and handsome Ibizan!" she remarked happily.

I shot her a look of question. "Hey, I'm not Beth; I didn't come on this trip just to get laid, you know."

"Yeah, but you never know. I think a holiday romance would be perfect to get you back in the saddle," she laughed.

"Are you wishing us all into bed with men, because you can't? Or is it just your dirty mind?" I then asked.

"A little bit of both I think. Hell, I would if I were you, as long as he hadn't just come out of nappies, which seems to be Beth's choice." She laughed a little more, which set me off too.

"Erm, hello, I am sat just here you know," Beth then commented as she punched Amanda's arm. Amanda however, carried on, laughing much to Beth's disgust, then she realised it was a little harsh as Beth too had recently had a pretty tough time.

"Hey, I'm just teasing, you go for it girl if you can get it," she finished as the air hostess arrived with more drinks for us. During all the conversation I realised I had been distracted from take-off, which I was now sure was Amanda's plan all along. She noted my realisation and tipped her glass to me.

"Chin chin," she expressed before chinking my glass. I reciprocated.

The flight was pretty quick in fairness, the food not bad either and before we knew it the captain had announced that we were descending towards the airport. Beth rubbed her hands together; during the flight she had moved the curtain behind her numerous times to try and see the young men she had accosted earlier. Every time she turned back to her chair with a grin on her face after miming God knows what to them in economy. Rose was busy getting things ready for our airport pick-up and, as she was super organised, she had booked a car to collect us and take us to the hotel. When the wheels hit the runway, Amanda let out a small whoop and Beth then high-fived her. It was obvious they were very happy to be here and that was great, although I hoped that the behaving like eighteen-year-olds would settle down just a little!

The carousel beeped and then the handlers started to feed the bags through very slowly, after fifteen minutes everyone's bag had arrived except mine. I was just starting to panic slightly when I saw it appear at the top of the belt and slide its way around to me. It didn't fill me with confidence to think that I may have to share everyone else's eclectic choice of clothing, so when I pulled it from the carousel I patted it in appreciation that it hadn't got lost in transit.

"Right, let's go," Rose instructed as she marched on in front. We all followed feeling happier than when she first told us where we were going. Beth suddenly then spoke turning to us first;

"You know that film '*The Hangover*'? Maybe this is our kind of version of that," she laughed.

"I bloody hope not, I don't think I would survive that," I replied honestly.

"Well, unless Bradley Cooper is around… then that could change the decision?" Amanda enquired.

"Will you lot stop going on about getting drunk and getting laid? If we attempted anything like that quantity of drinking it would probably take about five days for us to recover… Well, it would take you three that long, being older of course," Rose then chipped in smiling from ear to ear.

"I've just decided that I don't like you anymore," Amanda said with a tone of sarcasm.

"You'll be this age at some point you know," Beth then added. Rose just shook her head and laughed;

"Well, as long as I act my age and certainly dress my age I'll be fine," she mimicked at Beth's appearance.

"Yeah, yeah – you're only jealous that I can pull this off," she replied while straightening her blouse.

Beth had for many years been very subdued in her clothing department. As her marriage started to fail a few years ago she started doing more of what she wanted, rather than what her husband expected. It had resulted in a very flamboyant and colourful Beth which I liked, actually. She was now dressing more like her personality and for all intents and purposes it made her happy. I linked arms with her in reassurance and continued dragging my bag. As we walked through the exit to arrivals, the brightness of the sun hit us all straight away and so we quickly reached for our sunglasses.

As promised there was a luxurious air-conditioned car waiting for us, which was a welcome retreat from the intense heat. The driver placed all of our bags into the boot, and just as I was about to climb in behind Rose and Amanda there was a sudden barrage of questions from the same group of young men that had caught Beth's eye in Manchester.

"Hey sexy lady with the big hat. Where are you going?" the tall blond one asked with expressive confidence. Beth turned and looked at them and I turned from the car door.

"Why, do you want to join us?" she quipped.

"For goodness sake, Beth, I didn't come on holiday to babysit for two weeks," Amanda chided her. Beth turned to the car and shushed Amanda which made both Rose and I laugh.

"My holiday is just not going to be the same without you," he then shouted as he held his hands to his heart and mimed undying love. "When will I see you again?" he asked as his friends simply laughed and pushed him to keep going.

"Oh honey, you couldn't keep up with me; not enough stamina, but if I bump into you I promise to let you buy me a drink," Beth then finished before blowing a big kiss and then climbing in the car.

At this point the driver was laughing to himself, and Rose, Amanda and I were simply staring at her. She let out a deep breath and then took off her sunglasses and looked at us, before banging her feet simultaneously on the floor and giggling like a schoolgirl. "I'm loving this, it's so much fun," she confirmed as she threw her head back and laughed. What else could we do but join her. We took in all of the sights on the way from the airport as we travelled toward our destination for the next two weeks; the scenery, it had to be said, was stunning.

Chapter 2

The car slowed at the impressive entrance of the Golden Palm Hotel. We all stared at the grand facade and then commented on how well Rose had done getting us into such a place on our budgets. Although San Antonio was well known for its clubbing and party scene, I have to say that this hotel had completely changed my opinion. It only got better as she then told us we had a two-bedroom suite, one of only four. The driver kindly gave us our bags and told us to have a good holiday, and then he left to continue with his day. Our bags glided over the cool cream marble floor, and as we walked to the reception we were very impressed with the overall look of the hotel and commented many times at Rose's fine decision.

Once checked in we rode the lift to the eighth floor (the top floor) and entered the room. It was very white: white leather sofa; white walls; white voile curtains; white linen; white tiling. The only thing not white was the cream carpet, which somehow looked like a mistake alongside everything else. It was however spacious, it had a small tea and coffee kitchenette area and the bedrooms were big and cool. Amanda slid open the doors to the balcony and then called us.

"Wow! Guys, you have to look at this view!" she said as we all made our way over. It was beautiful; a white sandy beach, shallow water leading to moored boats and some of them expensive looking too. The pool was below us and palm trees surrounded one side creating some welcome shade I suspect. There weren't as many people on the beach as I had expected for early afternoon.

"Have we arrived out of party season?" I asked innocently. Rose laughed;

"No, Jenny, you have to remember that people here party until six in the morning or later – so they sleep most of the day."

"Ah of course, stupid thing to say." I shook my head.

"Well it actually may work in our favour, being older and obviously unable to take in the party scene as Rose suggested, will mean that we have our pick of the sun loungers," Amanda then said.

"Very true, but surely young people wouldn't be able to afford to stay here?" Beth asked as she turned to Rose. Rose replied honestly;

"Well, in fairness, I was surprised at the deal I did receive on this. It has great write-ups, so I can't understand why more wouldn't stay, there seemed to be plenty of rooms left."

"Maybe it's a little too minimalistic? I mean, if you were twenty-one you would want to be in the centre of all the action, surely?" Beth then commented. We all agreed that she was probably right, as this hotel was a little way from the main areas. "It may mean that we have more exclusive men staying here," she winked at us.

"Oh God, we're back to sex again," Amanda said and we all sighed and laughed a little and left her on the balcony.

"What?" she asked. "I don't know what your problem is," she said as she followed us. We didn't comment but simply went to our rooms to unpack.

I had drawn Rose's name out to share a room with, it only needed me to pick being only four of us, but while on the plane Beth had moaned about Amanda's snoring and Rose had said she didn't want to share a room with Beth and a bevy of men, so while up in the air Rose wrote our names on a piece of paper shook them up in her hand and asked me to pick one. She seemed happy with my selection, and as much as Beth and Amanda moaned about each other they were only jesting as they had been close friends for nearly twenty years. Initially they met at work, a large insurance brokers in which they worked in the same office for nearly eight years. Amanda then decided to move to a smaller firm and Beth fancied a complete change two years after that and was offered a job with a client as a personal assistant. Beth still maintains to this day, that this was the best decision she ever made as she loves her job. Amanda still finds it difficult to find any excitement in insurance these days but continues to work in the same industry for fear of finding nothing else.

I had met Amanda in my late teens; she was dating Jonathan, who was one of my best friends at the time, and so we spent many weekends together along with my boyfriend, Matt. That was a long romance for me of nearly two years, but then he moved down to London when he was offered a unique opportunity to finish his architectural qualification with a large London-based firm. Commuting from Manchester to London every weekend we knew was never going to viable while I was studying, and so we ended our relationship amicably and kept in touch and still do, remarkably. Amanda's short-lived relationship with Jonathan, of only nine months, was a shame, but Amanda and I got on really well and so had been friends since then. Jonathan had drifted a little after their break up as it was awkward for him to be around me and her at the same time. I hadn't heard anything from him after he joined an accountancy firm in Leeds, which I always thought was a shame and it wasn't from not trying. He'd found a new life and a new circle of friends but I always wished him well.

We unpacked, got our swimsuits on – or in Rose's case, bikini – and with covering beachwear we headed straight down to the pool. The poolside grill meant we could eat first after having been on the go for so long and then we lay down and soaked up the rays for about three hours. We had all taken an array of books with us; this was good as I never seemed to be able to focus long enough to read at home. The silence in the house meant I ended up looking around for something physical to do. I craved our regular girls' Wednesday lunches and every other Friday or Saturday night we tried to meet for a meal or drinks. I didn't realise how much I relied on these meetings with my friends until Paul had died; listening to my best friends and their troubles for a few hours was a great escape from my own.

The beach had become crowded from around three thirty onwards, and it was alive with the voices of the young people who had emerged from the rooms of the neighbouring hotels, after a long session of alcohol and dancing among other things I suspect. They were starting to get rowdier as the day progressed and this highlighted to us that the best time for peace and quiet was obviously mornings and early afternoon. By six o'clock there was music and more noise and suddenly it felt like we were in Ibiza!

We decided to retreat to our rooms and take a shower, so that we could venture out into the town and see what all the fuss was about. By the time we were ready to leave it was seven thirty and we decided to have a drink in the bar first. Beth ordered us all cocktails and insisted that they were her treat; after recent events she was just glad to have us all there with her. We laughed and talked and had another drink before deciding to venture outside. Amanda asked the barman which was the best place to start and he briefly pointed us in the right direction. I suppose we should have half expected to know what to see, but being out of the loop for so long made the venture into town a complete eye-opener.

To say that we got a few funny looks was an understatement, probably due to the fact that we obviously had far too many clothes on based on what these young girls were wearing, which boiled down to something about the size of the hand towel in my room – and that was a dress! We must have been staring as much as them: there were boys necking shots faster than you could count, girls doing pretty much the same, people falling over so drunk they couldn't stand at only nine fifteen pm. I cannot tell you how many couples we counted who were aiming for death by tongue-down-your-throat, and the hands that were wandering were embarrassing for me to even look at. The music was loud from one bar to another and hurt the ears at times as each bar competed for a louder environment than the next.

We didn't even think about stopping, we just walked and watched and walked some more. As the street we were on started to quieten just a little and we felt like we had just left a war zone, Beth spotted a little bar by the beach which looked quieter and far more civilised so she pointed and grabbed Amanda by the elbow and dragged her along as we followed. She ordered us all beer and said that we needed something to quench our now dry mouths from so much gawping; at this point we still hadn't spoken and were dazed. We all drank quickly and then Amanda spoke. "Well, I wasn't expecting that! I mean I've seen it on TV and I thought I knew what was going on at places like this – but witnessing it is another thing entirely. I feel exhausted just watching them – I'm sure our partying days at their age weren't that bad."

"Oh I don't know, Amanda. You've recounted numerous times of being drunk and making out with guys in your teens while dressing inappropriately." Beth reminded her.

"Yes, but at least I was dressed. I had clothing on. Inappropriate or not it covered the essentials – but these girls?" she relayed to us. We all looked at her for a minute and then started laughing and reliving what we had just seen.

"I don't know why you're laughing Jenny, your boys will be on holiday living it up like them,"

Rose then said while raising her eyebrows sarcastically. I threw my head in my hands and grimaced. "Oh please, I hope not – I don't want to think about that!"

"Well I know my son lived it up on his holidays, and he had no problem telling me about each time he did either," Beth then added.

"Great," I said before taking another large gulp of beer. "My only concern is that we have to walk back through that." They all then sighed.

"Well, can I make a suggestion then?" Amanda asked. We all shrugged and said why not. "Let's get out-of-control drunk ourselves and then it may not bother us as much."

"Oh I don't think that's a good idea," I replied, thinking it had been a long time since I had consumed a lot of alcohol in one sitting.

"Well, I think it's a great idea. Let's get our party started," Beth agreed and Rose seemed intent on drinking a ridiculous amount too. I decided that I was not going to get my own way on this and I would have to join in.

Five drinks down in the small beach bar gave way to a slightly bizarre head rush. We laughed, laughed some more and by the time the sixth drink came which was another cocktail, I was fast becoming drunk. I could feel my legs doing that slightly merry little dance they do when your head's not quite telling them what to do properly. Rose had been dancing in the middle of the floor to the numerous better songs that were played. It was commented on many times that apart from the few good songs around today, most of what they played in these bars, classed as modern pop, was like a head-pumping noise and nothing more. We craved some good old eighties music, something that we could dance to. So we took the brave decision to move back into the hustle of the town, knowing damn well that we were going to get more inquisitive stares.

"On the bright side, they are probably so drunk now that they won't even notice us," Beth stated hopefully.

"Sod them, we are here to enjoy ourselves just like them. However, you will not be seeing me in a dress like they're wearing," Amanda insisted.

"Thank God for that!" I piped up with a slight slur. "Mixing these drinks is not a good idea," I then finished while I leant on Amanda apologetically.

"Hey, don't be leaning on me after that," she laughed pushing me upright again.

"I'm heading down a slippery slope," I informed them.

"Good," Rose laughed. "It's great to see you letting your hair down."

I scowled. "You may not agree in the morning."

We finished the drinks and stood and decided that we would make our way back to the main street that we had first walked down. It was noisier, and busier than previously, but on the plus side I didn't care and they did look far drunker than us. It was eleven thirty now and I knew another hour of this would see me needing to head back; the last thing I wanted was to be sick for the next two days, which at this rate was looking likely. Amanda was talking to everyone and anyone with Beth. Rose walked along with me but she was obviously scanning the crowds, and who could blame her? She was only thirty-five and had the body of a twenty-one-year-old; an exercise fanatic. That, mixed with her long brown hair and the skin of a woman ten years younger, was a combination causing attraction. I was just about to ask where we were heading as the bright lights and head-thumping noise were fast adding to my feeling of complete lack of control, when Beth shouted, "Yeah" and started heading toward a bar called Liquid Disco! I understood why as we got closer and caught them up; Madonna's 'Holiday' was playing and it instantly lifted my mood.

We walked inside and although not huge in comparison to some of the other bars, the atmosphere was great. There were some slightly older people in here which made us feel a little less alien. It was my round and so to ease the heavy alcohol I ordered four Sol with lime. It was necessary at this point to have something refreshing and that seemed like the perfect choice. With bottles in hand, Amanda manoeuvred us to the dance floor, the song had nearly finished and so our hope was that the eighties continued...We weren't disappointed when Soft Cell's 'Tainted Love' started which pulled most of the bar onto the dance floor with us and made for a great start to our dancing. It was like reliving our days of partying in our teens and twenties and suddenly

I felt far happier being here, so I told myself to just enjoy it.

Around seven songs later I had to take a break with Beth. We went to the bar and got a diet coke just to quench our thirst; it was heaven to my taste buds which were now getting that acid kickback from too much alcohol. We laughed at Rose and Amanda who were now in full swing, dancing around the floor with two guys who were probably in their early thirties. It was obvious what the guys were thinking as they were grinding close and Amanda's face was a picture as it started to dawn on her, so she made her excuses and made her way to us. I quickly told Beth not to let on we only had coke – Amanda would not be impressed with us if she realised this. She slumped herself across the bar;

"Holy crap. I thought he was going to just get his penis out right there!" she joked. We laughed agreeing that it was steamier than she realised. "What you drinking?" she then asked looking at me, but Beth was quick to answer.

"Rum and coke."

"Excellent idea." Amanda slurred a little as she leaned over and asked the barman for one. I looked at Beth and she just winked at me.

"We hopefully will recover quicker in the morning," she whispered.

We sat back and watched as Rose was getting attention from around four guys now that seemed intent on surrounding her. She could handle herself and this we knew, but as they started manhandling her, we all decided that we should step in. So we manoeuvred our way over and surrounded her and then mimed that it was probably time to leave and move on. We all exited into the humid hot air and realised how nice it had been to be in the cool air inside. Walking along Rose then spotted a tequila bar. I grimaced as soon as she said it but we were already heading that way; two rounds later and that was me done. I could feel things starting to go out of focus slightly and quite honestly I needed my bed. As we had walked to a point where you could walk on the beach back to the hotel, I made my excuses and decided to head back. They did their best to deter me, but I just couldn't consume anything else. I told them to enjoy themselves and as I could see the hotel which didn't look too far I made my way back, which, truthfully, I soon realised was not as easy as I'd hoped, walking in sand with wedge heels on. As I made my way across the beach and they shouted goodnight I could hear Amanda; "Okay, just for the hell of it let's have one more shot here and then move on," she insisted. I was suddenly very glad that I was leaving.

Mumbling to myself and probably looking slightly insane, I struggled slowly through the sand, trying not to make eye contact with the many couples and crowds that were still partying hard. Sun loungers were now makeshift beds for making out, and I knew that I was staring occasionally. I now knew that I had enjoyed far too much drink, and that this dress was probably not the best idea, because if I fell arse over tit then I was sure going to be giving this whole beach a view of my knickers. I was trying my best as it was to hold it down in the cooler sea breeze and this was taking far too much concentration. I was so close to the steps that led to the hotel, but I could walk in those wedges no longer and so I stopped and bent down to take them off. Not my best decision of the night it would appear. I had just managed to unhook the strap from my heels when that nauseating dizziness hit me from being bent at a completely inappropriate angle after alcohol. I steadied myself by placing one hand out onto the sand and then as I lifted my feet to slip them off I felt myself going… sideways! I couldn't do anything but laugh, and as I sat up and took hold of my shoes, sand in my hair and dress, not in the most ladylike position, I wondered how the hell I was going to get up. I didn't think for long: as I rested my head on my knees looking toward the steps that I was aiming for, I saw two feet skip down them and appear in front of me;

"Are you alright?" a very smooth sounding voice asked. I followed the linen trousers up his legs to an open necked shirt, and then grimaced knowing someone had just witnessed all of that. But then his face, oh my God his face; chiselled, tanned, dark blond hair and piercing eyes. I swallowed but hadn't answered.

"I'm sorry what did you say?" I asked, not sounding too slurred.

"Are you alright? I was just sitting here with my friend and noticed your unfortunate tumble," he said in an understated way. Now I was embarrassed.

"Oh God, I am so drunk. What was I thinking?" I said disappointed at myself while hiding my head in my hands.

"If it's any consolation, I have seen worse," he then said with a tone of sarcasm, but it eased my embarrassment. I looked up from my hands and he had both of his reached out toward me. "May I help you?" he asked as he smiled and then he bobbed down a little nearer to meet my eyes.

He had very fine lines around his eyes, but they looked kind and genuine and as I took the sight of him again, I realised that he was probably in his forties like me. I smiled; I was at the hotel anyway so I had nothing to lose. I reached out my hands and placed them in his. His skin was warm and soft and as he squeezed my hands lightly he pulled me to standing. "Thank you," I quickly said as he let go of one hand and reached for my shoes.

"My pleasure. Are you staying here?" he gestured to the hotel.

"Yes, unfortunately for you it would seem," I replied. He laughed as he guided me up the stairs. His friend was stood at the top and also asked if I was alright. It was getting worse – two witnesses to my drunken state. I nodded sheepishly.

"I'll be with you in a minute, Josh," he then said as he continued past him while placing his arm around my waist.

"Sure, no rush," his friend replied.

"I'm sure I will be fine now, honestly," I remarked, but I knew without his help I would probably be taking one step forward and three to the side. He looked at me and smiled;

"Let's make sure you reach your room safely," he simply said, and knowing he was helping me I leaned into him a little, grateful for the support.

We entered the reception and then he asked which room I was staying in and I told him knowing I probably wouldn't get there alone. He pressed the button for the lift and we stood and waited when I caught a glimpse of myself in the reflective doors. I sighed.

"I'm not usually like this you know," I tried to convince him, he just smiled more. "My friends Amanda, Beth and Rose drove me to this," I added honestly.

"Well, you are in Ibiza, in one of the biggest partying towns," he remarked.

"Yes and think how much worse I would have been had I stayed out with them!" I then insisted as I prodded him on his chest – his very taught and firm chest which I stared at for a moment. Thank God the lift arrived right then, I knew I was blushing.

"They left you to make your own way back?" he asked sounding concerned.

"I insisted. I could see the hotel, I wasn't far away but it's just taken me longer than I thought walking in those stupid shoes," I replied tapping the heels that he held.

"You should be careful you know, these young men are out trying to grab anything they can. A beautiful woman like yourself could end up with too much attention," he then said. I smiled and looked at him.

"You're quite charming, aren't you?"

"I like to think so," he replied as he smiled more. I suddenly realised I had no idea who this guy was, and I was taking him to my room. What was I thinking? The lift stopped. "So, here to unwind for a while then?" he asked.

I tried to stand up straight and replied. "Just a girls'

holiday. It's been too long since we last did it for various reasons which I will not bore you with, but this is our first night here, so I'm not doing too well, am I? I never drink this much, I didn't want to drink this much because of this…" I then gestured to my state as we arrived at our room door.

"If this is a much-needed break, then I don't think there's any need to worry. No harm done, eh?" he kindly said. "May I?" he then asked as he gestured for my key. Slightly reluctantly I gave it to him, but I had no need to be nervous. He walked me in, placed my shoes on the floor and then turned to face me. "It was a pleasure meeting you," he remarked. I rubbed my forehead.

"Now I know you're being charming. I'm sure I looked a real sight," I replied sobering up faster than I could have hoped for.

"You definitely looked a sight, but not in the way that you're thinking," he said and I blushed again. I reached out my hand as a gesture of thanks to shake his, he took it and shook it willingly, looking at our hands all the while. "I didn't catch your name, only your friends'," he pointed out.

I smiled. "Jenny. It's Jenny," I said, a little flustered.

"Well, Jenny. I hope to see you again." He sounded hopeful.

"Preferably not like this!" I remarked. He laughed as he made his way out of the door.

"Goodnight. I hope tomorrow isn't too painful," he grimaced while still laughing. I rolled my eyes at his comment, and then he tucked his hands in his pockets and left towards the lift. It suddenly dawned on me that I had no idea what his name was, so I leant out from my door. The sight of him was delicious, cool and casual as he stood there and waited patiently.

"Hey!" I called as the lift arrived. He looked at me. "I didn't catch your name either?" He smiled.

"It's Ethan," he called back. "Good night, Jenny," he quietly said as he stepped into the waiting lift.

"Goodnight, Ethan, and thank you," I called back and then like a dream he was gone.

I closed the door, managed to pick up my shoes and went to get my pyjamas on. I thought about Ethan for a while as I drank a glass of water and then I looked through the window to the beach below that was still bustling with life. As I watched, I saw Ethan make his way back to his friend and while I stared from my unlit room I smiled. He sat and continued his drink and seemed deep in conversation, which was when I decided that the room was swaying a little again and my head was thumping. *Two paracetamols and bed,* I thought. *I need to switch off.* And as my head hit the pillow I was out cold.

Chapter 3

As I reached across to my nightstand to pick up my watch, I scowled at the sunlight that came through the voile curtains. No one had closed the blackout blinds and after that had hit my tired eyes and I managed to focus at my watch, it surprised me to note that it was nine thirty, later than I've slept recently. I sat on the edge of my bed and stretched, noticing then the bitter aftertaste of stale beer and other alcohol, which was still present even after managing to brush my teeth the previous night. I needed the bathroom, and wondering how badly the room might spin, before I stood I turned to see that Rose was fast asleep and still in her clothes. This made me believe that I was probably the best one out of us all this morning. I never heard them come back so for all I knew they may have only been in bed for a couple of hours! I sighed at my sorry state, took a deep breath then stood. Remarkably, I felt better upright than I had lying down. I made my way to our en-suite and splashed some cold water on my face, brushed my teeth brushed my hair and took a very much needed call of nature. Just as I was exiting the bathroom the doorbell rang. I froze, who could that be? Then I looked at Rose who had in her hand an ornament of some description.

Thoughts quickly raced through my mind and as the doorbell rang again she stirred, but I ran across to Amanda and Beth, both with eye masks on and both snoring. It rang again and then someone knocked, and as I shook them wondering if it was hotel management or the police after their long night partying, I started to panic when Amanda sat bolt upright and simply lifted her eye mask and scowled at me;

"You're up, will you please answer that bloody door?" she unhappily cried at me.

"Who the hell should be knocking on our door? What did you guys get up to last night? I hope you haven't invited the whole of Ibiza to our room," I remarked, now annoyed that none of them were moving. I placed my hands on my hips and stared at Amanda as the bell rang again, but this time someone called:

"Room service."

I paused and then walked toward the door, "Did you order something last night?" I shouted to Amanda who replied in a half state of waking.

"Not to my knowledge."

I slowly opened the door and there stood a very happy and bouncy waiter who pushed a large trolley into our room, filling the suite with the smell of bacon and warm pastries. Just as I was about to close the door another arrived filled with teas and coffees and juices. I looked at it all and then at the waiter;

"I'm sorry, we didn't order this," I said feeling sorry for his effort.

"You are Jenny?" he then asked as Amanda appeared.

"Yes, I'm Jenny," I nervously replied.

"There is a card with your breakfast, it is with compliments," the waiter said and then turned to leave the room. I was dazed. He had already left after telling us to enjoy when I realised that I never even tipped him.

With all the noise and the delicious smells, the others now appeared. Amanda just stared at me with her eyebrows raised, Rose was rubbing her eyes and yawning asking what all the fuss was about and Beth walked straight over and poured some coffee.

"Well?" Amanda asked as she looked at me. I shrugged and reached for the card. Opening it curiously I then smiled at the neatly written words.

Jenny, I hope that you can manage to eat something this morning. I promise it will help you feel much better. With compliments to you and your friends – please enjoy and recover well. I hope to be able to help you again soon! Ethan.

"Ethan," I remarked as Beth grabbed the card from my hand and read it out loud.

"Bloody hell! We leave you for a few hours and you find a man!" Amanda remarked walking over to read the card again herself. I blushed, remembering my embarrassment last night.

"Who the hell is Ethan?" Rose asked.

"It's a long story. What did you guys get up to anyway?" I asked.

"Stop trying to change the subject," Amanda insisted, waving the card in front of my face. "Let's get some breakfast – we need to hear this," she insisted as we all suddenly felt the need for food and vitamin C.

We sat in the lounge. I had pancakes – an all-time favourite but rarely did I make them. Tea had a medicinal quality after a few sips, and as I sat with all eyes watching me I knew I was going to have to tell them what happened. I relived the embarrassment and told them everything. It didn't sound that much of a deal to me, and I remarked on that.

"Well he definitely took a liking to you," Beth stated. "I hope you got his number?" And it suddenly dawned on me that I hadn't even thought to ask in my drunken stupor.

"I want a full description of him, right now – warts and all," Rose insisted. I thought instantly about his eyes.

"There's not a lot I can remember. He was tall, dark blond hair, in his forties I think. Chiselled, good-looking, tanned, really lovely eyes, he's well-toned and he dresses well," I then found myself relaying a long list to them.

"And that's not remembering a lot?" Amanda laughed. "I'd say someone is a little smitten."

"Don't be silly. I only met him once and, let's face it, I don't think he will want to see to me again after last night's embarrassing spectacle," I concluded.

"Hence this breakfast…?" Amanda sarcastically gestured with a grin from ear to ear.

"I want to know how you know he's toned," Rose then asked innocently.

"It was nothing like that. I poked his chest. He was really nice, a real gentleman," I finished, smiling.

"Do I detect a hint of wishful thinking here? I suspect you would like to meet him again," Beth then said. I looked at them all and then took a bite of my pancake. Then a sip of my tea. They stayed silent.

"Maybe? I didn't think I could see anyone else after Paul, let alone want to see them. It feels like a betrayal of sorts," I replied honestly.

"Are you kidding me?" Amanda burst out. "It's been three years and we know that you loved Paul, and it was the most unfortunate thing to happen, but Jenny you deserve to be happy. You're only forty-three for God's sake and Paul would not have wanted you to live alone forever. He'd want you to be happy again." She moved across to sit next to me and placed her hand on mine. "You're not doing anything wrong, that's if you even decide to see this Ethan again or anyone else. You have to carry on living," she finished.

I looked across at them all, and then at Amanda and she simply smiled and repeated, "It's okay." I suddenly felt like a weight had been lifted.

"I think I needed to hear that!" I replied honestly, and then Beth and Rose came over and we had a group hug. As we embraced Beth then started the comments;

"You know, Jenny, how we recommended you get back in the saddle? We didn't actually mean as soon as you stepped off the plane on our first night here!" she laughed. "But hell girl, you go for it. I'm impressed." And suddenly we were back to the cheap digs!

Breakfast was delicious; it did the trick and although we all felt a little jaded we put on our swimsuits and shorts and headed down to the pool. The lift took no time to reach the reception and we stepped out feeling better than we expected. The reception was busier than normal and it seemed to be mainly business people, which made us think this was a conference-type of hotel. Rose and Beth were checking out all of the men – I wasn't trying to look but someone caught my eye and as I stood watching I knew he was making his way over to us. I gasped, turned to the others and stopped dead in my tracks. "Oh crap, it's him!" I told them.

"What? Who?" Amanda probed and I gestured to where he was and quickly mimed, "Ethan". They all did what was to be expected and peered around me in his direction and then they all gawped. Beth lowered her sunglasses;

"Holy crap, is that him? He's delicious, Jenny," she stated while drooling, as Rose prompted pretty much the same response. Amanda just stared and as she started smiling I knew he was close. She nudged me, so I took a deep breath and turned quickly. With his hand in his pocket he had casually strode across the lobby straight to me.

"Jenny. Nice to see you again so soon and you're looking far better than last night!" he smiled. He didn't even look at the others to start with.

"Ethan. Yes, I am much better, thank you, and thank you so much again for last night, and for the amazing breakfast this morning," I was saying when Amanda elbowed me to introduce her. I grimaced, "These are my friends," I quickly said while gesturing to each of them, "Amanda, Beth and Rose."

"It's a pleasure to meet you all," he simply replied as

they gushed their thanks for breakfast. "So, what are your plans today?" he asked.

"Oh after last night I think that we will be taking it easy until tonight, where these crazy friends of mine want a re-run of the whole thing," I joked as they just kept staring.

"Well, a word of advice – make sure you stick together this time," he requested at all of us. I found it amusing that they all nodded but said nothing like good children. They were embarrassing.

"So, I never asked if you were staying here," I enquired as Rose poked a 'good question' acknowledgement finger in my back. He smiled.

"Unfortunately not. I have a business meeting today and possibly a couple more in the coming days," he replied, as the other guy he was with from last night turned up at the side of him.

"Ah Jenny, right?" he asked as he shook my hand. Beth and Rose both perked up as he was handsome too.

"Yes, I'm sorry I cannot remember your name," I admitted in embarrassment.

"Hardly surprising… but forgivable. It's Josh," he happily replied. Beth pushed her way forward.

"Beth," she quickly said as she shook his hand. He smirked as Rose then did the same, followed by Amanda. I looked at Ethan and mimed, "Sorry", trying to point out their obvious attention to his friend. He smiled at the remark.

"Are you ready, Ethan? The meeting is about to start," Josh then asked.

"Of course." He turned to me and kissed the back of

my hand. "A pleasure again, as always, but I am sorry I have to leave now," he finished. I smiled.

"A pleasure to see you again too. Perhaps we may bump into each other again?" I hopefully stated. He started to walk away;

"I do hope so," he called back and then he was gone. We all watched them walk away and then a gaggle of excitement ensued.

"Jeeze, he's gorgeous!" Rose stated. "I'm going to try falling over tonight and see if I can get one," she giggled. I laughed at her.

"I have to agree with Rose," Amanda then said.

"Me too," Beth added.

"Hell, make sure you bump into him again," Amanda then prompted.

"Make sure he brings his friend too," Beth added while licking her lips.

"I wonder if he has any more," Rose pondered. I scowled at them all and turned to go to the pool, and then smiled to myself as I listened to them chatting about him all the way there.

The feeling of warm sunshine on your skin does wonders for the mind and soul. I found myself drifting a little and daydreaming about Ethan. He was definitely stirring some emotions and it shocked me a little, as I had only seen him twice; well, one and half times really because I wasn't focusing properly last night! I sat up to find the others lying still and so I decided to cool off for a while in the pool. I'm not sure why they don't heat pools at hotels in hot countries; the shock is enough to shrivel your breasts to the size of walnuts! I braved the sharp contrast though and eventually immersed myself and started swimming. There were only a couple of others in the pool and it was still quiet due to the party people still sleeping, but it was relaxing and relatively tranquil. A waiter walked over to me and asked if I would like a drink from the poolside bar and I decided that flushing out most of last night's alcohol was probably a good idea, and so I asked for an orange juice, which was delicious and freshly squeezed.

I bobbed around near the edge of the pool and when Rose sat on the edge and dangled her legs into the refreshing water I swam to the side of her and rested my arms on the edge. We chatted for ages, about work and life and relationships and after we had downed another glass of orange I decided it was about time I got out. Rose stopped me.

"Stay there," she insisted while I asked her why. "He's here again and I do not want you getting out of the pool ungracefully. He won't be seeing any of your good sides otherwise," she commented, grinning.

"What do you mean 'he's here'?" I asked as I followed her gaze. It was Ethan who, with Josh, was strolling to a table outside. He looked across at us and smiled, but seemed deep in conversation. "Oh crap, I have to get out of this pool, I'm shrivelling up," I remarked. Rose in her elegant way stood and told me to sit on the side so that she could give me a hand up. "Does this costume look okay? I don't look old and frumpy, do I?" I whispered. Rose was now laughing and Beth had looked up to see what the fuss was about. Rose happily mimed to her why we were behaving slightly irrationally. Beth laughed and nudged Amanda and whispered to her.

"Are you worried you'll fall over again?" Amanda asked louder than I hoped she would have. I grimaced while Rose told them my worries. "He can't hear us, you know!" she then said before Beth finished with.

"Well, I think there's definitely some sort of sexual attraction then if you're worried about how you look. We should get you a sexy bikini," she suggested.

"I can't wear a bikini, I'd look terrible." I was now standing and reaching for my towel.

"Well that's the most ridiculous thing I've ever heard. You have an amazing figure and you should show it off," Beth then said.

"Definitely need to get one, Jenny; in fact there is a shop that we passed yesterday that sells swimwear. We'll go tomorrow," Amanda then pointed out. I had the feeling that they weren't going to let me get away without making a new purchase.

I popped my sunglasses back on and climbed back on my sun lounger hoping to warm my skin with the hot sun as it was now goosebumped and not the nicest thing to look at. I found myself spying at him through my glasses and I watched more intently as he seemed deeper in conversation, although he did look across a couple of times. Then after he had finished his coffee, he stood and started walking back indoors. A break in the meeting was my only thought, and so once the coast was clear I relaxed and closed my eyes. The day was moving nicely along; it was getting noisier now and we decided to have a late lunch – almost early dinner – as we couldn't squeeze two meals in after the large breakfast. We sat by the beach bar and ordered grilled chicken and salad all around with more fries than you could possibly eat, but they were so good here as we found out yesterday. We were happily chatting when Amanda nearly choked on her drink. She put her glass down and smiled from ear to ear;

"Ethan alert," she simply whispered. As I had my back to him it disguised my panic. He strolled along alone, she informed me, while Josh waited by the door.

"Ladies, I'm sorry to interrupt your meal. I was wondering if you weren't doing anything on Friday evening, whether you would like to go to the annual fund raising dinner at the Golden Coast Hotel. It is usually a really good evening and the food is well known for its outstanding quality," he commented.

"I think that would be great," Beth quickly answered. "Will your friends be going?" she then quickly asked. The others agreed while I dared not say anything.

"Jenny?" he then asked me as he placed a hand on my shoulder. My heart was racing. I looked at the others who all sat there patiently waiting for my reply, so I sucked in a large breath and turned to face him.

"That sounds... lovely," I said. "What's the dress code? I don't think what we have with us would suffice," I then pointed out.

"Speak for yourself," Beth chirped.

"It is quite formal, but I could recommend a few

shops within the area if you would like to go shopping," he then replied. Rose clapped her hands together.

"Ooh shopping, what a fantastic idea! We can get that bikini for you while we're there," she then finished, aiming her last comment toward me. I scowled while Amanda tried not to laugh.

"It will be a far more interesting night for Josh and me and our two other colleagues, if you are sure. These events can sometimes be a little dull otherwise," Ethan then said. I smiled at him.

"It sounds great, thank you for asking us, Ethan, but I think some of us had better go shopping, so if you could point us in the right direction?" I then asked. He paused for a minute.

"Better still, why don't I take you all? I have a free afternoon on Monday, so it would be my pleasure," he suggested. Beth raised her eyebrows at me, almost hinting that I should answer.

"We really do not want to take up your precious time, you seem so busy," I replied honestly.

"You are observant I am quite busy, but I would much rather enjoy a free afternoon with you ladies, than being on my own," he kindly said.

"Well, in that case, as you asked so nicely that would be really lovely," Beth quickly confirmed, before I had even digested what he had just suggested. I think that Beth knew I would try to get out of it due to nerves.

"Alright, I shall pick you all up at around one thirty after lunch," he insisted. The girls all looked at me for some response. I turned and smiled at him again.

"Fantastic, thanks, Ethan." I was trying my best to hide my nerves. He nodded and then turned to leave. The girls all waved to him and Josh, who seemed happy at the attention. Whereas Ethan was cool and collected as he strode back indoors, I started to breathe quite rapidly. "What am I doing?" I asked them.

"I'd say you're aiming for a date," Amanda happily replied as she took a sip of her water.

"Well, I could think of worse things, Jenny," Rose chipped in. I placed my head in my hands and a sudden wave of nausea presented itself.

"I need to just cool down a second," I informed them as I rose from my chair and walked toward the hotel, trying to stop any forthcoming panic attack.

The need for air conditioning was a thought I relished right now. The girls didn't follow me; I think they knew that I needed a couple of moments alone. I walked inside made my way to a quiet corner in the reception, sat down and placed my head between my legs. I mumbled to myself hoping to try to find some logic in how I was feeling about this man, and the fact that I didn't feel that it was right for me to feel anything for another man after Paul. I knew that the girls were right and I had to live, but how long is long enough, or the right time to move on? I sent these thoughts around in circles in my head and continued to feel as nauseous, making myself take some deep breaths. I felt the sofa I was sat on dip at the side of me, and I knew that it was more than likely Amanda coming to give me 'the talk' again! "I know what you're going to say." I remarked without lifting my head; "I just keep thinking it's not right somehow, and that I shouldn't feel like this," I continued. I felt a hand of reassurance place itself in the middle of my back.

"Feel like what? Are you alright, Jenny?" the smooth voice of Ethan suddenly asked me. Oh my goodness, could it get any worse? I grimaced and cursed between my legs, what was I supposed to say to him. I had to be honest I thought it's always the best way. I raised my head and looked directly at him;

"I wasn't expecting it to be you!" I replied.

"So it would seem," he smiled, and then he rubbed my back. "Are you unwell? I could get a doctor?" he asked. I shook my head.

"No, not unwell, just feeling… guilty." I replied honestly. He looked at me inquisitively with those gorgeous blue eyes.

"Guilty? For what?" he asked curiously. I sighed and rubbed my head and thought that I needed to tell him why I was behaving like a crazed woman, especially if I did have the courage to make a date with him, should he ask me. I closed my eyes and took a deep breath, then looked at my hands. *Just tell him,* I thought.

"It has been a long time since a man has been kind to me or shown me any attention, or that I have dared let him." I started and then I looked at him again from my fidgeting fingers. He was still looking at me with worrying but gorgeous eyes, which didn't help my tummy one iota. "You see… I was married for eighteen years to Paul, and then three years ago he died suddenly," I gushed out. Ethan looked down and sighed. "I, I… I keep feeling like I'm letting him down somehow if I don't stay on my own," I finished, wondering why the hell I had just told him all that. *Be realistic,* I then thought, *you're telling him because you like him, and you don't know what to do.* I've probably told him enough to scare him away now anyway! Now I feel like I've made a terrible mistake. I rubbed my forehead feeling more uncomfortable now. He said nothing for a minute, so I did, "I'm sorry I don't know why I just told you all that," I said. He placed his hand on mine.

"Because you felt that you needed to? I'm sorry, Jenny. That must have been terrible for you; I can't imagine what you've been through. One thing I do know though is that you have no need to feel guilty. If my attention toward you and your friends makes you uncomfortable then I will leave you alone, but how can I avoid paying you attention when you now look so vulnerable as well as beautiful?" he asked with a voice like melted chocolate. I smiled at his remark then looked toward him, but I caught Amanda staring at us; she had obviously come inside to see what was taking me so long. She held up her hand to say that she was leaving and did just that with a huge smile on her face. I reverted my eyes back to Ethan who looked at me intently.

"Thank you," I simply said.

"For what? Being honest?" he asked.

"No, for listening to me blurt my tragic life story to you," I gestured.

"I'm sure it wasn't all tragic, but obviously the last few years have been difficult." He stopped for a second and stared directly at me. "You know, I think that it's time you took a break from torturing yourself." He raised his eyebrows at me in question. I laughed a little.

"Maybe you're right; this holiday was certainly a good start." Then he looked toward Josh who was beckoning him. He released my hand and then looked hopefully at me.

"So, would you still like to go shopping with me on Monday, with your friends of course?" he asked. I couldn't believe that he still wanted to take us out. I thought that my outburst was sure to have made him cautious.

"Yes, I would like that," I exclaimed honestly, because I did want to spend some time with him. I wondered briefly if you could honestly be attracted to someone after only meeting them a couple of times, but my racing heart was proof that it was possible.

He stood from the sofa on which we sat and fastened his jacket and then reached out his hand to help me stand. I was hopeful that we had just made a small connection, and was glad that he still wanted to even talk to me. At the very least, it would be nice if we could be friends. I stood and stared at him for a second and then he leaned in toward me and whispered, "Now go and enjoy yourself, and try not to get too drunk tonight."

"But when I get so drunk that I fall over, I meet very nice gentlemen." I smiled, he laughed.

"Maybe one nice gentleman on your holiday is enough?" he winked at me.

"Probably," I laughed.

"I have to go, but I will see you on Monday at one thirty?" he questioned. I nodded.

45

"I'll see you then. I hope that your meeting goes well," I said trying to sound like I was concerned.

"Thank you." And then he turned and walked away and I looked around feeling like the entire world had just witnessed that, but in fact everyone was just continuing with their own day. I walked back toward the door and pushed it open and felt the sudden intense heat, but at least I didn't feel nauseous anymore.

When I returned to the table and sat down, they were all smiling. I carried on eating my salad and then looked at them all and smiled back.

"Feeling better?" Amanda asked sarcastically. I shrugged. "You looked to be having a very intimate conversation," she then said.

"I told him about Paul," I stated matter-of-factly. Amanda sat up and looked at me more intently.

"What...? Why?" she asked. Rose just looked at her and then Beth.

"I didn't intend to, I felt sick and so I had my head between my legs. I wasn't looking and I thought it was you that came to sit with me, so I started explaining something that I couldn't finish without being honest. I kind of just blurted it all out!" I replied.

"What did he say?" she asked curiously.

"He was really nice about it. He said that I should stop torturing myself and that there was nothing to feel guilty about," I informed them. Amanda sat back in her chair with a look of surprise and then folded her arms;

"I'm liking this Ethan more by the minute. He didn't

run the other way, thinking that you are still emotionally scarred?" she asked.

"No, he wanted to make sure we still wanted to go shopping."

"Well, well, this is going to be interesting isn't it?" Beth then said.

"I'm not saying that I want to get serious here, I was simply giving him all the facts," I tried to convince them.

"Yet still he wasn't fazed by what you said?" Beth smiled.

"It would seem that way," Amanda replied. I smiled at them.

"He just seems really nice and friendly," I shrugged.

"He could be a serial killer!" Rose then joked.

Beth shot her a look of dismay. "Really?" she asked her. "Do you have to spoil it?" she then commented before bringing the tone back down to her level. "I think it's great that you're even talking to another man, so if he becomes another friend then that's great for you. If it becomes more than that… then you best get your KY jelly out, because you've probably dried up love by now!" She said it so seriously, and then she smiled at me and started laughing, which set us all off giggling with hysterics.

"Thanks for your continued support, Beth," I managed to get out. It took us some time to calm down.

Chapter 4

Back in our room sometime later, Amanda had ordered a bottle of rose wine for us to enjoy while getting ready to go out again. I had found a new spark of confidence this evening, and was looking forward to having a few drinks with my best friends. We had already got to the point of borrowing items from each other, as we always did, and after last night's trip out we decided a slightly more casual approach would probably be better for us. Cropped chinos, pumps and a nice top were the necessary clothing for our venture out, makes it far easier for dancing. We finished the wine and decided to go back to the bar in the hotel to start with. We had made the remarkably sensible decision to stick to the same thing tonight, and so I bought another bottle of rosé which we sipped and enjoyed with the various peanuts and nibbles that kept arriving.

We decided to eat lightly, something to soak up the alcohol, and it was a great decision by Rose when she spotted a small bar that sold the most amazing fish platters which we shared. Another bottle of rosé later and we were ready to do some serious dancing and drinking. I had told myself before we left that I would definitely drink a glass of water every once in a while, but my plan didn't seem to be working at the moment. By the fifth bottle of rosé, I knew that I was back on that slippery slope. This was more than I had consumed in a long time, well apart from last night. We decided not to care what all the other younger people were doing or thinking, we just went with the flow – *our flow* – and boy did we make the most of it. As we walked back to the hotel along the beach it was a relief to take our pumps off and feel the cool sand under our feet. Hot feet from dancing was not the nicest sensation, but we were all grateful for wearing flats. We laughed about our night, in particular about the poor eighteen-year-olds who seemed to want to hook up with us, because no other girls were hooking up with them. It didn't take them long to move on when Beth started giving them tips and advice on sex! I think that she scared the poor boys to death!

At least this time I could focus on the stairs of the hotel when we reached them. After learning our lesson last night, we had chosen to drink some water while dancing which had helped, but I could feel the last drink of Amanda's choice repeating badly already, tequila shots were not my favourite, I decided. We helped each other up the stairs and past the pool, I looked across to where Ethan had been sat last night and I smiled but wished that he was around again. I had that Dutch courage after my wine and tequila, but then thought that after earlier I may embarrass myself and tell him more about me than I would wish him to know really, so it was probably best that he was not here.

We had stocked our fridge in the suite earlier with soft drinks and we all reached for one and collapsed on the sofa. We laughed a lot and talked openly, discussing an abundance of personal things. I always said it was good to get things off your chest with your girlfriends, and I seemed to be right yet again as the discussions changed rapidly but seemed necessary for each of us. My best friends were just that, I thought, as I sat and looked at them all, and my gratitude for that friendship could never be measured; it was boundless. Once we seemed to have put the world to rights we aimed for our beds as tiredness and alcohol were taking over. I have to say that I felt better than I had last night but desperately needed some sleep. Once my head touched the pillow I was out like a light, and this continued until I woke at five thirty to go to the bathroom.

I wandered back and lay in bed for a while, but suddenly felt wide awake and so I went into the living room and grabbed a glass of water from the kitchen area. I think I was dehydrated and it was making me restless. I pulled the door of the balcony open and stepped outside; the warm breeze was making my skin tingle and as I inhaled the sea air I noted the activity that was still going on. Crowds were singing and dancing in the streets, and in the grounds of the hotel next door they continued drinking and playing silly games. Maybe the noise had woken me? I looked across to the beach and saw a young couple making out and I found myself staring. My thoughts jumped to Paul; I had spent the last three years grieving so intensely that I hadn't realised how lost I had become myself. I missed the intimacy of being with someone. I wanted to be held and touched and then my thoughts turned to Ethan and I had butterflies and felt warm inside as I continued to watch the couple stepping things up. *Oh my God, I was attracted to Ethan and I wanted him, which was the first time I had felt like this in three years!* I stepped back and averted my eyes from them and took a few deep breaths. I ran my conversation with myself through my head again; *Is three years long enough? Should I allow myself to feel like this at all? What would Paul think?* I stopped and rubbed my forehead and drank half the glass of water in my hand. I was torturing myself again; after all, I was a woman and I can't deny these needs forever, can I? *Go back to bed, then you don't have to think about this,* I told myself, but then I found myself looking back toward the couple on the beach and could feel myself heating up again. I turned and walked back inside to the cool air of the suite, finished my water and then refilled the glass before walking back to my bed. I lay on top of the cool sheets and pondered for a while and then smiled because Amanda was right; Paul would want me to be happy. He was always so generous and loving and he wouldn't want me to be without that for the rest of my life. Not that I think Ethan is the next Paul, but I made a decision right then that I needed to start looking after my own needs now and I suddenly felt calm, and slowly drifted back to sleep.

When I woke in the morning and turned, Rose had already woken up and left the room. I sat up and stretched, my mouth felt like parchment paper and I needed to drink the rest of the water I had on my bedside table. It was instant relief to my taste buds. I went to the bathroom and tidied myself up a little before going to find the others. Remarkably they'd ordered some room service and we had breakfast in the comfort of our room again, although not as much as yesterday. I did worry though that if I continued to eat like this every day I was likely to gain a stone. It was Sunday, and we hadn't even explored the island yet so today we decided to take a bus to Ibiza Town, where it had been recommended that we visit the castle with its sixteenth century walls. I had to say that we were all looking forward to venturing out upon the island that we had decided to holiday on – it would be nice to see some of the more traditional towns and visit the local shops.

Sundresses and sunglasses on, along with Beth in her large floppy hat and we were ready to set off. As we boarded the bus it became obvious that Beth's hat was going to be a pain after firstly nearly trapping it in the bus door, and then managing to poke pretty much most of us in the eye with the brim. Amanda hit it numerous times telling her how ridiculous it was, which Beth just laughed at stating she was setting a new fashion trend. I don't think that locals were overly impressed with it either, but she sat happily and refused to take it off. We reached Ibiza Town, and it was so worth the trip. The boutique shops were great little Aladdin's caves and we bought local jewellery and small items of clothing and nicknacks that we probably didn't need but fancied anyway. The cathedral was amazing as were all the little red tiled cupolas of the churches, which were a typically imagined old-town sight and we loved it. We found a lovely area of restaurants and so sat and had lunch and more wine. The owner of the restaurant was lovely, a man named Miguel who made it his sole duty to look after us speaking his pidgin English as he went, but he was obviously enjoying the practice none the less! We had a lovely time, and the food was delightful. We meandered through the streets and soaked up the traditions and had the best day that I had experienced in ages.

When we slumped back into the chairs in the suite we were exhausted. After the last two nights we thought that we would stay in the hotel and dine in the restaurant, which meant that we could stay casual and drink less – that was music to my ears. We continued the stimulating conversation of the day, which kept reverting inexcusably to me and my sex life – and Ethan. It didn't seem to bother me as much now though; I had found that I could give as good as I got and this made me feel more like the old me. I went to bed that evening having had a brilliant time and other than a few nerves about going out with Ethan tomorrow, I felt like I had it all under control.

We all woke feeling refreshed and glad of the break from the excessive alcohol consumption. We decided to have breakfast downstairs this morning as we were up and ready early. A couple of hours by the pool, lunch and then get ready to go shopping was our plan. It was a perfect warm sunny day, the pool felt refreshing and I managed to read another four chapters of my book. When it got to twelve noon we all had a quick sandwich and then retreated to the suite to get changed and then the butterflies returned. I sat on the edge of the bed after drying my hair and took a deep breath in and out. Rose watched me intently.

"Nervous?" she asked smiling. I nodded.

"It's silly really," I replied while I slipped on my wedges. She sat beside me.

"Despite all of our jabs at you, you know we're only joking, don't you? We just want to see you happy again, get a little of the old Jenny back," she smiled.

"I know. It's just taking a little getting used to having… you know… those type of feelings again," I told her honestly.

"I can imagine, but on the flip side, it's nice to have those feelings, isn't it?" she asked with a hopeful look. I thought about it for a moment and it was good;

"Yeah, it feels great," I replied before she stood quickly and gestured to the door.

"Come on, it's time to go."

I agreed and walked toward the door with her trying to ooze confidence, the other two were already waiting. Beth had an even more flamboyant outfit on which made Rose and I instantly smile. We rode the lift down to the reception and as we stepped out talking rather loudly we were met by the sight of Ethan, who was sitting patiently waiting. He stood when he saw us, my heart skipped a beat; he looked remarkably hot in his casual trousers and a t-shirt that emphasised his muscle tone. The others excitedly hurried over and greeted him.

"Ladies… Are we ready to go?" he asked looking toward me. I had slowed and hovered at the back while my adorable friends smothered him a little. I tried not to laugh as he looked a little crowded. "My car is outside," he then stated as he gestured toward the door. The others started in that direction, I waited a second and then started following while he waited for me; "Shall we?" he smiled.

"I am sorry about them; they obviously don't get out much," I smirked.

"Don't apologise, they obviously make you happy and they are quite amusing," he replied. As we walked I looked at him.

"I am sorry too about my outburst the other day. I don't know why I felt the need to tell you my life story," I confirmed. He placed his hand in the small of my back as we neared the door and simply replied.

"I find it far more attractive for a woman to be honest, rather than try to be something she is not. Shall we say no more about it for now?" he asked.

"Alright, it's a deal." I caught him smile at my reply just briefly.

The girls nearly drooled when they saw the lovely convertible car that he had arrived in to take us for the afternoon. I was prompted to sit in the front next to him, and with sunglasses on we set off. He pointed out various sights along the way, as did the girls with every passing male that stood out to them. I shook my head numerous times at their comments but Ethan simply laughed. I do believe that he was enjoying our company. When we arrived at the first small street that had numerous clothing shops, some of which were designer, Ethan released his seat to let the girls out of the back and then quickly walked around to my side and opened my door. He was quite simply an absolute gentleman besides being generously easy on the eye. He explained which shops were the best in his opinion in this area and then asked which one we would like to go to first. We set off in the direction of a larger designer-fronted window which displayed a bright pink dress and had taken Beth's eye.

"Looks like we're going there first!" I exclaimed sarcastically to Ethan. He laughed, and said that he would wait outside.

"Absolutely not!" Amanda called out as she linked arms with him and marched him inside. I grimaced. "We need some advice on how dressy we need to be," she then said.

"At least point us in the right direction?" Rose asked.

"Very well." He looked back over his shoulder at me with a worried look which made me laugh.

The boutique designer shop we were in had some amazing dresses. I wondered around browsing at the racks, but most things I picked up looked only big enough to dress one of my thighs, let alone my body. Rose found a beautiful peacock blue dress which was mid-length and she was desperate to try on, and while she did so we looked at the shoes and bags. When she stepped out she did look amazing and as she did us a turn Beth clapped.
"Wow that really is your colour, it's gorgeous," she told her. Rose was very slim, and the dress showed off her figure perfectly. She looked across at Ethan;

"Is this not dressy enough, or is it alright?" she asked him.

"It's perfect," he simply said, and I suddenly had a pang of jealousy – what the hell was that all about?

"Okay, I'll get it," she smiled and she returned to the changing room to re-dress. Rose had always been great at knowing exactly what would suit her off the peg. As her figure was so toned and perfect she slipped into pretty much anything, and I did envy her a little for that.

Ethan had made his way over to me and smiled; "Nothing you like in here?" he enquired. I shook my head;

"Nothing my size in here, we don't all fortunately have perfect genes like Rose," I smiled as I gestured toward her.

"Really – interesting, and there I was thinking that your genes were perfect," he replied and I blushed. "I think I know just the place for you," he then said and he shouted across to the others, "Just popping into another shop, ladies. Shall we say that we will meet by the car in an hour?" he asked them. They stopped and looked at us and as I was behind him I shook my head in protest.

"Yes, that would be fine, have fun," Amanda replied smiling directly at me. I could have killed her! I replaced my grimace with a smile as he turned back around and then opened the door for me. I walked outside reluctantly, but then realised that if I needed them the girls were not far away.

"So, any colour preference in mind?" he asked as we walked.

"Not really, I usually stick to black to be honest."

"I think that we need to change that. I always find that black is a little sombre," he smiled. I nodded in agreement. As we walked it struck me that I knew nothing about him;

"So where are you from, and why are you here in Ibiza?" I enquired. He looked toward me.

"Originally I'm from London, grew up there and stayed there until I was around twelve, but then I travelled with my father and we moved around a lot," he started.

"That was because of his work?"

"Yes. He was a great hotelier; he owned three in London and a string of them in other countries. I was tutored in my final years while travelling around the globe, which was not as glamorous as it sounds," he informed me.

"Wow, that's quite a unique upbringing. It must have been quite difficult making friends?"

"It was hard but I learnt so much from my father, and, as it was just the two of us, I thrived in his company. I don't regret it," he then stated. I smiled.

"So you're in Ibiza because…"

"Well, business mainly. When my father died eight years ago he left everything to me, but the large hotel business is tough these days and it's difficult keeping things ticking when you're hopping from one to another, country to country. So I decided that I would sell up and open up smaller boutique-type hotels in the countries and places I love."

"So you have one here that you are buying or selling?" I asked with interest. I wouldn't have placed him as a hotel owner, but now that I knew I was intrigued. He laughed;

"So many questions," he replied. I was interrogating him a little.

"I'm sorry, just interested I suppose. Never met a hotelier."

"It's okay," he laughed. "I have a new smaller place out

here which is opening next month so I am checking that everything is complete, and I am in the process of selling the other large hotel that I have here," he confirmed.

"That's impressive – is it looking like you are going to sell it easily?"

"It's not easy convincing someone to buy a large hotel these days, but the owner of the hotel that you are staying in wants to buy it, hence the many meetings there," he concluded. "Anyway, enough about me for now. I'd like to hear more about you." I gulped.

"What would you like to know?"

"Where do you live when you're not getting blind drunk and partying in Ibiza?" he sarcastically asked. I nudged him with my elbow.

"Manchester. I live in a reasonably sized house – on my own now, of course. I have two boys; James is nearly twenty-one and Mark is just nineteen, both at university and I love them dearly. My favourite food is definitely Thai, my favourite colour is green and I am forty-three years old." I bombarded him with as many things as I could think of. "Do you want to know anything else?"

"I think that is enough to digest for now!" he laughed. "Anyway we're here." He pointed to the shop we had stopped at the side of.

If the window was anything to go by then I was sure to find something in here. He opened the door and we walked into the cool and very minimalistic shop. There were some vibrant colours along with black which I started to aim for, but Ethan surprised me when he grabbed hold of my hand and led me toward the colours, starting with green.

"I thought that we were going to aim for something other than black?" he reminded me.

"I'm really not sure what suits me anymore," I sighed as I slid each coat hanger along looking aimlessly, and with his one look at the assistant she came over.

I stood stunned for a second as he started speaking fluent Spanish, I presumed, and as the assistant smiled numerous times while he gestured toward me I felt extremely uncomfortable knowing that he was talking about me. I smiled nervously back and then she quickly came to my side looked at me and then started taking dresses off the rack.

"Well, she's in agreement with me that you'll probably suit pretty much anything, Jenny. So take your pick and if you want to try them on then go ahead," he encouraged me.

"You just happen to speak perfect Spanish?" I remarked at his conversation. He shrugged.

"It is Spanish with a bit of Catalan thrown in the mix. I did say that I travelled," he then smiled.

"So how many languages do you speak?" I had to know as I was now feeling slightly inferior having never learnt any. He stood and thought for a second;

"Not that many. Four including English fluently, but with the pidgin Italian and Portuguese I know, then six," he innocently replied.

"Six?" I asked with feeling. "Well you beat me hands down, I only speak two."

"Really?" he asked genuinely.

"Yep, English first and drunken slur the other!" I

joked at myself. He burst out laughing, which made me laugh.

"Your answer was far better than mine," he said while still laughing.

"Well, I aim to please," I replied as I was shown six dresses, two of which I actually liked: one lilac and one a lovely shade of green. "I think I will try these on." I smiled at the assistant and she pointed to the changing room.

"Please do, I will wait for you." He leaned against the counter by the accessories.

In the changing room I slid out of my sun dress and tried the green one first. It was lovely, but it just didn't seem to sit properly around my neck, and it was making me fidget so off it came. The lilac one was very plain, but it had a bit of stretch in it and the neckline and arms were really flattering. It did go with my sun kissed skin and blonde hair, and as I stood and turned to look at myself the assistant appeared at my cubicle. I opened the door and showed her and by using sign language I asked her if it looked okay. She did the traditional kiss of the fingers perfect signal and smiled intently which kind of gave me the vibe that it was a good decision. Then I looked at the price tag; two hundred and forty Euros for a dress, for dinner with a man I hardly knew! I realised the assistant was watching me so I smiled at her and nodded to save any embarrassment she clapped her hands in delight and left me to get changed. When I appeared back in shop Ethan stood up and looked at me for a reaction.

"I'm going to take this one, it's really nice," I informed him.

"Excellent!" he smiled, then he started talking to the assistant again as she wrapped it neatly in tissue paper. I reached in my bag for my purse, but he stopped me. "Please, allow me?" he simply said.

"What? I cannot do that, I mean I hardly know you – I cannot let you buy me an expensive dress."

"Well it does seem fair, after all I am kidnapping you and your friends for one night from your holiday," he smiled. "It would be my pleasure," were his finishing words, as he handed his credit card to the eager waiting assistant.

"I don't know what to say. Thank you, but you didn't have to," I tried to insist.

"I wanted to," he smiled again, and then they were back… those butterflies.

We left the shop and as we had only been around half an hour, he asked if I would like a coffee. I agreed as I felt that I owed him now. We sat at a small cafe and enjoyed watching the world go by. The conversation was moving along, mainly me asking about Ibiza. "I never asked you how old you were?" I suddenly said and then thought that probably wasn't the best thing to ask. He placed his cup back onto the saucer and replied happily;

"Forty-five next month," he sighed. "I really worry about how fast the time goes."

"Not married?" I then asked hoping not to hear the worst. He looked at me.

"I was very briefly when I was twenty-nine. Thought it was the right thing to do, but I realised very quickly that my father was ruling my head on that one! I don't think he wanted me to be alone like him, he never allowed himself to let anyone in after my mother died when I was eight. Then after three years we were pretty much living apart with me travelling and so we separated. She wasn't happy and neither was I, but we are friends," he concluded.

"I'm sorry about your mum," I told him. I felt sorry for him.

"Thanks, but it was a long time ago. We both know all too well that sometimes our loved ones die too young, and for reasons out of our control," he kindly said, and I agreed. "Your marriage sounds like it was a good one, though?"

"It was. Met him when I was twenty-one, fell pregnant a few months later – not quite what I had planned for myself – then we got married had another son and everything was great. When the boys started full-time school and I had managed to finish every other course possible in floristry I opened my own business, which was something I had always wanted to do. I love being in that environment – helping make other peoples' day brighter and happier, and being allowed to be part of the special days like weddings. It is just… amazing," I gushed, then I realised he was staring at me.

"That's great; it sounds like you've found the perfect job that you love," he remarked. I was confused.

"You don't like your job, or owning hotels?"

"It's what I know. I do love it sometimes, but other times it gets tiresome. Spending so much time alone in hotels isn't that exciting, I assure you. Josh, who you met earlier, is my overseeing general manager and personal assistant. He travels pretty much everywhere with me and he thrives on it; but he's only thirty-one and has no intentions of settling down at the moment so we work well together. He certainly makes my job easier." He was quite open with me.

"You could always sell them all and do something else, even settle down?" I suggested. His eyes met mine;

"Hard to do that when you cannot seem to find the right woman." I knew I was blushing at that comment. I looked at my watch as I didn't know what to say. He obviously noted that too. "So do you need shoes?" he suddenly asked to break the silence.

"No, actually I have some shoes with me that will match, don't really know when I thought I would wear them, but I do have them."

"Perfect," he said and then he stood and we started walking back to the car.

"So how long will your business take here in Ibiza?" I asked him, suddenly thinking that he could be leaving anytime soon and jetting off somewhere else.

"I'm not sure. The buyer keeps changing the boundaries and wanting to offer less, but he knows that he's getting a fair deal. I hope to have that finalised by Friday, then there is the fundraiser and then I actually have ten days to kill so I may hang around here." He almost made it sound like a question.

"That's great, some time off, sounds like you need it," I confirmed. He nodded then asked me.

"You?"

"We are here for two weeks, and then back to reality,

unfortunately," I frowned. He raised his eyebrows and simply said one word.

"Right!" He nodded at his confirmation, and then we arrived at the car and the others were stood waiting. Rose and Beth had bags but Amanda did not.

He took us to two other areas and eventually Amanda who is the fussiest of all of us found something that she actually liked. We had been nearly three and a half hours at this point and Ethan had taken two business calls giving the girls chance to quiz me while he waited outside. We were just walking back to the car, the girls were in front of Ethan and me, when Rose spotted a swimwear shop. She simply pointed and started across the road toward it. Beth turned and gestured to me that I was needed. I knew they would make me get one but I wasn't that bothered about buying it right now. I looked at Ethan and shrugged.

"It would seem like I'm wanted," I implied as I looked at Beth. Rose was now calling to me too. He gave me the cheekiest grin and stepped closer.

"Looks like you're definitely going to be made to get that bikini then!" he whispered and then he winked at me. I gasped.

"You heard that the other day?" I asked with embarrassment, I was definitely going to kill Amanda and Beth and their loud voices now!

"Let's just say I agree with them. You have a great figure you should show it off a little now and then." His eyes bore into mine. I was melting, and not just from the heat. "Off you go now, don't let them down," he then finished as he stepped back and gave me the same grin.

I smiled and then shook my head at him; if that wasn't coming onto me after everything else then I was way off the mark. I walked to Beth and then we crossed the street and I turned once and looked at him, he was still staring and it made me want to teach him a lesson by doing exactly what I think he was implying I was afraid to do. Bikini it is then, I thought to myself, and we all went inside.

After being bombarded with suggestions from all of them I actually settled on two. It was hard to focus while I was getting interrogated from every direction about what we were talking about. I tried to politely tell them that they would have to wait until we were back at the hotel as I didn't think it was nice to talk about him while he was in close proximity. I chose a very nice coral red bandeau bikini which you could wear with straps if you wished and a blue and white stripy one which was cute. The girls were ecstatic that I had decided to buy them as they thought it was likely I'd choose not to buy any, let alone two. Secretly my reason had become solely to show Ethan that I wasn't afraid to wear one, and my fear of showing my body would have to take a back seat for this holiday.

Chapter 5

Ethan looked at me numerous times on the way back with the biggest smirk, particularly after I had waved my bag at him confidently which held my new purchases; I think he had found me quite humorous, something I felt I had not been for a long time. He dropped us back at the hotel; the girls all one by one kissed him on the cheek and thanked him, and then like giggling teenagers went inside and left me alone with him.

"Thank you for today, it was really nice getting to know you a little better."

"Likewise," he smiled. "So I hope to see you before Friday, but if not I will make sure I leave details for you at the reception," he then said. I didn't even think, the words just popped out of my mouth;

"Would it be easier if you had my mobile number?" I asked. He looked surprised that I had offered.

"Yes, that would be much easier. I shall give you mine," he said as I took my phone out and punched his number in, saved it and then sent him a text.

"There, you have mine now," I smiled at him. "Thank you for the dress, I look forward to wearing it for you." I then stated, and in quick succession tried to correct myself. "Well, not for you but with you, you know what I mean?" I blushed. He stepped closer placed his hand on my waist and then lowered his mouth to my ear;

"I look forward to that too, but I think that you're other purchases will be far more interesting," he whispered, and then he turned his head and kissed my cheek hovering there for a few seconds. I closed my eyes and inhaled his scent, he smelt as gorgeous as he looked and then my body betrayed me and started throbbing in places that I thought had long since shut down! I quickly kissed him on the cheek and stepped back.

"Until next time, then?" I asked him trying to slow my heart rate with no success.

"Until next time," he repeated with a huge smile. I turned and walked through the door into the cool reception and took a few deep breaths trying to control my now twitching body. This was not what I had expected from this holiday but I was feeling more like the old me with each hour that passed, and I hadn't realised how much I needed that.

The girls beckoned me to hurry up so that they could get all the juicy information they so craved, and once inside the lift they started their million and one questions. I tried to tell them everything that had been said between us – particularly the part just as we returned to the hotel – but Rose interrupted me;

"So hang on a second… he bought you the dress? I can't believe he bought you the dress," she kept repeating.

"I insisted that he didn't need to; I was happy to buy it although it was a bit more than I was expecting to pay. But he said that he wanted to because it was fair as he was hijacking us all for one night," I informed them.

"Well, in that case he should have bought us all a dress," Amanda replied. I gave her a look of annoyance and she smiled.

"You looked very cosy before you parted ways," Beth then nudged me as we entered our room. I nodded.

"Yeah it was a bit intense, and then I had a panic attack because my body started throbbing in all the wrong places," I laughed.

"Oh you've definitely got the hots for him," Rose stated as we slumped onto the sofa. "Hell, why shouldn't you? He is a dish, and it's obvious that he is into you."

"Do you think?"

"Hell yes!" they all replied in unison. Then we burst out laughing.

"Oh you're so going to get laid this holiday," Beth then concluded. I threw my cushion at her. "What?" She carried on laughing; "I have some catching up to do," she then decided.

"You three are a bad influence," I said about their behaviour.

"That's why you love us," Amanda winked at me.

We sat for the next hour simply looking at our purchases, and the girls all loved my new dress. I tried it on for them with the shoes that I had brought and they looked just fine, so I hung it in the wardrobe ready for Friday evening. I still found my thoughts reverting to Ethan, and it made me question how silly I was being. I mean me – a holiday romance – and at my age? Who am I trying to kid? I have never done anything like this before and, let's face it, once I leave it's not like I'm going to see him again. Is a one night stand bad at my age? In fact, hell, why am I even thinking about that? What's wrong with me?

I stood looking in the wardrobe when Rose appeared.

"Are you okay, hun?" she innocently asked. I turned and looked at her.

"Yeah, just thinking this holiday romance stuff isn't really me."

"Jenny stop torturing yourself will you. He's a nice man, he's asked you out and you need to look at it as nothing more than that. The fact that we happen to be on holiday is a coincidence," she concluded as she gave me a hug. "Plus we get a nice meal out," she added. I laughed at her and decided that she was right.

We chose to eat at a restaurant recommended to us by Ethan, which was a little way inland, so we hired a taxi and travelled there, and that too was so worth the trip. The food was gorgeous; it was a family-run place and so their attention to customers was just perfect. They spoke good English and played great traditional music. By the time we left we decided that we probably wouldn't need to eat for a week. Once back at the hotel, we went to the bar to have a drink before retiring for the night. It was cool in the hotel and there was music playing in the background. It wasn't too busy and so we sat at a table and relaxed and chatted some more. It was nice to have a night away from the town and not be so drunk that we couldn't see properly – recovery at our age was far worse than I remember it being. So after a long spell in the bar, we went to bed early and made the decision that we would get some serious tanning time in tomorrow and Wednesday, while most of the people holidaying here were still sleeping.

Hot, bright and great for the skin. Sunshine is definitely medicinal and makes you feel amazing. As I lay there in my new stripy bikini with my eyes closed I wondered when the last time I felt this relaxed actually was. After a cooling dip in the pool and a glass of refreshing orange juice I took out my latest Nicholas Sparks book – I always was a sucker for a love story. I read it happily and as the other girls either sunbathed or read too – our Wednesday morning quietly rambled on. As it neared lunchtime we moved over to a table near the poolside grill and ordered a salad as before; at least we felt like we were trying to be good and it counteracted all of the drinking. We were sat contentedly eating when the waiter brought our next round of drinks, then he smiled at our enjoyment.

"So, will you ladies be going on the Sunset Party Cruise this evening?" he asked us. Rose's ears pricked up instantly as did Beth's.

"What's that?" Rose enquired. "We don't know about that."

"It leaves the bay at seven pm. It costs thirty-nine euros each and besides all of your drinks being included and some food, there is a DJ on board who will take you on a cruise that allows you to party through sunset. It arrives back at the dock at one in the morning," he informed us.

"Let's do it that sounds fun!" Amanda suddenly shouted, which took us all by surprise.

I have to say the sunset and cruise parts sounded delightful, it was the drinking and partying until the boat gets back at one that made me grimace a little. Beth pondered the idea as did Amanda. I think that the young waiter had his eye on Rose and I half wondered if he was going and that was the reason for him asking. Rose gave us all the 'puppy dog' eyes and we knew that she was going to be disappointed if we said no. So reluctantly we agreed, and she clapped her hands together with delight.

We had a leisurely stroll along to the bay and found it easy to see where we needed to buy tickets from with all the posters on display. We stopped and had a drink at a very nice wine bar that overlooked the bay and we had a great time eyeing all of the beautiful yachts and boats plus, much to Beth's delight, an abundance of men dressed in not very much at all. We enjoyed the stroll back and decided to retreat to the room and do those girly things like painting nails and straightening hair before the big night out. We made an effort but tried to dress it down a little wondering what the hell all of the eighteen-year-olds would be wearing. By the time we set off to get on the boat, Amanda and I were wondering what we had let ourselves in for.

It had to be said that the boat was quite impressive – fairly new, decorated party-style, plenty of staff watching and serving drinks – but we suddenly felt like chaperones, as most of the girls were between the ages of eighteen and twenty-five and wearing nothing more than very short shorts and bikini tops. I instantly felt like someone had put a spotlight on us, as most of the girls and the men had turned and were staring directly at us. Feeling like a fish out of water, I turned and started to walk back off the boat but then out of the blue the music started, most people started to talk and dance and then we heard a relatively familiar voice; "Hey! It's the lady with the big floppy hat," a young male voice called. As we all turned we couldn't believe it when the young men off the plane were stood staring at Beth. She instantly smiled and walked over to them and we quickly followed, not quite what I was expecting but it took the emphasis off our ages – thank God!

"Hey, hi there. Are you following me?" Beth chided him.

"You know you'd love that," he replied as he put out his hand. "Tim," he simply offered. She smiled.

"Beth." She shook his hand. Then without any extra effort, introductions were done.

It pleased me no end that one of the group, Matt, had a steady girlfriend and even though he was only twenty-six he was far more sensible for his years than I would have expected. So it was a relief to end up chatting to him for most of the cruise. The music played loudly, the younger people partied hard, drank litres and there were more excuses for people kissing anyone and everyone, than I care to mention. The only good thing about the whole situation was that I was managing to drink mainly soft drinks, while the girls were talking endlessly to the rest of the group who now were starting to think that my friends were actually great fun! We danced in a crowd far too busy to notice us after numerous alcoholic drinks; it was so crowded there wasn't exactly a large amount of space to move anyway, so I happily bopped along with them all.

The sunset was stunning, the people were interesting to watch for various reasons and Matt had been a pleasure to speak to. I was feeling cooler now and as I saw the lights of the bay flickering in the distance I felt relieved to be heading back. The younger end of the group had now taken to being ill over the side of the boat, and the staff were carefully making sure that no one fell in. Girls were in precarious positions with boys, mainly with their tongues down the boys' throat. Intimacy I did crave, but this visual representation was not exactly top of my list. Amanda stumbled over to me, rather badly I might add. Matt nudged me and laughed as he wasn't too drunk and had witnessed her wobbling.

"Heeyyyyy… What you talking about?" she slurred.

"Various things actually; Matt and I have had a very stimulating conversation," I replied as she fell alongside us. "Are you alright?" I quickly asked as I helped her sit squarely.

"Yep, I am just great," she laughed as Beth approached.

"Oh my God, how drunk is she?" she remarked at Amanda's state. I grimaced a little.

"Pretty darn drunk I'd say!"

"Hell, and I thought Rose was bad – have you seen her?" She then gestured to the very happy Rose who was being spun around the dance floor by Tim.

"He is known for his dancing," Matt then laughed, and both Beth and I joined him – dancing is not quite what I would call it!

I felt remarkably well apart from being tired. The boat docked and we started to disembark very slowly, mainly due to the fact that two people fell into the water as they tried being clever getting off, which was amusing to most of us, but the staff now looked a little fed up with the drunken commotion. We decided that the walk back to the hotel would do Rose and Amanda the world of good and we had docked a whole half hour early, so the probable thirty-minute walk back seemed like a great idea. Arriving back at our hotel after being serenaded by Rose and with Amanda trying numerous times to get yet another drink, both Beth and I were relieved to have made it back. We walked into the reception area trying to get them to be quiet, and at the same time realising that was near impossible, when I spotted a group of men near the front entrance and felt happy to see Ethan was with them. He looked over and so I decided to hover a little just to say hello.

"Beth, can you manage on your own with these two for a few minutes?" I asked her hopefully. She looked a little confused but then I bobbed my head toward Ethan and when she spotted him she just winked at me and tried herding the others toward the lift without saying anything – she just waved her hand to usher me away, and I smiled.

I stood near a pillar and then leaned against it hoping that I wouldn't suddenly feel like a fool if he left, but as the men shook hands and said their goodnights he smiled at me and started to make his way over. I stood and straightened myself and remarkably my tiredness suddenly faded.

"Hey, Jenny. How nice to see you," he said as he kissed me on both cheeks. "… and at this unearthly hour!" he then remarked as he looked at his watch.

"Yes it is. I'm quite surprised to see you too."

"Well, I'm closing this deal on Friday morning for definite now, and it seemed right that as we've agreed on everything I should take them out to dinner. I've known the buyer since I was around seventeen so it felt a necessary close to the sale," he replied. Then he looked at me with raised eyebrows, "Have you had an eventful night?" he enquired, I presume remarking at Rose and Amanda's drunken state. I laughed lightly.

"If you are referring to the rather boisterous friends that I am here with, then yes we have had an eventful night, but I would like to add that I am actually fine." I smiled. He looked toward the bar.

"Do you fancy a drink with me before retiring?" he kindly asked. I had those returning butterflies and hesitated for a nano second.

"I'd love to, if you're sure that you have the time?" I replied as he gestured toward the bar. We walked together and he asked me to sit at a table while he ordered. I felt it polite to leave the choice with him.

He sat next to me and unfastened his casual jacket and then smiled at me.

"So, please do enlighten me as to how your friends are so very obviously rather intoxicated and you are not."

"Yes, again…" I shook my head slightly embarrassed.

"You are certainly seeing the best side of us." I laughed. I sat back against the sofa and faced him. "We somehow, after the suggestion of a waiter this lunchtime, ended up on the Sunset Party Cruise," I started. He burst out laughing;

"Well I bet that was an experience for you all!" he remarked as the barman appeared with two champagne flutes and a bucket with a bottle of Cristal champagne within it. I took in a deep breath for a second as I looked at it which he saw. "Do you like champagne?" he asked hesitantly.

"Yes, yes, I'm sorry; I think that I have only ever had Cristal once before, it just surprised me," I told him.

"Panic over then." He smiled as he leaned forward and passed me a glass that the barman had poured. He sat back and faced me and then raised his glass; "To meeting new and interesting people," he smiled. I nodded and then chinked glasses with him. "Please do go on." He gestured for me to continue.

"Well, there isn't much to say really. Rose and Amanda were partying hard, particularly after we bumped into a group of men that we had been talking to on the plane. In fact I will rephrase that; a group of men that Beth had been talking to on the plane. The music was loud, I managed to drink mainly soft drinks due to the fact that the others were pre-occupied and Matt, one of the group, had a serious girlfriend and was more sensible than I could have hoped for," I finished as I took another sip.

"You know, if you all wanted a boat trip you should have just said. I would have been happy to take you," he replied before sipping his cold champagne.

"You have a boat? Why does that not surprise me very much?"

"Well, I spend so much time on land – in hotels, of course – it is really nice sometimes to look at the island from the sea. I would be happy to have you all on board, perhaps on Friday after I have signed all of the necessary paperwork here?" he asked. I was starting to feel more relaxed around him now. I took one long sip and then replied.

"You know, I think that I would like that. It would be a nice celebration after your sale." He seemed happy at my response.

"Nearly a whole day with you, and then a whole night. I am one lucky guy!" He was admirably polite.

"Well it is probably better that you suggest one of the days after tomorrow, as I suspect my friends are not going to be on good form for at least twenty-four hours. They will, however, need plenty of time to get ready for the evening," I informed him.

"That isn't a problem; I should be finished here by ten thirty so we can be on my yacht by eleven thirty."

"Yacht?" I replied, nearly choking on my champagne. He reached for the bottle to refill my glass.

"Does that worry you?" he asked.

"No, I've just never been on a yacht," I was quick to say.

"Ever? Well we definitely need to remedy that. We can all have a really nice lunch and also a swim in the sea after a sail around the north of the island," he smiled. "I may have to invite Josh – not sure I can keep four women entertained all afternoon!" he then added.

"Sounds perfect," I tried to say with confidence while trying to convince myself at the same time, after I'd run through my head that I would have to wear a bikini near him.

"See if your friends are happy to do the same. We can finalise arrangements later," he replied calmly, probably reacting to my nervous reply.

We sat for nearly an hour talking and enjoying each other's company, and when I yawned slightly, I realised how tired I had become with the adrenaline rush of being with him again. He asked me to wait while he paid the bill and offered to take me to my room. I knew that this was all that was intended as he knew all too well that my friends were sharing my suite with me. We stepped into the lift, and I suddenly felt very light-headed and my heart was racing – not sure if it was the champagne, but it was like being a teenager again about to have that first kiss. We were quiet as he pressed the button and when he leaned against the rail that ran around the edge of the walls and crossed his legs, I had to fight the urge to pounce on him, which surprised me a little.

"Thank you for a lovely end to my evening," I said to break the silence.

"I was just thinking the same thing," he smiled as the lift stopped and the doors pinged open. I stepped out as did he, but as I started to step away he took hold of my hand and pulled me back toward him;

"Would it be very inappropriate of me to ask if I may kiss you goodnight?" He asked with his face inches away from mine. I didn't want to say no, I had no reason to. So I took a tiny step nearer to him.

"I think…" I swallowed hard as his eyes bore into mine, "… that a kiss would be very acceptable." I smiled. He pulled me into his chest and placed his feet either side of mine. My breathing was faster and my heart was in my throat and felt like it would explode at any moment, but he just smiled at me and took my face in his hands. His warm breath on my lips made me close my eyes and as his lips delicately brushed against mine I melted.

His kiss was intense but not forceful, and as we both sank into it my arms found their way around his neck. One of his slipped around the back of my head and the other around my waist. We were definitely wrapped up in the sensual way our bodies were responding and when he ended it he rested his forehead against mine, and simply said. "Wow!" I placed my hand on his cheek and smiled. "My thoughts exactly." I paused for a second and took a deep breath, "I think I had better go to my room."

"I think that may be very wise." We stepped apart and I started to move away, our fingers being the last thing to disconnect. He pressed the button to call the lift and continued to watch me as I did him. When its door opened and before he stepped in he just said, "I'm very glad that I met you, Jenny." Then he paused briefly. "Say, what is your last name?" he enquired and I realised that we didn't even know each other's full names. I laughed.

"It's Walker." He nodded;

"Then I am very pleased to have met you, Jenny Walker," he smiled.

"Likewise Ethan… Actually, what is your surname?" I asked. He then laughed out loud.

"It's James, not too exciting." I stood very straight.

"Then it has been my pleasure to have met you Mr Ethan James," I smiled. He stepped into the waiting lift.

"I'll be in touch," he called as the doors started to close.

"I'm counting on it!" I shouted back. I smiled to myself – *what the hell had come over me?* I jumped around the corridor like a giddy school girl. *Oh my God, that was amazing.* I tried to control myself and then leant against our room door and took a deep breath in, when I was brought back to reality.

The door unexpectedly opened and I tumbled in backwards and fell on my back, to look up and find Beth hovering over me. I burst out laughing.

"What time do you call this young lady?" she said in a serious tone, and then she started laughing. She helped me up; "Well? What happened?" she asked as I threw myself onto the sofa.

"We had Cristal champagne in the bar, and talked and laughed and then he walked me back to my room," I gushed.

"Is that it?" she asked, like her life depended on it. I smiled again.

"He asked if he could kiss me goodnight."

"I hope you bloody said yes!" she shot back at me. I nodded. "Jesus, I'm impressed – I want to know all the details. How was it?"

"Amazing, and I don't feel guilty at all," I replied. She punched the air with excitement;

"Yes, I knew it – I thought you looked happy. Just

think how giddy you'll be if you have sex!" she quickly interjected. I sat up.

"Hey, one step at a time, Beth! I did however find out his surname this evening."

"Which is?" she asked.

"James – Mr Ethan James," I said with feeling. Beth sat a minute and then started laughing uncontrollably. "What?" I kept repeating.

"It's nothing," she kept laughing.

"Spit it out!" I shouted at her.

"It's just, if things pan out and go well, then you could be Jenny James," she replied.

"… and that's funny because?" I asked getting slightly annoyed now.

"Well – Jenny James – it sounds like a porn star name." She kept laughing "Ethan and the busty Jenny James," she said in a funny voice and then burst into more hysterical laughter. I tried not to laugh, but she was infectious. I thanked her for finding me and my life so amusing, and poked her numerous times. After an outburst of ten minutes I suggested we go to bed. Beth in her infinite wisdom had put the two drunken bums in the same room, and so we retreated into mine and had a good night's sleep.

Chapter 6

The early morning sunshine on the balcony was blissful. Beth and I had ordered breakfast in the room again, and decided we would take a bit longer before going down to the pool or beach, just to give the other two the chance to awaken from their drunken coma. Beth remarkably, given she had been drinking, was not bad at all. She tried to explain that was mainly due to the fact that she had stuck to wine, and not tried every cocktail that the group we were in tried to coax her into having. Rose and Amanda, not wanting to disappoint and trying to behave like the younger part of the crowd, tried everything they were given. It did not bode well for the rest of the day as a group, I decided.

We took a mug of tea onto the balcony and took in the view. In the distance there were boats bobbing around which reminded me of the offer from Ethan.

"So, Beth – Ethan found it highly amusing last night that we had tried our first boat trip out here on the Sunset Party Cruise, in fact he nearly choked on his champagne," I commented, reminiscing.

"It wasn't that bad, it was a change. Anyway what would he suggest?" she asked as she turned to face me.

"Well, that's just it. He's invited us all on board his

yacht on Friday after he finishes the closure of his sale here at the hotel. Do you want to go?" I casually took another sip of tea.

"Are you kidding me? Hell, I'm in. This man is proving more likeable by the minute. A yacht, eh? Wow, he obviously has some serious cash," she replied smiling.

"I'm not bothered about his money," I remarked. She stopped drinking her tea and placed her hand on my arm.

"No, I know that, honey. It's still nice though," she said before winking at me. "So what does he suggest?"

"Well, we need to finalise. He told me to ask you guys first, but he suggested being on board at approximately eleven thirty and then having a celebratory lunch, and then a swim in the sea after sailing around the north of the island," I informed her happily.

"Sounds lovely, I'm sure the others will want to go. In fact I don't care if they don't want to go, I definitely am."

"He says he's going to invite Josh too; thinks it will be hard trying to entertain four women on his own." I told her knowing that she liked Josh.

"Hell, it would be entertainment enough Jenny just watching him dote on you all day, or better still stick his tongue down your throat. It would make a change from watching the eighteen-year-olds," she teased.

"Yeah, thanks for that. You're really good at lowering the tone!" I laughed with her.

"What time is it? I think that we should wake them up and start the paracetamol and coffee drip feed now, or they are never going to move today. Anyway, we have exciting news and an invitation for them," she said with excitement while bouncing back in the balcony door. I smiled: this holiday, even though I didn't know it at first, by my own admission was just what I needed.

"I agree," I answered. So we went into their room and started jumping on the beds to wake them, much to their disappointment. Amanda sat up; "What the hell are you doing?" she enquired with dismay as we continued by dragging their covers off.

"Oh no, no, no…" Rose interjected sounding worse than we imagined.

"Right, both of you up and have coffee, paracetamol, food and a shower," Beth insisted in a motherly tone.

"In that order?" Amanda asked as she staggered her way to the bathroom. Both Beth and I laughed at her. When she reappeared moments later she insisted on the coffee first, Rose then made a move.

"Maybe you need orange juice first, Rose, a little vitamin C," I grimaced. She turned and looked at me and then held her hand up and did that infamous wretch before dashing to the toilet. I looked at Beth.

"And there is our cue to leave!" she said quickly exiting the door. I must admit I was never one for being able to be around sickly people. Even when the boys were ill, it took all of my focus to stop myself from being sick.

I followed Beth, and we sat and had another cup of tea while Amanda slowly picked at some sweet American pancakes. I think her thought was definitely to soak it up as soon as possible. Poor Rose appeared and slumped on the sofa.

"Well, I feel much better now. How the hell did we get back last night?" she then asked.

"My feet hurt – I suspect we walked," Amanda moaned while rubbing at the soles of her feet.

"Oh my God, you two were obviously obliterated last night. Thanks to both Jenny and me, you were brought back to your room, *'yes'*, walking, *'yes'* – well staggering, pain in the arses – *'big bloody yes!'*" Beth told them.

"Oops, I can remember snippets of the night. Was I talking to some guy who was trying to drag me to a tequila bar?" Amanda grimaced.

"Oh that was one of many, but don't be embarrassed, honey, I think that you offered your company to everyone you passed, insisting that you weren't drunk and that you could definitely keep partying all night," Beth informed her. Rose laughed. "I don't know what you're laughing at, young lady, you had your tongue down the throats of three men that I saw and two of them, one after the other in the group on the boat!" she finished before then taking a sip of tea.

"I'm sorry, guys, why the hell did I drink so much?" Rose then said as she made her way to the breakfast trolley, taking forever to decide what to have first.

"I'm not so sure it was just the quantity, Rose, but the quality. I mean you did pretty much drink only spirits in cocktails galore. It doesn't really matter as long as you had fun." I tried to say that hoping it would help make her feel better.

"I cannot believe that you two are alright. It's like you didn't drink at all," she then said before forcing a piece of toast into her mouth. She slumped back on the sofa with her coffee.

"I had enough, but not as much as you," Beth happily quipped. While I just shrugged at them, I wasn't about to start telling them that I had mostly soft drinks. "So, while you two were up here with me in your alcoholic coma when we got back, Jenny here was having champagne with Mr Handsome downstairs in the bar." Beth then winked at me, Amanda instantly sat upright with interest.

"Ethan?" she enquired. "What the hell was he doing here so late? Stalking you?"

"No, it's not what you think. He had been for dinner with the owner of this hotel – he's actually bought Ethan's hotel. Anyway, we saw each other and he asked me if I would like a drink with him before retiring, so I agreed," I tried to explain. Rose smiled at me.

"…and?" she quizzed.

"Well, actually, funny that you should ask, but he has invited all of us on his yacht on Friday," I smiled as I looked at Beth.

"Yeah right, funny – pull the other one!" Amanda replied, thinking that I was being sarcastic.

"No, honestly, Amanda, he really has," Beth confirmed for my convenience.

"You're bloody joking," Rose then replied as she sat forward. I shook my head.

"Well, after witnessing you two last night, he asked where we had been," I started.

"Oh, please tell me you didn't tell him," Rose then grimaced.

"I did tell him, much to his amusement, and he said if we had wanted to go on a boat then we should have just asked him. He's here Friday morning closing this sale and said we can be on his yacht for eleven thirty and then have a celebratory lunch, before sailing around the north of the island and taking a swim," I explained again, for their benefit. "Of course, that's only if you want to," I said very matter-of-factly.

"This bloody Ethan is turning out to be a real winner. Hell, I'm in. It's like winning the lottery," Amanda smirked.

"Fine with me." Rose replied. "Do we get to watch you making out?" she then grinned. Amanda nearly choked on her tea;

"Hey, I'd not thought about that."

"I did, I asked the same question this morning," Beth added laughing.

"God, we've managed to lower the tone again," I said as I sighed and sat back.

They carried on laughing for a minute and then they all piled on me, rubbing my arms and head in a sisterly fashion and saying "It's great. We're only jealous you know – he is really hot." It didn't last long before Rose sat back up and insisted; "Oh crap, right that's enough of that; don't know if the room is spinning or it's just my stomach." She blew air out fast and we all quickly moved away from her thinking she was about to be ill again. She just made a whimpering sound; "Please don't let me drink that much again," was all that she could say. We carried on drinking tea and giggled at her very sorry but highly amusing state.

By the time we had managed to get downstairs to the pool, and Rose had made a point of saying that she wasn't moving once on a sun lounger in the shade, it was nearly eleven o'clock. Beth and I had a stroll on the beach and dared to brave the sea, which was actually very refreshing. Once back we ordered lunch – sandwiches and drinks around our loungers – and simply chilled. I hadn't felt this relaxed in such a long time, and to be quite honest, despite the late and drunken nights I was having the most amazing time. As the others kicked back and started reading, with the exception of Rose who was simply sleeping off her hangover, I reached for my phone and decided to text Ethan our decision;

'Ethan, thank you for last night – it was lovely to see you. I have raised the suggestion of joining you on your yacht tomorrow with the others, and they would love to, if that is still alright? Let me know what we need to bring, and what time to be in the reception and I will make sure I organise them all! Jenny.'

I toyed with the idea of putting a kiss at the end, but then wondered if that was too much, so I just hit send and then realised that I had those butterflies… again. I sat back and picked up my book, but no sooner had I opened to the next page and started reading, when my phone pinged. I smiled and reached for it.

'Good afternoon, Jenny, I hope that you are enjoying the day and your friends were not too worse for wear this

morning? It was my pleasure to see you last night, a
perfect end to a long day. How about you meet me in the
reception at 11? You don't need to bring anything, except
probably your swimwear! I'm fairly certain that none of
you will want to be skinny dipping! Look forward to
seeing you, Ethan X'

I blushed instantly and laughed out loud just once at his reply, which made Amanda look up at me and she just smiled. He sent me a kiss, so it would have been perfectly alright for me to do the same. I replied quickly:

'I am looking forward to it already, I hope today passes
quickly. J X'

I hit send and then smiled to myself, I was being absolutely truthful. I really couldn't wait to see him tomorrow and so the sooner it came, the better. I longed to be in his company again, as he made me feel so important and worth spending time with, and quite honestly I had really missed that feeling.

I managed to read another six chapters of my Nicholas Sparks book, *The Longest Ride* which was just adorable, and a true love story of two couples that was rich with warmth and character. When it reached four o'clock and the pool had become a hub of noise now that more people had woken from the night before, Rose decided that she needed a hot shower and her bed for an hour. Amanda thought that it sounded like a great idea too, and so the two of them disappeared upstairs.

Beth and I ordered a glass of wine – it seemed the right time of day, and we were on holiday. We sat there in the sunshine and sipped slowly while chatting and people watching. When we reached the last half-inch in our glass she suggested that we go upstairs and repaint our nails. She was sweet in pointing out that she wanted me to look my best for tomorrow, and she always travelled with an array of beauty products, so I agreed that would be a nice thing to do and we packed up and retreated to the coolness of our room.

The others were fast asleep still, and so we sat in the lounge and embarked on a mission of painting each other's toes and then our own fingers. We had music playing lightly from Beth's iPhone, as there was a docking station in the room and it actually was a pretty delightful way to spend the rest of our day. She managed with wet nails to pour us another glass of wine from the fridge, and as we sat laughing and joking about her love life and while waiting for our nails to dry, Amanda appeared.

"Sounds like you guys are having a blast."

"Yeah, do you want to join us?" Beth enquired.

"Maybe the painting nails, but not the wine drinking," she said touching her obviously still delicate tummy.

"Take your pick." Beth gestured at the many bottles of nail vanish in all the colours of the rainbow and more.

"Bloody hell, Beth. How do you manage to get everything within your weight limit in your case?" she replied as she sat and looked at all the many bottles. I have to admit it had crossed my mind also.

She grabbed herself a coke and then sat and did her

own nails, toes and fingers the same colour. She laughed at herself saying it looked like a five-year-old had painted them, and just as she finished and we all got another drink, Rose walked in looking better than earlier. She fell on the sofa beside Beth.

"Hey, what you all up to?" she asked innocently. We all waved our nails at her and she smiled. "Not got the bloody patience!" she simply said.

"What do we fancy doing tonight?" Amanda asked us.

"Something simple, that means minimum effort," Rose chipped in.

"Why don't we watch a girly movie and get some room service?" I suggested, they all looked at me.

"Bloody brilliant idea, I like it," Amanda said before leaning back into the sofa.

"Agreed," Rose said sounding relieved.

"Beth?" I asked hopefully.

"Fine with me! Let's all get our pyjamas on and veg out in front of the television," she smiled.

The thought of chilling in our room the night before I saw Ethan was the best outcome that I could have hoped for. As I sat with my newly painted toes stretched out on the footrest in front of my chair and I sipped on my wine, I let out a contented sigh. We sat and talked for a while, I had more digs thrown at me about tomorrow, involving bikini wearing and making sure that my bikini line was trimmed to perfection. I was interrogated as to whether or not I would kiss him again, and would I do it in front of them and so on... I was starting to just brush their remarks off, but as they kept coming I decided to take my leave for a while and take a hot shower.

"Not a cold one then?" Amanda chided me.

"No need for one yet, Amanda, but give me time," I joked with her.

I pushed my door closed and set the shower running. The girls were singing along to music and chatting, and so I knew that I could switch off for a few minutes. I lay quietly on the bed with my underwear on and just closed my eyes and then felt myself drifting; you know that boundary of not quite asleep but not completely awake either? My thoughts were of turquoise water and yachts and Ethan. I opened my eyes and made myself go and jump in the shower before I started dreaming about more intimate things, which did in all honesty scare me just a little. The shower was divine and soothing and once dried and moisturised I was happy to see that I had a deeper glow about my skin from the sun today. Knowing that we were staying in meant that I could leave my hair to dry naturally which did it the world of good. As I carefully brushed it through I smiled, listening to Beth and Amanda trying to sing along to the songs that were playing, I was brought back to my senses when I realised that my phone was ringing. I ran to the bedside table and looked at the caller id and was happier than ever to see that it was Ethan. I quickly answered:

"Hey. Hi."

"Hi, I'm sorry to call unannounced, I hope that I haven't caught you in the middle of anything?" he said, and his voice had my body tingling again. I sat on the bed and screwed my toes up in the carpet nervously, then hoped I'd not ruined the newly painted nails.

"Not at all, I've just had a shower and I'm happy that you called," I replied, then grimacing wondering why the hell I needed to give him an itinerary of my movements.

"Getting ready for a night out on the town again?"

"Actually no, we are going to have a quiet night in our room tonight, watching girly films and getting room service. I think last night's drinking binge by some of my friends definitely took its toll. I am actually quite glad about it – but don't tell them," I tried to say with humour. He laughed.

"Sounds perfect."

"Did you need to tell me something about tomorrow?" I asked wondering why he had called in the first place.

"Yes and no. I just wanted to say that I was glad that you had all accepted my invitation, and that I was looking forward to it," he sounded a little embarrassed.

"Well I am very glad that you asked us, I'm looking forward to it too. I seem to be indulging in some very new experiences on this holiday and I actually cannot wait to explore the island from your yacht tomorrow. Sounds idyllic."

"Well, I better do a good job then," he replied and I knew that he was smiling. "So until tomorrow then?" he said, and then I was sure that I heard Josh call him and I knew that he had to go.

"Until tomorrow. Have a good evening, Ethan!"

"You too," he replied, and then he was gone.

I placed my phone against my chest and took in a deep

breath. I was certainly back on the path to normality. I had just put my phone back on the side table when Rose came bouncing in announcing that it was time to get casual, and that we were going to order in some room service and wine. As it had been my suggestion to have a night in, they wanted my input into which movie to pick. It was nearly seven o'clock and so I slipped into my shorts and vest top, loosely tied up my hair and went back to the lounge.

We all huddled on the large sofa opposite the television; we had some wine in the fridge but had ordered more to come with our dinner. As the opening scenes unfolded and the music started to *Hitch* – which we decided would be a good laugh to start with – Rose and Beth started doing a little seated dance and I knew that the night was going to be fun. We laughed, sighed a lot at the romance and as there were so many lines in this film that we loved, we decided that we would try and take a line from every film we watched that night and somehow make it work with our day tomorrow. The first from *Hitch* was;

'Life is not the amount of breaths you take, it's the moments that take your breath away.'

"I reckon you're going to be breathless by the end of this holiday, Jenny," Rose gestured, doing what I can only describe as some kind of grinding action, but it wasn't flattering in any way.

"Yes, thanks for that. It would seem that this is what you all want me to aspire to during this holiday – a night of passion with Ethan. He may not even be thinking about me in that way," I proposed.

"Don't be stupid, he has the serious hots for you. I have no doubt about that," Amanda said, as there was a knock at the door.

"The bloody service in this hotel is amazing. I only ordered that food about fifteen minutes ago," Beth was impressed as she stood up and went to the door.

She stepped back once she had opened it and glared for a moment, then she looked at us and with arms crossed she gave me that *'We told you so'* clever look. She made a gesture at the open door and beckoned for me to go over, which I did. There was a barman stood there, with a tray on which stood a bucket holding a bottle of Cristal champagne on ice and four glasses. A card stood in the middle with my name on it. The barman just stood and smiled at me;

"Jenny?" he enquired. I nodded. He handed me the card.

'Enjoy your night in ladies; I look forward to seeing you all tomorrow – Ethan.'

I curled my lips in trying not to smile, but blushed and then asked the barman to bring it in and open it.

Both Rose and Amanda had now shuffled to the end of the sofa and as music drifted from the television while the film carried on playing, Amanda snapped the card from my hand. She read it and then threw it to Rose, who just sighed heavily and exclaimed, "Oh my God, we told you he was into you."

"I want to know how the hell he knows that we were staying in tonight. Is he spying on us?" Beth then interjected, and they all turned toward me, eyebrows raised and glared.

"I will leave you to it ladies, enjoy," the barman said as he exited the room. The girls all continued to stare at me, waiting for an answer.

"He called me while I was in my room, he was glad that we had accepted his invitation, and then asked what we were doing, so I told him," I explained.

"Well, I think he's a real gentleman then. It's a nice gesture, sending you gifts to share with your friends, but I swear to you he will be expecting something in return," Amanda then said which kind of brought me down to earth with a thump.

"I'm not going to do anything that I don't want to, Amanda. If he wants to spend his money doing nice things, who am I to stop him? I didn't ask for this," I tried to tell them. Beth had heard the tone of irritation in my voice, and as always she neutralised the situation;

"Hey, guys, come on. It's champagne, not a request for one of her kidneys or anything," she said humorously.

Rose leant forward and picked up a glass; "Yeah, sod it – it's only champagne. Let's enjoy it." She held up her glass and Beth reached for one too. Amanda then realised that she was being a little too protective, I suspect. She picked the final two up and passed one to me;

"I'm sorry, I don't want to spoil your fun. I think

97

I'm jealous," she said, and then she looked at me with apologetic puppy dog eyes.

"Can we promise to say no more about it, me and Ethan that is? I like him, I'm not denying that, but I am not saying that means I'm going to jump into bed with him, whether he buys me gifts or not! Can I just see how I feel as we go along?" I asked trying to be as honest as possible. Amanda smiled at me.

"Of course, it's great that you are finding it easy to be in the company of another man, and honestly I am just being a cranky middle-aged woman. I mean, my relationship isn't exactly electric, is it?" she said.

"Maybe that's just what yours needs, Amanda. Some jump leads on Gerry's penis might just give him a kick start again!" Beth said trying to be serious, but it ended up with us all having hysterics. "To friends," Beth managed to say laughing, and we all chinked glasses and continued with our film watching until the food and yet more wine arrived.

By the time we had watched *Pretty Woman*, we had had a few happy tears, drank the champagne, eaten the food and opened and started on the wine. Beth had managed to scroll through the pay TV and found *Dirty Dancing*; yet another favourite movie of ours from an eon ago. She started it going and we all moved the plates, and I could feel a dance along coming on! It was turning into one of the funniest nights I had spent with the girls in a long time. Our selected lines from *Pretty Woman* (as we could not just stick to one) were: '*In case I forget to tell you later, I had a really good time tonight.*' and

Beth's favourite: *'I'm gonna treat you so nice, you're never gonna let me go.'*

Beth was finding an inordinate amount of pleasure in trying to make up scenarios where these lines could be used during the holiday, and of course they all pretty much involved me.

"Oh, the line from this film, girls, has to be…" Rose shouted as we all replied in unison:

"Nobody puts Baby in the corner."

Then Rose started laughing, and suggested for the sake of ease of use that we should change it to: *'Nobody puts Jenny in the corner.'*

I didn't have the patience or straight head to argue the point, I just waved my hands in the air and said, "Whatever."

The dancing (if you can call it that) was the number -one priority while watching this film; every time a great song came on we all jumped up and bounced around the room. It was tiring, but fun and at the same time hysterical in so many different ways; Rose and Beth tried dancing together, Amanda did her impression of Baby learning her dance steps to 'Wipeout' and Rose at one point stood on the sofa and said she wanted to jump into our arms so that we could lift her above our heads like the last lift of the film. We quickly sat her down and told her that was an absolute no. By the time it ended we were exhausted; it was after midnight and we had drunk far more than we wanted to, so we decided to retire hoping that we could get ready in the morning without feeling too hungover. The room unfortunately now looked like it had been the base for a party hosted by a famous pop group and I grimaced a little at the mess, but we promised each other that we would straighten it out in the morning, and with that we all collapsed into bed for a good night's sleep.

Chapter 7

We woke up refreshed, tidied the room, showered and then put casual clothing on to go down and eat breakfast. I kept tentatively looking around hoping that Ethan didn't appear seeing me with no make-up or with my loose trousers and t-shirt on that did nothing for anyone's shape. However, I had no need to panic. It would seem that he was obviously busy in his meeting, and I hoped it was going well for him, or our trip on his yacht would not be as enjoyable as we hoped. It was now nine thirty and we had just returned to our room. Hair done, minimal make-up on and a nice little sundress later and then it was decision time on the bikini. Rose insisted on the coral red one, and I to be honest had chosen that one too – it was just a little sexier than the other. I packed it into my bag along with a beach towel, sun cream, my sunglasses and some extra make-up for touching up after a swim. My brush was the last thing to go into my bag, after I had checked and re-checked I didn't look like I had just woken up, or been dragged through a hedge backwards. I had left my hair alone after drying last night; it was slightly wavy but I felt like it looked more natural, like I hadn't taken too much time. The same with the tinted moisturiser; better than none and I save something for later tonight! I hadn't realised I had thought about this in such detail. I slid my wedges on and stuffed my flip-flops into my bag and then went into the lounge to find the others fussing over what they should take.

"Are we ready?" I asked to stop them flustering.

"Think so," Beth replied winking at me, before whistling loudly to usher the others to the door.

I was the last one out of the room and as we all stepped into the lift I decided to give them a few ground rules. "Right girls. Number one: no sexual references or innuendos on this trip, particularly you, Beth," I said as I pointed at her. "Number two: no purposefully leaving us alone, because that will be so obvious and probably uncomfortable for both him and me. Number three…" I started.

"God, there's more?" Rose asked, as Amanda sniggered.

"Yes, and this one applies to you too," I said looking at Rose. "There is to be no fighting over, slobbering over or touching up of Josh, by any of you and certainly not all at the same time," I insisted.

"Bloody hell, you're like the fun police," Amanda stated sadly. "I tell you what, don't worry about us; we will entertain Josh as we see fit. You concentrate on spending some quality time with your beau," she smiled at me before high-fiving Beth.

"Too bloody right," Beth agreed, and I knew even though I had said what I had wanted to, it had probably fallen on deaf ears!

The doors opened and I took a deep breath; it was

now ten to eleven, and we wanted to make sure we were down in the reception on time to be on his yacht for eleven thirty or thereabouts. As I walked scanning the reception area, the others seemed happy to chatter away and discuss how much fun they were expecting to have. I gave a little sigh of relief to myself when I saw both he and Josh already near the entrance. He looked gorgeous, he had taken off his jacket – dark blue, which matched his trousers – and had started to roll up his white shirt sleeves. He turned and faced us once he spotted that we were walking toward them, and smiled. Josh gave one of the girls behind me a large grin; I didn't turn to see which one of them, perhaps they didn't know either.

"Ladies. A pleasure to see you again," Josh smiled as he then kissed every one of us in turn on the cheek. My friends, of course, were giggling like small schoolgirls now. Ethan walked straight up to me.

"Jenny, how are you?" he asked as he placed one hand at the small of my back while he kissed me gently on the cheek, lingering for just a second or two. I smiled.

"I'm very well, thank you. More to the point, how did the meeting go?" I asked hopefully.

"Very well indeed, thank you for asking," he smiled. "All squared away, so let's not talk about that. I think that it's time to have some fun," he grinned.

"Oh yes, fun time it is. Let's go!" Beth shouted out as she started making her way through the doors with a slight salsa move. Josh laughed at her and then held the door gesturing for the others to go through after her, which they did willingly.

Ethan looked at me and then asked for me to follow on, making sure that he kept his hand right where he had first placed it in the small of my back. I had to admit that it sent shivers up my spine, but I tried not to show the fact that his touch could do that to me. As we stepped out into the bright sunshine I reached for my sunglasses and put them on. When I turned to look at Ethan, he had done the same and I nearly gasped but quickly stopped myself. Oh my, oh my, it was like a moment from a film with an actor you find attractive and would most probably be drooling over, while thinking you'd say yes to anything – if he were real and could actually ask you! But Ethan was real, and he was standing right in front of me. I quickly looked at the girls and then remembered our pact the night before and so I made the most of this moment. I leant toward him touching his arm and whispered in his ear;

"In case I forget to tell you later; I had a really good time today and tonight." Not quite the *Pretty Woman* line but close enough. Then I kissed him on the cheek. He looked at me and then swallowed hard.

It was a shall I or shall I not kiss you right now moment, which was broken when Josh shouted across;

"Come on Ethan, or we will never get to the yacht." He had a hint of sarcasm in his voice, and I knew they were all watching, which made me blush. So I quickly turned after smiling back and walked toward the car that the girls had hopped into. It was not the one from shopping the other day I noted. Josh put his hand up and stopped me as I got closer; "Ah sorry, full up over here. You, Jenny, will be travelling with Ethan," he smiled as he pointed to the car that was more familiar.

"Race you there!" Amanda then called happily as Josh jumped in at the side of her and started the engine. I pulled a face at her and walked to Ethan's car.

Ever the gentleman, he was stood waiting and threw his jacket onto the back seat before opening my door. I carefully slid into the luxurious leather seat after placing my beach bag behind it first. By the time he had walked around to the driver's side, I had re-straightened my sundress and run my fingers through my hair. He started the engine and looked at me, tanned, smelling gorgeous and with sunglasses on making him look hotter than you can imagine – he simply said, "You look beautiful today." Needless to say I melted again.

The journey seemed quick and was nothing resembling a race. Although we could see Josh ahead of us, Ethan had no intentions of racing on the coastal roads. We neared the far side of the bay and then went just beyond it where they both parked next to a jetty where a speedboat was waiting. I grabbed my bag and as we walked to the waiting boat I felt a little nervous. Josh jumped in and helped the girls onto it with ease, each one of them swooning in the process. Ethan got me to wait while he jumped on board and then with hands around my waist he lifted me down.

"I suggest you take a seat, ladies; our captain here likes to travel with speed," Josh then informed us. The girls took his advice and sat quickly looking slightly nervous. Ethan grabbed my hand and pulled me to sit next to him.

"Hold on," he said as the engines started. I moved in

closer to him and he responded by placing his arm around me. I felt safe in his arms.

By the time we had left the jetty the girls were squealing with delight at the exhilarating feeling of speed, along with the breeze and the water spray gently covering the skin. Josh laughed at them as did both Ethan and I. We did not travel long before we were winding through a multitude of expensive boats and yachts, and I suddenly realised that Ethan must be wealthier than I had ever imagined: to even hire one of these must cost a small fortune. We made our way through them and continued toward a yacht sat way out in the sea, quite a distance from the others, but as we neared it was easy to see its size and quality. The captain pulled up to the back of the yacht and waited for us to carefully disembark from what now seemed a very small speedboat in comparison. Ethan tipped him, and the captain thanked him by saying to just call when he was needed again. That was fairly impressive, I thought; everyone seems to want to bend over backwards to do things for him.

We made our way onto the top deck, and it really did not disappoint. All four of us stood and turned, taking in the whole luxury that surrounded us. Josh had moved to the table where a chilled bottle of champagne stood and he started to pour us all a glass;

"Well, Ethan. I'm loving you more every minute, and I now agree that the 'party boat' we were on recently was like the cheap first car that you buy. Whereas this… well it's like a bloody Ferrari. There's even a bloody jacuzzi!" Beth then stated.

"Glad that you like it, Beth, but it is only on hire though so don't get too excited," he told her.

The girls happily flopped down onto the seating on the large sun deck, and took a glass of champagne from Josh. Ethan had poured both himself and me a glass and we stood for a second and chinked glasses;

"This really is beautiful, Ethan," I remarked, because it was. "I feel like someone is going to wake me up in a minute!"

"Would you like a tour?" he asked smiling.

"I'd love one," I happily replied as he took my hand and led me through the top deck of the boat.

"The best views are from here, small relaxing area, along with the Jacuzzi, total chill-out area," he started before we took the stairs. Once on the deck below he continued; "So, al fresco dining, large lounge area, Josh's room next to the gym of course, but then it's fairly serious stuff. Come on, I will introduce you to the captain," he said, as we strolled through sipping our champagne.

The bridge was like something from NASA. I'd never seen so many gadgets and instruments. It looked like you needed some serious qualifications to sail this thing, and as it glided through the water like a knife through butter you could hardly tell that we were moving. I happily shook hands with the captain, who seemed equally happy to meet me. Then after looking at the view through the bridge windows, Ethan bobbed his head toward the door and gestured that we continue the tour. We made our way to the floor below, and before we knew it we stood in the middle of the master suite. The bed was huge, the linen was expensive and there was a large television on the wall opposite. A bar housed spirits, a velvet-covered sofa filled a wall… it was seriously expensive furniture. I stood and turned to look at him, he looked a little flustered and so I turned back and followed the wall to a large en-suite, the shower was bigger than any I had ever seen. All of his toiletries stood neatly on the marble-topped sink. There was still a lingering smell of his delightful aftershave which I inhaled deeply. I walked out through another door and into his dressing area. His suits were neatly hanging, shoes aligned underneath and then I smiled at his casual clothes that were folded and neatly placed on the shelves to the side. I walked back out, and had the biggest urge to just have him right there, but it really wasn't appropriate timing. He was stood waiting for my return; he held his champagne nervously in one hand and had his other in his trouser pocket.

"Well? What do you think?" he asked with a hint of a quiver in his voice. I suddenly had an overwhelming amount of confidence. I placed my glass on the table near the sofa, and smiled at him. I walked across calmly and we simply looked at each other until I was stood directly in front of him. I swear that I could almost feel him trembling.

"It's better than the recent boat that I partied on!" I joked. "It's really amazing, Ethan, more impressive than I was imagining. I particularly like this room," I then grinned.

"My room?" he confirmed. I nodded.

"I have a question for you," I then asked needing to get this initial heat out of my system before I embarrass myself and pounce on him.

"Go ahead," he smiled nervously. I took his glass off him and reached to the nearby furniture which housed the television and placed it carefully down. I could tell by his body language he had no idea what to expect, so he placed his other hand in his pocket and watched me closely.

I returned to where I was stood and took in a deep breath. I smiled, and even though I had butterflies I felt in control of them;

"I want you to know that I'm really glad that you asked me to spend more time with you," I started and he smiled. I placed my hand on his chest and I felt him inhale quickly as he looked at my hand and then back at me. I continued; "So while we have a moment together without those rather rowdy friends of mine watching my every move, would you allow me to kiss you, by way of a thank you?" I asked as I stared directly into his eyes.

He didn't move initially but simply replied, "I think I would find that acceptable," before giving me a wicked smile almost in appreciation of my request. I stepped closer and slid my hand up to his shoulder and around the back of his neck, and without seeing it move his hand was around my waist and the hairs on the back of my neck stood to attention. I smiled again and then slowly moved my mouth toward his.

We were breathing more deeply and the intensity was at exploding point, so before our lips touched I whispered, "I'm really glad that we met, Ethan James." I hesitated a moment and then I couldn't resist any longer. The moment that our lips touched, it was like an electrical current running though our bodies, his hands pulled me closer and we both gasped for air between each synchronisation of our lips. My hands were around his neck and his tongue delicately probed mine as he gently but with commitment kissed me in a way I hadn't experienced for a very long time. Within seconds his hands were across my back squeezing me closer to his body. Aroused was an understatement; I think that went for both of us. We continued for a few more seconds, then as if we both read each other's minds we slowly but reluctantly pulled away. He continued to hold me close and his hand moved to my cheek, he kissed me gently again on the lips, and then looked at me.

"I'm really glad that I met you too, Jenny, and I really have to say that I was slightly nervous about what you were going to ask me then, but that was a question that I loved answering," he whispered back. We were still within inches of each other's faces and my breathing was still faster than it ought to be. I laughed and rested my forehead on his. We were stood embracing, and it was a sensation that I was enjoying when we heard voices.

"So this is where all the action takes place?" I heard Beth saying slightly louder than normal; I knew she was giving me a heads up. I stepped back and straightened myself up then picked up my glass as did Ethan, and I returned to the dressing room but not before smiling at him and the thought of what we had just done. "Ah here you are!" she then said to Ethan.

"Hey, girls, you'll like it in here," I called from the dressing room, and within seconds they were in there with me. They gawped at the immaculately tidy area.

"Ethan, I'm impressed," Amanda called before they all then wondered into the bathroom, continuing their expressions of amazement. I wondered back into the bedroom and looked at Ethan. I licked my lips, which still tasted of him, and then realised that Josh was stood staring at me, and so I blushed a little. Ethan simply continued smiling and then threw back the rest of his champagne walked toward me and grabbed my hand and marched me past Josh stating, "Let's continue our tour; it's nearly lunchtime."

As we passed Josh I curled my lips in feeling the slightest bit like I had been caught with my hand in the biscuit jar. Josh, however, just winked at me and smiled as if he knew what had happened and gestured for me to continue. With the girls following along close behind, the rest of the tour seemed slightly less fulfilling. The yacht, however, was like a luxury mansion and every bedroom and room on board was more impressive than I was expecting. One of the stewardesses of the boat came to find us to announce that lunch was ready to be served and so we made our way to the third deck to the al fresco dining area. It was a relief to be out of the intense heat while we ate. Ethan was attentive as ever, making sure that I was happy and well fed. It was the most enjoyable experience despite the many questions that the girls threw at poor Josh, asking any personal thing that they could possibly think of that he may be willing to answer. He seemed completely unphased by the whole experience and their intense attention and took it well within his stride, which I remarked about to Ethan a couple of times. "Don't worry about Josh; he knows how to handle himself," he told me with confidence, and so I left them to it as his replies were quite humorous.

Josh completely held us all in conversation. He seemed to know what to say, how far to take it, and when to change the subject. I fast understood why Ethan liked him so much, and I suppose if they were always travelling around it would be fairly lonely, despite having each other, so the girls were probably a nice distraction from his usual business talks. I smiled at them all and closely watched, then had a distinct feeling that he was favouring Rose.

After a delicious lunch and some relaxing in the sunshine watching the island pass by, the engines eventually came to a stop. The view as promised was spectacular and quite honestly I don't know what I was expecting from Ibiza, but the image of the island from here was far more beautiful than I had allowed myself to imagine. I leant on the gold rail that ran around the deck of the yacht and breathed in the warm sea air. As I stood there watching the island dip and rise a little with the movement of the sea, I suddenly felt someone stood very close behind me and then his hands were either side of mine.

"Are you alright?" he gently asked. I smiled and turned my head to catch a glimpse of him.

"I'm more than alright. It really is beautiful viewing

the island from here. I can understand why you like it so much," I replied.

"I can't seem to focus on anything after earlier, but I'll take your word for it!" he joked and I slid my hands over his and stood up so that he could inch his body a little closer. "The others are wanting to take a swim; can I interest you in joining them?" he asked. I turned to face him and stood between his arms.

"Will you be joining us?" I asked. He smiled.

"Would you like me to?" he smoothly asked. I was melting again.

"It will be more fun if you do. Perhaps Josh too, so that the girls can keep drooling over him!" I replied sarcastically. But no sooner as I said it than he appeared in the smallest James Bond-type swimming trunks and the girls sat there with their mouths wide open, which prompted me to laugh.

"Come on then, girls! That blue sea is calling!" Josh shouted loudly. Rose stood first and retrieved her bag;

"Where can I get changed?" she quickly asked as she stood in front of him, not hiding her excitement at looking him up and down.

"My room or one of the others downstairs is fine. I wouldn't suggest Ethan's room though," he smiled. She scurried away like a girl about to be first in line at a Victoria Beckham sale. I continued to chuckle at her and then the others quickly followed along behind, giving Josh the serious head-to-toe check.

Once they had disappeared and I tried to stop laughing, Ethan looked at me; "I love to hear you laugh."

"At Josh's expense," I gestured as Josh had now walked across to us, nibbling on something from the table.

He shrugged his shoulders; "It's fine. I can handle them!" he smirked. He oozed confidence and I liked that about him. "Are you two going to take a dip?" he then quizzed us.

"Absolutely," I said as I retrieved my bag. "After all I have a new bikini to wear!" I smiled and then I winked at Ethan and wondered off to find the others.

I could hear Josh ribbing Ethan a little, and the more I got to know them both the more I liked the relationship that they had. They seemed to be more like brothers than work colleagues, but I knew when he had to be Josh was extremely professional. As I neared the downstairs bedrooms I could hear whispering and giggling and a whole load of Beth making noises that no man should hear, so I went in asking her to quieten down. Rose had already got her bikini on and was desperate to get back up to the deck to be with Josh. I moved quickly out of her way. Beth was doing her best impression of fanning herself to calm her obvious hot flush.

"Bloody hell, Jenny. You are proving to be a diamond on this holiday with meeting Ethan. Did you see those swim trunks? Hell, they don't leave a lot to the imagination. I think I might orgasm when I see him for a second time," Beth said almost palpitating.

"Bloody hell, Beth. Really didn't need to know that – you must be sadly frustrated," Amanda replied with disgust.

"Actually, Amanda, I think looking at Josh, he could probably take all three of you on – one after the other," I sarcastically replied. Beth in response high-fived me. She too changed quickly and went upstairs. Both Amanda and I took our time.

I had to check and re-check about three times from every angle that I looked alright. Amanda found it highly amusing that I asked her about my appearance numerous times. I scooped up my hair and placed a bobble around it, popped my sunglasses on my head and tied my sarong around my middle. I felt decidedly naked, and I was sure that was showing in my body language, but I swallowed hard, put my flip-flops on and took a deep breath before Amanda left the room. We talked all the way up to the deck. As I approached the others, Ethan was there and had changed. His torso out and tanned, it was obvious he relaxed in the sun more regularly than I would have suspected. He had longer swim shorts on than Josh, they were a nice electric blue, and when he turned with his sunglasses on Amanda elbowed me very obviously. I grimaced under my glasses at her.

Ethan passed me a refilled glass of champagne and then after a couple of sips we walked down to the lower deck where the platform and steps were lowered to the sea. A stewardess stood there with masks, snorkels and plenty of towels for when we decided to get out. Ethan leant over and asked her for more champagne to be brought down. Josh, Rose and Beth all jumped in without hesitation. I took off my sarong and sunglasses and then looked at Ethan. He raised his eyebrows at me almost looking like he suspected I would change my mind and so I stood on the end of the platform and dived in. The water was cool and refreshing and as it ran across my skin it felt calming. There was something about swimming freely under the water that made you feel quite serene; perhaps it was the lack of sound. When I surfaced and turned back to the yacht, Amanda was deep in conversation with Ethan, but thankfully they were smiling, albeit staring at me. I bobbed around for a while and then Ethan took off his glasses and dived in too. I was slightly shocked when he surfaced directly in front of me. He placed a hand on my waist, and that skin-to-skin contact made me shiver, then he smiled.

"Nice bikini," he grinned. I blushed.

"Thank you," I laughed. "I hope Amanda wasn't embarrassing me with whatever she was in deep conversation with you about?" He pulled me closer for a second and I found myself bobbing with my arm around his neck.

"Actually, she was singing your praises and saying what an amazing person and friend you were," he started.

"Really? It's not like her."

"Well, I have to agree, so stop worrying. Come on let's swim, or at least try to get that ball off Josh," he then said as he made his way to the others.

We tried to have our own game of some kind of water volleyball, not very successfully, although it was fun all the same. We swam, played, bobbed and floated for a long time. I was starting to feel tired and swam to the yacht and Ethan was quick to follow. I perched on the edge of the platform with my feet dangling in the sea. No sooner had we been sat there when a stewardess appeared and offered us a towel and champagne. Ethan and I laughed at the others for a while, but before long they all felt the same tiredness and they started to swim back. Josh, however, seemed to have other ideas, and managed to coax Rose out on one of the jet skis with him while Ethan and I watched them from the comfort of the seating on deck. Amanda and Beth were quick to stand and watch from the platform. Josh certainly knew how to handle the ski, taking her in circles, across waves and going faster than I would like. When he came back he asked if any of the others would like a try. Beth being Beth held her hand up with excitement and begged him to take her. He did, much to her delight, which she squealed at with complete satisfaction. This I knew I had to watch. He turned, went faster, did circles just as he did with Rose; however, on the third circle Beth, in her excitement obviously, lost her grip on Josh because quite spectacularly she went flying backwards into the sea. It wasn't very ladylike and I knew she would be feeling slightly embarrassed, but nonetheless it was so funny. Amanda and Rose had collapsed on the platform with laughter, I couldn't stop myself and even Ethan laughed as Josh realised that he had lost her. He circled around with a huge grin on his face as she tried to get back on which was even more amusing.

By the time they had returned to the yacht, we were all completely laughed out. Amanda and Rose had joined Ethan and me with a glass of champagne, trying not to make it too obvious at their amusement. It didn't work, however, when she stepped back on deck and made her way to us, trying to act cool and calm she simply said,

"Well, that didn't quite go to plan did it?" We were all quiet for a couple of seconds and looked at her, but then Amanda burst into laughter again and it set us all off. "Oh well that's just great, now I'm the laugh of the afternoon!" she unhappily said. Amanda ran around to her and gave her a huge hug. Beth did laugh a little and could see the funny side.

"In fairness, Beth, at least you had a go. I wouldn't dare!" I replied. "Come and get a glass of champagne," I insisted, as Ethan reached for the bottle to pour her one.

She slumped down on the chair as Josh arrived, still smiling. Beth wasn't looking but Ethan made a gesture to stop him from taunting. He simply placed a hand on her shoulder and asked her if she was alright. She nodded and drank her champagne down pretty much in one. We sat and talked, had nibbles, drank champagne and when a member of the crew came to speak to Ethan I knew that it was time for us to return. I suggested that the girls get changed, but they didn't seem to be in too much of a rush to leave Josh and so I excused myself and went to get dressed. Once I had changed, let my hair back down and brushed it through, reapplied mascara and sprayed some perfume I was good to go. I was so relaxed that I kept my flip-flops on and left the room. As I reached the stairs and was about to go back to the others I heard a noise from Ethan's room, I toyed with the idea of going to look, and after nearly going, then not, I shook my head and just went toward his master suite. He was just finishing up putting on his t-shirt when I neared his door. He looked up at me and smiled.

"Everything okay?"

"Great. It's been a really good day, Ethan; I've had a lovely time," I replied as I placed my bag down by the door.

"I'm glad to hear it." Then, without hesitation, he walked across to me and took my hand to pull me closer.

"If today is anything to go by, I cannot wait for this evening!" I then informed him.

"Ah, well – not quite the same is it at a charity dinner. It's all about money and not as much fun. It will be far better for me and the boys though, with you girls sat at our table," he laughed.

"Well, as you can see we're certainly not boring!" I remarked at our mishaps. He laughed in agreement.

"Tonight is too far away for me," he then said and he looked at me with those gloriously alluring eyes.

"Maybe something to leave you with so you don't forget me then?" I asked him. He didn't need to ask. His hands were on my face and his lips on mine faster than I could think about it. I wanted more of this feeling it was exhilarating and I loved it.

By the time we went back on deck, the girls had decided that we had been up to no good. If that was their look at me for just a kiss, I dread to think what they would do if I admitted anything else. Josh stood to go and get changed; the yacht had been moving for a while and miraculously the girls suddenly moved when he did. He lingered behind Rose and she gave him that look – I knew that they had hit it off. Ethan and I sat and talked, I snuggled up into his chest and just once turned and kissed his neck. That set us off kissing again but we were caught out this time by Beth and Amanda who must have been stood watching us for a few seconds. I knew I blushed, Ethan asked if they would like another drink, which they didn't turn down, and then we all sat together once Rose and Josh appeared with us, both of them looking a little flustered. I smiled at her knowing she had probably been up to the same thing as me; although with Rose's track record a quickie was never out of the question, so I knew we would hear all about that once back.

We dropped anchor offshore, and the speedboat appeared to take us back. I insisted that Ethan and Josh need not come back with us, as they themselves had to get ready, but Josh insisted on driving us back to the hotel, which Ethan seemed pleased about.

"There will be a car collecting you at seven forty-five," Ethan said as we started to step into the speedboat.

He kissed every one of us on the cheek, and as the time was now a quarter to six, it didn't leave us ladies a lot of time really. I reluctantly let go of his hand and stepped into the boat and waved to him. Josh amused us all on the way back to the hotel and simply stated that he looked forward to seeing us later. I somehow had the feeling that tonight was going to be rather amazing as far as my nights go.

Chapter 8

We waved to Josh and all excitedly entered the hotel, the ride in the lift to our room resulting in Rose being quizzed intently by Beth and Amanda about what she had been up to with him. It was a refreshing change from them interrogating me, and as we entered our room she disclosed that nothing more than some heated kissing had happened between them, much to my surprise.

"I'm so pleased that you could contain yourself," I mocked her. Then Beth looked at me.

"Unlike you, young lady, who happily had your tongue down Mr Handsome's throat on one occasion that we saw, and probably not the only time!"

"I hardly had my tongue down his throat, did I? It was more sensual than that." I hoped.

"Oh, it was sensual alright. The way he was looking at you as you left, I bet he is seriously offloading some frustration right now before he sees you again," Rose interjected. We all looked at her with a little bit of disgust.

"Jeeze, Rose, you really know how to paint an image in someone's mind, don't you?" Amanda confirmed.

"That really was something that I didn't need to think about, thanks, Rose," I complained.

"Oh come on… he's a hot-blooded male. He wants you, that's obvious; don't you think that a bit of release from his right hand may be a possibility?" she asked us. We just shook our heads.

"I'd like to think he's saving himself for a magnificent night of passion with our Jenny here, so no, not really," Beth then said, but did so in such a tone that it was like shutting a door on the whole topic, which I was grateful for.

"I'm off for a shower. We don't have that long, do we?" I said as I sloped off to my room, with an image of Ethan in my head that wasn't quite what I had hoped for earlier!

The hot water was like a massage to my skin. I washed my hair as the salt water that had drentched it had not done it any favours, and was feeling very refreshed when I exited the bathroom and Rose stepped in. Moisturised to perfection and with the added help of Beth's illuminating highlighter brushed up my shins and arms, I felt like I had a lovely glow. I finished my hair and make-up and before I knew it, it was seven twenty. Amanda had appeared suggesting that it would be a nice idea to have a quick drink in the bar before we left and so I reached in the wardrobe for my dress and slipped it on. This shade of lilac looked even nicer now against my bronzed skin, and the shoes were just perfect. I grabbed a small clutch bag, filled it with essentials and walked into the lounge. When I looked up the others were staring at me.

"What?" I asked innocently.

"You're going to blow his mind!" Beth stated, as I looked down at myself.

"Most definitely, and possibly blow something else too!" Rose then chipped in, but she was then in quick succession smacked around the arm by both Amanda and Beth.

"For goodness sake, Rose," Beth chastised her. Then she realised what she had said.

"Oh God, I didn't mean that, you know, that you were going to do him. I just meant that he probably had something in his pants that was likely to blow besides his mind! Oh this isn't sounding any better is it?" She quickly stopped herself, but somehow her flustering actually amused me no end and I started to laugh.

"Let's go and get a quick drink," I suggested.

"Yes, please get me out of this verbal nightmare," she scowled and so I linked arms with her as we walked down the corridor.

One quick glass of Prosecco later, and it was seven forty-five so we headed out to the front of the hotel. The lovely concierge seemed to know that we had a car arriving to pick us up and he directed us immediately to a car that was waiting. The driver was chatting to one of the valet parking attendants, and he quickly opened the door once he saw us manoeuvring toward him. It was a large black car; very new – it had that strong smell of leather still inside. He closed the doors after us and ran around to the driver's side and quickly set off. The car was luxurious and comfortable; we didn't need to tell the driver where we were going he simply knew.

"I have a really good feeling that we are going to love tonight," Amanda suddenly said.

"I really hope so. Looks like Josh has picked his girl though," Beth glared at Rose. She simply smirked at the remark.

"Oh, don't be too disappointed, Beth. Ethan has two other friends coming tonight so I am sure that you and Amanda will be thoroughly entertained," I happily told them. Beth suddenly cheered up.

"Well that is good news, I'd forgotten. I was starting to think that Amanda and I would have to sit and watch you four all night," she concluded.

"Well, now that other men will be on our table, you will probably keep us entertained, Beth," I smiled, knowing that the slightest inclination of flirting from one of the other men would result in Beth pouncing on them.

"Damn right!" she replied with glee.

The streets were bustling with life, and as we arrived and queued in a line of cars, waiting to stop outside the entrance of the Golden Coast Hotel, it was obvious that there would be some serious money raised here tonight. The driver pulled up and then walked around to open our doors, and he kindly helped us out with a little more grace than was probable on our own. We made our way up the stairs and as music played from within, and we looked at all of the people attending, we felt happy that we blended in quite well. Even though some women had chosen to completely overdress, the majority were in stunning cocktail dresses just like us.

The hotel didn't disappoint in any way – it was impressive and had been completely overhauled with decoration for this fundraiser, which seemed to be for a children's orphanage and a local hospital. We were directed towards a huge dining room and when we entered there was a long bar which both Rose and Amanda made a beeline for, while Beth and I followed along behind.

"Have you spotted him yet?" she asked.

"No, and it's making me really nervous," I replied as I scanned the room.

"Hey, he's going to show you know," she tried to reassure my obvious looming panic attack, and then she took my hands and continued. "Okay, honey, face me and take a deep breath," she smiled. I did as she asked and re-asked for her confirmation that I looked alright. As I watched her grinning at my obvious and acute nerves her glance went beyond me. "I need you to relax and turn around smiling," she then stated.

"Why, it's not a photographer is it? I hate having my picture taken," I reminded her. She gave me that stern motherly look again, and stepped closer to me.

"He's here," she simply whispered, and I suddenly felt like my feet were glued to the floor. She nodded as if to prompt me, so I shut my eyes and took a deep breath just as he spoke.

"Jenny, I'm glad that you arrived safely," he said. The sound of his voice suddenly soothed my nerves and I turned to face him.

As I took in the sight of him cleanly shaven, in a dark suit with a slim black tie and a very crisp white shirt, I almost didn't register his response toward me until I realised his smile was growing, and then he said, "Wow, you look stunning." I did a very cute dip of the knees and then did him a turn so that he could view every angle.

"I'm glad that you like. It is, after all, courtesy of you," I replied.

"I didn't supply the amazing woman within it though!" he then grinned and I blushed, so I was grateful when Josh passed him on the step and walked up to Beth and me. He gave us both a very subtle kiss on the cheek repeating the compliments that we looked stunning, and then he passed us to find Rose at the bar. Ethan made a move and stepped closer to me; he placed his hand again on the small of my back and kissed me tenderly on the cheek. Before he pulled away he whispered in my ear, "I'm honoured that you came tonight, and you do look exceptionally stunning."

I placed my hand on his waist and kissed him back on the cheek and then whispered, "You don't look too shabby yourself." Then I inhaled. "And you smell amazing," I pointed out as his aftershave hit my nostrils giving me that instant tingle through my body that completely betrayed me! He smiled and then greeted Beth.

Rose, Amanda and Josh returned with champagne and handed Beth and me a glass. Rose nodded her head toward Josh and I can only assume that she was making me aware that he was at her side, or that he had bought the drinks – either way, neither surprised me.

"So ladies, let me introduce you to the other two gentlemen joining us tonight," Ethan then said as he took my hand and led me to our table, with the others following along behind.

I felt like the whole room had their eyes on me, like I was here with a man they knew and respected and they wanted to know who the girl he was holding hands with could be. He seemed oblivious to any worries that I had, and as he passed various people he greeted them happily with me alongside him. We reached a table near to the staged area and as we approached the two gentlemen stood alongside turned to greet us.

"Gentlemen, it is my pleasure to introduce to you; Jenny, Beth, Amanda and Rose," Ethan kindly said as he gestured to each of us while he spoke our names. Both of them stepped forward, and then he returned the introduction. "Ladies, these are my friends Rafael, and Hernando." The men then took our hands and gently shook them in response, one after the other.

"It is a pleasure to meet you. I am Rafael." He was very smooth and polite and was dark-haired with very dark brown eyes. He was very powerful looking, and very business-like. He seemed nice enough though.

"Ladies, it is my pleasure to be spending the evening with you. I am Hernando." The blond-haired gentleman then followed suit. He was slightly younger, and I noticed Beth swoon a little toward him.

We had not long being introduced when it was announced that we should take our seats for dinner to be served. Ethan pulled out my chair and prompted me to sit, which I did happily. The other men took hold of Beth and Amanda's chairs and asked them to sit, and then sat either side of them, and as I expected Josh was not letting Rose sit anywhere but right beside him. A waitress appeared asking if we would like wine, or champagne and Ethan took charge and ordered some of each. It would appear that this was his table, and I did dread to think how much the price per plate must have been. As we started conversing and finding out more about Rafael and Hernando, the drinks were poured and the starters appeared. Ethan had not been kidding about the quality of the food; the half lobster that appeared in front of us was impressive and I hoped it tasted as amazing as it looked. Ethan leaned toward me;

"You like lobster?" he enquired.

"I love lobster, I just don't indulge very often!" I replied and I touched his arm to acknowledge that I was fine.

He made sure that he had the whole table speaking together and I was amazed at how easily he managed that. The men were enquiring about what my friends did for a living, and Beth quizzed Hernando more about his yacht business, which was emphasised when he admitted that Ethan had hired the yacht we had been on today from his company. Her eyes were ablaze with the possibility, I suspect, of luxurious travel of the seas with the blond-haired, young Spanish male in front of her. I leaned into Ethan and whispered my thoughts and he touched my shoulder where his hand rested on the back of my chair and he agreed that she looked pretty smitten.

During the meal numerous girls walked around the tables, showing us some of the items up for auction tonight. There were such beautiful things including a very nice Bottega Veneta tote bag that Beth had her eye on, an impressive diamond bracelet, a day on a yacht fully staffed (courtesy of Hernando's company), a whole host of spa days and champagne and wine from a vineyard. Then one item caught my eye. It was a five-day stay for two at a new boutique hotel in Ibiza: the leaflet that accompanied the auction item included photographs and a very full description of what was available, and it looked absolutely gorgeous. I read it intently and it was only when I got to the bottom and read: 'This auction item – a stay at The Gessami Residence – is donated by Mr Ethan James.' I stopped reading and stared at him. He smiled and raised his eyebrows in question.

"What?" he asked innocently. I waved the leaflet at him.

"This is your hotel? Your new hotel? It looks amazing, Ethan. I had no idea that this was the type of hotel that you meant you had converted to when you told me about it." I looked at the pictures again. "I'd love to stay there, it looks beautiful," I stated. He leaned in with his mouth next to my ear;

"It could be arranged," he simply whispered, taking no credit for his hotel or anything else that I had just said. I waved it at Rose.

"Hey girls, look at this place. It's Ethan's and it looks amazing," I insisted, but I didn't need to push the point – they were as impressed as I was.

"I could sell holidays to this place through my company," Rose stated with interest.

"A business venture?" Ethan enquired. "Interesting, we must have a chat about that," he answered back.

The others commented on the quality of the hotel from what we could see in the pictures. Ethan, it was obvious, did not like to be the centre of attention, and tried to change the subject. I was quick to keep asking questions.

"I thought that it wasn't quite ready to open yet?" I said.

"It's ninety-nine percent ready. This donation is for anytime after the official opening date which is in about two weeks' time. It will be ready by then, I'm not worried," he casually replied. I smiled at his response. It was obvious that he was proud of the hotel, and also that he didn't like to promote himself personally as amazing, but I was starting to think that he was.

"I'd like to see it before I leave, if you wouldn't mind showing it to me?" I asked hopefully.

"It would be my pleasure. I will make sure that we do that within the next week," he quickly replied, and seemed happy that I wanted to see his recent acquisition. I nodded in response and then took another sip of my champagne.

The whole meal had not one fault. The food was of a quality that I did not have the pleasure to partake in regularly, but my taste buds were very appreciative of the whole three-course experience. As coffee was served, the auctioning of items started. It was quick and the amounts being bid were breathtaking. Beth bid for the bag as expected. Hernando found her unique way of bidding by ferociously waving her hand in the air amusing. It did not help her at all however, as she was outbid by nearly five hundred euros. There were so many items to auction that I lost count. Ethan bid on a white gold and diamond pendant necklace. It was stunning and he seemed happy that he had won it. I hoped that it was for someone special in his life, but then that also worried me a little, mainly because there was the possibility that such a person existed and all of this casual fun with me was just a distraction from his work. I decided not to dwell on the thought; whatever this was it was making me happy and I knew that he was no longer married, so I wasn't causing any foul play. He must have noted my vacant thinking as he asked if there was something wrong. I quickly replied telling him that I was more than alright.

The five-day break in his hotel raised five thousand euros, I was impressed and pleased at the same time that so much money was being raised for such worthy causes. Recipients from both gave speeches on how the money would help them, and quite honestly I think that most women in the room had tears in their eyes. We were all thankful when at nearly eleven, a DJ started to play some music. It was quite sedate, and Rose was longing for some good music to get the party going! As we sat and chatted and drank more champagne and wine, the few people on the dance floor seemed more than happy when the Bee Gees song 'You Should be Dancing', came on. I instantly stopped talking dead in my tracks to Ethan and looked at Beth who had already jumped up in the air and prompted Amanda and Rose. Ethan looked at me with reservation, and he had every right to.

At Beth's wedding many years ago instead of the

'bride and groom' crazy dance that seems to be normal these days, we did the 'bride and her best friends' dance to this song. It had become a tradition ever since then that wherever we were, we had to do *'the dance'* with no exceptions. It still wasn't that bad ten years ago, but now at our age it wasn't quite as flattering – it was embarrassing to say the least! As I tried to explain this to Ethan, Beth dragged me to my feet excusing me while I tried to down the half glass of champagne that I had. I passed Ethan my glass and grimaced miming that I was sorry but he seemed intrigued by the whole situation. When I reached the dance floor, staring at Beth and wondering if she had managed to ask the DJ to play this song before the evening even started, I stood in the usual line with them and we proceeded to start the cheesy dance moves we had taken from *Saturday Night Fever*, incorporated with our own. To our surprise though the people on the dance floor cheered us along and as we got into more of a rhythm, it amused us that they were trying to join in. We turned again and ended up facing Ethan and the rest of our table carrying on with the moves, they were whistling and cheering us on. (Or more likely hoping that we would stop!) I shrugged my shoulders quickly at him, and he responded with a smile of appreciation. We seemed to have the whole room bouncing along with us, and as I expected, the girls loved the attention.

Once the song had finished, I excused myself while the others stayed and carried on dancing. Josh and Hernando joined them on the dance floor while Rafael talked to an acquaintance. I sat next to Ethan and quickly started to apologise, but he grinned at me and then pulled me in close and kissed me on the lips meaningfully. I looked at him and then nervously looked around to see if anyone had seen us, but they seemed oblivious.

"Alright, that wasn't quite the reaction I thought that display would have had!" I remarked at his now grinning face.

"Well, you keep surprising me with your talents," he said and I couldn't tell if he was being sarcastic or he meant it.

"Yeah well, it's a terrible necessity of Beth's, unfortunately," I sighed as I reached for my now refilled glass of champagne. He leant in closer to me.

"A necessity that surprisingly makes me like you more," he replied as the music changed to a slower pace, being that of Michael Bublé.

Rafael was now free and he looked at Amanda on the dance floor. He excused himself and walked straight toward her, taking her in his arms which made her swoon a little. The others had already been swept up in the arms of Josh and Hernando, so when Ethan suddenly stood and looked down at me, I was filled with knotted nerves.

"Would you like to dance with me?" he asked smiling.

I slowed my breathing and placed my glass on the table and replied, "I would love to." He reached out his hand and I placed mine in his and he led me to the others on the dance floor.

The girls were quick to touch my arm, smile, and wink at me as I moved closer to him resting my cheek against his. He wrapped one arm around my waist and wound his fingers through mine then pulling our hands close to his chest. I closed my eyes and inhaled his aftershave, the hairs on the back of my neck stood proud as I felt the air from his mouth run past the skin over my shoulder.

He whispered in my ear, "I was not expecting to meet anyone on this trip, Jenny Walker, but I have to say that I am very glad I met you. It has made me happier spending time with you these last few days than I have been in a very long time, and I thank you for that," he kindly said. I pulled back and looked him in the eye.

"Yeah well, you're only saying that now because you've seen my wicked dance moves!" I said with sarcasm and he laughed. As we resumed our dance position I whispered to him, "I told you that I would have a really great time today and tonight, and I have – it has been beyond any expectation. I am also really pleased that I met you," I finished as I ran my hand to the back of his neck, and he responded by pulling me closer.

The lights dimmed toward the end of the song and the bright sparkling raindrops of light reflected from the chandelier above were scattered across the floor. His face moved slowly to face mine, and there was no need for words – he just placed his lips millimetres away from my mouth and without any prompting we eased into a sensual and mind-blowing kiss. I smiled as it ended and he pulled me back close to his chest. I looked over his shoulder and the others watched us closely. I noted Josh's look of surprise at Ethan's obvious gesture and liking toward me. I could do nothing but smile in return; I suspected from Josh's reaction that he has not seen Ethan this intimate with anyone in a long time, and for some reason that pleased me.

As the evening started to draw to a close, I was disappointed that we would have to leave soon. The room was emptying and it was now well after midnight. The men had other ideas though;

"So, Ethan, firstly thank you for your hospitality this evening." Hernando stated as we finished our drinks, before carrying on. "Can I interest anyone in joining me on my yacht, which is conveniently moored at the edge of the harbour and so no need for speedboat travel?" he enquired hopefully. "I think that a little more champagne would not harm anyone." Amanda, Beth and Rose were quick to say yes. Josh looked at Ethan for approval, while he looked at me.

"Would you like to?" he asked me.

"Well I'm not tired yet, so why not? That is if you want to?" I asked him, secretly hoping he would say yes.

"If it means spending more time with you then, yes, I would be happy to," he happily whispered before shouting back. "Thank you, Hernando, that would be acceptable by all, it would seem."

"Excellent!" Josh replied.

I had noticed Rafael's wedding band on his finger, and I think that this was why Amanda was so calm around him – she had no need to worry as he was already committed to a relationship just as she was. She was simply enjoying his company. We stepped into the chilly air about ten minutes after deciding to continue partying, where two cars awaited us. The quick response to their calls when needed was impressive to say the least. Amanda and Beth along with Hernando and Rafael climbed into the first car, and so the rest of us climbed into the second. Ethan held my hand on top of his knee, it was a touching gesture.

The yacht… Oh my! I thought that the one Ethan was staying on was impressive, but this one was the yacht of all yachts! Champagne was chilling on ice when we arrived and the staff had canapés ready. The lounge area was bigger than the ground floor of my house, and the furniture was comfortable and the sofas plush and expensive. I took off my shoes and snuggled into Ethan who had removed his jacket and after some time put his feet up on the stool in front of him. We were all settled; we laughed, talked, the girls did some dancing and both Hernando and Rafael remarked to Ethan a couple of times that we were all so much fun and they desired to know where on earth he had found us.

"It was by sheer luck," Ethan replied both times before smiling at me.

The early hours drew in, and I didn't want to leave. It was obvious that Rose and Josh had disappeared below decks, and Beth seemed keen to disappear with Hernando. Rafael and Amanda and the two of us continued to talk until tiredness came to us all. I looked at my watch.

"Well, I don't know about everyone else, but I am tired now," I explained trying to stifle a yawn.

"I do not think that we will be seeing the others anytime soon!" Rafael convincingly replied, and we all agreed.

"I think at this time it is probably wiser to just stay here. We have blankets and throws – we can just stay put, or find a room downstairs?" Ethan then suggested. I retracted a little feeling nervous and I knew that he felt this. "Not a room together of course!" he then quickly added and I relaxed and melted back into his chest.

"I am pretty sure that I do not want to walk in on any of them downstairs, and I have no idea which rooms they are in. I think picking the wrong one would scar me for life!" Amanda then dryly proclaimed. We did agree though.

"I'm happy just crashing right here," I told them while looking at Ethan. He stroked my hair.

"Are you sure?" he asked. I nodded and yawned again, with Amanda following suit.

"Yes, sod it," Amanda was quick to say grabbing a velvet throw and snuggling down on the sofa. "I'm not promising that I won't scare you to death in the morning guys with my make-up half across my face, but I'm damn happy staying put right now," she finished as she closed her eyes.

"Perfect," Ethan sighed as he snuggled down with his arm around me. He pulled a throw over the two of us, and then pressed a button on the elaborate remote and dimmed the lights. The stars twinkled in the sky and the water rippled around the yacht, it was the most soothing sound. I turned and kissed Ethan on the cheek and as my heavy eyes closed and I wrapped my arm around his chest where I could hear his steady heartbeat… I slept like a baby.

Chapter 9

I was awoken with the sound of a spoon swirling in a cup. As it chinked on the edge after stirring, I slowly opened my eyes. It disappointed me to find that Ethan was no longer at the side of me and I was lying on the very comfortable sofa on my own. I sat slowly and stretched as I looked across to Amanda who was happily sipping coffee, the smell radiating around the large lounge. She smiled at me. "Morning, sleepy head," she called as I tried to focus. I think I had indulged in more champagne than I had realised.

"Where is everyone?" I asked looking around the room, and then I spotted Ethan and Josh chatting out on the deck.

"They're around; Rose has been prancing around in Hernando's guest t-shirt like the cat that got the cream. Beth, well, I think that she's pretty much feeling the same and Hernando is showering while Rafael is eating breakfast out on the sundeck," she concluded.

"Right – Am I the last to wake up?" I grimaced.

"Yeah, but don't worry only by about twenty minutes. I can't wait to get out of this dress now though," she complained as she pulled at it numerous times.

I stood and stretched again and walked to the table where the stewards had placed fresh coffee and tea; I couldn't wait to get a cup down my throat and get rid of that aftertaste of stale alcohol and locate a toothbrush. It was divine, and as I reached for a croissant I felt someone stood behind me.

"Good morning," Ethan said quietly, and the hairs on the back of my neck stood on end. I turned.

"Good morning, handsome," I confidently replied hoping that I had wiped any smudged mascara from under my eyes before I had gone for the coffee. He smiled and reached for a cup too. "Everything alright this morning?" I enquired as I looked across at Josh.

"Yes, why shouldn't it be?" I swallowed the mouthful of croissant and shook my head.

"It was just that I noted you looked deep in conversation with Josh. I was worried it was something to do with the sale?" I pointed out.

"Oh it wasn't business, so no need to worry," he grinned. He took a sip from his cup and I really found myself wanting to just throw my arms around him as we just stood and stared at each other. "I will talk to you about it when the others surface properly," he then said and I looked at him curiously and wondered what on earth it could be. He gestured for me to sit and finish my breakfast, and as we sat with Josh, Amanda and Rafael it was very calm and relaxing and a relief to wake up slowly.

After what seemed like a long time, Hernando, Beth and Rose made an entrance. Rose was wearing shorts and a t-shirt that I assumed were available for guests in the room she had shared with Josh – she carried her dress and shoes. Beth had her dress on still like Amanda and

I, but looking at Hernando I don't think his t-shirts would squeeze over Beth's ample chest without looking like something from a Playboy magazine, so I assume she had decided against it! As the girls grabbed a cup of tea or coffee and then sat with us out on the deck, Ethan took my hand in his under the table and I looked at him nervously as he prepared to say something.

"So, now that everyone is here I have something to ask you all," he started. "As Josh and I have concluded business, and I know both of you have no further business," he gestured to Hernando and Rafael, "I want to ask you all if you would do me a favour actually." He looked directly at me and I swallowed hard. "Ladies, I know that you have probably spent an excessive amount of money to stay at your hotel, but Jenny gave me an idea last night," he continued.

"I did?" I enquired. He nodded.

"My new hotel, which is only small I might add, is due to open in a couple of weeks' time. I could really do with some honest reviews before I open it to the public, and as we are all getting along so well I wondered if you would all consider joining me there for a week. Your input would be invaluable and the staff will get the chance to have a 'run-through' so to speak," he finished. The girls were buzzing a little. I looked at him genuinely;

"Really? The Gessami Residence? You want all of us to come and stay there with you?" I repeated finding it hard to take in. It was an exclusive hotel to say the least. He smiled.

"Don't sound so surprised. You will be helping me

out, and of course there will be no cost to any of you," he confirmed before squeezing my hand.

"Will they be ready for us?" I asked.

"Don't worry about that, I'm on it," Josh interrupted, and I suddenly realised what they had been planning on the deck this morning. I smiled in response.

"Well, I'm happy to leave you in the hotel, but I'm going!" Rose then informed us while grinning at Josh, who winked at her.

"Well I would love to, but what about letting our hotel know?" Beth then asked.

"You will have to retrieve all of your belongings, so we will have to go back. If it worries you, then I will speak with the manager. It isn't as though they are losing any cost; they could resell the rooms," Ethan said trying to ease any worries that we had. He turned and faced me. "So what do you think?" I placed my coffee cup back on the table and looked at the others; they all seemed to be waiting for a positive response as if it all depended on me. I thought about it for a few seconds longer and then looked at Ethan. Could I possibly spend a week in close company with him, and feel comfortable with that? Or was it going to turn into something that I wished it hadn't? I really wasn't sure, but one thing I did know was that I was tired of being alone, and tired of no intimacy or no one paying attention to me, and so I squeezed his hand and then smiled;

"Well, I would love to stay. It would be my pleasure to try to find fault in you, which seems pretty damn difficult to be honest!" I replied with a hint of sarcasm.

"Touché," Amanda agreed happily.

141

"Well it's fine with us, if these lovely ladies don't mind our humour and company," Hernando gestured to himself and Rafael.

"I will make arrangements then to get us all there," Josh announced as he sprung to his feet, suddenly eager to get things moving.

"Well, it seems logical for me to sail the yacht around to the north of the island and moor it there. So if anyone would like to sail around with me, you are very welcome," Hernando offered. Beth clapped her hands with delight.

"Oh goody! Yes please, can I come with you?" she bounced around in her chair. Hernando laughed at her.

"Of course," he said, and then he looked at Rafael and Amanda. "Would you like to sail around with us?"

"Yes, that would be lovely. I do need to retrieve my belongings from my hotel, though," Rafael replied.

"Likewise," Amanda confirmed, smiling at him.

"Right. I suggest that we all get our crap together and then meet back here at, say, two o'clock?" Josh said as he punched a number into his mobile to arrange details.

"Can we sail too?" Rose then enquired hinting to Josh that she would really like that. He nodded and seemed very cool and confident with the whole plan. He started talking to whoever he had called.

"How would you like to travel? We can take my yacht around the island or we can drive?" Ethan then asked me quietly while the others became more vocal about the unravelling arrangements. I leant into him and placed my hand on his knee.

"Can we sail on your yacht? It would be nice if you can relax too, and it will be far quieter on yours I suspect than with this rowdy lot," I gestured to them. He laughed lightly;

"Perfect. I will give the crew a call and make sure that they are ready. I can meet you at your hotel, as I would like to speak to the manager anyway," he then remarked. I instantly thought about the added cost.

"Are you sure about all of this? It's going to cost you a small fortune," I grimaced. He kissed me on the cheek and whispered into my ear.

"I cannot think of a more perfect way to spend my time here than with you and your friends and mine. Cost is of no consequence." I returned the kiss on his cheek and he pulled back and smiled as he stared into my eyes.

Beth then shouted across the table. "Okay, Jenny. You need to get your arse moving. It's now eleven o'clock and we have a lot of packing to do. So let's get this show on the road. I can't wait to get sailing and get to the new hotel."

I stood and paid a quick call before retrieving my shoes and meeting them back on deck. Ethan was on his telephone organising what sounded like the speedboat back to his yacht. Rafael had ordered us a taxi back to the hotel along with his own, and I was glad of that; it was nice to pay for something. We thanked Hernando for his hospitality and Beth, as was to be expected, gave him the kind of goodbye that looked like she would eat him for breakfast. We dragged her away making the point that she would be seeing him later. Ethan stepped off with us as a speedboat approached, and I knew it was both his and Josh's ride. I turned to him before walking to the taxi barefoot.

"So I will see you in a while?" I re-confirmed.

"You bet. I will be in the reception at around one thirty," and I nodded in confirmation and then hopped in the back of the taxi.

When we arrived back at the hotel, we had some curious looks from some of the younger guests. They had that 'Oh yes, and where have you all been since last night dressed like that?' look. It amused Rose and Beth no end, and actually made me feel remarkably young at heart and so I laughed along with them. We rode the lift back to our floor with the voices of the girls getting higher pitched with excitement the more they talked about our arrangements. Amanda put her arm around me as we walked to the suite.

"You, young lady, as I have already pointed out, have made this holiday an absolute pleasure so far," she grinned. Rose and Beth turned and agreed.

"I second that. Hell, I thought that I had done well with this hotel, but I can't wait to get to Ethan's place and the yachts, the dinner – it's all turning out pretty damn fan-tas-tic I say, so thanks, Jenny," Rose happily chirped, and then Beth was more matter of fact.

"Well, it's proved a point that if you want to make a fool of yourself and get blind drunk, then have someone pick you up and help you, then you need to make sure you do all of that in front of a wealthy, handsome gent!" she laughed.

"Beth!" Amanda replied, hitting her arm. "Jenny didn't come out here just to cop off with someone, you know, wealthy or not."

"Yeah, but I am quite enjoying his company," I replied. "So I get what you're saying Beth, money aside he just seems to be a pretty decent guy." Beth winked at me and then hugged me too.

"That's my girl. I reckon by the time the end of this week arrives, you will be well and truly back in practice!" she remarked as we entered the room.

"What practice exactly are you implying?" Rose enquired. Beth stood with her hands on her hips and glared at her.

"Of all people you're the one to have to ask me that?" she started. "We can start with making out, but sex is a definite I reckon and goodness knows what sort of practice her mouth might be getting – I think she is going to go home exhausted," Beth giggled. After we had all stood and glared at her for a moment, we each picked up a cushion off the sofa and threw it at her before making our way to our rooms to pack. "What?" she called to us all. "It's only what you all really think."

"Don't judge us all based on your track record lady!" Amanda shouted back.

"Well, you only live once. I just think she should go for it," Beth replied sounding a little deflated at her outburst. So I popped my head around my door and just said, "I might just go for it!" She meant no harm, she was just trying to get me back in the saddle it had been a long time, and I did have those feelings when I was near him. I needed to just go with the flow; if it felt right, why should I stop it? She blew me a kiss as if to say thank you and waltzed off into her bedroom.

We all showered quickly and changed. Packing became a bit of a nightmare, particularly for Beth who had somehow managed to get the equivalent of two suitcases full of clothing and beauty products into one. Rose and I seemed to be managing nicely; I suggested a glass of diet coke while we finished and she agreed that some non-alcoholic fluid would be a good thing after last night. As I started to walk back across the living room, glasses in hand, I could hear her laughing uncontrollably and she was hailing the others to come and see; I already had a bad feeling about this and as Amanda and Beth stopped for a while to come and see what the fuss was about, Rose appeared at our door with a pair of my knickers in her hand.

"What the hell are these, Jenny?" she asked while waving my large and not very sexy control knickers around in the air. I quickly put down the drinks and asked for them back.

"Yes, alright we don't all have your figure some of us need some help," I tried to insist. She in turn threw them to Amanda who held them up and laughed out loud.

"Jesus, Jen, you can get sexier control pants than these," she said stretching them between her hands. I frowned at their behaviour. Beth snatched them off her.

"Bloody hell, you're not going to get any practice in this week if he sees those beauties, only one thing for them," she stated as she walked to the balcony and I had a sudden panic attack… she wouldn't dare…would she?

Oh yes, she bloody well would! Beth opened the balcony door and stepped out and then turned to face us all. I pleaded with her to give them back, but she simply gave them their last rights.

"I condemn these unflattering hideous knickers to the bin; they can never be worn again and certainly not retrieved. This is the start of the new thong wearing Jenny," Beth declared as she launched them from her hand off our balcony and they fluttered away in the breeze.

We all leant over the railing to watch them float down toward the pool, which wasn't the best outcome as it was full of young people, men included. I frowned again and sighed at the sight of my underwear in full view for everyone to see. I slumped back onto the floor behind the railing and put my head in my hands.

"Could you embarrass me any more than that?" I asked her.

"Probably, I reckon I could have held onto them like a parachute and landed safely in and among everyone," Rose then added seriously. They were all very quiet and when I looked up at them they were trying not to laugh. As an almighty roar developed from below we all peered over from the balcony and were surprised to find some of the young men waving them around and looking up. We all quickly ducked beneath the railings and rested against the wall and then after a moment's silence we looked at each other and burst into hysterical laughter. The comments being shouted were cringe-worthy and then Amanda in all seriousness suddenly said, "I hope that they were clean – please tell me you've not worn them yet this holiday?" That started us off again.

"No, I haven't worn them yet and I am so pleased that I amuse you all so much," I cringed as I started to crawl back into the suite hoping no one could see me. They followed me inside, laughing all the way.

"I bet you're not going to retrieve them though, are you?" they all asked. I sat and looked at them.

"Absolutely no way on this earth am I going down there," I admitted and then Beth reached out her hand to help me stand. They all gave me a group hug.

"Hey, we're only looking out for you. You'll get laughed out of the bedroom otherwise. They were worse than the ones Bridget Jones wore," Amanda then said and I knew that she was right. There was no way that I would have worn those knickers in the company of Ethan.

"Crap!" Rose suddenly shouted. It's twenty past one. We have ten minutes left to be downstairs!"

The whole suite suddenly became a frenzied place of panic as we tried to make sure that we had everything packed and ready to go. It was like a sped up scene from a comedy sketch. I was remarkably organised and as I had packed with minimum effort I found it amusing to watch the others. I even had the time to pin up my still damp hair, apply lip gloss and walk my suitcase to the door calmly. It was a refreshing change to say the least. I had my bikini on and a simple pair of jean shorts with a white linen shirt. I felt suitably dressed and at the same time relaxed. At half past I gave them a loud whistle. They all came running, dragging their bags like school children, and it made me giggle.

Beth had opted to wear her ever so large hat again, Rose had the skimpiest sundress on I had seen her wear to date, Amanda had opted for shorts like me. We did a quick sweep of the suite and then made our way down to the reception. There was a mixture of giggles, expectations, excitement and competition about everything to do with sex, mainly – in particular how many possible places and positions Beth and Rose could squeeze into the time they had. They had already suggested fun in the showers, pool, on the yacht, in their rooms at the hotel, on the beach and anywhere else they could think would be suitable. Beth and Rose were obviously on some kind of competitive mission and I felt sad for Amanda. I made the point of miming "Sorry," to her and she simply mimed back "I'm fine." As the lift doors pinged open, I was glad to exit – there was so much excitement from them that the whole space had filled up with masses of hot air. I took a deep breath and then waited for Amanda.

"I am sorry about their obvious and blunt sexual intentions," I remarked. She just laughed.

"I feel quite happy that I don't have to think about it actually. I'm also glad it isn't with a bunch of eighteen-year-olds though," she winced. "I just hope that the walls in his hotel aren't paper thin, or I'm going to be exhausted. May have to enquire if the hotel has ear plugs!" she winced a little more as we spotted Ethan. "Promise me that you'll make sure that this stay is about your enjoyment too?" she then said, and I was grateful for that.

"I will, I promise!"

Ethan was in deck shorts and a polo shirt; he looked hot as always and he was getting some serious attention from a few young girls that were hovering so obviously close to him. It was to my absolute delight that when he saw me approaching he walked directly to me, threw his arms around my waist and kissed me once – firmly but with intention. The young girls then sloped off mumbling to themselves; I looked at them and winked, which seemed to amuse Ethan no end.

"Bothering you, were they?" I asked a bit tongue in cheek.

"I'm not good at unwanted attention; never know how to deal with it!" he honestly replied.

"Well, it looks like I am going to have to keep you close then."

"I was hoping that you would say that," he winked.

"We just need to settle the bill, so just give us a minute," I then told him as the others patiently waited for me.

"It's all sorted nothing to pay," Ethan stated as a matter of fact.

"What?" Amanda asked. "You can't pay our bill," and we all agreed.

"I am changing your holiday plans, so it hardly seems fair that I don't look after you. Come on let's go, the car is waiting," he replied as he gestured for us to leave.

Once the girls and I had picked up our mouths from the floor and started walking quietly toward the door, I just stared at him. It was even more impressive when the hotel manager was waiting by the door to wish us a good remainder of our holiday. We shook his hand and thanked him for a wonderful stay, and then Ethan shook hands with him and said that he would speak with him next week. Business I am sure, but he seemed to have everything in order.

Our bags were packed into the car; Ethan was driving us back to the bay to board the yachts. I slid my sunglasses on and wondered how I had somehow found the most generous man I have had the pleasure of meeting in such a long time, while in Ibiza, extremely drunk – what are the odds of that happening? Then I had a quick flashback to that film with Liam Neeson in which his daughter is kidnapped on holiday and sent to be sold as a sex slave. I had a momentary lapse of confidence, but as the yachts came into view and Hernando, Josh and Rafael were stood with champagne on deck, I felt a little more relaxed again.

Before the car had even come to a standstill Josh was at the boot helping lift out the bags. Rose had her hands on his arm in appreciation and Beth grabbed her case after putting back on her hat, and swaggered toward Hernando who had a glass of bubbles waiting for her. Ethan came around to my side of the car and even though I had stepped out he still offered his hand as we walked toward the others. Josh had kindly taken my case to Ethan's yacht, which was now moored directly behind Hernando's. The staff all stood on the jetty waiting for us to board. Rose and Beth had already boarded Hernando's yacht and Amanda looked back at us two.

"Are you joining us, or travelling in peace and quiet?" she asked almost reading my mind.

"It's entirely Jenny's choice," Ethan remarked stepping back a little. I had my confidence back.

"Yes – we're going to follow on Ethan's yacht," I quickly replied before I changed my mind and she smiled at my response.

"I don't blame you," she grimaced as Beth shouted her to get on board so that they could set off. "I suppose someone needs to keep them in check!" she then said.

Ethan laughed a little, "Yes, well – good luck with that one!" She gave the expected 'thanks' look. "It will literally be an hour or so of sailing, that's all, and then we should be around to other side. It will be cars the rest of the way then into the hills," he tried to convince her of the short trip. She nodded in response and took Rafael's hand as she stepped on board.

Ethan gestured to walk toward our yacht. The staff had drinks ready for us too; I felt like royalty and it was a strange feeling. I wanted to keep thanking them consistently for all of the attention, although I knew it was not necessary.

As we walked up the stairs to the deck the others shouted to us. "See you at the other side!" they called and we waved back happily knowing that we could have some time alone.

We made our way to the middle sundeck and sat on the comfortable seating in the sunshine. The staff had made afternoon tea, I suppose at Ethan's request. The sandwiches were neat and small and there were cakes and chocolates, champagne and tea. It was like being in an elaborate tea room with the most amazing view. He sat down beside me and leaned his glass toward mine.

"Cheers," I toasted.

"Cheers," he repeated before we took a sip. "Are you sure you are comfortable with this… us being alone?" he asked very meaningfully.

I turned and ran my fingers along his chin then looked at his eyes. They longed for me to say yes, I could read them so easily. I smiled at him and then without any hesitation I kissed him with real intention. My tongue delicately flickered across his and it made my stomach tie itself up in knots. He gasped for breath as he pulled me closer and then we melted into each other not wanting our lips to part. The gentle hum of the engines and the sound of the sea rippling around the yacht was like a subtle lullaby and as he pulled me to sit across his lap I jumped when I stupidly spilt my champagne down my shirt. He stopped and looked at me as I gasped and then I simply said, "Oops!" and we laughed.

"Good job that your case is on board."

"It is, but I am not exactly over worried about it, I'm just wet," I tutted at myself while brushing the excess off. I did have my bikini on after all.

"Here, let me refill your glass," he said as he reached to the side of him where the ice bucket stood. It was sorted in a flash and so I stood up took a sip and then placed my glass on the table.

"Where is my case? I may just quickly put a t-shirt on before I start to smell like a beer mat!" I joked, not wanting to sit in only my bikini just yet.

"It will be below decks. Shall I go and get it for you?" he offered.

"No, I'll find it honestly. I will be two minutes." I turned and walked toward the bedrooms.

I checked the guest rooms, but it was nowhere to be found, it certainly was not in Josh's room, and then I had that gut/nerve wracking feeling that the staff had been presumptuous and placed it in Ethan's room. I gingerly walked to his suite and peered in the door. Nope – not there either. Then I looked toward his dressing room – it had to be there. The one obvious place for clothing, I'd left my flip-flops on deck and so I tiptoed across his carpet to look and there it was; placed neatly on a bench in the middle of the room. I unzipped it and found my red t-shirt, it was loose and expensive as far as t-shirts go, but it felt amazing against the skin. As I stripped off my shirt and threw it in the case I heard him calling me.

"Jenny? Are you okay or did you get lost?" he enquired. Crap – I didn't want him seeing the entire contents of my case, not that there were any more control knickers to be found! I quickly zipped it back up and started walking out of his dressing room to find him stood at the door.

I looked down at myself, bikini top and shorts with t-shirt in hand. Then I looked at his bed and back at him. He moved closer. "Are you alright?" he asked again.

I pointed toward his dressing room and then raised my t-shirt to show him, I couldn't speak but my body was doing that betrayal thing to me again. He stood inches away from me and I could hear his breathing was quickening with mine. We stood and stared for a minute.

"I couldn't find my case. I think your staff presumed I was staying in here. I'm sorry I didn't hear you, I hope it was alright me coming into your room." I babbled nervously, but he just stared at me and me at him. Then like a wave of heat coming over me I dropped my t-shirt on the floor and threw my arms around his neck.

His arms embraced me tightly as I felt this absolute need to have him, right now. He was very obviously aroused, and I was feeling so turned on again. I found myself reaching for the bottom of his polo shirt and then pushed it off over his head. All the time our lips were entwined, but it didn't stop me from running my hands down his tight muscular chest. Oh my God, he was amazing. I moaned with pleasure – this was really happening! He scooped me up and wrapped my legs around his waist and he carried me to the bed. As we landed in the soft coverings, his lips moved to my neck and I found myself gasping for breath as my heart pounded in my chest. I pulled him back to my lips and as his hand ran over my breast and then my waist and to my hips I wrapped my legs around him wanting to pull him nearer. I was lost in a moment of intimacy, it was stimulating and sensual and it felt so right, so you can imagine my disappointment when he suddenly stopped. With one hand on my waist still he propped himself up on his other elbow and looked at me.

I was still gasping slightly and a little confused. He ran his fingers around my hairline and swept strands behind my ear and then looked at me, he looked lost for words and so I spoke first.

"Everything alright?" is all I could think to say. He smiled and then pushed his face into my neck and growled a little before he sighed. I placed a hand behind his neck, wondering what the hell to do. Then after a few seconds he looked at me.

"Jenny, I am so sorry," he started, and then he sighed again and carried on. "Truthfully, I am more than alright, but I would be no gentleman if I let this go any further right now," he stated. I, however, was still confused and heated with desire.

"Oh God, are you still married?" I asked feeling awkward, but he laughed.

"God no," he replied. "Definitely single, but I am aware that you have had a tough time in recent years, and you haven't known me that long. This is a big decision for you and I would hate for you to feel forced into anything," he then stated, and I suddenly felt calmer and comforted by his chivalry.

"You're not forcing me into anything. If I remember correctly I actually jumped on you first," I replied. He looked me up and down.

"Well, it was a little hard to resist with you looking like this," he gestured and then we laughed before he became more serious. "Look, there is nothing I would like more, than to make love to you, but I need to make sure that it's absolutely what you want, and not something that you feel you have to do. I couldn't live with myself if you felt pressured in any way." And that's when I realised why I liked him so much. He was everything that I hadn't had in my life for so long. More than anything though, he actually had a huge amount of respect for me, and that was irresistible.

He had already thrown himself alongside me on the bed, slightly frustrated I presume, because I sure as hell was. I found myself however smiling and then to kill any embarrassment or feeling of letting each other down, I rolled over and lay on top of him.

"You're really going to have to stop all of this chivalry and kindness, generosity, respect, admiration and so on, because it's just making me like you even more," I smiled. We kissed again, then when we finished I looked him up and down. "Plus if you're going to go around looking like this it isn't going to help me one little bit; a daily pounce on you may become inevitable!" I smirked and then we laughed again.

"Trust me, no one has seen me looking like this for a very long time, nor are they likely to, perhaps with the exception of you," he replied.

"Right," I said with feeling.

I stood up and pulled him to standing. He kissed me again on the lips and then we reached for our tops and slid them back on. I felt slightly flushed, but I was more than happy that he had just done what he had. I also knew that it wasn't an act; his eyes never lied, and he meant every word. As I straightened my t-shirt and ran my fingers through my hair, I caught a glimpse of him in the mirror.

I had just seen a very private side of him that I liked more than ever. He gave me the impression too that I was the first to see this side of him for a long time, and it made me feel comfortable that I wasn't the only one who was out of practice! I turned and we smiled at each other and then he suggested music and more champagne and I was certainly not going to turn that down. As he took my hand and we made our way back to the sundeck he turned and looked at me.

"I feel very relaxed and comfortable around you, Jenny, like I can simply be myself!" he exclaimed. I knew exactly what he meant because I felt the same way, and I suddenly realised that I didn't want that feeling to stop. I had, without realising it, being craving it for a long time.

Chapter 10

I laughed consistently more than I had in such a long time. He was funnier than I had realised in previous meetings, mainly I suppose because we were both a little nervous. I could tell that he was completely relaxed due to his body language, and as we sat together talking I could quite happily have continued sailing for a week and left the others to it. After saying my thoughts out loud I realised that wouldn't be the kindest thing to do as he was the host; so we stood to see how far away we were. He pointed out parts of the island as he stood behind me and rested his chin on my shoulder. The other yacht was in view and we felt sure it was rowdier than ours, but I couldn't have been happier than being right here at this moment with Ethan. As he pointed out a small bay and he made a comment that we would be mooring somewhere close I knew that we wouldn't have much longer alone. This was confirmed when the stewardess appeared asking if we would like anything else bringing before we made our way nearer to shore.

Ethan said it wasn't necessary, we still had water and tea and champagne and that was enough. I turned between his arms to face him and as the wind blew my hair across my face, I scooped it to one side while I said what I wanted to get off my chest.

"You've made me feel alive again!" I remarked. He raised his eyebrows at me slightly shocked.

"Well, I cannot say that anyone has told me that before," he said as he looked down for a second and then swallowed hard. "I suppose the same could be said for me. You are making me feel alive, relaxed and comfortable and more like... well... me, and it has nothing to do with business for a change, which is definitely not normal for me." He smiled nervously. I placed a hand on his cheek and just looked at him as that's all that we needed to say for now, and we meant it. I kissed him gently on the lips once and then we simply embraced, holding each other tightly. It felt warm and safe and I wanted more! Could you possibly have more than one soul mate in a lifetime?

He made a light humming sound as he rubbed my back, and then he eased back and tucked my hair behind my ears. I found that I could do nothing more than smile at him, it made me wonder how he had not managed to find anyone to spend his life with, as to me he seemed perfect! I had to ask him more.

"How can you possibly not be attached to a woman? You seem to have the complete package." His hands were now on my shoulders rubbing them gently.

"Ah, I wondered when that question may pop up," he gestured with his head that we take a seat. I followed willingly. "Where should I start?" he sighed. "Well, you know about my failed marriage, which I will add is the only one I have ever had. We still remain friends; I owed her that much as my work was the thing that caused us the most problems. After we divorced I found that I didn't want the pain of a failed second marriage and so I was happy dating if you can call it that. Travelling from country to country doesn't particularly help anything endure."

"They could have gone with you." I pointed out. He nodded.

"That would have been the easier option – yes. My problem was that I kept dating women with the same driving business ethic as myself and none of them wanted to give that up. There have been probably three women that I have had the pleasure of dating since my marriage, which I would have been happy to have travel with me, but none of them was interested in accepting my offer. So for the past eighteen months I have been focusing more on consolidating my business and getting it to a place where I maybe don't have to travel quite so often, then freeing up some of my personal time. I can, in all honesty, say that I haven't been on a date since then," he finished.

"Well we certainly make a pair, don't we?" I replied before sipping some more champagne. "I can't believe that no one took up the offer of travelling with you; there are so many places that I would love to go and have not had the opportunity to do so. It seems such a waste, particularly if you can travel in luxury," I said as I snuggled into the chair. He grinned at me.

"Yes well, I don't like to point out what I can afford as I feel that it attracts the wrong kind of attention firstly, and secondly it seems that then they are just there to take advantage. It does leave you in a bit of a quandary because I find that then you don't ask people out – too worried that you'll find that is the only reason they are with you.

It is easier being on my own," he openly confirmed, and then as if he was saddened by his statement he reached for his glass and took a sip.

"It may seem easier to be on your own, but it isn't; I can vouch for that. I think that you just switch off that emotion and try to ignore it – that's what I have been doing. You know that if you avoid getting yourself into a situation with the opposite sex there can be no disappointment. But it makes for a very lonely life, and that's not easy for anyone. I think everyone deserves to be happy and in love," I quietly spoke.

"You were happy though and then look how unlucky you were," he said as he pulled me closer.

"I was really happy, that's true, and then I've never been sadder than when Paul died. What I've learnt is that I wouldn't trade any of the time that I shared with him for anything; we were good together and I am grateful for that. I do, however, miss that intimacy and closeness with someone. It is lonely sometimes and with that comes that feeling of unhappiness. I would like to think that I can experience that connection and happier feeling with someone again someday," I honestly replied.

"I am sure that you will; you have everything to offer that any man would be desperate to have. Even with your slightly crazy friends being a part of you!" he then joked.

"Yes, well, I should apologise for them being attached to me really!" I laughed. "I did choose them as my friends."

Then he was serious again. "So, how many men have you dated since Paul died?" he enquired and him asking that made me grimace a little, as I was so out of practice being in any man's company even to have a mere conversation. I looked at him with reservation before I answered.

"None! I just couldn't bring myself to go through with any offers for dinner or anything else," I frowned. He squeezed my shoulder.

"You worried me a little then with that look, I thought that you were going to say you were inundated with offers… and it wouldn't have surprised me in the slightest. You're a beautiful, good-hearted, funny, generous young woman and it has been sheer luck that I met you." he complimented me.

"Yes, maybe we should both be grateful for my crazy friends and their bad drinking habits, or I would never have fallen face first into the sand that night which ended up being our introduction." I smiled. He nodded in agreement and then we both had a sip of champagne. "I am sorry to have quizzed you so much about previous relationships – I'm not even sure why I needed to know. It was just that you seem to have everything to offer. You're handsome, and good-natured and funny… It surprises me that a man can feel the way you do about relationships and, well, I can't honestly believe that I met you and you're single," I confessed.

"Well, there is nothing sinister or of intrigue, I promise you. I felt after my divorce that I needed to think twice before any long-term commitment again and to date, I haven't had the inclination to want to completely give myself to anyone else."

"So no one has captured your heart yet then?" I winked at him.

"Well, why don't you ask me again at the end of this week?" he smiled. I decided to pull his leg as he caught me off guard with his comment and I knew I was blushing.

"Why? Are you going to ask Beth to date you?" I asked trying to be serious. He nearly choked on his champagne.

"Please no! She is lovely and rather exuberant, but I think that she would kill me with her expectations," he laughed nervously. I turned and knelt to face him.

"I'm sorry, that was unfair. I don't want to frighten you. I love her to death, but I know what you mean." Then we just looked at each other. "I am having the most amazing time on this holiday," I finished, and then without hesitation I leaned in toward him.

We kissed, but then were interrupted by one of the crew who had obviously come on deck to speak to Ethan; he made us aware of his presence by coughing lightly into his hand. He told us that we were close to the shoreline and would be mooring at the furthest jetty alongside the other yacht in approximately ten minutes. I sighed as I didn't want to move, but Ethan asked that my case be brought onto the deck while he quickly packed a bag to take with us. I wanted to help, but he told me to stay put while he quickly rushed to his suite. I decided to lie on the sun lounger and looked up at the sky through my sunglasses. It was clear and the perfect shade of blue, and that bright sunshine, which was warming my skin, was becoming very hot. As I thought about how beautiful I was expecting Ethan's hotel to be, he suddenly appeared with a medium sized leather bag and a suit bag which he handed to a stewardess as he walked over toward me.

I stood as he neared me, I didn't want to appear rude. He reached out his hand for me to take and I had to admit I loved his gestures.

"Are you ready for a short drive?" he asked.

"I am. I can't explain how excited I am." I smiled. He started to lead me toward the stairs, so I quickly bent down and picked up my flip-flops and continued.

"I just need to talk to the crew while Josh sorts out the cars. Do you want to wait for me on the jetty?" he asked as we reached the lowering steps.

"Yes of course, you do what you need to." I replied not wanting to get in the way of his organisational skills. As I lifted my hand to point out that he needed to let go, he lifted it to his lips and kissed it once. When I turned to disembark I noted that the stewardess at the top of the steps had a cheeky smile on her face, almost as if she found his attention to me amusing, and it made me wonder how many times she had been on a yacht with him while he was alone. Had she tried flirting with him? Had he turned her down in the past? Or was she simply happy that he seemed relaxed and happy? As I walked down to the jetty toward the others I realised that it didn't matter either way; that was then and this is now and I had a new confidence that told my inner self that I was going to make the most out of this whole experience.

The men had gone with Josh and taken all of the bags to the car, so the girls were waiting for me. They all had that inquisitive look about their faces and I knew exactly what they were hoping I would say.

"So? How was the intimate travelling experience with just the two of you?" Amanda enquired first. I found that I had a huge smile increasing across the width of my face.

"Oh I think that you need to spill the beans with that look, young lady," Beth then announced looking me up and down. "You definitely did not have that t-shirt on when you left!" she finished as she crossed her arms.

I sighed and started to walk away explaining that I had spilt champagne down my shirt and as we walked Rose swooned at the sight of Josh.

"God, he is absolutely gorgeous, isn't he?" she almost sang.

"Oh shut up, Rose, we want to know what Jenny has been up to," Amanda snapped as Rose just frowned in response.

They weren't going to drop the questions and so I gave them a quick synopsis which including the pouncing on him. Probably not the best idea as they all started giggling like immature teenagers and I had to silence them. Amanda gave me a big hug like I had just achieved something huge, Rose clapped her hands in delight while I just thanked them numerous times asking them to settle down. As I tried to quieten their excitement, I asked how their trip had been.

"Anyway, less about me how was yours? I expect you've all been drooling over them."

"Oh, besides the champagne drinking? Drooling, obviously. We have been chatting really and listening to music, dancing a little and generally having a bloody fine time." Rose then informed me.

"Well, had you not had sex with Josh this morning you probably would have disappeared this afternoon. The poor guy is going to be useless this week if you don't let up on him a little bit!" Beth then stated. I shot her a look of surprise.

"You've had sex already? Hell, Rose, you're a fast mover." I was a little shocked.

"Yeah and once last night too," Amanda then grimaced. I looked at her again, but she just shrugged.

"Well, technically it was twice this morning as once was just before bed in the early hours, then again just before Josh came up for breakfast," she corrected us all.

"Well, that would explain the big grin on his face then," I smirked as I nodded toward him leaning against the car waiting for us. Rose turned and looked at him and he instantly grinned more which made us all laugh a little.

"Poor guy, he is going to be good for nothing by the end of this week!" Rose whispered, and we knew then that she had no intentions of easing up on him.

"Well, just make sure that you don't keep all of us awake during your sex marathon. I did come for a holiday and that included sleep," Beth sarcastically replied and Rose just glared at her.

"Says the woman who shagged Hernando last night," she let slip, and Beth clipped her arm.

"Well, we didn't think you were just sleeping in his room," Amanda confirmed, trying to make a point that we weren't completely stupid.

"Yeah, alright. I was trying to be mature about the whole thing. I mean he's ten years plus younger than me, so what the hell would he want to be with me for?" she said with dismay, but I hated that she put herself down. Beth was nearer to fifty than the rest of us, but she was very beautiful, had a gorgeous curvaceous figure and was sweet and funny and sensitive and the type of friend anyone would wish to have. I rubbed her arm.

"Why wouldn't he want you? Look at you – you're gorgeous," I tried to convince her, and after an initial look of 'thanks for that' she smiled and then chirped on about wanting to get going.

I stopped before walking to the cars, and turned to find Ethan heading down the steps of the yacht and so I waited for him. He smiled as he neared me.

"Ready to go?" he asked as he reached me and walked alongside with his hand in the small of my back again. My body did that little flutter deep inside at his touch.

"Yes, I am. I have a picture in my head of how it's going to look and I am desperate now to see if it mirrors my thoughts."

"Well, let's hope that it lives up to your expectations then, or else I'm in big trouble!" he smiled calmly, probably knowing that it would not disappoint. It simply made me more curious.

The winding roads to the small town where his hotel was situated were quiet and narrow at times, but charming none the less. The scenery was beautiful and an abundance of colourful flowers and shrubs lined the roads. I closed my eyes and took a few deep breaths as we travelled and the wind blew across my face. I felt serene and at peace with everything in my life at this moment in time and that feeling was more than I had ever expected to find on this girls' holiday. It occurred to me how much I had let my life continue to pass me by after Paul's death, and that meant that a little of me had died each day in the process. I used to love life, and certainly made the most of it at every opportunity, but I had, in all honesty, during my grief, forgotten how to live. I hadn't realised until this exact moment how utterly miserable I had become.

I suppose anyone would say that my misery was a normal process after sudden grief like I had experienced. However, I had suddenly turned a corner and the girls knew that I needed to, and so I made a deal with myself that this was the new, improved me. I did not want to go back home feeling like I was when I left (I had lost three years of my life pining after Paul) but I needed to move on – after all it is what he would have wanted. I looked across at Ethan who in return looked at me and smiled, and that was all that I needed to make me accept my new pact with myself. The way he made me feel when he looked at me was with a warmth that I didn't want to ignore or leave out of my life anymore, and with that I smiled back and placed my hand on his knee, which made him flinch just a little, but he didn't remove it.

Josh was driving the car in front – he suggested doing so as he knew the way after being here with Ethan many times before – and while Beth and Hernando chatted in the back of our car I waited with anticipation for the sight of The Gessami Residence. We drove for approximately twenty minutes and then as we turned a tight corner high up in the hills with a beautiful traditional town below Ethan announced, "We are here." For some reason I could feel my heart racing as if it was going to be a nervous experience, but it wasn't nerves; it was anticipation and excitement.

He pulled the car up outside an old high wall, the bright purple and orange shrubs that climbed it were stunning, and as I stood and stretched my legs I did a turn and took in the surroundings. There was an old tall ornate iron gate, with one side open, and the beautiful italic name plate to the side of it simply stated 'The Gessami Residence'. It didn't look like a traditional hotel and I suppose that was the whole image that Ethan was trying to portray. It looked like a beautiful old Spanish household and in its original day it probably was: the renovations that had been carried out changed no original features and were done sympathetically toward the building itself. The men took the bags out of the car as a very nervous looking member of staff appeared to great Ethan. He spoke briefly with him as the others walked through the gate and beyond, I was simply taking in the view across the town below until Ethan appeared at my side.

"You like it so far?"

"It really is beautiful and the location is amazing. Far better than the busier hotel that we were at," I remarked.

"So may I show you inside?" he gestured toward the gated entrance. I nodded and we walked together slowly.

I was wrong about my original thoughts of how it would look, so very wrong. It was far more visually stunning than I ever could have imagined. The gated entrance opened into a beautiful courtyard filled with flowers and an ornate fountain, which sprinkled drops of water onto the small pond below cooling the fish that swam there. It made me smile at its simplicity yet it was captivating. The main entrance of the hotel greeted its guests with a large oak door adorned with intricate ironwork, and as we were about to step through it I turned and looked at the little windows that were all looking across the courtyard, all of which had shutters painted in a subtle green hue. They made the whole place seem inviting somehow and I couldn't wait to go inside.

"You're not saying anything," Ethan suddenly said. I looked at him and touched his arm.

"Not because I am disappointed, far from it. I just cannot find the right words." He smiled and then we turned and walked inside to the nervous staff member from earlier.

There was a buzz of excitement from the girls and Hernando and Rafael were talking to Josh and openly praising the quality of the place. It didn't disappoint. The old stone walls and the smooth marble return staircase edged with a twisted iron balustrade was visually stunning. The entrance and rooms beyond were filled with beautiful furniture, and pictures that were in-keeping with the ambience dressed the walls. Ethan spoke in Spanish with the staff member who was obviously being given instructions on who was sleeping where. He clapped his hands and ordered the young men at his side to take the bags upstairs while chattering to them with speed. As I started to walk toward the others, Amanda appeared at the end of the corridor and requested that we all come and see the pool. Rose and Beth were quick to walk toward her as I followed along after the men. We turned into a room that had doors to the outside and as the men parted and started to walk down the steps toward the pool I gasped a little.

The sun was high in the sky and reflecting on the rippling water, which was crystal clear. The pool was not the traditional rectangle, but a large and impressive kidney shaped pool. There was a hot tub at the far end, which the girls had made a beeline for, and the men slowly followed. I, however, stood on the steps and looked at the view of the sea, which was visible over the most amazing blanket of shrubs on which blossomed beautiful small white flowers – I suspected they were jasmine. These shrubs dressed the pool area in a way that made you feel like you had been transported into a scene from *Alice in Wonderland,* and the smell was sweet and perfumed. I sat on the step on which I stood and felt with all honesty that this was the most beautiful hotel that I had ever been to, and I was privileged enough to be able to experience it. As I sat contemplating its elegance and attraction Ethan appeared at the side of me and sat. I had the feeling he was nervous for my thoughts.

"So, what do you think? Does it live up to your expectations so far?" he enquired hopefully. I suddenly felt like I was in a dream bubble with him and didn't care who was there or watching. I looked at him and just kissed him in reply. "I'll take that as a yes then?" he smirked.

"Ethan, it's amazing, it really is. The location is stunning, the view of the town on one side and the sea on the other is exceptional. The work you have done is of a quality that I have not experienced before in a hotel, and this pool area is like complete tranquillity. I love it, I really do. The shrubbery looks like something that you have had designed just to suit, they're so pretty," I rambled on. He jumped to his feet and quickly went to pick one flower off the nearest shrub, then he returned and placed it into my hand.

"Jasmine," he simply said. "It is very beautiful, and the previous owner admired them so much that he had them planted everywhere," he explained as I examined the flower. "I suppose that you knew what they were though, being a florist and all?" he then asked.

"I thought that's what they were, but I don't think that I have actually ever seen so much jasmine in one place. Not as uniform or in such quantity and all in bloom." I smiled as I pushed the flower head into my hair just above my ear. "I can understand why the previous owner liked it so much. The flowers are enough to be stunning but not so large that they are overpowering, and they smell divine," I smiled.

"I agree – hence the name for the hotel; Gessami in Catalan means?" he looked at me inquisitively as the penny dropped.

"Jasmine," I replied suddenly realising the thought that had gone into the name. "Good choice," I confirmed and he smiled at my recognition.

We sat there talking about the pool and the hot tub and the view of the sea until Rafael and Amanda walked over to us. "Well you've certainly excelled yourself this time, my friend!" Rafael acknowledged before shaking Ethan's hand in appreciation.

"Thank you. I have to admit that this hotel to date is fast becoming my favourite," Ethan told him.

"Well I can see why. It really is very kind of you to invite us all here for a week." Amanda was grateful.

"It's my pleasure, Amanda. After all please don't forget that you are doing me a favour." He wasn't one to take any credit for his generosity. She smiled at him and then looked at me as if to ask for a response. I stood and rubbed my hands together.

"Well, I for one cannot wait to look at the bedrooms and then sample the food. If what we have seen so far is anything to go by, then I suspect that we are in for a real treat," I said with enthusiasm, looking at Amanda for confirmation.

"Ooh yes, absolutely. Can we see our rooms, Ethan?" she asked as he stood.

"Yes, of course." He laughed a little. "You're all very easy to please. Come on, I will show you all which room is yours."

Amanda was quick to call Beth and Rose to follow us. She knew that they were impressed too and as Josh and Hernando hovered behind them chatting and looking at the outside of the building, we all followed Ethan upstairs. Due to the fact that the building wasn't a traditional rectangular shape in its footprint, there were corridors and small facets and parts of the building that hid the doors to bedrooms and made the whole hotel have a magical feel about it. He showed each of us one by one which room we had, and as we progressed along I could tell that he had put a great deal of thought into who was in which bedroom. They all had the same luxurious fixtures and fittings, but he cleverly put Beth and Rose and Hernando and Josh in close proximity so that if they had the urge to want to spend the night in each other's room they were not likely to disturb anyone else.

Amanda and Rafael had been given rooms in a slightly quieter end of the building, and I knew that Amanda would love that. Her window overlooked the town and you could see one of the lovely churches as the bell tower protruded over the trees. Ethan commented on the fact that it had beautiful murals on the walls inside and there was an interesting vault which would make it well worth a visit. I found the fact that he had taken the time to sightsee the area quite endearing; it proved to me that he was not just passionate about the hotel, and his business, but the surrounding areas too.

We went to Rafael's room, which was as stunning, and then we left them all and he led me to a room at the corner of the hotel which was his. It was the most simplistic room and the smallest, and even though it had the same charm as the others I was touched by the fact that he had given all of us the bigger and more extravagant rooms instead. I stood there and then realised that I had not seen mine yet and he obviously registered that thought with my look.

"Would you like to see your room?" he suddenly asked as if he had read my mind.

"I'd love to." I couldn't wait. He took my hand and led me out of his room.

We walked a few steps down the corridor and to a very narrow staircase that had a rope handrail attached to the stone wall with metal rings. It curved up and around until we reached a small open area that had only one huge oak door. Ethan stopped and squeezed my hand a little tighter, then he looked at me with caution.

"I don't want you to think that I mean anything by this, but I want you to have the best room. This is the grandest room in the building, and most probably the one that will be used as a bridal suite should the need arise, but it is the best and I wanted that for you," he sincerely stated. I became more excited and released his hand asking if I may go inside, which he gestured for me to do so.

The large heavy door opened easily as I unclicked the latch, and as the room came into view I found myself holding my breath a little. The main feature of the room being the large twisted oak frame bed, which had carvings like nothing I had seen before, except maybe in houses like Chatsworth. The furnishings were of the highest quality, including all the pieces of furniture that filled the room. I would imagine that most were antiques and as I looked at the paintings on the wall and moved toward one of the full-length windows, the voile curtain blew in the breeze. I stepped out onto a small balcony and had the most impressive view of the sea which made me release a small laugh of sheer delight. The balcony was so small that it made me feel like Juliet, or a princess from a fairy tale. I suddenly found Ethan at the side of me.

"The view is impressive isn't it?" he asked. I found myself grabbing his hand without looking.

"I am overwhelmed at the beauty of this place, Ethan, and I am so happy that you invited us here with you. I never realised that Ibiza was so breathtaking," I told him, then I stepped closer and we kissed.

Had it not been for the ringing of a church bell that chimed across the warm breeze, I would more than likely not have ended our embrace, but the sound was as I would imagine from a small old town and as I hugged him I smiled. I happily released him and went to the window on the other side of the room, as I pushed one of the full-length wooden shutters open I was more impressed to see the old town below. This room had the best views of both the sea and the town, and it made it a room which was going to be delightful to spend time in.

He walked across to me and pointed out some interesting areas of the town below; it was very small and looked quaint and yet intriguing and I longed to explore it in greater detail. The whitewashed church, from where the bell tolled, was just visible and Ethan, as I expected, offered to show me around anytime that I should choose, and that made me happier still. He remarked that the old town, although it was still there, was becoming surrounded with more modern additions, but this I fear tends to be the same for most historical and old places today: societies are modernising to suit. Regardless, he commented on the narrow cobbled streets having coffee shops nestled within small buildings and the bougainvillea covered walls that bordered the streets; it sounded charming. The warm breeze blew gently as we stood together, the sea rolled on the shore in the distance and the church bell still rang – the scent of jasmine was sweet in the air, the whole experience was tantalising to the senses and it was a great start to our stay.

He showed me the en-suite which had the most elaborate large roll top bath along with beautifully tiled floors and walls, and a huge shower with a curved glass screen filled one corner. The sink was oval and a continuation of the marble top in which it sat. New white fluffy towels were soft to the touch and it was nice to know that they had not yet been used. My suitcase was stood at the bottom of my bed and as I looked at it I couldn't wait to unpack. We stood facing each other and that electricity from before had started to build when we heard some of the others approaching, Beth called us in an almost 'we know what you're doing' voice, and it made us laugh.

"We're up in my room," I called, just as Josh appeared at the door. He obviously knew where we were and where to look. As Beth, Rose and Amanda followed him into the room they simply gawped at how big it was and how amazing;

"Wow." Rose was in awe.

"This is amazing, Jen. Look at the view." Amanda said as she stood on the small balcony that looked out to sea.

"I know, I know it's breathtaking. I'm speechless." I was smiling at Ethan. He simply stared into my eyes and then repeated.

"Yes breathtaking."

"Well, we definitely know who is favourite then!" Beth said sarcastically, Ethan looked slightly vexed.

"Are you not happy with your room, Beth? We can change it to one of the others," he told her, not realising she was just pulling his leg.

"Oh Beth's happy, Ethan. She's simply jealous," Amanda called from the balcony. "I don't think anyone has call to complain about any room in this place; they are all just perfect." She walked back toward us.

"I bloody well hope that you are happy! Josh said with sarcasm. "The time we have spent on this place should reflect in the quality and finish. Even the chef was brought in from another hotel of Ethan's to finish the package. Speaking of which, I am starving again – shall we eat?" Josh then enquired.

Everyone started to walk and talk from our room and I just briefly caught Josh nod once at Ethan almost as if to say, "*you're welcome*" and I suddenly realised that part of Josh's role was to dilute any stress, tension or worries that Ethan may have, and he had just proved that he was able to do that with ease – whatever the situation. Ethan quickly spoke with him as we exited the room and as I listened, I smiled while Josh kept telling him how well the job had come together, and he was one hundred percent correct. It had completely excelled all of my expectations and if the chef and the food were as good as I now anticipated they would be, this was going to be one mind blowing week.

We sat out on the terracotta-tiled terrace and ate the most amazing paella, along with salads and breads. The wine was refreshing and although this dish was simple and satisfying it was the perfect meal. I looked at all of the happy faces around the table, laughing and relaxing and being at ease in each other's company; it felt like we had been friends for many years and I loved the atmosphere that it created. Rose enlightened us with stories of her travels to secure exclusive hotels for her company. She was amusing to say the least and had the men in hysterics; even Ethan laughed at her antics. She kept asking for his opinion on various matters of the hotel business that she struggled to understand, and he was happy to make sense of them for her. It made my floristry business sound remarkably dull by comparison, but I did however have the same passion about what I did for a living and so I was happy.

We sat for nearly two hours before Amanda decided to go and unpack. She was the most relaxed that I had seen in a long time, and that was pleasing. She stood and stretched and then looked at Ethan.

"I think that you need us to visit this place once a year, Ethan, just to make sure that the consistency and quality are uninterrupted." Ethan swallowed the mouthful of wine that he had just taken and replied.

"Well, that could be arranged, Amanda." She smiled at his response and then continued.

"Actually, why stop at just this hotel? How many do you own? We could be your own personal critics, Ethan, and an absolute advantage to have around," she smirked.

"I really don't think that Ethan would be too happy with the bar bills if we stayed regularly. You do all drink like fishes," I joked with them. Beth nearly choked on her wine.

"Hey, don't you be judging us, young lady! Just remember that you're the only reason we're all here, after you drank so much and then fell head first into the sand, meaning that you had to be helped to your room," she said with authority. I scowled at her.

"Well, in fairness to Jenny, it was the highlight of our evening wasn't it, Ethan? Our business conversation had just concluded anyway and there is nothing more inspiring to send you off home, than a pretty woman face ploughing into the beach – and sideways, I might add!" Josh laughed as did Ethan, lightly behind his hand. I elbowed him.

"Hey, you're supposed to be on my side," I remarked. Everyone was now laughing, so I sat back and folded my arms feeling slightly embarrassed. Ethan noted my rebuff and so reached out and rubbed my arm.

"Hey. Thank God that you were inebriated, as otherwise I would not be sat here with you all now," he replied sensitively before winking once at me. I half smiled in return.

"Oh God, get a room," Beth chided, mimicking sticking her finger down her throat before quickly saying, "Oh yeah, that's right – you have got a room, in fact you've got about ten of them… Cheers!" She toasted after her obvious statement which made me cringe just a little. Before Ethan or I could reply, everyone toasted him along with Beth, and thanked him for the invitation this week. I joined them and let the comment from Beth pass.

It was now six thirty and as most of them strolled off to unpack and Ethan went to speak to the chef about a late al fresco bite at around nine or ten tonight – anticipating that we would be up until after then – I found myself sat with Josh chatting in the warm, jasmine scented air. He gave me the biggest smile as we sipped the remainder of our wine. I in return gave him an inquisitive look;

"What?" I asked, but he just shook his head as if to be happy about something.

"I have been working with Ethan for a number of years now, and I have to say, Jenny, that I have not seen him this happy, or chilled in a very long time. You are good for him, it's nice to see him like this – not so orientated around business," he finished and I blushed a little.

"Well, all that I can say, Josh, is that I feel the same way. I like feeling like this too – chilled and relaxed. He's a really great guy," I confirmed.

"Long may it continue then I say, for both of you." Then he stretched out his arm to meet my glass. We chinked the glasses once in agreement just as Ethan reappeared.

"Did I miss something? What are we toasting now?" he enquired. I gave Josh a pleading look to not tell the truth.

"Toasting new friends," he said and I sighed with relief and then turned to smile at Ethan.

"I will definitely join you in that," he replied warmly.

The waitresses came to clear the table and I found that was my cue to go and unpack too. Ethan walked with me and when we reached the bottom of the narrow staircase he stopped. I stepped closer.

"If you keep this up you know I am not going to want to go home."

"Well I would be happy for you to stay as long as you like," he said softly and then we kissed tenderly, but parted lips breathlessly. If he keeps this up I think that the girls will be correct in their assumptions – I will want to have sex with him. I am finding that I am aroused every time I go near him, and the kisses are getting more intense.

He gestured for me to go to my room and as I started up the stairs I had to stop myself from taking his hand and leading him there with me, and I was sure he could sense that was how I was feeling. This was just not like me at all, but these feelings were making me feel youthful and enthused about life, and that surely had to be a good thing. I closed my door and took in a deep breath and then strolled onto the small balcony for a few minutes. I was having an amazing time, and I intended to make the absolute most of this week, starting with the rest of today. If it continued as it had been, I would be one happy lady.

Chapter 11

I stepped into the delightfully hot shower; the jasmine-scented products were a lovely touch and completed the luxury of the place. As I stood and combed through my hair wrapped only in my towel, Amanda and Beth appeared in my room. They both threw themselves onto my large bed and sighed in unison. I turned and watched them mimic sleeping for a second before Beth then propped herself up on her elbows.

"I knew that we were going to have a great time away, but I never expected to be enjoying myself this much!" she grinned as she banged her feet together, I smiled at her.

"Yes, and that would have nothing to do with the fact that you've been humping a young thirty-something-year-old man would it?" Amanda laughed. Beth reacted by smacking her across the leg. "Hey, you know I'm right." Beth just shrugged her shoulders.

"I would hardly say 'humping' – we had great sex. Yes he's young, but he is very attentive and we know that it's never going to be madly serious. We are having a little bit of holiday fun," she concluded looking at me for reassurance. Amanda was still laughing a little.

"Beth, if he gives you that spark of confidence that

you need to be yourself and have fun, then I say go for it. If you both know where you stand and you are after all consenting adults, I think you're doing alright." I tried to convince her, but she didn't need me to at all. As Amanda sat up and calmed herself Beth then said;

"Well, I'm not that old, Amanda, if I want to shag the brains out of some young man willing to let me, who am I to turn him away?" She gave her that cocky *'you're only jealous'* look and I chuckled to myself and carried on combing my hair. Amanda by now had realised that Beth didn't give a flying fig what she thought, so she stopped taunting her.

"This room is amazing, Jen." She then changed the subject as she walked to the large shuttered windows. "I really don't think that I'd have ever thought to look for a place like this in Ibiza, but my God I am pleased that you hit it off with Ethan. What a great place to spend some time together."

"I wonder how much a standard week here would cost. It must be a fairly expensive place. I mean the quality is exceptional, the food looks great so far and the setting is simply perfection," Beth added as she went to the other balcony.

"It just feels so tranquil, not like our last hotel at all. I love it here and you are right, I have missed the feeling of having a man around," I honestly confirmed. They both stepped back into the room and looked at me.

"Do I detect a hint of lust here?" Beth enquired hopefully. I felt my face heating up and I started to mess around with the things on my dressing table.

I knew that they were giving each other that hopeful look, but I tried to ignore it, they, however, had other ideas as they came closer toward me.

"Are we? I mean it is so obvious that he likes you," Amanda asked again. I took a deep breath and looked at them both.

"I really like him, he's just... just... perfect so far," I managed to say, then Beth put her arm around me and walked me to the bed where we sat down.

"But?" she asked. She always knew when I was holding something back. I grimaced a little.

"Do you think I'm being stupid? I mean he's the first man I've even allowed to be anywhere near me since Paul died. Maybe I am wanting him to be all the things I've missed and more, but perhaps I'm just jumping in with size ten shoes and this isn't what I think it is," I tried to explain. Amanda plonked herself down beside me.

"Do you honestly think that we would let you do something that we did not think you could cope with, or that seemed unacceptable by us? We're always looking out for you, Jen; you've had more than your fair share to deal with. We know that you like him as you have that look when you're with him, and truthfully we love seeing you like this. Even if this holiday with Ethan is just that, time shared with him on a holiday, is that a bad thing? You like him, and we're damn sure he really likes you otherwise we wouldn't be here now – what have you got to lose?" she asked me. I smiled at them both, I loved them for always being there for me and this was no exception.

"You're right, it's time for me to start trying to live again. If that means enjoying this holiday with Ethan, then I cannot think of a better start."

"That's my girl!" Beth replied as she slapped me firmly on the back. "Now get your hair sorted and let's get moving; we're having cocktails on the terrace in five with music," she happily informed me while clapping her hands together with delight.

They scuttled out of the door chatting away and discussing what they would like to do over the next few days. I actually took my time and put on a pair of white linen trousers and a simple pale blue strappy silk camisole, and after applying a light spritzing of perfume and some lip gloss I felt ready to return downstairs. As I ventured back down the narrow staircase I could hear subtle music from the terrace, it was soothing as it carried along the breeze that blew through the open doors, and as I neared the stairs I spotted the candles that glowed on the tables lighting up the coloured glass lanterns in which they stood. The subtle outside lighting that circled the pool lit up the jasmine shrubs in a hue of blue light and as they glowed it was like a scene from something magical. I carefully made my way down the steps and looked across at the others who were happily sat talking and in Rose's case swaying along with the music. When Ethan saw me standing there he made his way over.

"Hey, I thought that you had changed your mind for a second and opted for some sleep," he said as he kissed me on the cheek.

"No, I just enjoyed a hot shower and then took a while

to finish unpacking. It didn't help that Beth and Amanda came and took over, which sidetracked me," I informed him again before inhaling his aftershave for a second time.

"Well, I am glad that you are here, and you look lovely," he remarked as he stepped back slightly and looked me up and down.

"Thank you."

"Drink? The others are a couple ahead of you," he then informed me. I leant into him and whispered;

"I am actually glad about that, this pace of theirs is killing me!"

We sat and talked, danced a little, and ate some light snacks at ten thirty which were delicious, and by midnight I had simply had enough. I was extremely tired and after yawning numerous times Ethan had noted my desire to retire to bed. It had been a busy day after a late night, and so I excused myself from the others who seemed happy to keep partying, with the exception of Amanda. We walked indoors together, and as I hugged her goodnight at her door Ethan appeared. She winked at me and then released me and gestured that I should be prepared, I replied with a quick elbow in her ribs. After closing her door, I turned to him and smiled.

"I am so sorry that I'm so tired, the whole day has just been delightful. I am not going to be much use to anyone tomorrow though if I don't get some sleep." He took my hands in his.

"I just wanted to say goodnight without the others around. It's nice knowing that you are in the same building as me," he said but then he looked embarrassed.

"Well, should I need anything I have a telephone at the side of my bed and I know where you are," I said. He nodded and then started to turn away, but I thought about what I had said to the girls earlier and quickly reached for his arm. "Ethan," I softly called. He turned back to me. "I hope that you are not leaving without kissing me goodnight?" He stepped closer;

"I thought you'd never ask," he said with a softer voice than I had. Then he smiled at me and took my face in his hands and let his lips seal mine. What a way to say goodnight!

I sank into the cool sheets of the soft bed and sighed. That kiss had left me knowing that I would definitely have pleasant dreams. I lay there and thought about me and my life, and then the boys sprang to mind again. It had been two days since I last text them, and so I dropped them both a quick message making a mental note to call them soon. I pushed my head into the pillow and even though I could hear subtle music and laughter from the others outside, the sea beyond lulled me to sleep – and it was the best night's sleep that I had experienced in a very long time.

I bounced down the stairs in the morning feeling completely energised and refreshed. It was only nine thirty, and stupidly I hadn't thought to ask what time breakfast would be served. I did feel however that with Ethan around, timings wouldn't be strict. It was very quiet apart from two voices outside through the doors of another room. It was a beautiful balconied area on the opposite side to the pool and as I neared a member of staff appeared and smiled at me gesturing for me to join them. It was a relief to see Josh and Ethan sat with their laptops and talking business. Josh stood as I approached and greeted me with a good morning. But before Ethan attempted to stand, and as he had his back to me, I placed a hand on his shoulder and then slid my arm around his neck and kissed him on the cheek.

"Good morning." I said with enthusiasm. His hand reached up for my arm.

"It would seem that someone slept well last night?" he remarked at my perky disposition. He was right though, I felt amazing.

"Yes I did. That is the most comfortable bed that I think I have slept in for years." I sat just to the side of him. He was grinning at me, and he looked so desirable right now in his plain white t-shirt and shorts. I am sure that he noted my appreciation as he gave me a slight 'and what are you thinking right now?' look! I curled my lips in and smiled to myself and then reached across the table for a slice of toast.

"So shall I tell them that you will be there next week?" Josh then said, continuing their discussion. Ethan closed his laptop.

"It appears that I am going to have to be there, so yes you can tell them I will be there by Sunday and we will have the meeting Tuesday of next week," he replied.

I stood with my toast and looked at the view. It was so stunning, the air was warm and there was a hum of activity from the gardeners that were busy working. It was relaxing in a strange way to just watch them. I admired the many visual sights around me, paying attention to the beautiful climbing plant that so gracefully trailed its way up the hotel wall; its flowers were orange, and trumpet style and they vexed me for a moment as I studied them. Ethan had walked to me with a cup of coffee, I pushed the last corner of toast in my mouth and then took it thanking him. He looked at the flowers too.

"*Campsis grandifiora* – one of my favourites," he suddenly announced. I gave him a look of surprise, and in return he shrugged at me. "You weren't expecting me to know that, were you?" he grinned with confidence.

"Not really, but I like the fact that you do. It's beautiful, never seen it before though," I replied before taking a sip of the hot fresh coffee, which was delicious. "Oh my God, this coffee is divine," I announced.

"Well, you have Josh to thank for that; he certainly knows his coffee," he informed me as Josh smiled and nodded his head as if to thank us;

"Well, with this slave driver I have needed my fair share of it over the years!" he joked, and Ethan just shook his head at his sarcastic comment.

We returned to the table to continue breakfast and I nibbled on the fruit and other delights that adorned the large round tiled table. We were enjoying chatting, just the three of us, and as I sat there with my foot on the chair next to Ethan he reached across and touched my knee; "What would you like to do today? Josh suggested a trip down to the beach?"

"That sounds lovely. Can we walk a little too? There is so much to see around here," I enquired.

"Well if you fancy it, we can get everything ready and then walk down but send a picnic and our towels with Jose. He wouldn't mind coming down with everything in one of the cars," Josh suggested. Ethan agreed.

"Well, I think that sounds just perfect. It will be good to get some exercise and then we can chill on the beach for lunch," I replied just as Amanda, Beth and Rose appeared with the other men. They enquired as to what was being discussed and we relayed the plan to them – they were more than happy.

Breakfast became a bustling affair of chatting, drinking coffee and reading papers that were a day old, but none the less it was nice to catch up on them. I really couldn't stop picking at the food in front of me; it was delicious and it seemed that everyone else thought so too, as breakfast was consumed slowly over an hour or so. As it neared eleven, Josh tried to get us motivated to be ready to leave for a walk down to the beach. He had disappeared once or twice talking to staff, I assumed to sort out lunch and towels, and as everything seemed very well planned it only left us to get our sunglasses and sun cream really. Ethan had made a point of telling everyone not to take valuables or money as there was no need, and I was happy to walk in my converse pumps, as once I arrived at the beach bare feet would be just fine.

We all met back in the small courtyard near the entrance; the cars had been packed ready for driving down later and as everything was timed and planned to perfection, there was nothing more for us to do. We set off down the small track that had led to the hotel. Rose clung tightly to Josh's arm as it was a little steep to start. Beth had her ridiculously large hat on, which made Rafael laugh out loud: Amanda tried to apologise for her complete flamboyance which was not only radiated through her clothing but her whole being. Hernando however remarked that he would not like her any other way, which gave her the biggest smile I have seen in a long time.

As they all merrily walked, or in some cases skipped, down the track – Ethan and I hovered at the back of them. He was cool and collected as he followed along, but he also looked nervous and slightly out of place in all honesty and it gave me the impression that he didn't often do this as a form of relaxation. I felt bad for him that he seemed to give so much of his life to working and yet he never seemed to live much beyond that, through friends or otherwise.

He pushed both hands in his pockets as if he was, as I had suspected, nervous and that made him all the more charming. I smiled.

"Something amusing you?" he asked innocently.

"You look cute right now," I blurted out. God, he wasn't ten years old, but I knew what I meant. He laughed lightly.

"Cute?" he repeated nodding at the same time. "I don't think that I've been called that before," he continued. "How so?" I suddenly felt silly for saying it as now I had to elaborate.

"Well, maybe cute was the wrong word… Vulnerable would be better suited," I tried to explain. "You don't look very comfortable right now, which gives me the distinct impression that you haven't done this for a long time," I finished while gesturing to the fact that we were walking with friends.

"You are rather observant," he answered before looking down. "No, it's not something that I would ordinarily do to relax. Most people that I frequent with in my spare time are work acquaintances. Even Josh who I respect a great deal works alongside me. It's not quite the same," he honestly replied.

"Does this make you uncomfortable? If you would rather we can stay here," I tried to convince him. He moved a little closer and his shoulder nudged my arm.

"That's really sweet and I like the fact that you would do that for me, but I'm not uncomfortable and I am liking the change from my usually pretty boring existence out of work. This is a nice experience for me; I think that we should try to break my bad habits, so I am going to enjoy this." He was honest and so I smiled at him knowing that this was obviously a big thing for him.

"I hope I'm not being a bad influence, I do love the outdoors though – particularly in warm weather," I said as I looked up at the sun above.

"Well, if this is your idea of being a bad influence then I say bring it on. I am enjoying exploring this side of relaxing, especially as you are here."

"I am pleased about that then. Let's see if we can make this whole day completely enjoyable from start to finish," I dictated as I offered my left hand out for him to hold should he wish to. He looked at it for no more than a second or two and then smiled and took his hand out of his pocket and entwined his fingers with mine, then he looked up toward the sky and grinned a little more, and I knew that the gesture had been well received.

We saw many locals along the way, and we got some strange looks, it has to be said – especially Beth and that large bloody hat, which was almost giving us all shade. Amanda and some of the others had noticed our hand holding, but simply overlooked it, trying not to make a big deal of it which was appreciated. As we meandered through the streets nearing the beach, we passed a little cart and an old woman selling fruit and vegetables. I stopped thinking it would be nice to take some with us and proceeded to buy more fruit than was possible for the ten euros that I had in my pocket. She chattered away in Spanish to me and I just smiled not having a clue what she was saying, but Ethan replied a couple of times.

As we stepped onto the warm sand I took off my shoes, Josh was on the telephone and then waved to someone on the beach. The service that they had organised was second to none. Jose and another staff member had brought both cars it would seem, along with towels, a picnic, wine, umbrellas, beach chairs and sun cream. If only every holiday was as well organised as this! We walked across to the seemingly 'only us' area and sat down. The walk had taken about an hour with the stopping to look at things that were appealing, but it made it enjoyable none the less. Rose, before we could blink, had stripped her clothes off to her bikini and was beckoning Josh to go with her in the sea, which he happily did. Beth, Amanda and I went to dip our warm feet into the cool sea, and remarkably it wasn't as cold as I was expecting. When Hernando and Rafael appeared to do the same I turned to see that Ethan was propped on his elbows watching us. I quietly sloped back toward him leaving the others chatting. As I neared his grin widened.

"Aren't you going in?" he asked as I slumped down beside him.

"I might, but only if you join me," I pouted before turning onto my side and kissing him. We parted lips.

"That's coercing me, and not fair," he smiled.

"Well, I could beat you into going in with me instead if you'd prefer?" I suggested. He lay back and placed his hands under his head.

"I'd like to see you try," he cheekily replied, and with that I started digging him in the ribs which made him laugh out loud. It was the most addictive laugh and I wanted to hear more.

As I tried harder he sat and grabbed my arms and pushed me back onto the towels, he was now pushing against me and as I looked at him enjoying himself my fighting stopped and I melted into his grasp. He looked at me through his sunglasses.

"If you give up this easily, this wrestling is worthwhile!" he remarked.

"I like hearing you laugh, and for the record I let you win."

"Really? And why would you do that?" he asked while pinning my hands above my head. The position was intoxicating, and my body language was fearfully letting me down.

"I can't let you kiss me again if you're wrestling me." His grip loosened immediately and one hand slid down to my glasses which he removed before his.

"You are fast becoming addictive, Jenny Walker. What are you doing to me?" he asked. And suddenly, in that moment, I realised that I didn't want this holiday to be the only time that I ever see him again.

"Reciprocating!" I replied, and then he took my mouth and danced his lips across mine with an eagerness that made me think that he hopefully felt the same way.

I stripped down to my bikini and he to his swim shorts and that gave me an instant hot flush. Then we lay side by side after laughing at Rose and Josh who seemed intent on trying to drown each other. The sun again had that miraculous soothing feeling of melting your troubles away as it heated up the skin, and as I sighed heavily I was completely at the mercy of enjoyment and relaxation. Beth and Amanda went in for a dip too as did Hernando, but Rafael chose to soak up some sun for a while with us. After a long half hour of heat I sat and placed my hand on Ethan's tummy.

"I'm off for a cool down," I informed him while pointing to the sea. He nodded saying that he would join me shortly.

As gracefully as possible I stood and made my way to the sea edge hoping that my bottom hadn't eaten my bikini flashing my arse or worse still leaving that sweat streak from overheating! My aim was to get to the sea as soon as possible and then submerge without hesitation. As I held my breath and sank beneath the water I took a moment to surrender to the quietness. Once I resurfaced then slicked my hair back and opened my eyes, I turned and looked back toward the beach and Ethan. He was sat propped on his elbows again looking toward us. As I stared for a second I was pulled to one side by Rose.

"Hey, isn't the water great?" she asked as she splashed me numerous times. I agreed and splashed her back before we took a swim together. We talked and swam while Josh floated on his back. Beth and Amanda along with Hernando had retreated back to the towels but Rose was right, the water was delightful.

On our return swim toward Josh, I noted that Ethan had walked to the water's edge. He watched me closely as I swam, smiling and I think hoping that I would ask him to come in further. I was just about to beckon him, but he started wading in, much to Josh's amusement. He swam out toward me and Rose gave me that look.

"God, he is so into you Jen – make the most of it," she whispered before swimming back over to Josh and then hanging around his neck.

Ethan had disappeared under the water and resurfaced right in front of me. He ran his hands through his wet hair and then did a little shudder at the sharp contrast from the hot sun. I splashed him and told him not to be a softy! He bounced in the waves as we both faced each other and so I moved closer and placed my arm around his neck in sympathy of his shock therapy. His arm found its way around my waist and pulled me closer.

"Is it me or is being so close in the sea quite a turn on?" I confidently asked. He gave me a look of surprise.

"Perhaps it's being half naked and skin to skin contact?" I carried on;

"I know where you're coming from, but that sharp sudden contrast has made things shrivel somewhere they shouldn't, so just give me a minute to adjust and I'll probably agree!" he said nervously and I couldn't stop laughing.

We swam together for a while before deciding to get out and warm up in the sunshine. I nervously checked my nipples, just to make sure that they weren't like chapel hat pegs, and then walked back with him to the towels which were the perfect place to dry off. Hernando had dragged Beth again in her new bikini to the water's edge. She never really was one for swimming in the sea, but liked to stand waist deep in the waves and bounce around within the spray. As long as she had her feet in the sand she was happy. I reached in the basket for a glass and Rafael filled it with wine; I did the same for Ethan and passed it to him. The picnic was a medley of colourful food: salads; peppers; fruits; breads; chicken; olives; cheeses… It went on.

"I'm going to be the size of an elephant when I return home," I pointed out.

"Well, it will be winter before you know it and you can wear your baggy jumpers, so who cares?" Amanda sniggered.

"God, stop wishing our holiday away, Amanda," Rose insisted while downing wine and eating cheese and small tomatoes. I sipped my wine and listened to their bantering while watching Beth with Hernando.

The waves were getting a little bigger than before, mainly due to the speedboat that kept crossing back and forth. Twice now Beth had been overcome by waves while Hernando stood slightly shallower than her simply watching. I nudged Ethan who looked in the direction that I was.

"She's going to go way under in a minute if she isn't careful, and she won't like it one little bit!" I pointed out as I nibbled on olives, watching. Everyone else now had turned to watch her.

The bright yellow speedboat turned again and made its way back as someone happily water skied behind, this time they were much closer to shore and the waves came rippling in like the harsh Atlantic on the Portuguese coast. I gasped a little as Beth obliviously bounced in the waves looking at Hernando and shouting with delight, not realising that there was a huge wave approaching her. We all sat up a little taller wondering when she was going to realise, but it was too late.

As Hernando tried to point out what was coming it slapped her hard on the back of the head and pushed her under, it wasn't the first wave that worried us it was the following two that kept rolling her under. We knew that she wasn't going to be happy, and as the waves subsided and Hernando tried to make his way toward her she came into view on her knees gasping for breath. We stopped panicking from the moment that we could see her, but we were not expecting what followed. Ethan stood quickly thinking that she was in trouble and as we watched for a few seconds while she caught her breath she flicked her head back and started laughing.

"Oh my God, can you see that?" Rose called, as we all started to realise the worst had happened for her.

She crawled on all fours nearer to the shore, Hernando had his hand on his head slightly panic-stricken, and then Beth jumped to her feet and announced to the whole world in all her glory that one of those waves had taken her bikini top. She stood and threw her hands in the air and screamed in glee as if to have enjoyed the whole experience. Everyone was sat in silence for a minute and then Rafael started laughing which in turn made us do the same. I held onto Ethan's leg at the side of me and rubbed it in reassurance that she was alright. He sat back down and looked at me and I shrugged my shoulders to acknowledge the same shock.

Hernando had managed to find her bikini top and was trying to convince her to put it back on as numerous other people on the beach were suddenly interested. Beth frolicked in the waves with ease, and I wasn't sure if it was to hide any embarrassment, or the simple fact that she didn't care! Either way it had all of us in hysterics, and in particular Rafael who found Hernando's chasing of her funnier than anything else. Ethan looked at me.

"She's obviously not shy then?" he remarked and as I tried to stop laughing by taking a sip of wine. I shook my head in agreement. He looked slightly taken aback by her boldness and that made me laugh all the more.

Amanda by now was nearly wetting herself and Rose was simply pointing out that she was in fact an exhibitionist at heart. The men praised her confidence and self-loving, but more than anything found Hernando's worried response the funniest thing. By the time he had got her to put her bikini top back on and started walking her back to us, she looked liberated and he looked totally drained. As we composed ourselves for their return, Ethan leaned into me.

"This should be fun. Hernando will be ribbed by Rafael." I looked at him and gave him the 'why?' look. "They have been friends for years; it's usually Rafael that either says or does something embarrassing after drinking that gives Hernando reason for complete humiliation at his expense, so this should be quite humorous to witness!" he explained. "You know, roles reversed." I nodded realising what was to come, but felt for Beth.

They both arrived and collapsed on the towels, Beth laughing and Hernando looking like he needed to sleep. I laughed as Rafael laid into him asking what the hell he thought he was doing letting a young woman be in the waves on her own, and as serious as he tried to be while Beth helped herself to wine, Hernando could not be more apologetic. This in turn just made the men laugh even more, Beth stated quite openly that at first she wasn't sure of the situation but she loved the feeling and realisation that she could just bare all to the world.

"God, I have an ample bosom. Why not share it with everyone?" she declared quite happily.

Rose and Amanda told her that she needed to calm her enthusiasm to share so eagerly so she didn't scare off any children. Josh hinted that he'd quite enjoyed the whole thing, which Rose then quickly punished him for. I looked at Ethan and told him that he had no need to worry

202

that I was that outgoing. I think he was slightly shocked at Beth's antics even though he laughed. He leaned into my ear.

"Thank God for that!" he said firstly. "If you were mine, I would not want to share you with the world," he then finished. I smiled at him.

"Good!" I said and then I kissed him in, and among, all of the commotion. I looked across at Beth still revelling at her nakedness and Josh who was looking curiously at her.

"What I want to know is, how the hell did you fit those into that bikini top in the first place?" he then enquired with all seriousness pointing at her breasts. We all looked at him and were quiet for a moment. "Just asking!" he then continued when nobody replied.

"He does have a point, Beth." I agreed. She sat for a minute looking down at her chest then replied;

"Well I could take it off again if you'd all rather?" and then she started to reach behind her back for the clasp.

"No!" we all shouted in unison, and then proceeded to laugh a little more when she joked that she was kidding.

The afternoon was enjoyed at a pace I consider to be complete holidaying. We ate, drank wine, sunbathed, took a dip in the sea, played a little volleyball and football – badly I might add – and then we talked and laughed and enjoyed the whole afternoon in each other's company. When it was time to leave, I pulled my t-shirt back on and then let out a little high-pitched noise of sheer delight.

"Enjoy that?" Ethan asked. I smiled at him.

"I did, thoroughly."

"Me too," he answered smiling, and as Jose and the

others helped carry the things back to the cars, Ethan placed his arm around my shoulders and we walked back across the sand leaning into each other.

The ride back to the hotel was quick and an absolute relief that we didn't have to walk. Even though it wasn't far, I was now in complete *'can't be bothered'* mode, which was lovely to experience as we all seemed to be feeling the same way. When we arrived back it was almost five thirty, so as the staff unpacked the cars we made our way to our rooms. A shower was definitely in order to rinse off the sea, sand and sweat caused by the sun and my rising body temperature when near Ethan: it was starting to become harder to resist.

Chapter 12

The shower was again a blessing. As I stood rinsing the day from me I looked at the beautiful hand-painted tiles that dressed the walls; every detail had been carefully thought about even down to the colour of the grouting, which matched the tiles perfectly. I wrapped myself in a fluffy towel and patted my damp hair with another and I could have quite happily stayed curled up in the large comfortable bed and just snoozed the evening away, but I knew that the girls would not let me get away with that one little bit. I had taken an inordinate amount of time in the shower enjoying the cascading water, so I was surprised to see that it was already six thirty now. I reached for my after sun, I had that notable tingling skin after a day in the sun and as I rubbed it into my arms it felt refreshing as well as cooling. I continued to let it absorb and carried on with my legs, neck and body and as I started to rub in the droplets of cream that I had distributed around every exposed area, there was a knock at the door.

I placed the bottle down and walked over drying the cream off my hands on my towel before I touched the handle, as I opened it nervously with only my towel wrapped around me, I was surprised to see Ethan stood there showered, shaved and dressed.

"Oh God, I'm sorry, I've caught you at a bad time," he insisted as he blushed not wondering where to look. It was too late now; he had seen me as I was. I stepped back and gestured for him to enter my room;

"Please come in." He hesitated for a moment before doing exactly that. He ran a hand through his hair and his nerves made me smile.

"If this is a bad time, I can come back," he repeated. I quickly looked at the bottle of after sun on the small table.

"Actually, if you wouldn't mind I could really use your help." He looked at me curiously;

"How so?"

"That sun was stronger than I thought today, I have very hot shoulders and a hot back. If you wouldn't mind I'd appreciate it if you could rub some cream into my skin, it's a little difficult reaching on my own." I prompted him by reaching the bottle out to him.

He was speechless for a moment and held out his hand to take it, then retracted it, then placed it out again. To help his unease I took hold of his hand and placed the bottle in it. I smiled at him as he looked at me nervously.

"Are you sure about this, I could call Amanda or Rose?"

"It's only cream, and you're here anyway. I dare not even think about what Rose is up to right now, but if this makes you really uncomfortable then it can wait until one of them is free," I tried to convince him.

"No, it's fine. I'm happy to oblige if you are happy for me to do it," he then said as he flipped the top open. He stepped closer smirking a little.

"Am I amusing you? I enquired. He shook his head laughing still, then reached his free hand up toward my face.

"It's just that you look like something from an eighties band right now," he told me as he started to wipe the thick smears of cream from my cheeks. With all the excitement of him being at my door, I hadn't had the chance to wipe them away.

As his thumb pad gently swept across my cheek to rub in the cream, I closed my eyes and pushed my cheek into his hand in response. I inhaled his freshly showered skin and the hint of aftershave still present on his palm. When I opened my eyes he was staring at my face, and the moment took me unawares because even though I wore a towel, I really did feel naked, completely. I was opening up my emotions and feelings to a man I hardly knew and my body was informing him of all these responses quite freely. He smiled and then noting my shyness, suddenly he did a little circle gesture with his finger to get me to turn around. I was immediately grateful and did as he asked and lowered my towel down my back so that he could easily apply it.

"I will try and warm this up a little – don't want you hitting the roof," he joked.

"I think the contrast of the cool cream with my hot skin will be instant bliss," I shuddered as his hands touched my skin.

If he was enjoying this applying as much as I was receiving it, then we could've been in for some serious trouble. Was it not for the fact that I knew after recent events there was no way that he would break his promise to me as a gentleman, I may have been worried. But actually in all honesty if he did break that promise right now I would not find myself complaining. His touch was soft and consistent and he carefully moved his hands to the edges of my hips, my sides and my shoulders without overstepping any boundaries. When he had finished I pulled my towel back up to a suitable position and turned to him.

"Thank you."

"My pleasure… anytime," he replied with a cheeky grin. I bit the inside of my cheek as I knew he was toying with me.

"I suppose I had better get dressed then?" I asked looking at my current white towel dress.

"For me you can come to dinner dressed as you are – I think it may cause some serious questions from those girlfriends of yours, though," he laughed as he started to walk toward the door.

"Ethan," I called.

"Yes?"

"Did you want to ask me something?" I enquired. He looked confused.

"You came to my room first, before I so ungraciously gave you a task. You must have wanted something?" he shook his head;

"Oh, yes, sorry – I wanted to let you know that dinner will be at eight, that was all. We are going to have drinks outside until then," he waited a few seconds and then stepped closer. "So I'll see you downstairs?"

"Yes, you will," I replied raising my eyebrows happily, then he kissed me on the cheek and exited the room.

I closed the door and leant against it realising that my body was almost pinching me from the inside out, and trying to tell me to stop holding back and do what I want with him. It made me smile and as I rubbed my tummy trying to stop the butterflies that circled within; the thought of spending a night with him was starting to feel far more acceptable. I continued to get ready, and this time decided on a simple dress, it was only jersey cotton but bright in colour and very comfortable. When I arrived downstairs again, I was pleased to see that I wasn't the last. Both Beth and Rose had not appeared yet, but neither had Josh nor Hernando, and so as I approached Amanda I knew that she thought the same when she gave me that look of relief that I had arrived.

Ethan was quick to pour me a glass of wine, and I chose to sit next to Amanda and chat to her for a while as Rafael discussed some business plans with Ethan on expanding his company. I looked across at him numerous times, and every time that I did he was always looking back at me. Resisting was getting harder and harder and I wondered how much longer I could wait. I wanted to be held, and loved and make love with someone I was truly attracted to. I had never been one to have a one night stand, and so getting closer to Ethan plus the fact that he was so charming, was making this transition in my life so much easier.

Amanda and I nudged each other when Beth and Hernando appeared together, closely followed by Rose and Josh who looked exhausted. We shook our heads at her as she plonked herself down at the side of us. The men stood and talked, as did we until dinner was served. This time we had been given the opportunity to eat in a very elaborate dining room. It was stunning, fresh flowers adorned the table, candles were lit, and the aroma of fine food that filled the room made most of us hold our rumbling tummies and salivate a little. The fresh air during the day along with the walk had resulted in us all feeling very hungry.

The meal yet again was absolutely amazing. We all gave our compliments to the chef and after the three courses that were served, I think that I can safely say that we were all more than satisfied. We sat for a further hour, just talking and drinking wine and at around eleven o'clock Ethan asked if I would like to take a walk outside. I happily agreed as the others were fast reliving this afternoon's mishap with Beth, who then decided to start telling them stories of misfortunes that had fallen upon both Amanda and Rose. I was happy to escape any embarrassing tales that they may wish to tell about me.

Ethan placed his arm around my waist and we walked around the hotel and then out onto a quiet terrace. He summoned one of the waiters and asked that the bottle of the red that we were drinking be brought out to us. There was a large double sun lounger looking plush with thick cushions, and as he looked around for where we should sit, I suggested that. I took off my shoes and happily sat. He sat at the side of me and put his feet up and then placed his arm around my shoulders and pulled me to lean on him. I took in a deep breath of contentment and then placed my hand on his chest.

"That was a short walk!" I remarked, but I was happy that it had been.

"I just wanted to have you to myself for a while," he said, and then he squeezed my shoulder a little tighter. I liked his reply.

The waiter returned with an open bottle and placed it onto a table just to the side of Ethan. He poured us the first glass and then asked if we required anything else. We both replied with, "No thank you," at the same time which made us smile. I took a sip of my wine and then shivered a little; the night had turned just a little cooler, particularly after being indoors. Ethan reached behind my head and pulled a beautifully patterned throw which he spread across our legs and then pulled it up to our waist. I was in heaven right now.

"So I wanted to show you how clear the sky is up here," he then said as he pointed up to the night sky above. It was like a dark blanket filled with tiny sparkling diamonds and such an amazing sight.

"It's really beautiful, Ethan. I never take the time to look at the stars – not easy to see them from the centre of Manchester. I'm glad that you brought me out here, just being with you alone is more relaxing than I can tell you," I honestly told him, and then he placed his wine glass in the hand around my shoulder and placed his other on my cheek and kissed me for longer than I can recount, but I didn't want it to end.

We talked about my business, my plans for the future

and his, and about things that we enjoyed, things that we still wanted to do. Our favourite foods, drinks, places, people… It was only when Josh appeared that I realised that we must have been missing for some time.

"Hey, there you are," he chirped. "Most of us are retiring, bushed from today," he announced.

"Alright, Josh. We'll see you in the morning," Ethan replied, pulling me closer. Josh gave us an enormous grin.

"Okay, have fun, kids," he teased us. Ethan just shook his head at him.

I knew that if Josh told the girls where we were they wouldn't come and bother me. I was happy to be just having some quiet time with Ethan, and I wasn't about to go to bed yet.

"Are you happy with us being up together and alone?" he suddenly asked breaking my thoughts.

"I am incandescently happy," I smiled at him and we kissed again.

We carried on our conversations, laughing and drinking wine and then talking some more. He was so fascinating, and listening to his childhood and where he had been, what he had seen and who he had met was intriguing. My life in comparison felt slightly dull, and I made a point of telling him that. He told me that numerous times when he was younger he had craved what he classed as 'normality', that even though he had enjoyed growing up it had been slightly out of the ordinary. While we sat there looking at the sky and sipping wine in silence, there was no need for words. I snuggled down further into the throw as the breeze picked up.

"Cold?"

"I'll be okay, should have worn something a little warmer than this dress." I pointed out.

"Yes, I was slightly disappointed that the towel toga you had on earlier didn't make an appearance," he joked. I turned and looked at his face and he was silently laughing.

"Oh, a comedian, are we?" I asked before I reached across and placed my glass down. He must have panicked that I was leaving as his face changed.

"I was only joking, where are you going?" I pulled a face at him.

"You are not getting away with that comment, Mr James. Payback time." I took his glass from him put it on the table with mine and stared him in the eye.

He looked a little confused, and then I tried to get back the infectious laugh that he had from earlier on the beach. I started to tickle his ribs, but manoeuvred myself so that I was now straddling him. As he laughed and tried to take control of my hands, I kept on going. After a couple of minutes he pulled one of my hands to the side and I slipped forward inches away from his face. My body started throbbing, I was in a very sexual position, and we were both gasping for breath.

"You're pretty amazing, has anyone told you that recently?" he smiled. I shook my head.

"Not someone that I wanted to hear it from so desperately," I whispered back. He let go of my hand and simply looked at me waiting for any other response but I smiled. "I'm going to kiss you now."

"Oh God, I really hope so," he stated as his hands

moved up my waist and then to my face. I swallowed hard, and then let my lips gently press against his.

We both melted into the most sensual session of kissing. He sat up and took a firmer hold of my face as I slid my hands behind his shoulders. Things were heating up; he was aroused and the feeling of that between my thighs was exciting me more than I had realised. He lifted me and moved me onto my back, holding my arms above my head on the large lounger. I slipped my body into his embrace as he kissed my neck and then moved his hands over my body. I whispered his name and that seemed to inspire him more. We kissed again. Then I found myself unbuttoning his shirt and pulling him closer so that I could kiss his neck. He moaned gently as he kissed mine, sliding my dress away from my shoulder to kiss that too. We were just getting to that point where you won't be able to stop yourself, when he did stop. I was gasping and holding him and he looked directly at me.

"I'm sorry, I've done it again, haven't I?" he said. I pulled him back to me and kissed him again.

"I want to do this with you, I want you," I replied, and I really did mean it this time.

"Well, that's good for me to know, but I can't do this with you here. It's not fair to you, and I'd like to think that I'm slightly more romantic than this." Bugger – he was being that chivalrous guy again that doesn't usually exist.

"I love your gentlemanly ways, Ethan, but God I'm light-headed right now, you're working me into a frenzy." I took a deep breath. "I do love you for thinking so much about me though." I reached up and touched his cheek, then he pulled me back up and onto his lap.

"I just want to do this right. How about I take you out for dinner tomorrow night, and if you still feel the same way… well, let's see?" he asked me. I smiled knowing that I had now made a decision about how far I wanted us to go, and I wasn't going to change my mind. I just wasn't sure which was more nerve-wracking, spontaneity or planning the moment? I kissed him again.

"That's an excellent idea," I said, and then we heard someone coming, so I quickly sat and we straightened ourselves up.

The waiter from before arrived at the side of us and asked us if we would like anything else. I tried not to laugh, but found myself starting and I couldn't stop. The image of him arriving to ask a few minutes earlier would have been a completely different situation. Ethan looked at me, smiled, and then very seriously said that there was nothing else that we needed and made out that he had no idea what was wrong with me. Once he had gone I hit Ethan on the arm and laughed some more.

"Alright, I think that may have been a good call by you."

"Indeed," he replied before throwing the last mouthful of wine from his glass down his throat. "Maybe we should get some sleep?" he suggested. I hadn't realised that it was past one, and the thought of my bed made me feel sleepy.

We walked back indoors and toward our rooms. He left me at the bottom of my stairs after a long lingering kiss, and then I thought about tomorrow night. This could be the first night in three years that I was about to give myself to another man other than my husband, and although I was nervous, I felt slightly elated. I couldn't think of anyone better to do that with than Ethan whom it would seem I was fast becoming extremely attracted to. Mental note: before the liaison, de-fuzz, de-fuzz and then de-fuzz some more!

Chapter 13

When we arrived downstairs for breakfast the following morning, Josh had decided another short walk exploring the small town below was in order. We had enjoyed the fresh air yesterday, and the town he had said was so compact that it would probably only be a two to three-hour expedition.

"Maybe the four of us could buy you men lunch?" I announced hoping that the girls would agree; it was something that we could do as a thank you of sorts.

"That's a great idea. Please let us pay for something this week," Beth chipped in. I was glad for her quick response. Josh looked at Ethan and shrugged.

"It's not necessary, ladies," Ethan said.

"But we would all like to… please?" I pleaded as I placed my hand on his and squeezed it lightly.

"Alright, it sounds great," he conceded smiling back at me. We hadn't realised the rest of the table was quiet until Josh spoke up.

"Well, Jenny, if you can get Ethan to agree to anything that easily, I think that I should be taking you on all business trips with us!" he teased. I nodded my head back at him feeling satisfied that I had Ethan's full attention.

We ate breakfast and drank the delicious coffee, when

Amanda then enquired about plans for the evening; "I wonder what amazing delights your chef will concoct for us tonight?" The others then went into raptures about what we had eaten last night.

"Well I'm sure it will be delicious, but you are on your own tonight friends," Ethan then said. Rose and Amanda glared at me in question, and Josh and Hernando placed their coffee cups down and looked at Ethan too. He looked up at them, then at me. He squeezed my hand a little tighter; "I am taking Jenny out to dinner tonight, just the two of us," he simply said. It was a statement and not an invite for questions from the others.

Josh smiled at the two of us, and Hernando raised his cup at Ethan almost in a congratulatory way. The girls tried not to say anything but smiled at me and nudged each other repeatedly. It was a little uncomfortable until Josh broke the silence again.

"Nice. Where are you thinking of going?" he asked quite casually, before forcing a quarter of toast into his mouth. Ethan looked at me.

"Do you like seafood?"

"I love seafood, but don't eat it often enough."

"Ooh, take her to 'Delicies del Mar,'" Josh suddenly called almost spitting out his toast across the table.

"That's where I was thinking," Ethan replied to his suggestion. Then he looked at me again. "It's the best fish restaurant here on the island. People drive for miles to eat there. It is all seafood though – would you be alright with that?" he enquired smiling. I nudged him with my shoulder.

"Perfect," I answered happily. We grinned at each other knowing it would more than likely be the start to a perfect evening of seafood, snogging and sex, and secretly I really couldn't wait.

The trip to the town was blissful. Small quaint houses were abundant and Ethan was correct – the shrubs that gracefully dressed the buildings were beautiful. We visited the church and there happened to be a ceremony; a christening. The town was alive with excitement and laughter and singing for the blessing of the new baby, it was lovely to stand and watch. We stopped for coffee, then walked again. The girls and I bought small traditional trinkets, and enjoyed the whole experience of another small historic town. As Ethan and Josh had never really had lunch there it was a new experience for them too, particularly trying to decide on somewhere to eat. We stopped at a small family-run restaurant – the food was simple but delicious and Ethan complimented the very happy owner, then explained who he was.

Ethan was then introduced to the whole family of the restaurant, who seemed to work there. They all greeted him with kisses on his cheeks – the men too – and this amused all of us as it was so obviously uncomfortable for him. The owner's wife held his hands and spoke to him for a long time, looking like she was praising him greatly. He told us afterwards that she was very happy that he had saved the building and restored it, and that sometime in the past her mother had worked there when it was a family home. Ethan invited them all to come and take a look sometime at what he had done to the place, and they were more than happy at his invitation. Then we left and said goodbye and we strolled back to the hotel – Ethan and I were hand in hand. When we arrived back we changed into swimwear enabling us to take some time to relax by the pool.

Ethan and Josh had a small amount of business to organise, and so they excused themselves for a while. The rest of us collapsed on the very comfortable sun loungers, soaking up the sunshine and taking a dip in the pool. I opted for no alcohol this afternoon; I needed a clear head for tonight and was very aware that I needed plenty of time to get myself ready and be smoothed to perfection. I looked sideways at Amanda to find her looking at me.

"Nervous about tonight?" she whispered. I nodded before replying.

"A little, but I'm also excited about it." She rubbed my arm to reassure me.

"I am betting that you have an amazing time. I'm really happy for you." I touched her arm as a gesture of gratitude; she was sweet about my wellbeing.

"I think that you are right and I will have an amazing time. I just need to make sure that I haven't forgotten what to do, you know, with a man!" I then whispered back. She lowered her sunglasses to the end of her nose and glared at me.

"Are you going to spend the night with him?" she whispered back. I suddenly became all twitchy and then felt ridiculously nervous.

"I hope so, well – I think so. Oh God, now I'm not sure," I then flustered as I threw my hands up to my face. She leant across nearer to me.

"Honey, if it feels right you will just let it happen, and I assure you that you will definitely not have forgotten what to do," she smiled

"What if I disappoint, or worse still make a fool of myself? And what if Beth was right and I need lubricant and an instruction manual. Oh holy crap, I now feel a bit sick," I quietly said as I sat up. Amanda swung her legs around to face me while the others either snoozed or chatted oblivious to our discussion. She placed her hands on my knees as I now faced her.

"You always knew the first time after Paul was going to be a whole flood of emotions, right?" she asked. I nodded. "Ethan is a pretty amazing guy from what we have all seen, and it's really clear that he thinks an awful lot about you – look at the respect he has shown you so far." I nodded again. "Honey, I cannot think of a better man, or a better time than right now for you to move on and get your life back on track. Stop worrying, and enjoy it for what it is… a man and a woman enjoying each other completely. It would seem from your discussions that he is a little out of practice too, so I'm also betting that he is probably as nervous if not more so than you. So enjoy it and be nervous, and excited, and happy and completely lost in each other – you deserve it!" she concluded.

I thought for a second about what she had said, and then I told myself that she was absolutely right; I had to let go, and I had to stop worrying so much. I loved being in Ethan's company, and so why should being with him in the bedroom be any less enjoyable? Amanda was right, he was out of practice too and so the chances of him being nervous were high. I looked at her as she nodded at me for some response to her declaration, and then I reached across and hugged her. We embraced and she rocked me slightly side to side. I was so glad to have such a great friend that always knew what to say to me to put me at ease, and confirm what I was thinking. I sat back and looked at her.

"Thank you. I love you." I declared and she grinned back at me.

"I'm actually a little jealous if truth be told. He is pretty darn hot… so I want all the details later!" she then winked at me, and so I slapped her leg to give her the notification that I was not about to divulge anything. She chuckled lightly, just as Rose looked over.

"What are you two talking about?" she called. Amanda turned to face her.

"Nothing at all, just enjoying the sunshine, the company and the absolute relaxation," she answered happily. I was pleased to know that she wasn't about to run and tell the others what my intentions were.

The fresh juices were delicious and tantalising to the taste buds after days of consistent alcoholic beverages. I walked across and sat in the hot tub and put my head back on the tiles letting any remaining worries melt away. I hadn't even realised that Ethan had joined me until he kissed my cheek and asked if I was enjoying myself.

"I really don't think that another holiday will be any comparison to this. It is the most perfect place to spend time with friends," I told him before closing my eyes again as the water bubbled around my shoulders.

"It depends which friends," he whispered back. I opened my eyes and looked at him, he was being sincere and then he kissed me on the lips just once. "So I have booked a table for tonight at seven thirty, but I think that we should leave at around six forty-five," he then informed me. I sat up.

"Oh that early? I better start to make a move soon. I need to make myself presentable, and that takes a lot of beauty products," I joked.

"You could come to dinner as you are now, and you would still look perfect and beautiful to me," he then said and I felt a little embarrassed.

"If I have to go dressed like this, then you have to come dressed like that!" I hinted at his bare chest. He looked down at himself.

"Alright, point taken – I don't want to put people off their food."

"Highly unlikely." I moved in the bubbles to face him. "They would simply think that dessert had arrived," I seductively said as I ran my hand down his rippling chest. His hands found their way onto my waist and he pulled me closer.

"We are not having dessert at the restaurant, let's save that for when we get back," he whispered into my ear and with a little bit of giggling I nodded.

When Beth stood and stated that it was already after five o'clock, I decided to make my excuses to return to my room. I wanted to give my boys a quick call and take a shower, shave my legs and de-fuzz any other area that may be exposed later, then moisturise, apply make-up and so on… all of the things necessary and needed for a first real date. A date – I cannot believe that I was actually saying that. I smiled to myself.

I decided to indulge in a hot shower first, and shave to a smoothness my skin hadn't seen in quite a while. Then I could chat to the boys while the moisturiser soaked in. It was great to catch up with both James and Mark and they had an array of stories to tell me. I tried to explain how I was getting on. Mark seemed relaxed that I had met someone who seemed to be sweeping me off my feet, which made me feel a bit easier about everything. I sent them my love, and told them that I would be back during the early hours of Sunday morning. That unnerved me – I didn't have that long with Ethan really. It would be nice to see my boys though – they promised to visit me the weekend after.

I had just finished blow drying my hair when Amanda knocked at my door. I called for her to enter. She had wanted to know if I needed help choosing what to wear, and I was glad of the help. Then in came Beth and Rose, wanting to know the same thing. I already had my underwear on under my bath robe thank goodness, or I would have received no end of ribbing from them. They all agreed on the same thing – I had taken with me a very simple but figure-hugging navy dress. I never went anywhere without one decent dress! I had nude heels and Beth lent me a clutch bag that matched perfectly. Simple make-up and an understated pretty bracelet and I was good to go. I did them a twirl and then we hugged.

"God, he's going to palpitate when he sees you," Rose happily chirped. The others agreed.

"I promise you all that whatever tonight brings I will enjoy it – all!" I then stated for their benefit.

"That's definitely my girl," Beth said as she quite forcefully patted me on the behind. I grimaced at her, but then smiled.

"Just promise me that you girls will behave while we are out?" I pleaded. They just laughed and muttered something along the lines of, "Whatever– spoilsport."

I gave myself a quick spritz of perfume, grabbed my little cardigan and then followed them down the stairs. They were loud, excitable and as they were in front of me – it gave me the chance to stop and check myself in the mirror before we went down the marble staircase. The others almost ran down them to Ethan waiting at the bottom, as if to give me a grand individual entrance. I carefully held the iron railing and made my way down, my eyes not leaving Ethan's very lustful ones, and I am sure mine were telling the same story. He had a very nice beige linen suit on and a black shirt. He was casual, but smart and looked very handsome. I felt a slight hot flush coming on, and stopped myself from glowing like something from the Ready Brek advert, just before I reached the bottom where Josh, Hernando and Rafael appeared.

I was then greeted with wolf whistles and comments about how I looked. I made my way to Ethan and we greeted each other with a large smile as the others backed away a little. He took my hand, glanced at my choice of dress and then raised his eyebrows at me.

"Stunning," was all that he said. I moved closer to

him "Likewise," I whispered then we kissed each other on the cheek.

We stood a second and then Ethan made a small cough and looked at the others who were like an audience.

"Help yourselves to anything, and enjoy," he told them. I then turned and pointed at the girls; "But behave!" I added.

"Spoilsport," Beth muttered and Hernando nudged her once, grinning from ear to ear. I really dreaded to think what they were planning on getting up to this evening. Just as Rose winked at Josh, I looked at Amanda and hoped that she was not left feeling like a gooseberry.

"Shall we?" Ethan then asked as he opened the main door. I happily walked through it and to the car with him. He opened my door, and when he got into his side of the car, he looked at me. "You really do look stunning," he repeated.

"You look mighty handsome yourself," I replied. He seemed to like the remark and thanked me before starting the engine.

The road to the restaurant was winding, but quiet and we talked all the way there. He reached across and held my hand at one point and I found that adorable. When we arrived, the restaurant was more elaborate than I had been expecting. It was high in the hills, and not a small family-run business as I suspected, but it was very elegant. Not large in scale, but very well proportioned; it was a very busy place. When we walked through the large glass door we were greeted by who I can only assume was the manager. He shook Ethan's hand and they briefly spoke in Spanish before he then turned to me.

"I would like to introduce you to Jenny," he said happily.

The manager reached out his hand, and when he received mine, he kissed the back of it and said in his Spanish accented English, "*Hola*, it is very nice to meet your acquaintance."

I smiled and returned the sentiment shaking his hand. "It is very nice to meet you too."

He then proceeded to show us to our table, and made a point of telling Ethan that we had been given the best table with the best view. I had a feeling that Ethan was well respected here too. The menu was extensive; the fish that was available sounded amazing and quite honestly it was hard to choose. I asked Ethan to choose the starters, which he did, ordering an array of various ones to try. I could not find fault with any of them and as we sat there enjoying each other's company, the rest of the diners were almost drowned out because I was completely focused on him. The wine was tasty, and I tried to take it easy drinking plenty of water. I excused myself before the main course and went to 'powder my nose'. I stood looking at myself in the mirror and wondered how I had been so fortunate to find someone so special. I reapplied my lip gloss, and was glad to have left my phone back at the hotel, as I had not missed it one little bit.

When I returned to the table, our glasses had been refilled and when I sat Ethan reached across the table and took my hand in his. He gazed into my eyes for some time before I spoke; "Everything alright?" I asked him.

He looked at my hand and rubbed my knuckles with his thumbs.

"Can a man be so fortunate, that he can find a woman this way, and it be one that he admires so greatly after such a short time?" he enquired. I laughed lightly. "You find my question amusing?" he asked me further as he straightened his posture. I rubbed his thumb with mine.

"I am not amused at your question. I am amused because I was just thinking exactly the same thing about you, while I was away from the table." I replied. He smiled and nodded in confirmation.

"So my feeling is mutual?" he asks.

"Yes, it would seem so," I calmly replied then smiled back at him. He started to lean across the table to kiss me, but our main courses arrived and so we sat back. He placed his elbow on the arm of his chair and then put his hand against his mouth before letting a large smile escape the sides. He was happy at the outcome of our discussion.

The food was out of this world. I had never tasted fish like it. We tried each other's, and then the manager brought another dish – an octopus salad, compliments of the house. It was the most delicious octopus dish that I had ever tasted; the dressing was light, the octopus delicate. I sighed with contentment that my taste buds were having the workout of their life on this holiday. I wanted to finish everything – it seemed such a waste not to – but I was fast becoming full and I suspect that Ethan was too. Maybe we had over indulged a little too much and ordered too many starters? I was completely satisfied once finished, and as they cleared away the plates we were offered desserts. I had to decline, as did Ethan, but a refreshing cup of green tea seemed appropriate.

We had sat for over two hours, eating and drinking. Ethan had not drunk very much as he was driving. When it came to leaving, the manager thanked us for our custom, and I told him what a pleasure the experience had been. He in turn said that he hoped to see us again soon, and I really did hope for the same. The girls would love the food here. I rested my head back against the seat as we drove back savouring that full feeling, but still tasting the delights and flavours in my mouth. "That was amazing," I commented. Ethan agreed, and said that it was one of his and Josh's favourite restaurants. We arrived back feeling completely overwhelmed by our whole evening so far. As we walked back from the car to the hotel along the path of the courtyard Ethan stopped me. "Join me on the terrace?" he asked. I nodded in agreement, I didn't want to rush the remainder of the evening.

We arrived back on the quiet terrace from last night and retook our place on the large lounger from yesterday. I was amazed to find lanterns lit, music playing quietly and champagne waiting for us. I gave him a quizzing look, and he simply shrugged at my expression. He was remarkably good at organising everything to perfection. We snuggled into the throw again, the house was quiet, but it was now near eleven fifteen, and I suspect some of our friends were sharing rooms right now. We sipped the champagne that did what is always expected with me – it made me a little light-headed. We talked, kissed, looked at the stars, and then Ethan without any notice suddenly stood and held out his hand. The butterflies were back, was this it? The moment of getting it on? Then he said;,"Dance with me." I relaxed at his request and stood to take his hand.

As he held me close to his chest with our fingers entwined, I rested my head near his shoulder. The scent of his aftershave started to set my emotions stirring as we gently swayed along to the music. After dancing to a whole song with no words just the feeling of him squeezing me tighter, I took a deep breath and then lifted my head and pressed my cheek against his. Although we were still moving, my breathing was definitely quickening. I suddenly had the strong need to kiss him more intimately than I ever had, and as I moved my head to face him, he looked at me with longing in his eyes. Our lips touched for an instant and it was electric, but then as we took each other's kiss more intently it left us with a longing need for more, and had us gasping again for breath.

When we parted lips the first time, we both laughed a little at our desperation which was now very apparent. We stood for a second holding each other, then I looked up at him and swallowed hard. He noted my obvious sudden look of worry. "We don't have to do anything that you don't feel comfortable with. Just spending time with you is enough," he said kindly. I took a deep breath and then told him my feelings.

"I want to spend the night with you Ethan, I'm finding it so hard to resist," I started.

"But?" he then enquired sympathetically. I let it all gush out.

"I'm worried that I'll let you down, it's been a long, long time since I did this. I'm not that sure I will be very good at it," I said with embarrassment. Then I looked down at my feet. He placed his finger under my chin and raised it to eye level.

"Hey, how could you possibly think that? I am not here to judge you in any way and honestly, it worries me a little that I am out of practice too. You have no need to worry yourself about that. Let's wait, if you would rather?" he then suggested, and whether it was his complete understanding at my concerns, or the fact that I suddenly didn't care... I pounced on him!

I literally threw myself at him, as my chest hit his and my arms flung themselves around his neck, I found myself kissing him harder and faster. My tongue danced with his, my heart raced, my body ached for him in places that I had long forgotten about and I realised at that point that the need for lubrication (as Beth had put it), was definitely not necessary. As things heated up and my hands traced down his chest, his slid down to my buttocks. I parted our lips just as a waiter appeared asking if we needed anything else.

"Champagne!" Ethan said breathlessly, "Well chilled!" he then called. As the waiter turned quickly to do as asked, Ethan looked at me. "I wasn't expecting that reaction, but I like it," he grinned.

He took my hand and turned to retrieve the champagne flutes shaking out any excess while he carried them upside down by the stems. He then marched me back into the hotel squeezing my interlocked fingers. As the waiter reappeared Ethan turned to me and asked me to take the bottle. I smiled at the poor waiter who looked at us as if we were being slightly rude, but as we scooted past him I grabbed it and thanked him. We quickly walked to the stairs that led to my room, he stopped and looked at me again.

"Are you sure about this?" he asked. I had a sudden new found confidence, because I actually think that he was more nervous than I was.

I went past him, then turned back and grabbed the lapel on his jacket, pulled him closer and said, "Never more sure."

He grinned at me and laughed a little, then replied, "I thought that you were the nervous one?" I took his hand and led him up the stairs and suddenly found myself giggling as we fell into my room.

The champagne was quickly but carefully placed onto the nearest table along with the flutes and we went back to the intimate kissing. I pushed his jacket off his shoulders and then he squeezed my waist tighter than ever. We stopped and just looked at each other, he ran his fingers around my hairline and took a deep breath. I slid off my shoes and started to unzip my dress, he breathed out anxiously and I felt happy that I was taking control, which I would not have expected at all. He carefully popped his shoes off, and I moved closer and started to unbutton his shirt, he kissed my neck and shoulder while I did so, which made me inhale deeply. He reached around my back and finished unzipping me while I discarded his shirt to the floor. My hands ran down his chest while we kissed again, and when they stopped at his waistband and I started to undo his trousers he gasped a little.

I was more turned on now than I had ever expected to be, and Ethan certainly was, but we both remained a little anxious and that made the whole situation seem more special. Once I had unfastened his trousers I looked at him and placed my hand on his cheek. Our lips seemed to fit together perfectly, our tongues were delicate, and when I licked his bottom lip he let a small moan escape his chest. I took my dress from my shoulders and let it drop to the floor and then I felt sexier than ever when Ethan took a deep breath looked at my underwear and said "Wow, you really don't realise how sexy you are, do you?" I smiled and then he pushed his trousers to the floor and stepped out of them. We stood for about three seconds looking at each other and then we both pounced, he lifted me and wrapped my legs around his waist and carried me to the bed. We were breathless, naked in seconds and then it happened… It was sensual, and passionate and felt like the most mind-blowing experience that I ever recall having.

Chapter 14

When I opened my eyes the next morning to the gentle blowing breeze that came through the open window, I was pleased to find myself asleep on Ethan's chest. My leg was intertwined with his and my arm reached across his rippling abs and soft skin. His hand rested on my arm while his other was around my back. I lifted my head to look at him and it appeared he was still sleeping and so I propped my head on my hand and just watched him. He was gorgeous, but he looked serene and relaxed.

"Good morning," he then said with his eyes still closed. I smiled.

"I thought that you were asleep?"

"No, been awake for a while, but didn't want to move – too content and comfortable," he replied as he opened his eyes and looked at me. "Are you feeling okay about everything this morning?" he then enquired with a little apprehension. I was more than alright, I felt absolutely amazing. I rolled on top of him.

"I feel amazing. I suppose that I should thank you for such a wonderful evening," I said and then I planted a huge kiss on his lips.

"I think it is I who should be thanking you, Jenny," he

said as we parted lips and he pushed my hair away from my face. "You know – you are intoxicating and far better at that than you realise," he smiled. I looked at him for a second then replied.

"Hmmm, I'm not so sure. I think that I need to just check again," I found myself saying and then I sank down and started to kiss his nipples, kissing his toned chest and abs was all the inspiration that I needed. As Ethan took a deep breath in, I looked up at him as seductively as possible, it was all the confirmation that I needed to carry on – just seeing the look on his face. I found myself doing things that I had forgotten I enjoyed so much, and then I crawled back up to him and straddled him, making love for the second time within twelve hours!

We showered together, which was a fairly new experience for me. It was something that Paul and I never really did. I enjoyed it immensely – he washed my hair and ran soap down my body gently brushing his hands over my skin. We kissed and talked about the fun that we had sharing each other in every way. Ethan was getting aroused again: "You're going to kill me at this pace!" he suddenly said slightly embarrassed that he had little control right now.

"It's alright, I will let you recover. We need to get some breakfast, or we may have a room full of nosey friends wondering what we were up to last night," I pointed out as I rinsed and stepped from the shower, not before smacking him quite hard on his left buttock.

"I think those nerves that you were experiencing are well and truly gone!" he joked as he rubbed the slight red mark left behind. I laughed, I think he was correct.

After dressing and drying my hair while Ethan waited on the bed, we left my room and went downstairs. Ethan went back to his room to take off his clothes from last night, and dress in something more casual. I went down to the terrace, where all the others were sat having breakfast. Josh saw me walking toward them and gave me the curious 'Did you or didn't you?' look. I tried to keep my face neutral, but a large grin escaped which I tried to disguise by curling my lips in. Josh looked away from me smiling more than I was. I knew he had that strong suspicion.

"Morning everyone, how are we this morning?" I asked as I reached the table and sat down.

"We're fine, how are you?" Beth enquired. Then Amanda looked at me as did Rose.

"Great!" I said promptly. "Slept really well." The others smiled and then Josh spoke up.

"Hey, what did you think of the restaurant?"

"Oh God, it was amazing, Josh. The food was out of this world. You'd love it there," I told the girls.

"Sounds like you had a fabulous time," Rose then smiled, just as Ethan appeared.

"We did. That restaurant never fails to impress, does it, Josh?" he stated trying to deter the questions from me. Rose stopped the quizzing.

We had breakfast, and decided to have a day of reading and relaxing. I was happy with that – I rarely sat and read as my mind had too many distractions. Now I found that I had different but pleasurable distractions as Ethan was sat at the side of me – he kept touching me and talking to me. We all had a large lunch, we talked, swam, sat in the hot tub, read, laughed, a lot, but I was definitely distracted. Ethan looked gorgeous, I felt confident for the first time in ages, I also felt horny all the time which was a renewed feeling, and I felt happier than I had in ages. Eventually Amanda and Beth cornered me about the rest of the evening while Ethan went indoors.

"So, what happened, Jen?" Beth asked first.

"A lady should never tell," I tried to convince them.

"Yeah well, you looked pretty cosy dancing on the terrace," Amanda then said.

"What?" I wondered if they had been spying on me all night.

"I was having a night cap with Beth in her room as Rose was busy, when we heard music and laughing so then we looked out of the window. We saw you, it was sweet," she smiled at me.

"Well, it was sweet and Ethan was sweet, and then he was hot…"

"… and then…?" Beth asked inquisitively. I shook my head knowing that I wasn't going to get away without telling them something, but I wasn't about to go into detail as Amanda had suggested I should.

"Let's just say, I'm now back in that saddle and back in practice," I whispered. They unfortunately got a little excited, which I quickly shushed. "Let's not say anything else about it."

"For now," Amanda winked. "I want details!" she then said and I walked away and grimaced a little.

The day was a complete success as far as holidaying goes, but the sun was a little hot and so I tried to make sure I had plenty of shade too. Rafael and Amanda were enjoying each other's company more than I had noted previously – probably because there was no inclination to want anything more than friendship. He was teaching her how to play chess today, and it was frustrating her no end. Beth and Hernando happily frolicked in the pool and doted on each other, knowing that the week would be over faster than they would wish. Josh and Rose looked to be getting closer than ever – I wasn't sure if it was just a sex thing, or whether she was liking him more than just for the service he was providing.

As the day rolled into the evening and we all changed for dinner, it worried me slightly that the hotel staff had suggested to Ethan that they needed to know if their choices of wines were satisfactory. Ethan and Josh had agreed it would be an excellent idea to try pretty much everything that the hotel had to offer, and so the night started with a very nice bottle of red wine. Wine tasting had not been the best decision in the past for the four of us; after trying a couple of these intended evenings back home, we ended up so drunk that we couldn't even remember actually getting home. I decided to stay close to Ethan as I knew if I was struggling he would look after me, instead of making sure I would spend all the next day with my head in the toilet – which would be the girls option if given the chance!

The evening started off well with a delicious feast of more seafood, meats, salads and fresh breads. We had decided to be al fresco tonight with the amount of wine the men were hoping to drink, and so it was a nice change to be able to just keep nibbling away at the delicious foods and be a little less formal. The cheeses were an absolute bonus as I hoped that they would line my stomach. It was so enjoyable. Rafael and Hernando recalled stories that were embarrassing about each other. Ethan had a few about Josh, but no one seemed to have any about Ethan – he seemed to always be aware of his appearance when in public. The night rolled on and we became rowdier and more wine was opened, dancing ensued, in all forms. I was drinking more than I had wanted to and even though we had water, I was fast getting that feeling of alcohol blurriness where everything becomes a little hazy and hard to follow.

When it reached eleven thirty, my stomach felt like it had definitely had more than enough and I felt just a little queasy. I looked at Ethan and then leant into him almost falling on him to say that I needed to go to bed. He chuckled at me and said that he would walk me to my room. I really had no idea how the others did it – I was such a lightweight. I walked easily enough, but felt like I was slurring, and I apologised profusely. Ethan found this highly amusing and so I hit him on the arm to show my disappointment.

"You know you are quite 'cute' when you are drunk," he laughed as we reached my room.

"Ah 'cute', that's my favourite word for you," I pointed out as I jabbed him in the tummy. He just laughed. He kissed me and I swayed a little in reaction as he caught me off guard.

"I think that you, young lady, need to get into bed," he then suggested and I agreed without any protesting.

He lay me down and took off my shoes and my jeans and then sat me up and took off my top. He was now in front of me with his hands on my knees and he looked into my eyes while smiling at me. I know that we speak rubbish when we are drunk, but I really meant what I said next. I watched him as he poured me some water from the jug off the table at the side of my bed, then he insisted that I drink some. "Good job that you don't mind me seeing you like this," he smiled at my state of undress. Then he bobbed down in front of me while I drank and then my mouth opened and out it came;

"I think that I'm falling for you," I said, and he stopped what he was doing and stared straight at me. He licked his lips and then looked surprisingly at me like he already knew that.

"Well thank you for that, sexy. What a nice confession to make while you're dressed so provocatively," he smirked.

"Well I mean it," I said before leaning closer to him. "I'm not sure how much use I will be tonight though – provo…provocti…pro-voc-ative as I may look!" I slurred struggling to get my words out. Now he laughed at me even more and then I realised how drunk I was and how bad I must look. I gave him my glass and then I threw myself back onto the bed and fake cried, covering my face with my hands.

"Oh my God, what a mess," I complained at myself.

He climbed on the bed and hovered over me laughing at me still. Then he peeled my hands back and pinned them to the bed. I screwed my eyes tight shut and asked myself why the hell I had drunk so much… again!

"Hey," Ethan called down at me. I tried to wriggle free. "Hey," he said softly again. I reluctantly opened my eyes to find him just looking at me. He kissed me and I stopped wriggling for a moment.

"That's not fair," I then said, but he had my attention.

"Right, listen. Firstly there is nothing wrong with being a little merry. Secondly, you are not a mess, I love the way that you are dressed right now," he told me as he gestured at my underwear with a grin. I laughed as he tried to make me feel better. "As for your previous comment – I can understand how you feel, as I think that I am possibly falling for you too!" he then stated sincerely, and I froze and looked him in the eye. Drunk or not I definitely just heard that.

"You do?" I asked again.

"Yeah, and I didn't need to wait the whole week to tell you," he laughed nervously as he climbed back up from on top of me. He sat me up and gave me the water back. "I think that we should consider carrying on this conversation after a good night's sleep," he suggested. I nodded because I still hadn't really absorbed what he had said. Maybe he thought I had only said it because I was drunk?

He pulled the covers back and told me to slide underneath and get some rest, and I was right as I had thought earlier – he did look after me. I reached up my arms to him requesting a hug, and he obliged. Then I kissed him again before he left, but I knew that I needed to sleep this off. He stepped away looking like he wanted more but knowing that wasn't appropriate in my state. As ever – a complete gentleman – he then turned off my lights and left me to get some sleep, but not before saying, "You know where I am if you need me; I will leave my door unlocked." I drifted off into an alcoholic slumber faster than I could say Cabernet Sauvignon Shiraz!

I swallowed hard when I woke at around six; I had that dry, desert-like mouth and throat from too much wine. I sat up, felt a little light-headed and then made my way to the bathroom. Two paracetamol later and a large glass of water I lay back down, plumping my pillows numerous times like it would make me get back to sleep easier. I lay there for over twenty minutes, continually looking at the time on my phone. I never had quite worked out why alcohol put you in an instant coma but then seemed to wake you up at a ridiculous hour like it was tormenting you. Laying there studying the room in the now even lighter morning, I realised that I didn't feel quite as bad as I first thought – the tablets must have kicked in, or as per usual I hadn't actually had as much as I first thought. I got up again and wondered around my room. I looked at myself in the mirror, took last night's make-up off and then brushed my hair. As I licked my teeth I felt that fur coating so I made my way back to the bathroom and brushed my teeth – I cannot tell you how much better my mouth felt then. I looked at the shower and thought, *Why not?*

I tied my hair up and had a quick blast under the hot water. It was delightful and medicinal.

When I stepped back out and dried, I re-looked at my phone, it was now six forty-five. I thought about what I had said to Ethan last night, and about his reply – I smiled to myself. Then I wondered if he may be awake thinking about it too. He did say that he was there if I needed him, and his door would be unlocked and so I decided that I did need him – right now! I put on some jean shorts and a vest top – no underwear and decided to sneak downstairs. I felt like a teenager sneaking around her parents' house while her boyfriend was staying over – it was quite exhilarating.

When I got to his room, I stopped at the door. *What am I doing?* I questioned myself. I turned to walk back and then I told myself to stop being a chicken, that it was exciting. I clenched my fists and took a deep breath and walked back and placed my hand on the door handle. It quietly unlatched, and when I went in he was fast asleep on his back with his bare chest exposed, I knew that I had made the right decision when I started tingling. I closed the door behind me and tried to quietly lock it; it clicked and he stirred but he didn't wake. After tiptoeing to the other side of the bed I lifted the sheets and slid underneath. I screwed my eyes shut feeling so naughty and tried not to let a squeak of delight leave my mouth, and then I gently rolled up to him and placed my arm across his stomach. When he made a slight waking groan I snuggled into his chest and then he opened his eyes and looked at me.

"Good morning, and how are you feeling?" he quietly asked. I looked up at him and grinned.

"Better than last night!" I grimaced. He smiled and kissed me on the forehead.

"I'm glad about that, although you were quite amusing – and seductively dressed too," he joked.

"Yes alright," I replied, before he rolled onto his side and wrapped his arm around me.

"Well, this is a nice wake-up call. What time is it?"

"Actually it's only about seven, but I couldn't sleep – I've showered and everything already, so I thought I would come and see if you were awake."

"I'm glad that you did. Dressed too I see," he then remarked as he lifted the sheet to see what I was wearing, which gave me a thrill as he was naked. I smiled and ran my hand down his chest.

"Yes, but what you can't see, is that I am naked underneath," I confidently told him.

"Is that right?" he mumbled as he rolled on top of me. "I think that you just may have to prove that," he teased before kissing me and setting my body off on another roller coaster of sensations.

When we re-opened our eyes it was nine o'clock. He was pressed tightly against my back holding me close to his chest. We made love again, it was fun and thrilling, sensual and steamy and I loved knowing that I had sneaked into his room with others nearby – maybe it was a thrill of being caught. He had an air of youth about him and I liked him radiating that feeling. I pulled his arm tight into my waist, and then turned and faced him. He ran a finger around my hairline again scooping my hair behind my ear and I found myself running my finger down the side of his face and then pulling him closer for a kiss. He moaned contentedly afterwards and just looked at me.

"I had a feeling that you were going be addictive from the moment I picked you up off that beach, Jenny Walker."

"Well, that's alright with me as long as it's a positive addictive and not negative. You, I fear, were suddenly very prominent in my thoughts when I watched you walk back to Josh by the hotel pool after helping me," I replied.

"You were spying on me, eh?" he asked with a cheeky tone.

"Well, after realising how toned you were when I poked you in the chest and then how much of a gentleman you were when we got to my room, it was hard to resist watching you."

"You remember all of that? You were well inebriated at that point!" he sarcastically replied. I pulled him closer by his left buttock, which made him gasp a little.

"If you keep taunting me, I am going to have to punish you," I said as seductively as possible. He raised his eyebrows at me in surprise.

"Well now – you really shouldn't have said that!" he then remarked, me knowing full well that he wasn't going to stop now.

"Ooh you are going to wish that you hadn't started this, Mr Ethan James," I concluded as I rolled and sat on top of him. He looked at my body and then back at me.

"This is one punishment I would happily keep enduring," he said. I felt completely at ease with him, lowered my head and then kissed him.

I snuck back upstairs and took another shower, before putting on my underwear this time underneath my clothing. When I eventually bounced downstairs to find everyone else waiting at the table, the girls clapped.

"Well, hallelujah! She's surfaced!" Beth said.

"Yeah, and she looks pretty good too," Rose remarked at my non-hangover state.

"I'll second that," Ethan added and he winked at me making me blush. If only they knew where I had been half an hour ago!

I sat and poured coffee and had breakfast. There was a market on in the town where we moored the boats; it was supposed to be a complete mix of traditional and non-traditional items, from pottery to clothing, paintings to food. Josh had obviously discussed it with Ethan the day before as they seemed to have all the details planned again. We were to leave at eleven thirty and drive there in both cars, have lunch out and stay by the bay for some live music that played all evening and then drive back. Another perfect day, with the perfect group of friends.

Rose was sat eating while leaning against Josh and I had the impression that she was now very taken with him. As for Beth, well she looked a little worse for wear this morning, and I couldn't work out if it was the alcohol or too much sex, or maybe both, that had her looking a little out of sorts. I on the other hand felt amazing, and even though this holiday was getting nearer to the end – it felt like it was just the beginning.

Chapter 15

The drive back toward the bay was quiet until we neared the market and then it was like half of Ibiza had turned up to visit! Parking was a pretty hard task, and eventually Ethan managed to get a local restaurant to allow us to park for a fee. We had a short ten-minute walk back toward the hustle and bustle of the many stalls and many visitors that were there to enjoy the delights that it held. We all meandered buying small tokens of our holiday. Ethan held my hand as Josh did with Rose and it seemed to spur on Hernando and Rafael, as they did with Beth and Amanda. Even though she wouldn't admit it, I think that it made Amanda's day. Rafael was a handsome man, and even though I knew that Amanda had no intentions of taking things any further, the impression it gave to the gazing crowds made her feel special.

We sampled cakes, and wandered for numerous hours just looking and examining and enjoying the many different things which were on offer. We stopped and had coffee and there were small groups playing music and singing. When it neared two o'clock, Hernando started to walk us back toward the far end of the bay. I hadn't really noticed earlier, but his yacht was moored and then he informed us that we were having lunch on board.

"Oh really? That's a real treat, baby," Beth said as she trotted alongside him with excitement. Hernando put his arm around her waist and pulled her in tightly to his side.

"What another great day this is turning out to be," Rose chipped in, as we all followed along wondering what feast would be awaiting us.

Once we arrived on deck overlooking the hustle and bustle of the market, we were greeted by the biggest table of various foods: seafood, breads, cheeses, meats, rice dishes, a huge fresh whole fish (I had no idea what type), tomato salads, olives, some type of tortilla, potato croquette-inspired bites. It was a feast fit for any VIP and we were certainly starting to feel that way. The champagne was chilled and ready, there was wine at the table and water, and when Hernando told us to help ourselves no one hesitated. There was definitely something to be said about fresh holiday sea air and your appetite – I had never eaten as much on any holiday before, and this lunch was no exception.

We spent hours on board enjoying food and wine, relaxing and just being in each other's company. The noise of the crowds was growing as it neared early evening and then the live music started playing, it was dusky and the glow of the lights that edged the water and the crowded square along with the warm breeze had the ability to make it feel very romantic. We started to make our way back toward the staged area, where a small band played traditional and modern Spanish music. The crowd swayed along and then bounced to the rhythm. It was such a sensual experience having Ethan stood behind me, his arms wrapped around my waist swaying along too. After a while that band changed to another which played some more modern songs, and much to the girls' delight they had their own mini dance floor going on within our little group.

Ethan and Josh had drawn the short straw as they were driving, but this made me take it easy with the alcohol and I was glad of the rest from it after last night. After standing and enjoying the music for a couple of hours, we all made the decision to drive back to the hotel and spend the rest of the evening there; at least then Josh and Ethan could have a drink. It was a short ride back really as we were talking most of the way and by the time we got back to The Gessami Residence it was nearly ten o'clock. We all stayed up for another hour or so chatting on the terrace, before Hernando and Beth and Amanda and Rafael said that they were ready for their beds. Both Ethan and I had a drink with Rose and Josh as we were still talking.

Josh made it quite clear when he leant in and whispered to me, that I was the best thing to have happened to Ethan in years. It made me feel so significantly important, particularly when he then whispered that it was crucial that I didn't lose touch with him after this holiday. As we whispered and looked across at Ethan, he obviously knew that we were talking about him – he stretched out his arm requesting my hand. I happily obliged and reached mine out to him and as he entwined our fingers he then he looked at me just once, as Rose carried on enquiring about hotels with him. Josh nudged me on the elbow and so I turned and gave him a big smile. "Crucial!" he said again, as if to confirm that Ethan needed me to stay in touch with him.

Rose was yawning, but I had already seen her give Josh *the look* requesting that they retire. It made me silently laugh as she was so obvious. We all stood and went back indoors – they were down a different corridor to us, and so we said goodnight and parted ways. As we reached the bottom of my stairs again, I stopped him and then planted a huge kiss on his lips.

"Thank you for another lovely day."

"Every day is lovely when we can share it together," he replied before kissing me back. At that moment I didn't want him to leave me.

"We don't have many nights left," I pointed out; he shook his head looking slightly disappointed. "Stay with me tonight?" I whispered in his ear. He gave me that lustful wanting look again and I knew that he wouldn't say no.

I don't even remember getting from where we were at the bottom of the stairs, to my room. But somehow I found us with the door locked stood in the moonlight from the window, kissing passionately – that type of kiss that makes your knees want to give way. I was melting at his touch, and as we peeled each other's clothes off it was an exhilarating feeling I was getting used to. We were naked again, in my bed, and when he rolled on top of me he just smiled. Then he looked into my eyes and said, "I am definitely falling for you." I nervously licked my lips then pulled his head closer to mine and whispered, "And I you." Nothing more needed to be said in that moment.

We made passionate love and in many positions, and each one made me feel more connected and closer to him. It wasn't until I found myself straddling his lap, and he was kissing my shoulder while pulling me down deeper onto him that I wholly and completely gave myself to him. As I felt that ripple at the start of a mind-blowing orgasm he let go too, and the whole sensation we shared was more intense than I ever thought that I was capable of.

By the time we wrapped ourselves up in my sheets; hot, sweaty and satisfied, I knew that there was more to this than just a holiday romance. The thought of leaving on Saturday was making me worry – I didn't want to leave him behind. I was loving being in the arms of a man, Ethan was turning out to be everything and more than I ever could have hoped for. He pulled me close to him as we both started to drift off to sleep but not before he placed his lips against my ear and said, "You are the most amazing woman that I have ever met." I had my eyes closed but smiled and squeezed his arm tighter to my chest. Right here at this very moment – I was in heaven.

Thursday has already arrived I thought as I opened my eyes to the bright sunshine creeping though the shutters. I was happy to know that Ethan was still beside me, his arm was draped across my tummy, and as I turned my head he also started to stir. I turned into him and wrapped my leg around his entwining us. He breathed in and then made a little contented groan before opening his eyes, then he gave me a slow smile.

"Good morning, handsome," I said as he pulled me closer to him.

"Good morning, gorgeous," he replied before giving me a kiss on the cheek. I snuggled into his chest and inhaled his skin. "Wow, what a night. Completely unexpected, and I have to say one of the best nights of my life," he then said and I instantly looked up at him.

"Really?" I enquired as it shocked me a little.

"You sound surprised."

"Well, it was certainly one of the best nights of mine. I hadn't thought you would feel the same way," I replied, thinking that Ethan must have had some other sexual experience that had topped it. I mean – look at him! I kissed his shoulder after speaking.

"Hey," he said softly needing my full attention. I looked at him. "No one has ever made me feel the way that you do. I had no idea that it could be like this," he then said which surprised me even more. I kissed him softly before replying.

"Me neither. It was pretty amazing – you're pretty amazing," I smiled. He squeezed me tightly and groaned a little more.

"What are we going to do about it?" he asked as he twisted my hair around his finger.

"I'm not sure, but one thing I do know is that going home on Saturday will be difficult." I was being honest. He kissed my forehead.

"We'll think of something," he said and we just held each other for a time. "Are you hungry?" he then asked me.

"I am actually, but I don't want to move. What time is it anyway?"

"It's eight thirty, and I have to say that I've not slept as well for ages like I have these last few days. I wasn't thinking of moving though – I thought we could get some room service."

"Can we do that?" I asked. He laughed.

"It is a hotel," he reminded me as he rolled over and reached for the phone. He spoke in Spanish, or Catalan, or whatever it was – and ordered some food to be sent to my room. I rolled up behind him and let my hand wander across his hip and down to a now slightly aroused welcome.

When he replaced the phone back on the receiver, he lifted the sheet and looked at what my hand was doing to him and then he turned back to me, "I thought that you said you weren't very good at this? Let me reassure you that you are so much better than you think!" he informed me before some very heavy kissing and nibbling ensued, which had us both giggling with delight.

Before it went too far, I reminded him that this hotel was exceptionally efficient and it was likely that there would be someone at the door within minutes. We laughed at our newfound confidence with each other and made ourselves presentable, and sure enough, twenty minutes after he had put the phone down there was a knock at the door. Ethan insisted that I stayed put wrapped in the sheet where no one else could get a glimpse of my nakedness. He jumped out of bed pulled on his boxers and wrapped one of the fluffy robes around him before opening the door.

I instantly started salivating once the smells started to permeate around the room. The excitement and exercise from last night's intense sexual workout had me feeling hungrier than I had realised. The tray was placed onto the nearby table and then the waiter exited the room. Ethan removed the robe and asked me to make a space on the bed to place the tray, so that he could join me there, and I happily did so. We ate breakfast, I was wrapped up in the sheets, Ethan was perched on top of them, and we casually discussed the night and how amazing it had been, although I did blush just a touch as we talked. He told me that plans had been made for today, which was now becoming routine. I felt guilty that we were catered for in every possible form, I wondered if he would let us do anything toward the week – but then I realised that he wouldn't want us to and so there was no point continually mentioning it.

Once I had eaten and drunk the refreshing tea that accompanied the fulfilling breakfast, I threw myself back onto the pillows completely happy at that full feeling. Ethan moved the tray and climbed back under the sheets with me, pulling me close to him.

"Maybe we should just stay in bed for the day?" he happily said as we lay in each other's arms.

"That would be delightful, but perhaps you would get sick of my consistent expectations!" I cheekily remarked. I knew he knew what I meant.

"Not possible. I don't think I would ever get sick of any time that I spend with you," he smiled. "However, at the thought of Josh, Hernando and Rafael wondering where I am and trying to find me, perhaps we should make an appearance?" he suggested. I sighed heavily.

"Yes, as always you are right. I'm actually surprised that the girls haven't been up to my room yet to see where I am. It is however only nine forty-five. Some of them are probably otherwise engaged themselves," I then hinted and he agreed.

"How about we wake ourselves up with a shower together then, before venturing downstairs?" he asked hopefully. I looked at him.

"Perfect," I told him and then I gracefully slid out of bed and walked naked across to the bathroom where I stopped and leant against the jamb and coaxed him to join me. He grinned at me.

"You really are amazing, and pretty darn good at coercing me." He laughed again as he made his way over with the grace of a god. I sloped into the bathroom and turned on the shower; one thing I loved here was that the water was instantly hot. I stepped under and turned to him; he discarded his boxers and stepped under the cascading water with me. It was sensual, and more erotic than I had thought it could be – having sex in the shower was a first for me in all honesty, but I absolutely loved it.

After showering properly and drying, Ethan suggested that I wear shorts and a t-shirt with trainers today. I inquisitively looked at him wondering what on earth both he and Josh had planned today, but he simply smiled and told me not to worry. I went to his room with him while he changed and then we made our way down the stairs to the others who were sat in the hot sunshine sipping coffee. Ethan had pulled me in tight to his side with the arm that was now around my waist; he looked so damn hot with his crisp white t-shirt on and black shorts along with his aviator sunglasses. I had to stop myself from drooling as we approached the table.

Beth, I noted, looked at Amanda and then nudged her arm to acknowledge us. They just grinned at each other. Rose and Josh also gave each other a look once they saw us approaching, which was the 'Oh look at them' response. I suddenly felt like I was still naked again with all eyes on us, and I am sure that Ethan noted my slight wariness. I decided to just be casual and act as normal as possible.

"Good morning, everyone," I said as we reached a chair and sat.

"Well good morning," Josh then said in reply staring directly at me. I gave him a half smile as he knew exactly what we had been up to, as I suspect the others did too.

"You're a little late for breakfast; we were famished this morning," Beth then said as she gestured to the small amount of food left on the table.

"It's alright, Beth, we've already eaten, thank you." Ethan casually said and then he released my waist and reached for my hand and squeezed it lightly. Beth gave me a surprised look – I don't think that she was expecting that answer, whereas Amanda and Rose just looked across at each other to acknowledge his statement.

"Well, now that we are all here, I should tell you the plans for today," Josh said to break the silence.

"I am sure that it will not disappoint," Rafael replied before finishing his coffee.

"I have arranged bikes for us all today. We will be taking a bike ride along the coastline road to a town not too far away for lunch and then we can cycle back. I thought it would be nice to have a little exercise and see some of the island at the same time. So shorts and t-shirts today," he explained. Amanda leant into me as the others started to talk.

"Looks like some of us had a heads up!" she said looking at what I was wearing.

"Maybe," I replied and she laughed at me.

"You look so happy this morning; I like it, it suits you," she stated before winking at me.

"Thank you – I like it too." And I did. The sad me that arrived here in Ibiza was not me now, and I liked feeling like this.

Once ready we all went to the car parking area as instructed to find two men and a large van with eight bikes alongside. They were lined up in size order and looked brand new. Ethan shook the hand of one of them who seemed to remark at the building, which Ethan was happily talking to him about while we were each designated a bike. Everyone seemed thrilled to be getting out in the fresh air; the exercise was welcome after not really doing a lot over the last two weeks. As I fumbled around with my chin strap on my helmet, Ethan appeared in front of me and helped.

"Are you happy with this?" he asked genuinely.

"Yes, I am – I have to say that I haven't ridden a bike in years, but you never forget, right?" I asked hopefully.

"You'll be fine – I will be right alongside you," he replied. I nodded in response as he pulled the strap tight and then kissed me on my nose. "Cute," he said and I grinned at him.

"Thanks," I said as he pulled his own over his head. I have to say that even with a helmet on he still had that 'wow' factor.

There was a hub of excitement and chattering as we mounted our bikes and then readied to set off. Two waiters appeared with rucksacks for Josh, Ethan and Rafael and I assumed that they were filled with water for the journey. As we started off down the driveway, I was a little wobbly but braked to slow myself and as we reached the bottom and then started peddling down the road I started to feel more in control. After around ten minutes, Ethan cycled alongside me to ask if I was alright. So far I had no reason to complain as it had been downhill or on the flat, I hoped that the rest of the trip was as easy, realising that coming back was obviously in reverse.

The view along the coastal road was breathtaking – the breeze was cooling even in the hot sunshine and even though cars were passing us, there wasn't as much traffic as I had thought, which I was grateful for. We stopped after around forty minutes and had a drink, and then continued along to another town approximately thirty minutes further on. Josh had planned it well as there was a bike park, where you could leave them for a small fee. My legs were a little like jelly by the time I started walking – it prompted me to make a mental note to get back to the gym.

Josh had a quick word with Ethan who pointed toward a group of buildings, which looked exceptionally busy. I didn't worry as I knew the planning with these two was first-rate, and so I assumed that they had booked a table somewhere for lunch – and I was right. As we neared one of the shacks beside the sea, Josh pushed forward to speak to the girl at the entrance. She led us to a table that was on a terrace overhanging the water. It was all whitewashed and like something you see in the States, but it was a mixture of traditional Spanish food and seafood, with other European dishes in the mix. I think it was probably the busiest restaurant I had seen yet and obviously very popular. It wasn't as lavish as others that we had eaten at, but I liked the casual, relaxed nature of the place. We had beers today, something refreshing, and ordered buckets of shrimps and breads with olives and tomato salads to start.

We were all now so comfortable in a group that the conversation just flowed. Beth was sat next to me and rubbed her legs before looking at me and saying;

"God, I think I'm really out of shape. My legs feel like lead weights!" she moaned.

"Mine too, so you're not on your own," I replied as Amanda and Rafael moaned about theirs too.

It was obvious that Hernando, Josh and Ethan worked out and so it was probably nothing to them and Rose always worked out regularly too, so it was no sweat for her! The rest of us, however, felt very inadequately fit, which prompted Beth to say that there was no point starting now and she downed her bottle of beer. Hernando clapped and laughed at her, before pecking her on the cheek and saying that she was perfect as she was. I think it's the first time that we have seen Beth go a delightful shade of red. Ethan found her amusing and promptly passed her another bottle from the bucket that we had.

We sat for nearly two hours watching the world go by and eating delicious food and drinking beers. After realising that I had now had four of them along with everyone else, it dawned on me that I had to be in control of that bike and so I stopped myself from having another. By the time we were ready to go back, I have to admit that I was a little nervous – I was wobbly with no alcohol. We set off back along the same coastal road; the sun was warmer still and the now stale taste of beer in my mouth, was making me feel thirsty. Just as we had on the way there, we stopped to have a drink of water on the way back. I hadn't realised until I stopped that I was sweating quite profusely. I slumped under a tree with Amanda, we both felt overheated and dehydrated. As Rafael passed us both the other half of our water, we happily drank it and sat and watched as Ethan, Josh and Rose stood chatting and they looked like they hadn't even broken a sweat yet.

"God, this seemed like a great idea when we set off!" Amanda said. I placed my head against the tree and closed my eyes.

"Yes I know, I wish that I hadn't had those beers now," I replied feeling drained from the intense heat.

"I don't think it's the beers that have tipped you over the edge!" she then replied, I opened my eyes and looked at her.

"What do you mean?"

"I think that you are falling for this guy, you're worried about leaving, you're getting some hot stuff and this is the outcome," she then shrugged.

"Well, yes to the first two, but I feel like this because I have had some beers and I am in control of a bike! It's not the best combination," I admitted.

"Well, I'm just glad that you confessed. He is great and after the way you both looked this morning I can only assume that you had an amazing night?" she then queried hopefully before smiling. We both laughed a little before she leant her own head on the tree and placed a hand on my knee. "I'm really happy for you and the fact that you seem a lot more like the old you this last couple of weeks," she finished just as Josh walked over to us.

"Hey, are you two alright? We're ready to get going again now," he informed us happily, much to our disappointment. We helped each other up as Ethan then walked over;

"Ready to go?" he asked as he fastened his strap on his helmet. I grimaced a little but Amanda answered;

"Yeah it's fine, but you all go on ahead – we're going to take it slowly," she said and I was so grateful for her response.

"Okay, I won't be far in front so just shout if you need anything," he replied before kissing me on the cheek and then going back to his bike. Amanda looked at me with slight annoyance.

"How the hell can you wear a bloody cycling helmet and still look that hot?" she whispered, just before he turned back to look at us. We both waved at him before laughing under our breath. I agreed with her as she was right then, knowing that we had to get back, we remounted our bikes and set off behind the others.

Amanda cycled slowly at the side of me; she was laughing saying that it was the best view possible with four men's buttocks to look at while following along behind. I agreed as all four of them were in fairly good shape. We laughed at each other too as we kept trying to climb the relatively small hills – very badly. There were a few more cars on the road; I'm sure that we must have been a real sight to see huffing and puffing and generally looking out of shape. When we reached the brow of a hill the others were just disappearing out of sight around a corner below. I looked at Amanda and said that obviously they had turned this into some sort of a race. Beth and Rose were doing the same as us it would seem and cycling together at the front of the men, but Beth used to cycle a bit with her ex-husband in the early days, and it would seem that she still knew how to keep the momentum going.

"I would have preferred a moped, I think," Amanda said as we kept pedalling, hoping to catch the others.

"I agree, far more civilised. I feel a little light-headed. Can you get arrested for being drunk in charge of a bike?" I asked.

"Probably. Think I had too much too. It was great travelling there and having lunch, but I think that we should have re-thought our return."

We carried on following slowly and kept losing sight of the others regularly, then out of the blue a Jeep came around the corner behind us and without warning braked hard and swerved to miss us. It put the fear of God into us as it sped off and even though we managed to stop our wobbling, a bloody rabbit then ran out in front of us from the small forested area at our side. We both saw it, cursed, swerved, Amanda locked handlebars with me and even though we had both braked we knew it wasn't going to end well. We ended up heading straight off the road, Amanda hit a rut and started going sideways and then as we were now somehow locked together I started to feel myself going with her.

"Oh crap!" she called out loud as I let out a small yelp.

Amanda hit the ground with a thud, both bikes went and then I ended up thrown a little way over them but I hit my side and buttock on the now crumpled heap.

"Ouch!" I cried laying there motionless close to where Amanda had landed.

"That bloody hurt!" she then shouted loudly, before saying, "Bloody rabbit – I'll skin you alive if you show your face again!" She was obviously not amused, and I suspect sore like me.

I dare not move for a moment for fear of severe pain. I moved my head and looked at her – she was trying to sit up and she held her leg.

"Are you alright?" she asked at my unresponsive movement.

"I don't know, not wanting to move – but actually the rest is quite nice!" I then joked as I looked over at her again. She stood laughing at my remark and made her way to me holding her hip and limping a bit, then looking at her grazed knee. She slumped down at the side of me and sat pushing the bikes off the top of my leg. "You're bleeding!" I pointed out. Amanda rubbed the excess off her knee making a smear down her leg and hand.

"Yeah well, at least I wasn't absolutely paralytic and it's a genuine injury. Never mind me – how the hell are you?" she then enquired.

I managed to prop myself onto my elbows to try and assess the damage and my hip and buttock ached instantly. I moaned at the feeling of bruising, and then decided that I didn't want to look, but other than that I didn't feel it was anything serious. I lay back down – we were covered in dust and dirt from the edge of the road that led to where we fell and if anyone had seen us right now, they probably would've thought that we had been off-roading.

"How long do you think it will take them to realise we've disappeared?" Amanda then asked as she kept dabbing at her knee. I suddenly felt a little sickly – I think it was the mix of adrenaline, alcohol and seafood. I placed my hand over my face and simply replied.

"I have no idea, but I'm not in a rush to catch up really – what about you?"

"Well, Beth and Rose will be none the wiser that we are no longer with them; I imagine one of the men folk will notice first but if you think I am getting back on that bloody thing you can forget it, I'd rather push it back and walk!" she stated.

"It's the thought of walking that is making me not want to get up. Let's just wait a while, surely someone will realise we have vanished," I said not relishing the thought of moving really.

"Agreed," she replied as she lay down beside me and sighed. "Well it seemed like a great idea at the time!"

"It's our own stupid fault for drinking and then cycling. God, I haven't ridden a bike for a bloody long time, I don't know what the hell I was thinking," I sighed at our now sorry state.

"Well, in fairness you seem to be doing a lot of catching up on this holiday – that bike's not the only thing that you seem to be practising riding!" she then laughed, and without looking I hit her. "Ouch!" she quickly replied in response.

"Don't be so cheeky then – you deserved that," I commented, feeling no remorse.

"Well, come on. You may as well spill the beans while we are on our own – what the hell happened last night? You came down this morning looking like the cat that got the cream," she grinned. I turned my head and looked at her;

"Honestly – it was absolutely amazing. I know that Paul and I had great sex and I know that I have been out of the game for some time, but I'm not sure it was ever as good as last night – or I certainly cannot remember it being that good." I told her openly. She flicked the back of her hand against my leg.

"Good for you, honey – hell, I can only imagine how good he is. I think I could probably manage to orgasm if I simply sat and watched him long enough!" she then said as a matter of fact. I shot her a look of disgust, as I wasn't really sure I needed to know that, but it resulted in us just laughing uncontrollably which actually emphasised our soreness. As we lay there with cars passing us, we just laughed a little more remarking on the state of the two of us, at least we were in the shade.

We had been on the ground now for approximately fifteen minutes and I was just about to suggest trying to stand and start walking when Amanda suddenly stated that the cavalry had arrived. I looked up and felt completely embarrassed when Rafael and Ethan suddenly cycled into view. It was like a scene from a sporting triathlon – they both somehow spotted us, curved their bikes around in the road and, as they came near to us, managed to dismount and continue running without faltering steps once. I watched Ethan as I propped myself on my elbows.

"Jesus, are you alright, ladies?" he was quick to ask as he ducked down at the side of me trying to assess how injured I was. I tried to sit and grimaced a little – Amanda had now got Rafael trying to sort her knee out by pouring water over it from his rucksack. "What the hell happened? I shouldn't have left you," Ethan then carried on. I touched his arm.

"It's fine, you couldn't have done anything about it. A Jeep came past at a real rate of knots and sent us off on a wobble, and then a rabbit ran out in front of us and we ended up locking handlebars and landing here," Amanda tried to explain.

"That bloody Jeep – he did the same to us!" Ethan then said slightly aggravated. I grabbed onto his arm wanting to stand and prove that I wasn't as bad as he thought. It took some doing initially but when I got to my feet I felt better.

"I'm alright, honestly," I tried to convince him, but he simply unfastened my helmet and brushed the dirt from my face.

"Nice try," he said looking worried. He dropped my

helmet on the floor. "Are you bleeding, or feel like you've broken anything?" he asked inspecting every visible inch of me.

"Don't think so – just have a sore hip and my right buttock hurts. Amanda is worse than me – she's bleeding," I replied placing my hand carefully on my sore bits.

"May I?" he asked wanting to check that it wasn't anything too bad. I nodded and turned lifting my arm higher than my waistband so that he could check. He took a moment and then carefully replaced the fabric back to my skin.

"Hell, no more riding for you two today!" he then said as he took his phone from his shorts pocket and telephoned someone. He rang Josh, I presumed, and told him to make sure that the others got back safely, quickly explaining our situation. Then he turned back to me and took my hand looking around. "Do you want to sit?" he enquired. I shook my head.

"Sitting actually hurts. I'm okay, honestly. I shouldn't have had beer and rode a bike – the combination is obviously too much for me," I mocked myself.

"Me too, it would seem," Amanda then suddenly said as she was helped to her feet.

"Well, there's a car on the way and I have asked them to call the hire company. They should be here soon and will recover the bikes," he said anxiously looking out for them on the road side.

"God, I feel like such an idiot. I'm sure we could walk back if we went slowly." I then said.

"I think not. You need to get back and have these

wounds cleaned," Rafael then said looking at Amanda's still bleeding knee. "Besides, we were starting to feel like it was a competition with Josh way out in front," he then said, and I know that he was simply trying to make us feel better. I smiled.

We didn't have to wait long. Remarkably the van and the car turned up within minutes of each other and I was happy that I didn't have to walk now. Rafael and Ethan helped us into the car, and as we set off with Ethan in the back with us, I rested my head on his chest. He placed his arm around my shoulder and then ran his fingers through my hair, it was exceptionally soothing. Even hot and sweaty he oozed sex appeal, I looked at Amanda and she just winked at me and then placed her head back on the rest and closed her eyes.

The drive back to the hotel seemed relatively short, but I was glad none the less that we were back. Amanda made a point of saying that her knee was now stiffening up and I suspect she had bruised it quite badly. Rafael helped her out of the car and then without any hesitation picked her up and carried her toward the main door with ease, as the others appeared asking if she was alright. I smiled as she looked at me over his shoulder grinning heavily;

"Well, whatever has happened today, that has just made hers so worthwhile!" I remarked as I sighed a little bit – putting weight onto my right leg made my buttock ache greatly. Ethan scooped my weight up with his arm around my waist and walked slowly alongside me.

"I am so sorry about this, I can't tell you how sorry," he said again and again.

"Hey, this was not your fault. Actually, I blame Amanda," I joked.

"I shouldn't have let Josh organise bikes without checking you were all happy to ride them," he then said. I stopped walking and kissed him on the cheek.

"I love the chivalry, but stop blaming yourself. We both wanted to go and loved every minute of it – this was just a simple accident actually caused by both myself and Amanda. No permanent damage is done and believe it or not we did both laugh at each other before you arrived," I tried to explain. "The last thing I want after everything that you have done and given us this week is you feeling guilty, so I don't want to hear anything else about it okay?" I insisted. He nodded in response, but I had the distinct feeling that he wasn't going to feel that happy about it for a while.

We carried on walking and Josh ran over standing on my other side. He also wrapped his arm around my waist and walked me into the hotel. It was a flurry of attention and flustering around us. Hernando gave us both a glass of brandy saying it would help, and Beth and Rose in and among laughing at us sounded quite sorry at our state of affairs. Ethan crouched beside the seat I sat on and asked if I needed anything.

"Actually, can you take me to my room?" I asked him. I think I need to shower and just lie down for a while." The girls rubbed my back and told me to feel better soon. Amanda decided that was a great idea and Rafael helped her, telling her to ring down once she was ready and he would dress her knee for her.

When we reached my room Ethan locked the door while I tried to push off my trainers, with some difficulty. He stopped me and knelt down to untie them lifting each foot and discarding them. Then, while I peeled off my t-shirt he set the shower running. I still felt a bit of an idiot, only I, with the exception of Amanda, could manage to fall so fantastically off a bike. I suppose the only saving grace was that we weren't going too quickly. Ethan came back to me and unfastened my shorts letting them drop to the floor, and injured or not that had some feelings stirring. He suddenly looked uncomfortable and started to walk toward the door.

"Hey, where are you going?"

"I thought that you would want to shower in peace and quiet?" he answered.

"Absolutely not. What if I manage to fall in the shower? You're hot and sweaty too, so I'm hoping that you are going to join me?" I replied, which I think took him by surprise but it conjured up a smile from him.

"You're hard to refuse, also very easy to forgive."

"Why do I need to forgive you?" I asked. "Unless you threw that bloody rabbit in front of us?" I queried sarcastically. He laughed a little.

"I shouldn't have left you," he said again sounding disappointed with himself.

"Hey, enough of that. Even if you had been there I would have still fallen off, and you would be injured instead of Amanda. Now get your clothes off and get in that shower!" I finished smacking him on his left buttock.

"I think I like you being in control," he stated as we stripped off our remaining clothes and stepped into the hot spray. It was medicine itself.

Ethan washed my hair again and then after washing we embraced under the water. I could have quite easily started something else, and I tried to let him know this by letting my hands wonder, but he stopped me saying.

"Right, young lady. None of that just now. You've had a bit of an adrenaline rush and I think that you need to rest, just for a while," he prescribed, and I sighed – he meant it, and wasn't going to let me get away with having my own way.

I stepped out and dried myself, noting the soreness when I dabbed my buttock and hip dry. I stepped in front of the mirror to take a look and was quite shocked at the size of the bruise developing. Ethan stood in front of me to take a look. Then he gave me a huge hug. "Thank goodness it's only bruising – the idiot driving that Jeep could have made it so much worse than this," he commented with annoyance. I turned to face him.

"Why – would you miss me and visit me in hospital?" I joked. He held me tightly.

"Please don't say that – I would have been devastated if you'd been injured more severely. This is bad enough," he replied. I suddenly felt guilty for being so blasé about the whole situation – Ethan obviously felt terrible about it.

"I'm sorry, yes you are right – it could have been worse, but I am fine so let's not think about what could have been," I said before releasing him and walking naked toward the bed.

I climbed onto it after pulling the sheets back and then laid out on my tummy. Ethan walked over and gently ran his hands down my back and then my over my buttocks. He noted that I now looked a very lovely shade of blue and purple in certain areas. I effortlessly agreed with him – now that my head had hit the pillow I suddenly felt exhausted. I felt him pull the sheet over me, but other than that I do not remember drifting off to sleep.

Chapter 16

I knew that I had been sleeping soundly, as some time later I felt the bed dip and a hand was placed in the middle of my back. My name was called softly and when I started to stir and stretch and wake from my slumber, I found Ethan sat at the side of me with legs stretched out, dressed in jeans and a polo shirt. I looked at him with heavy eyes and propped myself up as I was still lying on my tummy.

"Hey, sleepy head. How are you feeling?" he asked. I rubbed my eyes and then scratched my head while yawning. Then, realising that my hair was now dry, it was obvious that I had been completely comatose for a long time.

"What time is it? God, I am so sorry – I didn't mean to drift off for so long," I mumbled rolling onto my left side to face him, still noting the sore right buttock. Ethan smiled at me.

"It's nearly eight thirty and dinner will be ready shortly, I just thought I would see if you were hungry. If you wish to stay up here though I completely understand," he said as his hand moved to my waist.

"Oh God, I had no intentions of being here this long," I replied, feeling like I was a complete liability now. The last thing I wanted was for all of them to feel like I was a patient. I buried my head back into the pillow and sighed.

"There is nothing wrong with resting and catching your breath after a minor incident. Plus it was a fairly long bike ride to get there and the sun was hot today. Amanda has had a short rest this afternoon too, plus Rose, Beth, Hernando and Josh have been snoozing on the sun loungers, so you are not alone I assure you," he replied. I loved that he always put me at ease. I shuffled along on my good hip so that I was right beside him and then I straddled him. It amused me that he didn't quite know where to put his hands with all of my bruising on one side.

"I love how you make me feel." I told him. He swept my hair back and kissed me. "You always put me at ease, and make me feel less ridiculous than I sometimes am, and I love you for that!" I then gushed. We both breathed in as though we were both about to say something, but it was in response to what I had just said. My mind started replaying… *Did I just say I love him for that?* He obviously noted my sudden realisation at what I had said and my worry that I may have possibly just frightened him to death, but he answered me by saying.

"I love the way that you make me feel too." He looked me in the eye, and more sincerely than I could have hoped for he then said, "And I love you for that." I hadn't realised that I had been holding my breath until I let it out in a sudden rush. He grinned at me knowing that I was relieved, and then I hugged him tightly. After about ten seconds though I had to ask him to move his hand as it had found its way down my hip and to my buttock and it felt worse than earlier.

Ethan would have been happy for me to stay put but I was insistent that I wanted to go downstairs and eat with everyone else. I asked him to pull something out of the wardrobe that was comfortable for me to wear while I put on some underwear. When I started walking toward him he just grinned at me from ear to ear, I gave him a *'What?'* look.

"Wow, I still cannot get used to being able to see you like that," he remarked at my lacy number.

"Really? You've seen me in less than this!" I grinned back.

"I know, and I am still realising that I really am one lucky guy," he smiled as he handed me a long jersey maxi dress.

I took it from him and pulled it over my head, and it was a great choice – there was nothing to press against my bruised bits. I brushed my hair and pinned it up loosely then sprayed on some perfume and I was good to go. Ethan was treating me like I had just had a major operation, and it made me chuckle. It made him laugh more when I then told him that I think my bottom hurt more from the saddle than the bruising, particularly along with my now tight muscles in my legs – I wasn't doing that well!

When we reached the table indoors tonight it was already complete with everyone else. They all enquired as to how I was feeling and I tried to assure them that I was fine. Amanda showed me her now dressed leg courtesy of

Rafael, which I think she was actually quite proud of. She apologised for her pulling us both over after the shock of a rabbit, which then set the men off in hysterics that something so simple could have sent us both spiralling out of control. It did sound pretty ridiculous when they obviously elaborated somewhat, and so I tried to point out that the Jeep had started the whole process. Rose then chipped in that the driver of that vehicle was a 'bloody idiot' and Ethan agreed.

We were all famished again, even after a large lunch, which we had actually managed to get Ethan to agree to let us girls pay for and so we were happy about that. As we were all brought a menu and had our glasses filled, I was glad that I had made the effort to join everyone. I felt refreshed from the sleep and the soreness was bearable, the paracetamol that I had popped before coming down probably added to that. I chose a chicken dish, no starter as I decided that a bit of sugar in the form of a dessert was allowed after my ordeal today. As always the food was amazing, the chef was excellent and nothing disappointed. When my elaborate chocolate dessert arrived everyone was in awe of the artistry that had gone into its creation, the plus being that it tasted even better than it looked. I shared it with Ethan and he agreed that it was pretty amazing.

It was going to be the last day tomorrow before our departure and as I sat and thought about it, I had butterflies again, but these weren't the beautiful kind – they were the dreaded kind. Hernando enquired as to what the plan was tomorrow and Josh confirmed that after today's events a nice quiet day here was in order. The thought made me exceptionally glad as not too much movement was necessary; the warm sunshine on my body while relaxing by the pool would be a delightful way to spend the day. Rose and Beth clapped their hands in appreciation of the suggestion as they wanted to top up their tans. All in all everyone seemed happy at the decision as they were also ready to have a complete chill out after all the cycling today. Amanda gave me a thumbs up that she was desperately pleased at the arrangements and I replied by doing the same back.

When I looked at my watch at around ten thirty I realised why I was fidgeting somewhat. My buttock even though it had been given a very soft cushion, was aching rather a lot now, and to add insult to injury I really didn't feel like chattering with everyone anymore. I kept looking at Ethan who was always staring at me when I did him, I had the sudden urge to want to take him upstairs and just be alone with him. It wasn't just sex, I wanted to be close to him and have him all to myself. It was selfish I suppose as he was the host, but I knew that two more nights were available to me and then it was time to leave him. He had noted my fidgeting and my look of concern and as the others chatted he leant forward and asked what was troubling me.

"Not having you to myself, and my right buttock!" I whispered with a small scowl. He laughed lightly.

"Well, not what I was thinking, but I like the combination," he joked. I pulled a face at him, so he continued on a more serious tone. "What were you thinking?" he asked. I thought for a minute, then smiled.

"You, me, a warm bubble bath, champagne and then… well, let's see," I replied. He raised his eyebrows at me in response and then whispered.

"I like the way that you're thinking – give me a minute to sort out the champagne and then I'm all yours." He leaned and kissed me on the cheek and then left the room for a moment. Just watching him walk away so completely cool, sexy and confident had me stirring.

I answered the questions being asked of me about my boys and university and Rafael pointed out that he hadn't mentally registered that they were that old as I looked so young! I told him that he was a charmer and good at making the right responses. Rose gushed about how handsome my boys were and that they were an absolute delight. Beth agreed, and then Amanda pointed out that it was due to the fact that their mum was so damned amazing. I started to feel a little embarrassed – but my boys were simply adorable; the fact that the girls acknowledged it made me feel very proud. Rafael then explained that he had a son and a daughter, but they were much younger at fourteen and eleven. Beth had a son who was older than my boys. Other than that no one else was in a relationship to warrant children, or like Amanda had simply not wanted any.

The conversation turned to personal study and first jobs and so on, and I was pleased when Ethan appeared back at the side of me. He placed a hand on my shoulder and then looked at the others. "I'm going to excuse both Jenny and me as she is feeling a little under the weather and so I am going to keep her company where she can unwind a little," he simply told the others. It was a statement that no one needed to question, and they didn't. Beth looked at me and then smiled. She curled her lips in trying not to laugh, and I knew that she instantly thought we were just disappearing to have sex. It was at the forefront of her mind anyway, but then I noted everyone else's look and they had a similar expression.

I started to stand as Ethan pulled out my chair, and then Rose said, "Well, I hope that you feel better tomorrow."

"Yeah, lightweight," Amanda then jested at me before taking a large gulp of wine. I laughed and shook my head at her obvious medicinal excuses this evening. She had been drinking faster than the others I had noted that, I think it was to drown both the pain and the embarrassment of earlier. Rafael chinked glasses with her and then the others started to refill theirs – it was a good prompt to leave the room.

"Well, enjoy everyone and girls, don't drink them under the table!" I joked. Hernando burst out laughing.

"Not very likely!" he said.

"You really haven't seen them try that yet, have you?" I then said as I passed the table, knowing that I had just set them all a challenge.

"I'm game if you all are," Josh then prompted them, and as a conversation erupted on challenges and preferred drinks I smiled to myself and left the room with Ethan following.

He placed his hand around my waist and turned back to look at the others who were already talking about what drinking game to play first – currently with Josh in the deciding seat. He started to laugh and then turned back to me. "You do realise what you've just done there?" he asked me, and I nodded.

"Yep, I've just made sure that we won't be disturbed. The girls love a challenge!" I informed him.

Then we both laughed as we heard Josh call *"One, two, three!"*

When we got to my room I set the bath running, and then went back into the bedroom. Ethan had already removed his shirt and had pushed the shutters almost closed. I kicked off my pumps and then walked over to him and tiptoed, the sight of his toned and tanned chest made me want to just forget the bath, but I knew that it would do me the world of good. I kissed him on the cheek and then thanked him for looking after me today.

"It was the least I could do, and my pleasure," he said. I lifted my arms up into the air wanting help undressing. He didn't need me to elaborate, he simply hitched up my dress and then slipped it over my head discarding it to the floor. Then he took a deep breath in.

"You have an incredible effect on me when you are this confident and yet vulnerable at the same time." he stated. I felt sexy around him, and he said things that made my confidence grow tenfold.

"Well, you have an amazing effect on me when you have your chest out on display," I grinned as I ran my hands down his pectorals then stopping at his nipples and rubbing my thumbs across them. He sighed, closed his eyes and then let a low moan rumble from his chest. "As I recall this was not on your list of suggestions while having me to yourself."

"I did say… 'and let's see'." I reminded him. He took my face in his hands and lowered his lips within inches of mine.

"Ah – yes you did," he replied happily before taking my lips with his and executing the kiss to perfection with his tongue just gently probing and leaving me wanting more. I was gasping a little, and I really wanted him and he knew that. "Before we get carried away, young lady, that bath is going to overflow and we need to relax those muscles in your legs. So let's bathe first," he suggested and there was no negotiation. He had already turned me around and was marching me to the tub.

While I sank into the hot bubbles, Ethan poured us both a glass of champagne and came back with them. He placed them on the cleverly designed shelf and then he slipped in behind me and I leant against his chest. This whole combination I could happily endure; it was bliss. "This was an excellent idea," he confirmed and I contentedly agreed. We sat and drank champagne and talked and enjoyed the whole process of unwinding in the hot bath, but as it started to cool we decided to get out. The iPod dock was playing when I exited the bathroom in my towel; it was a mixture of love songs and I informed him that I thought it was a nice touch. My glass was refilled and Ethan was stretched out in my bed fresh, content and looking oh so hot – the contour of his body very visible under the crisp cotton sheet. I had so much confidence around him, confidence that I didn't think that I would have with another man – particularly seeing me naked. But as he pulled back the sheet and gestured for me to climb in, I just unpinned my hair and then dropped my towel and did exactly that.

He asked me what my plans were for the coming weeks, and as I relayed the projects that I had coming up soon, they sounded so remote from where I was right now. He rubbed my shoulder, and I asked what he was likely to be doing. He told me that he had to be in Rome on Tuesday, and then stay for a few days before then going to London. The thought of him travelling alone and just having Josh for company made me frown. I didn't like the thought of him being alone and I told him that. After our second glass of champagne he dimmed the lights and just held me tightly… the music quietly continued and I lay there listening to his breathing, the melody of both made me want to seduce him.

"It's not a nice thought, knowing that this has to end in a couple of days," I honestly told him.

"Shhh, let's not think about that now," he said and then he rolled me onto my back and more passionately than before he made love to me, and it was the best feeling in the world.

We were woken at a silly hour with doors banging and laughter – the others had obviously gone to the complete extreme and taken the drinking games to a new level. I hated to think what state the girls would be in tomorrow, but then I realised that I didn't care as I was completely happy where I was right now. I turned and rolled back into Ethan's side and when I felt his arm curl around me I knew the noise had woken him too.

"I think that they are going to be in trouble tomorrow," I whispered.

"Well, that's their problem not ours. I do know if Josh and Hernando were challenged in any way though they will not have taken it lightly. I think your friends will have had a whole new experience tonight." he whispered back just as we heard Beth let out a shrill scream and then be shushed by Hernando. We both laughed.

"Oh dear! I think that you may be right. As much as I love them they never back down from a challenge either, and never know when to quit, which is why I end up in such a state sometimes. It will be fun to laugh at them tomorrow for a change," I told him. Ethan rolled over to the bedside table and looked at his watch.

"Well, at three thirty in the morning, it's unlikely they are going to see much of tomorrow," he grimaced.

"I hope you don't feel like you've missed out tonight. You could have stayed with them," I said while drawing circles on his chest.

"Are you kidding me? This is my idea of a perfect night, spending it with you. I've seen Josh and Hernando, and Rafael for that matter, drunk far too many times in the past – not that enticing I assure you. Anyway, your suggestion was far more encouraging," he finished. I propped myself up and looked at him in the thin stream of moonlight that filtered through the almost closed shutters.

"Well, top marks for that answer; you better be awake enough to claim your prize?" I then exclaimed as I climbed on top of him and sat up.

"My prize being...?" he asked with that lustful tone again. I leant over and kissed his neck then sucking the skin lightly and running my tongue along his shoulder, he let out a contented sigh.

"Your prize being me seducing you during the early hours," I replied as I readjusted myself and started to let my tongue continue to trace the outline of his muscles down his chest. He didn't speak but took a sharp intake of breath as I now reached his erect nipples – and then I noticed his hand fisting into the sheet as I flicked it gently and I knew that I had him exactly where I wanted him.

Sometime later after I had traced every inch of his body with either my tongue or with gentle kisses, I had him panting desperate for more and when I reclaimed my first position straddling him I felt his heart racing in his chest. He ran his hand down from my shoulder between my breasts and to my tummy before saying, "You are so beautiful." I was now breathing faster, and as I took him and claimed him, he pulled my neck down to him so that he could kiss me. I loved being in control with him, and more so I trusted him completely. He pulled me down tighter to him which made me gasp, and only minutes later did we both climax together. It was quick, hot, and deep, but still so sensual.

I collapsed onto him and he held me tightly and once we both caught our breath he then said, "I don't want to be without you... without this." I lifted my head from his chest and looked at him.

"I know, I feel the same way. Is it possible to feel like this after only a couple of weeks?" I asked as I detached myself from him and rolled onto my back. I was glad that he had said what he had and that he felt the same way, but I had no idea how to deal with it. Logistically it was a nightmare – him travelling the world and me with my business in Manchester.

"If you had asked me that question a week ago, I would have said no, but now…" he started, then he rolled onto his side and propped his head on his hand. As he traced his hand over my stomach I looked at him.

"I wasn't expecting this… us… it has taken me by surprise, but I have to admit I cannot stand the thought of going home and leaving you and this behind," I honestly told him. He kissed me.

"Well then, in my eyes this just means some adjustment in our schedules and constant contact until we can get back together," he said making it sound so easy. I lifted my head for a second and stared into his gorgeous blue eyes, and he meant every word.

"I can't ask you to do that. Your work, your hotels, Josh – they all need you," I replied.

"Yes, they do, but if I've learnt one thing this last two weeks it's that there is more to life than work and travel. You've opened my eyes, Jenny, and it's not something that I was prepared for, but it's now something that I want more of and don't want to live without. That's if you can put up with seeing me more frequently?" he enquired hopefully. "Plus hopefully… you need me too?" I in return now kissed him.

"I would really love to see you more after this holiday. Even if it means that I have to travel out and meet you," I smiled.

"Well, look at you! Ready to travel at my beck and call, and this is the girl who wasn't that keen on coming here to Ibiza." he remarked. I tapped his arm.

"It wasn't the travelling, even though flights and me aren't a great mix – the yacht I like," I replied. He laughed at me.

"Well that's settled then, flights out – travel by yacht when here. It's easy enough to arrange so let's not worry about Saturday – it's not the end, just the beginning," he said before planting a huge kiss on my lips like he had just accomplished something great. Secretly though, I have to admit I was glad that I knew I would see him again. It made the thought of departing on Saturday less sickening and more bearable. "Right, let's get some sleep as tomorrow is just hours away," he then insisted, and we settled into a deep slumber content and happy.

I had missed the feeling of waking with someone next to me; it was soothing and yet at the same time exhilarating. Ethan had obviously been stirring way before me as he had his eyes open when I finally prised mine apart and looked at him. He was just putting his phone back onto the bedside table as I started to stretch, that glorious feeling of waking up your muscles by excessive lengthening. Then I quickly retracted them as I realised that my legs still ached and my buttock was stiff. I rolled onto my tummy and pulled the sheet down to see whether my bruise was any better, but when Ethan said, "Ouch, honey. That looks sore!" I didn't know whether to be more taken by the fact that he was so concerned or the fact that he had just called me 'honey.' Either way, I tried to get a look at it and then laughed when I realised it had turned to a lovely shade of purple, black and blue.

"Well, I'm glad that you can see the funny side," he said as he rubbed his palm across it gently.

"I'm just thinking how great that is going to look in my bikini today," I mocked myself.

"I don't think that you need to worry about that – no one will be looking at the bruising, I assure you," he said sarcastically and we laughed.

"I don't think anyone else will surface for a long time, and so I'm not worried about that either," I told him. "I am very hungry this morning though."

"Well, it's all of this exercise that you keep doing," he said and when I looked at him he winked at me. "Not that I'm complaining…" he then quickly added as I started to play fight with him which seemed appropriate as he was teasing me. He ended up making me laugh hysterically when he started to tickle me. He planted another huge kiss on my lips, after telling me he was hungry too and so we got up and showered and changed.

When we arrived out on the terrace, the umbrella was up to stop the glare of the morning sun, which I was very grateful for. It was nine thirty – the waiters were very attentive as there was only Ethan and me as we suspected. I sat and retold him how amazing it was here: the jasmine bushes were rustling in the warm breeze and as the sea rolled in on the shore in the distance I closed my eyes, inhaled and then sighed heavily.

"I'd really like to come back here one day," I told him.

"I hope so – I'm counting on it," he replied. "Where else would you like to go?" he then asked. I sat and thought for a minute, then opened my eyes and picked up my coffee cup.

"Italy, actually. Never been, but love the history of Rome and would love to visit there and Florence and the Amalfi Coast and anywhere else in Italy really," I truthfully replied.

"Well that could be arranged too," he smiled.

"You have to go to Rome next week, so I assume you have a hotel there?" I asked.

"Yes, actually. One in Rome and two others in Italy. It's one of my favourite places too; you can always wander the streets and find something new to look at on every turn. Perhaps we could explore there together one day," he suggested. I reached across and grabbed his hand.

"Yes, please, I'd love that. Not that I'm trying to get free stays in your hotels everywhere I go!" I then made him aware. He laughed at my response.

"If you're away with me you'll be paying for nothing. I like spoiling you," he remarked as he entwined his fingers with mine.

"I can't argue with that then – it's a deal," I answered in an excitable tone.

After finishing breakfast we moved to the sun loungers – we had worn swimwear under our clothes in anticipation of sunbathing and swimming. Ethan peeled off his t-shirt as I took off my clothes and then he asked if I wanted some sun tan lotion rubbing into my back. I loved the feel of his hands on my skin, and he was very thorough. I reciprocated, making him jump by tickling him here and there. The new fluffy pool towels had been left on the loungers, and as we settled into position we were happy to have the peace and quiet. I had brought my book down to read and Ethan was catching up on yesterday's news. He checked his phone numerous times and answered one work call as we lay there. It was hard to focus on my book when listening to him talk business – for some reason it was a real turn on and I think I made it obvious when he caught me watching him and he gave me a look of 'What are you thinking about right now?' I simply grinned in response and then licked my lips and curled them in to stop from chuckling. He shook his head at my reaction, because I suspect he knew exactly what was on my mind!

Chapter 17

T he morning was gliding along beautifully. We were brought fresh fruit and juices, and after managing to read some of my book in the searing dry heat I decided to take a dip in the pool. It was a slight shock to the system on initial entry, but once fully submerged it was refreshingly cool and a perfect way to take the temperature of my skin back to a bearable level. I swam approximately ten lengths (or curves) of the pool before realising that Ethan was watching me over his newspaper. I made my way to the edge just in front of him and asked if he fancied joining me. To my delight he was already standing up to do just that before I finished my sentence. He sat on the edge and dangled his legs into the water. "Jeeze," he quickly remarked after jumping at the sudden contrast. I laughed at him and then with hands either side of his legs I pushed up out of the water and kissed him on the lips.

"Don't be a baby!" I teased him placing my wet arms across his legs so that I could prop my chin on them and watch him.

"It was just a tad cooler than I was expecting. I'm fine," he then stated, trying to act all brave. "It's hardly fair that you are covering me in drops of the stuff, I need to adjust," he remarked and that was it – I couldn't resist.

I placed my arms around the bottom of his back and as he moved at the chill of my hands and I caught him unawares, I pulled him in! He went under and when he surfaced running his hands through his hair he gave me the 'Right, just you wait!' look. I scowled knowing that he was going to either dunk me or something worse and so I started to try and swim away, but he caught my foot and pulled me back.

"You, young lady, are very cruel," he joked as he took me by my waist and then threw me backwards into the water. I surfaced laughing hard, which I think annoyed him even more, but this time as he came face to face with me he just hugged me and then span me around in the water.

"Well, you know these hoteliers they never like spending money on a heated pool!" I joked. He smiled at my comment knowing I was jesting. Then he answered;

"Yeah well, the laugh is it is heated, but I think that it needs turning up just a bit."

"You think?" I sarcastically remarked. "At this rate your testicles will definitely soon be in your throat!" I laughed, but then he did too.

"Yes alright, point taken!" he said in response, but then he ran a hand down to my left breast and rested it over my hard nipple; "Looks like it's affected you too," he noted and then he raised his eyebrows at me in question. I had my arms around his neck and pulled him closer.

"No, that's just the effect that you have on me." I whispered into his ear, and then I looked into his eyes and kissed him delicately on the lips which led to a very sensual kiss and him standing and lifting me, squeezing me tightly.

"Good answer," he said as we re-submerged.

We swam for a while longer, but then as we neared the hot tub at the other end of the pool it started to beckon us. Without having to say anything we both stepped out and into the warm water, which Ethan set off bubbling.

"Ah, much better!" he confirmed as we both closed our eyes.

"It is, but with that sun too I think we will be getting out again shortly." I was just answering as Josh appeared looking a little worse for wear, but never the less he was dragging Rose with him and she looked worse still.

"Morning," he said in a neutral tone. Ethan looked across at him as he sat Rose at the table under the umbrella and then proceeded to pour her some juice. She rested her head on her hand, and took it from him with no enthusiasm.

"Looks like you had an interesting time last night, Josh," Ethan enquired finding his state quite amusing.

"Well, it started off well... but when we opened that tequila and asked for some limes... that was a big mistake!" he concluded as he downed a glass of orange juice. Ethan shook his head and laughed;

"And who won the competition?" he asked him.

"We did," both Rose and Josh stated at the same time and then they erupted into a disagreement about whether the girls or boys had fared better. Overall, so far they were looking pretty equal as far as I could see. Ethan looked at me;

"And you thought I'd missed out? Thank God you suggested your alternative!" he grimaced at the state of them.

"Rose, you're not looking too great this morning and that worries me as you handle your drinks better than Beth and Amanda," I told her honestly.

"Yeah well, this is good," she gestured to herself. "Wait until you see Amanda," she then finished laughing into her juice.

"You see, that's what I mean – you girls were far worse than us," Josh then interrupted.

"Oh please! Did you see the state of Hernando and Rafael? They both fell asleep at the table at one point," Rose pointed out.

"Sounds like them," Ethan interjected. Josh at this point started laughing.

"Did you not hear Hernando trying to sing again, Ethan? He was loud enough to wake the dead at one point," he said with amusement.

"Oh dear – that's Hernando at his worst then. I suspect we will not be seeing him for a while either," Ethan confirmed as he reached for my hand under the water.

"I have Alka-Seltzer if you need them," I called across to Rose – but she held her hand up to stop the suggestion as if the mere thought of it made her want to empty the cocktail in her stomach.

"What time is it, Josh?" Ethan then asked.

"Eleven forty-five," he called back. "Nearly lunch time – great," he said and Rose suddenly excused herself with her hand over her mouth.

"That doesn't look good!" I remarked as I stood to exit the hot tub that was now overheating me. When I walked to get my towel, Josh commented on my bruise.

"Whoa – that's a beauty, Jenny," he called across and I turned and looked at the top of my leg and partly exposed buttock.

"Yeah, it looks worse than it is," I noted, even though it was unsightly.

"Well, it's a great holiday reminder for a couple of weeks until it fades," he then said jokily. I looked at Ethan;

"I have far better things to remember this holiday by than that," I informed him and as he watched me staring at Ethan who was staring back at me.

He smiled and simply said, "Touché!"

I excused myself after drying and sliding on my shorts. I thought I had better see if Rose was alright. When I got to her room she was lying on her bed and looked grimmer than a few minutes ago.

"God, you look awful!" I told her as I poured a glass of water.

"I actually feel a bit better now that I have expelled the contents of my stomach," she informed me as she sat up.

"Well, you obviously had a great time last night."

"Jen, it was so much fun at the time, and we had a blast. You know me – think I can keep drinking anything," she groaned. I patted her leg.

"Well, if you can manage to eat something, I think you will be a lot better," I suggested, hopeful that she might at least try.

"I know and I will. Give me that water, I need to re-hydrate," she said as she took it and started guzzling it down at speed. Then she stopped. "Anyway, less about us – how the hell was your night?"

"Amazing, he's really amazing," I smiled.

"So you managed to get on that bike then?" she asked before drinking more water. I pulled a bit of a face at her and then decided to tell the truth.

"I did that days ago." I admitted. She nearly choked on the mouthful she had just taken and as she wiped the remnants dripping down her chin, she elbowed me.

"Holy crap, that's great! I mean you couldn't have picked a nicer guy. So… how did it go?" she then enquired. I smiled.

"It was better than I ever could have expected and it keeps getting better – it's always just absolutely amazing," I informed her honestly just as Beth walked in looking a lovely shade of pale green. Rose burst out laughing.

"Bloody hell, you've just made me feel so much better." She laughed harder. Beth walked over and took the remaining water in Rose's glass then sat at the other side of me.

"Thanks for that – I hate you, Rose. Whose stupid idea was it to get the tequila out?" she asked hoping for sympathy, I placed my arm around her shoulder and then she let her head fall onto mine and did a short fake cry which made me laugh. "Anyway, what are you two talking so quietly about?" she asked, and before I could say anything Rose chipped in.

"Jen here has been making sweet love for the last few days with Mr Handsome out there," she casually said. I confirmed her statement with a smile.

"What? You didn't say anything!" Beth twittered at me.

"Well, it isn't exactly something that you just announce at breakfast or dinner is it?" I tried to tell them.

"So… how the hell was it? If he's anything like Hernando and Josh then I reckon we've had a pretty damn fine holiday all in all!" she happily continued.

"I am not going into details, but let's just say it's mind-blowing!" I stated again before standing and then turning back to them to give them some advice. "I think that you two need to get outside in some fresh air, plenty of juice and some lunch. Oh and please don't let on that you know anything," I pleaded.

"We promise we won't say anything if you tell us exactly what you got up to last night – we promise that it will only stay within these four walls." Beth then replied as she crossed her arms waiting. Rose looked at me in anticipation.

I had the sudden quick thought that if I said something now, I may not get the request to reveal all when we travel back. Reluctantly I went closer to them and whispered in brief;

"Alright, then I want to hear no more about it – I never ask what you two have been getting up to," I scowled.

"I'll happily divulge my sexual escapades if you wish to

hear them," Beth started. Then she pulled a face. "Actually just don't ask me about last night – there was apparent evidence of sex this morning, but I don't really remember an awful lot about it!" she finished. Rose reached across and hit her arm.

"Jesus, Beth. You're so bad. I can't believe you even tried after the skinful we all had last night," she remarked at her comment.

"You know me; young sexy male offering his body… it's hard to say no!" she laughed and then Rose joined her shaking her head at her obvious lack of decorum. I coughed lightly to interrupt their little form of amusement. Rose looked back at me.

"Sorry, Jen. Carry on," she insisted as she wiped her eyes dry.

"Right, I will say this quickly and only once so listen up," I commanded. "We took a bath together, drank champagne, dried, had sex, went to sleep – then some noisy guests woke us at three thirty, so we had sex again and then went back to sleep and that's as much as I'm saying."

"God, get her. She's turned into a little minx," Beth then decided. I groaned at her childish remark.

"I think it's bloody great. I'm so proud of you. Not only have you hooked a hot guy, but he's kind and sweet and he's given you your mojo back! Bloody awesome I say," Rose happily exclaimed, and for once I was happy at her remark which involved both Ethan and me.

Beth nodded after a few seconds and then added, "Not bad girl – it's about time, and yes, I am proud of you too. Big steps after everything, but we knew that you'd get there," she smiled.

"Okay, well that's me done explaining. Let's go and get some lunch," I ordered as I pointed to the door trying to get them both moving. They looked at each other and as they stood to do what I requested Rose made a comment.

"God, give her sex and she gives us a lecture." I smiled at her remark and as they started walking out of the door I followed them and placed my arms around their waists.

"I love you too!" I replied with a hint of sarcasm. Then as we walked toward the pool, and as bad as they were feeling we all laughed a little at the situation we found ourselves in.

When we eventually got outside I popped my sunglasses back on as the sun was more intense than yesterday, and it was blinding. Beth and Rose immediately aimed for cover at the large table umbrella where Hernando, Josh and Rafael were all sat drinking juice with Ethan; he seemed to find their sorry states highly amusing. They retold stories of last night, and even though they laughed Rose kept holding her sore tummy and asking that they stopped mentioning alcohol. It was obvious that they had enjoyed a great night together and I was glad about that. It did concern me slightly that Amanda hadn't surfaced yet; I was just thinking about going and seeing if she was alright and stood from my chair when I was stopped in my tracks.

"So, while we were getting completely intoxicated did you two enjoy your evening?" Hernando asked Ethan and me. I could feel myself going a lovely shade of red, but

Ethan answered him before I had time to think of a reply. It didn't help that I had Beth and Rose staring at me too, but as I was near Ethan's chair I felt much better when he grabbed my hand and pulled me onto his knee, almost as if he knew that I wasn't sure what to say.

"We had an amazing night, thank you. Quiet and very relaxing and even though we had champagne I'm glad to say that we were wise enough to stop at one bottle!" he replied with a hint of mockery.

"Yes, alright, Mr Sensible," Hernando replied smiling. "I admit that I probably wish I had your head today," he finished as he drank another mouthful of his orange.

"Has anyone seen Amanda yet?" I then asked with a little concern.

"Oh, I wouldn't plan on seeing her until this evening," Rafael mumbled. "She was setting the pace with the tequila and wanted to start on the rum but we had to stop her."

"Oh dear God, I do remember something about that," Beth chipped in, grimacing a little. "Was that before or after she tried to stick her tongue down your throat, Rafael?" she then enquired, and both Ethan and I shot an inquisitive look at him for a response. He noted our reaction and quickly replied – his hands held in a placatory gesture.

"Hey, I am a married man and she is a married woman – I was a gentleman and helped her to her room and that was all," he said trying to state his innocence. We all sat for a minute watching him flap slightly and then we all started laughing. I couldn't imagine for one minute

Amanda trying to do such a thing – so it only highlighted how drunk she had been.

Ethan squeezed his hand around my waist as he continued to taunt Rafael. I had the impression that he didn't get the chance to do it very often which had Josh in hysterics. I watched them all trying to get at each other but enjoying every moment of it and then I noticed Beth and Rose staring at me while I sat happily on Ethan's lap – they just smiled at me, and I was content with that.

After the cheap digs came to an end, we all chose lunch off the menu and decided to eat while our appetites seemed apparent – particularly those who needed to soak up some alcohol. I chose a salad which was crisp and refreshing, and as always my appetite was huge so I accompanied it with breads and olives. The girls laughed as they slowly ploughed through theirs and I seemed to make up for them with the quantity that I consumed, but it was too tasty to leave any morsel. Once I finished I sat back contently and held my stomach.

"Enjoy that?" Ethan asked, probably wondering where on earth I had just stored what I had eaten.

"Loved every bit of it," I replied, sighing at my fullness.

"I love a woman who enjoys her food," Rafael commented and I raised my glass of cool Sauvignon at him in appreciation.

"Our Jenny has always loved her food," Beth then said.

"Which is probably why I am the size I am!" I then joked at myself. Ethan reached across and rubbed my arm.

"You're just perfect the way you are," he said and without thinking I leant over slightly and kissed him on the lips.

"Thank you," I smiled.

"You're welcome," he smiled back and then we both turned our heads toward the table to see everyone staring at us. Josh gave us the biggest grin, and then broke the silence.

"Women worry far too much about their weight; as long as they aren't as thin as a pencil I'm happy," he honestly said.

"I agree. I'm not into seeing just skin and bone on a woman – it's not natural at all," Hernando added. Beth winked at him.

"Good job really!" she joked at herself, as Beth had a beautiful curvy figure with a more than ample chest. He gave her a huge smile back.

We sat and talked about last night some more, and then about tomorrow's return trip. The men seemed to decide on the spot that we would travel in luxury and go around the island on the yachts, which delighted us, and we were in complete agreement. Ethan said that he would get a car organised and drive us to the airport once back on dry land and that made me very happy. Beth and Rose decided to take a dip in the pool as a hangover cure – I decided not to tell them just how much of a contrast the water was to the air temperature as it would be funny to watch. I stretched back out on a sun lounger next to Ethan and made him aware of the impending swearing about to commence.

It took them some time just to strip down to their swimwear but as they started to go down the steps into the pool I started sniggering instantly. Josh and Hernando taunted their complaining at the coolness of the water as they started gasping for breath and then let the swearing ensue. After starting to swim and swearing profusely they started to calm down, but Beth insisted that her whole body now had a similar thing to brain freeze. Ethan laughed at them but then asked me if he had complained quite as much, I then taunted him by saying that he had been terrible too but not quite on their level!

They only swam about ten lengths and then decided that was cure enough, so they got out, dried and then lay out to warm up. The men were quiet for a change as they too caught up on sleep while they soaked up the sun. The waiter came around and offered us drinks, and then we simply relaxed. I read some more of my book and as the bell of the church rang in the town below and the sea rolled on the shore in the distance everyone seemed to be completely at ease. When three o'clock arrived, it brought with it one very tired-looking Amanda. She walked out in her shorts and sunglasses nursing what I can only imagine as the feeling of near death – she didn't look good at all. Rose burst out laughing, as did Beth – when the men turned to look at her they smiled, but Rafael did ask if she was alright and he meant it.

"I'm better now than when I woke at eleven." she informed us. "Why the hell did you keep plying me with more drinks?" she asked aiming that question at the men.

"Hey! You were doing mighty fine on your own."

Josh told her. "In fact you set the pace, Amanda. You wanted rum and we had to stop you at that. Besides, after sticking your tongue down Rafael's throat on tequila we dread to think what you would've done on rum too!" he sarcastically replied as Rafael dropped his head and shook it probably worrying about her reaction.

"I did what?" she said with added volume as she took off her sunglasses. "Please tell me I didn't – not that you're not a good-looking, really lovely guy, Rafael – but really? Did I?" she started to ramble. Hernando confirmed it for her.

"Oh, you most definitely did. Sorry, Amanda!" She shoved her sunglasses back on quickly.

"Oh dear God, I am so sorry, Rafael – I don't know what came over me. I don't actually remember that at all." she continued, but Rafael stopped her.

"I think it was the inordinate amount of alcohol that came over you actually!" he joked then he continued "Stop worrying, no damage done. It was, in a strange way, quite pleasant." The girls were now laughing at her complete embarrassment. Ethan was laughing at Rafael and I just found the whole situation amusing – it made a change for someone else to make a fool out of themselves, particularly Amanda.

The waiter appeared with a large glass of orange juice for her and a plate of food, which she must have ordered on her way out. She sat in the shade and slowly tried to nibble at it, but it was obvious that she was delicate. After a while she came and plonked herself down on a lounger and groaned at her own sorry state. Rose reached across and told her she would be alright and that she should get some paracetamol, and although Amanda knew that this was a good idea, she had no intentions of moving straight away. We all lay there quietly again for what seemed like a long time, but in reality it was probably only an hour or so. I could feel myself dozing slightly as there was activity at the side of me. Amanda had managed to get back up and she insisted on going and getting her bikini on and trying to snap herself out of it.

As Amanda walked back toward the door where both Rafael and Josh were stood, they stopped her and insisted that they needed a photograph of all four of us to remember the holiday by. She wasn't happy about it, but Josh called Rose and Beth, who were always up for fun photographs. I reluctantly went over as they kept calling and we all stood in a line trying to look better than some of us felt. They took a couple asking for silly poses and then as Rafael started to ask us to back up a little as he kept chopping one of us off, I had the sneaky suspicion he was up to something. Amanda kept doing as she was told just to get the task over with, plus her brain still hadn't kicked into normal working mode. Beth was acting like a model on assignment, and Rose just looked casual. As we backed up twice I started to see where this was going – we were inches away from the pool, and as he asked us one more time to just go back slightly further I knew what was coming.

"Amanda stop!" I called. But just as I did she lost her footing on the edge and started to fall backwards. It was almost in slow motion like a scene from a comedy sketch and no matter how much I knew it was going to happen – I couldn't stop it.

She started to fall in – it was inevitable – but then she reached out and grabbed Beth, who in turn grabbed Rose and then she reached out and pulled me in. In one almighty splash one after another we all landed in the rather cold water, which first had us obviously fully submerged and secondly woke us all up after lying in the sun. When we surfaced the men (even Ethan) were laughing heartily. I looked at the girls who were shocked, cold and cursing, but the sight had me laughing too. As they all adjusted to the incident they started to laugh a little and we swam to the side. The men pulled us out to standing with the exception of Amanda who started swimming lengths stating, "No need for my bikini now!" It wasn't so much her statement but the look she tried to portray of not being bothered by it at all that had us laughing more. After about three lengths she walked up the steps of the pool and Rafael graciously wrapped her in a towel. She laughed and said, "Well I suppose I deserved that after the tongue thing!" He gave her a big hug and said that it wasn't revenge, but a hangover cure. Whatever it was it seemed to kick start us all into enjoying the rest of the day regardless of our self-inflicted ailments.

Chapter 18

B y the time the sun started cooling at eight o'clock, I think it was fair to say that the others had recovered well. We were still sat outside and had done so all afternoon. Josh and Ethan had completed some work, and set up a meeting for next week. I played cards with Amanda and Beth while Rose just soaked up the sun. Rafael and Hernando played chess and then took a plunge in the hot tub and remarkably at seven o'clock they both asked for a beer, which impressed me to say the least. Amanda had sworn numerous times over the day that she wasn't ever drinking again – we didn't comment as we'd heard her say it so many times before.

Ethan was sat making a quick phone call a short distance from us when the manager of the hotel came to ask him what our dinner plans may be. I heard him suggest nine thirty and a late meal as we all needed to change and that made me stretch on the sun lounger and finish my cool Sauvignon. I stood and walked across to him and while he was on hold on the phone waiting to speak to a manager of another hotel, I whispered in his ear that I was going for a shower and I expected him to be joining me ASAP! He smiled at me and nodded in acceptance. I made my excuses and told the others that I was going to my room where I quickly undressed and set the shower running. After my hair had dried itself last night and was quite unruly, I decided to wash it again – after all it was the last night and I wanted to look as stunning as possible.

I stepped into the shower and started to relax under the warm spray. As I leant against the tiles letting the water cascade down my body rinsing all remnants of sun tan lotion away, I sighed. The Gessami Residence had been the perfect holiday retreat, and knowing that I had to leave here tomorrow was saddening. I washed my hair and then conditioned it and as I let the water rinse it clean, two arms suddenly wrapped themselves around my middle from behind.

"Hey, I thought that you had changed your mind?" I said as he kissed my shoulder.

"Not likely – how can I turn down an offer like this?" he asked as he turned me around. He kissed me and then embraced me under the warm spray and then he sighed. "I'm finding myself getting nervous about you leaving," he admitted and that made me smile.

"Well, as we said this isn't the end. Just think how exciting it will be when we meet again soon," I tried to convince him, which was hard as I was trying to convince myself too.

"Yes, I know. I'm simply enjoying this new me, and that's because of you. It's going to be strange after tomorrow getting back into work and not having you around," he said with feeling. I held him tighter.

"I know, I'm thinking the same. So my suggestion would be to make this the best night tonight and best day tomorrow," I smiled before stroking the sides of his face and then kissing his chest with meaning while the water ran down our faces.

He ran his hands down my body and I found myself doing the same to him, and as the kissing became more sensual and our hands caressed every curve of each other's body, there was no stopping us. He lifted me and wrapped my legs around his waist, and then pressed me against the tiled shower wall. It was unbelievably hot and was sex on a different level – it was needy and although still passionate it was fast and hard and almost like a desperation for us both to climax as quickly as possible. When we came back down from the spiralling sensation and he lowered me to the floor, resting his head in the nape of my neck, I felt him trembling a little. I pulled him close to me and he responded by pulling me tight to him.

It suddenly dawned on me that he was suffering worse than I was about having to part ways tomorrow, and it made me feel sure that this was meant to be. I was never a big believer in fate, but for once in my life I was starting to think it was a possibility. He had saved me from being miserable and alone when I arrived, and it would seem I had done the same for him whether he had realised he felt that way before we met or not.

After a minute or so he snapped his head up and moved me back under the spray. He delicately washed every inch of me looking appreciative of our silence but smiling all the same almost with gratitude that I was letting him. I found it touching that he cared so much about looking after me, and as I smiled back at him it was obvious that we had complete respect for one another. Once clean and rinsed I had to break the silence.

"You're pretty amazing – do you know that?" I asked honestly as I wrapped a large fluffy white robe around myself.

"That's funny, I was just thinking the same about you," he replied as he pulled me closer and then tied it pulling the belt in a tight knot. I lurched a little at the force.

"Hmm, that's definitely tied," I joked as he pulled my long hair free from inside it and let it fall loosely down my back. So I reciprocated and tied his, but then smiled as I had a wicked thought. He noted my expression and looked at me curiously. "I think that I may like to tie you up!" I explained as I played with the ends of his belt. He raised his eyebrows at me but gave me a huge grin.

"Let me guess – you've been reading *Fifty Shades of Grey*," he mocked me. The fact that I had did highlight my thoughts more. The girls had bought it for me to try to 'inspire' me. I laughed nervously just a little.

"Maybe," I commented as I then winked at him turned and left the room.

It was only eight forty-five, and so I sat up on the bed and took out my phone, he came and sat beside me. I had received a message from my boys, and it instantly made me want to speak to them. I looked at Ethan who had rested his head back and closed his eyes.

"Do you mind if I just call my boys?" I asked him. He looked surprised that I had asked.

"Of course not. You don't need my permission to

speak to them – please go ahead," he smiled. "I am sure that they miss speaking with you, and want to just check that you are alright," he finished and then he replaced his head against the headboard.

I hit dial and called Mark first; he had started a new part-time job to make some extra cash, and although I knew he would be fine I was interested to see how it was going. We laughed about the fact that he was loving it, mainly due to the excessive amount of attention he was getting from females. He was great at striking up conversation with anyone and I knew that this job would be ideal for him. His course work was going well, and when he confirmed that he would be still coming home the following weekend I was more than happy. James being the oldest was a little more inquisitive as to what I had been doing and whether I was enjoying myself. I explained that we had made some lovely friends and that I hoped to see more of them and keep in touch. He asked if a man could be involved in the mix, and as I looked at Ethan at the side of me with his eyes closed I decided to be honest.

"I've met a really nice guy actually, James. He has been nothing but kind, charming and an absolute delight to have spent time with," I told him. He asked me his name. "Ethan, and I hope that you can meet him soon," I then said, which had Ethan opening his eyes and looking at me.

He reached across and held my hand. James then highlighted that his name didn't seem very Spanish and I laughed explaining that he was just travelling, with a brief synopsis of what he did and where he was from. It was only brief, but James had always been slightly more protective of me after Paul. He said that he was glad that I was opening up a little to the possibility of not being alone forever and that made me smile: I was so lucky to have the support of my boys. James confirmed too that he would be back next weekend and was looking forward to seeing me and meeting Ethan sometime and so after leaving Ethan tomorrow I now had the confirmation that I definitely had something to look forward to.

When I had said my goodbyes and placed my phone back on the bedside table, I turned and found Ethan who was still holding my hand staring at me intently. I smiled at him and he said nothing; "What?" I asked him.

"You told your son about me?" he questioned. I rolled over and kissed him.

"Yes, well why wouldn't I? I wouldn't lie to them – and I do hope that you can meet them sometime," I explained. He pulled me close and wrapped his arm around me.

"I'm honoured. I didn't think that you would want to mention me – I mean it cannot be easy for them either, thinking of you being with another man." He tried to express his concerns.

"They're big boys now – I think that they can handle it. Anyway, James just said that he is happy that I am opening up to the possibility of not being alone forever, and he looks forward to meeting you." Ethan seemed happy knowing that.

"Well, I'd better be on my best behaviour then, hadn't I? It seems that it's them I need to convince that I am serious about you," he laughed nervously.

"They are a little protective of me I must admit, but I am sure that they will love you just as much as I do," I told him, meaning every word, and then I pecked him on the cheek – he was happy at my response. He took a deep breath.

"Well if we are being honest and – after Josh making me admit my feelings for sure this afternoon – I need to tell you… that I think I am falling in love with you," he stated nervously, and I sat up and looked at him. He sat and met my shocked expression at his revelation. He took my hands in his; "I know it's early days, and I don't want to scare you, but I honestly have never felt like this about anyone before – you've bewitched me, Jenny Walker – and I am not going to let you leave tomorrow without you knowing that." Then he smiled. I slowly digested the realisation that he had just confessed that he was in love with me.

I know that he had said he thought he was falling for me before, but I wondered if it was the whole ambience of this place and we were just wrapped up in the romantic fantasy of what it could be. I knew for sure that I felt strongly for him and it did feel like a love that was growing for me, but for him to admit it? It took me by complete surprise, let alone the fact that he had obviously been discussing it with Josh, his confidant.

"Say something – you look like you're about to go into shock," he panicked, squeezing my hands.

"I, I was just assimilating… I know that I feel strongly for you, and it's not just the sex – which is mind blowing by the way – but it's you. It's everything about you. Who you are and what you do, what makes you tick, your personal vulnerability, while being so completely in control with your business. I love it all! I understand what you are saying as I feel the same way – it was just a little bit of a shock to hear you confess it first," I tried to explain nervously. He smiled at me as his hands reached my face and then to calm my apparent mild panic attack he kissed me fully on the lips.

"I like that answer," he laughed lightly. He grabbed me and pulled us back down onto the pillows. "I feel this is the start of a new chapter for us, and it's going to be awesome," he then decided with a very excitable tone. Even though I had butterflies from the whole conversation I smiled uncontrollably and then I agreed with him.

We lay there for another few minutes in silence and then I asked him what time it was. Ten past nine was not what I was hoping for. I jumped up stating that I needed to blast my hair with the dryer, apply make-up and get dressed. Then he informed me that as he left the others earlier, they had decided to make it a slightly dressier dinner. My head kicked into gear trying to decide what I was going to wear. I wanted to look stunning, Ethan found my scurrying around the room amusing as he walked to the chair where he had laid out clothing from his room. I scowled wishing that he had given me more notice to prepare – and twenty minutes at the best of times wasn't a great deal of time to get ready in.

With the help of the sunshine giving me a deeper glow, I knew that make-up could be kept to a minimum and so I set about drying my hair. Ethan casually got dressed and then dabbed on some aftershave which was my favourite on him. It gave me that instant lustful sensation – it was a clever trick which the brain allowed to happen, all from the simplicity of a scent. After standing in front of the wardrobe for a while, I remembered that I had a very pretty plain green wrap dress with me. It wasn't casual, but it wasn't over dressy either – *perfect,* I thought. I took it with me to the bathroom and promised Ethan I would be ready shortly. He sat on the chair in the corner of the room and told me not to rush, which made me feel better.

Once make-up ready I quickly ran a few curls through my hair with my straighteners which took seconds. Ethan patiently waited, smiling every time that I appeared. Then I slipped on my dress in the bathroom, applied lip gloss, sprayed my Chloé perfume and checked myself in the mirror. Classy and understated, but it held me in in all the right places. I felt sexy and confident – I slipped my feet into my shoes and exited the bathroom looking across at him for some response.

"Will I do?" I asked hopefully. He let a sharp whistle leave his lips.

"Oh boy – wow – you look gorgeous," he replied and I knew that I was more than presentable – I was only bothered about his reaction anyway. "There is just one thing missing." he then added as he stood and gracefully glided over to me. He handed me a box, and I instantly recognised it from the auction. My heart leapt into my throat and started beating with such an intensity I thought it could possibly leap from my chest.

"What's this?" I asked breathing faster still while I held it tentatively in my hands.

"I think that you know what it is, and it's yours – I'd love it if you would wear it tonight," he asked with large puppy-dog eyes. I swallowed hard.

"But it's too much – I know how much you paid for this," I remarked. He took the box from me and opened it taking from it the beautiful white gold chain with diamond drop pendant and then he asked me to turn while he placed it around my neck.

When I turned back to him my hand found its way to my neck to feel it. It was heavier than I had anticipated, and so I looked in the mirror. It was stunning.

"I don't know what to say, Ethan. It's beautiful." Then I found a small tear leave my eye. He stepped closer.

"Hey, this wasn't meant to upset you – it's just something that I wanted to give to you. After all I did buy it for you, I just didn't know when the moment would be right, but this is the perfect time. Hopefully it will help you remember me, until we can be together again after you leave." He wiped my tear away. I leaned my cheek into the palm of his hand.

"It's not a tear of sadness, it's a tear of appreciation that I somehow found you. You do the most thoughtful things, and it's overwhelming sometimes," I confirmed. He simply smiled and kissed me once.

"Well, it suits you well and I am glad that you like it, but we need to get downstairs for dinner," he then prompted me gesturing toward the door.

I walked slowly toward it and turned the key when

my hand reached the handle, but I froze for a second and turned back to him. Without any warning I threw my arms around his neck and embraced him tightly. He laughed lightly at my reaction.

"Thank you for being so generous and being you," I said with absolute loyalty. He groaned a little and squeezed me even tighter.

"It's my absolute pleasure," he replied and then I planted a rather large kiss on his lips to confirm my statement. He reciprocated by patting me hard on my left buttock and telling me to get moving, which made me laugh.

When we arrived downstairs at the large terrace outside by the pool, the staff had decorated it quite elaborately with lanterns, flowers and bigger candles – it was really pretty and as the evening air was humid and warm but the breeze had dropped it was the perfect atmosphere. Everyone else was there with the exception of Rose and Josh and I knew that they were probably making the most of tonight also. Amanda remarkably was having a glass of champagne along with the others and as we reached them Rafael poured a glass for us and handed them to us. Beth gave me a huge hug and told me I looked lovely and then Amanda did and said the same. They looked gorgeous too and I made sure that I told them that. Amanda then reached up her hand and took my pendant in her fingers and looked at it inquisitively knowing exactly what it was, as we all had taken a look at it once Ethan had bought it at the auction. As the two of them inspected it more closely and just as Rose and Josh appeared alongside us looking smug, Amanda then spoke.

"That looks… stunning!" she said meaningfully, as I went a slight shade of pink and looked over at Ethan. He just winked at me and then continued his conversation with Rafael.

"Yes, I know – it was a gift from Ethan," I replied as I looked down at it. Josh looked across at me and raised his glass and then winked once at me, as if he knew everything about the whole conversation that we had had prior to joining them. I raised mine back at him, in thanks that he was such a good friend to Ethan and that he had accepted me and made me feel so welcome too.

As we sipped champagne, Rose and Josh stood hand in hand which made me smile. I think that she was as smitten with Josh as I was with Ethan, and that would make for an interesting relationship between us all. When the manager appeared we knew that we all needed to take our seats. It was nice to sit next to Hernando and chat to him about his yacht business; he really was an enthusiastic young businessman and I could understand why Ethan got on so well with him – they had the same aspirations about their work. We were given a choice at dinner and it was a menu of so many delicious choices. I chose fish again – it was so magnificent here – and tonight's dish didn't disappoint. We nibbled at a selection of starters, had our mains and then desserts were plentiful in choice – I had an orange Catalan cream, a kind of crème brulée but the orange zest that ran through it was tantalising and refreshing to the taste buds. It was amusing to find everyone so remarkably quiet during the eating of the desserts and we took it upon ourselves to try each other's, which added to the delightful experience.

The chef made an appearance tonight, I assume at Ethan's request, and we all stood and applauded him – he seemed very humbled at our attention, but it was so well deserved. We sat and talked for some time after eating and then Josh stood and walked toward the nearest open doors by the table and suddenly there was music. Not pop or anything heavy, but Frank Sinatra and other classics. It surprised me even more when Rafael stood and asked Amanda to dance, she gladly accepted and they walked to the open area behind the table and gently swayed. It wasn't long and the others joined them. I sat watching and reached my hand up to my neck and held the pendant in my hand, then Ethan touched my arm.

"Is everything alright?" he asked. I considered his words for a moment and looked back at the others then replied.

"Perfect." He smiled at me and then stood and reached his hand out for mine.

"Dance with me?" he requested and I stood placed my hand in his and kissed him on the cheek and answered immediately;

"I'd love to."

He walked me to where the others laughed and danced and as we joined them he pulled me close I couldn't think of a more spectacular way to finish our last night here. It was quite simply one of the most enjoyable evenings of my life and mainly because my best friends were here, but so was Ethan. We had cheeses and breads with more wine, and continued talking until the air grew significantly cooler and then we moved indoors. Coffee was served along with handmade chocolates which the girls and I commented were heaven themselves. As we sat there on the comfortable sofas and chairs relaxing, the men with either brandy, whiskey or some other spirit of choice, Beth asked what the plan was for tomorrow as we had to pack again and get ourselves ready. Ethan and Josh then looked at each other.

"I will let you relay the plans, Josh," Ethan happily said as he leaned back into the sofa next to me.

"Well, Hernando has kindly organised both yachts to be at the bay for eleven, so we can have a nice leisurely breakfast and then drive down to meet them. We can organise the finer points of who is on which later, but the plan is then to sail back down from where we set off. I have booked a table for dinner at a lovely hotel near the bay and then unfortunately we will have to part ways people!" he concluded and we all went a little quiet; the time had nearly arrived for us to leave. "But!" Josh then said with volume registering our quietness. "That is not going to spoil our fun tomorrow. I insist on that," he finished.

"Indeed," Rafael agreed. "While we are all here I would like to propose a toast to our most generous and kind host, without whom we would not have all had so much fun this week," he said and I looked at Ethan who now looked a little embarrassed. "To Ethan, we wish you good health and success in your business, as you seem to be very good at it!" he joked raising his glass and we all joined him.

"To Ethan," we all toasted and then took a sip. He was quick to take the emphasis off himself.

"My thanks to Hernando for generously giving up his time and his yachts for our short trip, and to all of you for being my critics this week. I couldn't have chosen a nicer group of friends to spend the week with – so big thanks to you all," he finished and he raised his glass to us.

We all repeated the toast and particularly thanked Hernando as Ethan was right – his yachts were amazing. I turned and kissed him once on the lips telling him that was a lovely thing to say and to also thank us. He nodded in acceptance and then everyone continued talking. Rafael was saying it would be nice to see his children who had been visiting his wife's family this week while he was away. Ethan whispered in my ear that he was a very devoted father and hated being apart from them, which I found adorable, as Rafael sat and showed Amanda pictures of them from his wallet. We had made some good friends on this trip and I hoped that everyone would keep in touch.

When the clock chimed one and after a long night last night, everyone started to make their excuses to retire and as I was feeling tired too; I was glad that it was suggested. We all made our way to our rooms bidding the staff goodnight along with each other. Ethan took my hand and walked me up the narrow staircase to my room. When we arrived at my door he stopped and said that he would understand if I wanted to have a night alone if I was tired. I opened the door and grabbed him by his shirt smiling and simply pulled him into my room with me.

"I am not letting you out of my sight until that flight tomorrow, so if you think that you are leaving me alone tonight you are sadly mistaken," I told him as I unfastened my dress and dropped it to the floor. He placed his hands on my cheeks and kissed me delicately.

"I was hoping that you would say that." He smiled and then he started to unbutton his shirt while I unfastened his belt and trousers.

We were on the bed before I could blink, and as we lay there with me underneath him looking into each other's eyes, I let myself melt completely into his body. We gave ourselves to each other knowing that this would be the last time for a while, and as intense and mind blowing as it was we didn't lose sight of each other the whole way through. We watched each other intently as we both reached the point of climax at the same time. Our heated bodies entwined we didn't move for a few minutes, but just watched each other and kissed numerous times.

When we eventually started to drift off, him snuggled up behind me, I raised my hand to my neck which still had the beautiful necklace he had given me upon it. I touched it and then smiled knowing that I had a special token of our little adventure together – an adventure that had led us to finding ourselves through each other. I drifted off happy and content and as I squeezed his arm he pulled me tighter to him. It was the most perfect place to be.

After such an amazing end to the evening, I was surprised when I woke startled at around four in the morning. I was sweating a little and remembered the nightmare I was having being along the lines of not seeing

Ethan, and in some strange way it brought back thoughts about my loss of Paul. I lay there with my heart pounding and gasping for breath a little. I had at some point managed to move away from Ethan during the night and he was fast asleep on his back. Luckily my restlessness had not woken him too. I lay there for some time, but found that I couldn't get back off to sleep and so after staring at the ceiling, I decided to get up and go to the bathroom.

I splashed some water on my face and also had a drink of water and then as I exited the bathroom before turning off the light, I looked across at the godly figure that lay in my bed. He was magnificent in every way, and the dim light emphasised the curves of his bare chest, along with his muscular legs that the sheet clung to perfectly. I breathed in deeply and smiled – I knew that I would get to see more of this even if it wouldn't be for a few weeks. Glancing around the room which had been my home for the last few days, I realised how easily I had settled here. I wondered around quietly and as I passed the desk which had headed paper and envelopes upon it – I had the brilliant idea of writing a letter for him explaining how I felt. I sat quietly after putting his shirt on and put pen to paper.

Dear Ethan,

When I arrived in Ibiza a little apprehensive about our holiday, I had no intentions of even thinking about looking for any type of relationship. The night that you saved me from making a complete fool of myself was a major milestone in my then miserable life. I did not expect to feel so strongly for you so quickly, but as I have spent more time with you and now know you better, I would not wish it any other way.

You are the most generous, charming, intelligent, handsome, charismatic, kind, thoughtful and sexiest man that I think I have ever met. The more time that I spend with you, the harder it is not to be with you. I really was not expecting to find such a connection with anyone, but after being here with you, I know that I now feel confident enough to tell you – and I mean it with all my heart – that I do love you.

I know that it may be hard to believe and to others it may seem a little crazy, but I cannot deny how my heart feels toward you. The days, hours and minutes until we can be together again will be hard to bear, but know that you are in my every waking thought and clearest dreams.

Thank you for helping me find myself again, making me extremely happy, and for being you. These last two weeks have been two of the most memorable of my life and I cannot thank you enough.

With my love and affection to a very special man…

Your Jenny X

Ps…Thank you for my beautiful necklace; I promise to wear it every day until I see you again.

I spritzed it with a light covering of my perfume and then sealed it in the envelope and smiled. I did mean every word, and I hoped he didn't find it too intense or overbearing. I wanted to leave him with something from me, and this was the best thing that I could think of; my personal thoughts and words that were only for him to read. I hid the letter in my bag, thinking that I could give it to him at the airport and then I climbed back into bed in his shirt and inhaled the lingering aftershave around the collar. I didn't want to wake him and this was the next best thing. After what I guessed to be around twenty minutes I started to drift while hugging a pillow tightly to my chest and then thankfully fell into a deep sleep with no nightmares.

Chapter 19

I was awoken to the sensation of Ethan tightly squeezed against my back and his arm sliding over my hip and around my tummy. As I opened my eyes he had propped himself up to see what I was hugging. I stretched and turned onto my back and then rubbed my eyes as I released the pillow.

"Hey, I'm right here – no need to be hugging that!" he joked, but I just sighed and looked at him.

"Bad dreams – it was my comforter," I tried to explain. He stroked the side of my face sweeping my hair away.

"Do you want to talk about it?" he asked. I smiled at his concern.

"Just dreams about leaving you – it brought back thoughts about losing Paul that was all. Made me wake in a hot sweat," I explained. He frowned a little.

"You should have woken me, honey," he said in a smooth, calm tone.

"You looked too peaceful to wake."

"So you substituted me with a pillow?" he smirked.

"It wasn't ideal, but it helped along with your shirt," I replied as I pulled the sheet down and revealed his now crumpled expensive shirt which I still wore. It made him grin from ear to ear.

"It looks far better on you than on me," he said before kissing me. I turned into him and entwined my legs with his. I didn't want to dwell on my dream – I just wanted to lie quietly holding him and I think he could sense that. So he gently stroked his hand down my hair and then my back and he did just that – he held me tightly.

After lying there for a while listening to his heart beating calmly but strongly, I looked up at him and asked what time it was. I was relieved to know that it was only eight thirty. He pulled me directly onto him so that my body was stretched out over his and he just looked at me.

"Let's make today a great day," he said smiling. I agreed and then lifted my arms up hoping that he would get the hint to take his shirt off me. He did and then hugged me tightly; "I love feeling your skin against mine." He squeezed me and breathed in deeply – I knew what he meant as I loved it too.

We lay there for a while just talking, no sex, but being this close and this intimate was just what I craved right now. When it got to nine o'clock I decided that I needed a nice hot shower to wake me up properly. Ethan, as always, joined me and we continued our discussion in the shower – for all intents and purposes it felt like a normal relationship. We dried, dressed and then he suggested that we have breakfast and I agreed I was hungry again. A few of the others were already down eating when we arrived at the table. The first cup of coffee was just what I needed – and as I started on the fresh fruit I realised that I was going to miss this in Manchester; my usual morning bowl of porridge and blueberries seemed remarkably dull compared to this regular feast.

It wasn't long before everyone else appeared for breakfast. Amanda and Rafael surprised me saying that they had already packed; Beth scowled as she wasn't looking forward to trying to get everything in her case again, but Amanda offered to help. I ate, drank another cup of coffee and then excused myself and went to pack. I was fairly good at folding and packing and so thirty minutes and I was done. I wondered out and stood on the balcony that overlooked the town it really was extremely pretty. Rose then appeared in my room.

"Hey, gorgeous. You look organised," she said as she joined me on the terrace.

"Yeah well, the sooner I get this goodbye over with the better," I honestly replied. She looked at me with a slight look of worry.

"I know – I really like Josh and I'm not looking forward to saying goodbye either. I can't believe how much we have in common and how well we get on," she started. "It probably sounds a little stupid I suppose, but I feel like I'm really falling for the guy, which isn't like me at all," she gushed. I laughed at her and she shot me a look of annoyance and so I placed an arm around her.

"It's not stupid – I know exactly how you feel, I've definitely fallen for Ethan," I tried to tell her to put her at ease. She let out a large sigh.

"Oh thank God. I knew that you'd understand."

"Have you told him?" I enquired.

"No – don't want to frighten him, but he has mentioned meeting up again soon which is positive."

"Well, I think that's a great start, Rose. Just take it a day at a time, that's what I intend to do," I smiled and then she hugged me.

"Thanks, Jenny. I really needed to offload these thoughts before I physically burst," she now said, giggling at her confession.

I told her, "Any time," and then we stood and looked at the view of the town below.

After both agreeing that we would miss it here – and not just because of the men that we had become attached to – we were interrupted by Josh who had obviously been looking for her. He saw my packed case and offered to carry it downstairs, which I allowed him to do. I had decided, like the others, to wear shorts while on the yachts and then change before flying. Josh had told us earlier that jeans would be perfectly fine in the restaurant that we were going to if we wished to travel casually and so that had become the plan.

I took my on-board bag, checked that I had everything and then walked out of the room, stopping and glancing around it just once more before closing the door. As I followed Rose down the narrow staircase while she continued to chatter away to Josh in front of her, I sighed heavily – it was the start of things coming to an end, and I wasn't looking forward to it one little bit. When we arrived in the entrance hallway there was a hub of noise and organising and for some reason it made me panic somewhat, so I quietly walked out through the doors that led to the pool while they decided what bags were going where and with who in what cars. I hadn't noticed Ethan yet, and so I knew that I had time to just stop and reflect for a moment.

I walked across to the jasmine shrubs and inhaled the soft scent and then picked just one to take with me. The petals were soft and cool against my hand and as I closed my eyes and inhaled the sweet smell as it sat in my palm I could feel Ethan behind me. His breathing was heavy but calm and his aftershave had now been picked up on the morning's warm breeze. I smiled.

"I'm really going to miss it here," I said as I turned to meet his gaze. "I thought I would take something to remind me of its beauty besides the photographs." I told him as I raised the flower in my hand and showed it to him. He did nothing but pulled me in close to him, and wrapped his arms around me. Then he sighed.

"The only beauty that I am going to miss is right here in my arms," he said and I gave him a huge smile.

"You are quite the charmer, aren't you?" I grinned with a hint of sarcasm.

"I honestly meant that!" he replied sounding a little disheartened that I obviously hadn't thought so, and that he was just being humorous in some way. So I reached up my arm and draped it around his neck and kissed him.

"I know that you don't just say things for effect, it just makes this separation process easier to deal with if I try and find the funny side in things," I tried to explain. He kissed me in return.

"This 'separation' as you call it is only going to be for a short time; I will see you soon," he insisted with conviction.

"You sound very sure about that, but you have lots of business to attend to," I reminded him.

"Well, it's not going to stop me from seeing you if you are worried about that, I promise." And I knew that he meant it. He was as desperate for us to get back together as I was and that made me exceptionally happy.

He put his arm around my shoulder and then walked with me back indoors. The others, it would seem, had now all but finished packing the cars up and were laughing about the whole week and some of the funnier points. We all chatted to the staff and told them that they had exceeded all of our expectations and that the 'trial week' had been out of this world. The manager seemed overwhelmed at our thanks and as we said our goodbyes and started to walk across the courtyard, Ethan quickly had a conversation with him and then shook his hand. I was glad to see that Ethan seemed as pleased at the service we had received as we all were – I am sure he must have been very proud of what he had achieved here.

The drive down the coastal road found us all fairly quiet. I think that everyone was sad to be leaving, and I was sure that the other car would be the same. Amanda and Rafael had chosen to travel with us including on the yacht – she made it quite clear that she didn't want to be stuck on the 'love boat' for the day, as she knew exactly what the others would be up to and it made it awkward for both her and Rafael. Having them with us, I decided, would be a good distraction from wallowing about the departure and so I happily agreed after checking with Ethan first.

As expected, when we arrived at the bay the yachts were moored one behind the other and stewards were ready to help with the bags. Two men then walked across to Josh and he spoke with them, signed some documents and then handed his car key over. Attention to detail was still second to none; Josh had everyone perfectly organised and on cue and I was still impressed at how smoothly things ran when he was in control.

"Is he always this efficient?" I stated while looking at Josh but aiming the question at Ethan. He answered in a cool crisp tone.

"Always – that's why I like him working for me." Ethan stepped out of the car and then walked across and handed his key over too.

As the rest of us exited the car and then made our way with only hand luggage toward the yachts, Ethan came back over to me and we walked behind Rafael and Amanda. He wrapped his arm around my waist, and I smiled at his almost protective gestures. Amanda turned and looked at us as everyone started to make their way onto the yachts. She gave me a look of concern that she dare not tell the others that they were sailing with us, so to put her out of her obvious nervous misery I shouted across to them.

"Hey, Amanda and Rafael are going to sail with us – you know, even the passengers out just a bit," I explained.

They all nodded and seemed happy with the

suggestion. I think knowing that they could do whatever they wanted probably had them happier than they were letting on. Amanda gave me a look of relief and then mimed the words, "Thank you," before turning back to make her way up on to the yacht. Ethan leant in and whispered into my ear.

"It's nice to have guests on board, but it means that I don't have you to myself." He sounded just a little saddened at that, but reminiscing about the trip here I knew why he felt that way.

"Well, I am planning on changing later – I will have to use your room and possibly shower," I replied giving him a very lustful look. He returned a searing sexy look.

"You're on – just give me the nod and I am all yours," he winked, looking happy at the suggestion.

I then whispered back, "It's kind of a turn on, don't you think? Knowing that others are on board and we could be up to very naughty things?" I knew that I had a glint in my eye. He laughed lightly and then shook his head.

"You are highly addictive, young lady, and you have some wicked thoughts in that head – but I am enjoying every single one of them!" he grinned. Then he tapped me on the buttock and told me to get on board.

I loved the cheeky playful side of him that he allowed me to see – along with his cool crisp business demeanour, the combination was quite intoxicating and also very addictive. I simply couldn't get enough of him.

On board there was tea and champagne along with fresh fruit. We were told that lunch would be served at approximately twelve o'clock and that suited me perfectly. The men kicked back and put their feet up and Amanda and I sat chattering about the whole holiday. She too, it would seem, had enjoyed every minute. I hinted that I was sorry that the rest of us had hooked up, but she really didn't seem to mind and admitted that even though she hadn't expected to, she had missed Gerry, particularly after talking to him last night before dinner.

Ethan kept refilling our glasses and after around forty minutes of sailing he pulled me into his side and wrapped his arm around me. I looked across at Amanda and she just commented how cosy we both looked. Ethan carried on talking to Rafael not acknowledging her remark, but I was cosy and I told her that I was perfectly happy right where I was. When the stewards announced that lunch had been served on the upper deck, we all moved to the table where it had been laid out and boy, oh boy was it spectacular. Lobster and shrimp were the main focal point and they looked delicious, along with salads and rice dishes – I was salivating already. I did wonder if Ethan had requested fish knowing that it was one of my favourite things. If he had thought ahead I was touched by the fact that he had selected my probable choice.

Both Amanda and I made sure that we drank plenty of water as we didn't want to be too merry by the time we boarded the plane. We were also bearing in mind that we may want a glass of wine with dinner, so it seemed the most sensible thing to do. We did highlight the fact that Rose and Amanda probably hadn't thought that far ahead, but they would have to deal with that issue later. Lunch was highly satisfying – the quality was first rate and as I sat and held my now contently full stomach I looked across at Amanda.

"Lunch and dinner back home after this is going to be miserable."

"Damn right – plain old egg and chips or salad just doesn't quite cut it, does it?" she remarked and I laughed at her.

After resting from lunch and chatting with the men too, we decided to chill in the sun and relax for a while. Hernando had suggested the long way around the island which was due to take some time yet, and so I was happy at the chance to just switch off. Ethan had joined us along with Rafael and he took the sun lounger next to mine. Even though they continued talking about work and other business-related matters Ethan reached across and took my hand in his, resting it on my hip. I smiled to myself, I loved his touch in any form and this was just perfect.

Amanda started to overheat a little and went to sit in the shade, so Rafael challenged her to a game of chess hoping that she had now mastered the rules. Hearing them laugh and mock each other was delightful; they did seem to have become great friends. I rolled onto my side and looked behind me at them; this holiday had simply been a great escape for all of us. Ethan turned and looked at me.

"What are you smiling at?" he enquired.

"The fact that those two get on so well – no sex involved either!" I remarked sarcastically.

"Yes, well he did tell me last night briefly that he thought Amanda was a very charming, intelligent and fun person to be around."

"Really? Oh, she would be really happy to know that."

"Well, you can tell her on your way back. May be something to make her smile if she isn't looking forward to going back to her normal life," he then said. I rolled back onto my back.

"She may complain about Gerry, but I know deep down she loves him dearly," I said. He reached across and grabbed my sun lounger and pulled it closer to his.

"I have the strong need to kiss you right now," he then said smiling and he rolled on to his side now that I was closer and I did the same.

Our lips touching was like an electricity surge, and as we sank into a deep and longing kiss I knew that I wasn't going to be able to let the day go by without having him completely again. The timing right now wouldn't be appropriate but it was definitely going to be included in my day somehow. I hinted at Ethan that these were my thoughts and he agreed, stating that he was somewhat turned on right now. I found it highly enjoyable insisting that he would have to wait – something that I think Ethan was not used to hearing. Everyone that he came across business-wise jumped to attention and did exactly what he wanted with no waiting involved, and when he scowled at me a little I found I couldn't do anything but laugh at him.

"You really enjoy being in control, don't you?" he said with a hint of frustration. I thought about it for a minute and then replied.

"I didn't think it was in me, but actually when it involves you, I find it highly satisfying that I can resist for a while!" I smirked. I think he was surprised at my response but nodded.

"Well, I would be highly satisfied to just let you take control completely. I find it both stimulating and very sexy watching you," he replied confidently and with that remark he had immediately turned the tables on me – I was now desperate to have him and as he grinned at me and my response, I knew that was probably his intention all along.

We had afternoon tea and cakes as before, and when the stewardess informed us that we would be mooring at our intended destination at around five o'clock, it gave us an hour to sort ourselves out, shower and get ready to disembark. It was at this point after finishing my tea that I looked at Ethan and could wait no longer. He looked across at me and I gave him that 'I'm ready to have you all to myself' look, and he knew instantly what I meant. I made my excuses to go and shower before dinner and the flight, and get changed. Ethan suggested he should do the same. Amanda asked if she could use one of the other rooms, which of course Ethan was happy about. So as we all started to make our way below decks I could feel my body responding instantly to the anticipated time alone with Ethan.

I went into his room first and walked straight to the bathroom, quickly stripped off my shorts and bikini underneath and then while he locked the door and was still talking to me – I walked out and leaned against the bathroom door jamb, completely naked and trying my best at looking sultry. When he turned back and saw me, he stopped talking instantly, gave me the biggest smile and as he glided across the floor stripping his t-shirt off as he moved, he said nothing but simply scooped me up in his arms and started kissing me.

As he moved to my neck he whispered, "You are so sexy, confident and hot – I need to satisfy that lustful look you have and give you something to remember for the rest of the day." He said it in the horniest and sex god-like way. I was panting and desperate now. He had an intense desperation about him, still sensual and still considerate to my every need, but I liked this hot needy passion that he was exuding.

He carried me to the bathroom marble counter and lowered my buttocks onto it which made my hot body jump as the coolness touched my skin. I unfastened his shorts and let them drop to the floor, pushing his boxers down with my hands and then my feet. He stepped out of them and kicked them to the side. We were kissing, our hands were gently exploring and when I leant and sucked on his nipple he let out a small but sexy whimper. I was into this whole needy and desperate passion, which was heating me internally to a whole new level. He slid me down to my feet and then turned me away from him. Scooping my hair from my neck he kissed it and then parted my legs slightly. I reached out my hands and held onto the rim of each sink knowing that I would have to steady myself and then as we watched each other intently in the mirror, he entered me deeply and I groaned at the sheer pleasure.

I slid his hands to my breasts and made sure that he took in the full experience of having my body for himself. He then turned me and lifted me to his waist and after leaning me against the tiled wall for a few moments taking a minute to just slow things down, he held me tight and lowered himself to his knees still holding me and then lay me on my back on the warmth of the fluffy bath mat and then continued his hot and passionate love making. I writhed underneath him feeling my climax build and then he whispered in my ear: "Give me everything you have – I want it all!" And that was it, all the encouragement I needed. I couldn't help myself I let out a small cry and as I let it spiral out of control and then start to come down I looked into his eyes, pulsing and desperate I reiterated the comment to him; "I need everything from you too, let me have it!" I said this as I pulled his head to mine and kissed him. He carried on with two maybe three more thrusts and then he gave in to his climax and collapsed on me both still pulsing. We lay there hot, sweaty, panting like we had just run a marathon. I pulled him tight to me and held him as he did me.

"Jesus – I think that has to be the most intense we have been yet," he remarked and I laughed lightly at his comment. "Was that too much for you? Was I a little forceful?" he then asked as he looked at me.

"Are you kidding me?" I was still panting. "That was… amazing – more than amazing, I actually have no words to describe it," I started. "No, you weren't forceful and I did entice you first," I then reminded him.

"Well, how do you expect me to react when you stand

there naked looking so hot and wanting?" he smiled questioning me before kissing me.

"I like you needy and desperate for me," I told him and he smiled.

"I have never, nor do I want to behave that way with anyone else – ever," he then said sincerely and I knew he meant it.

"I hope not, because I know that I have never, nor do I want to give myself to anyone else like that," I then repeated and he smiled. I carried on, "Well, thank you – I won't be forgetting that in a hurry. Great thing to recall for the rest of the day." I smiled at him and he laughed.

"Well where you are concerned – I aim to please."

"Oh – you definitely did that, and more," I replied. He knelt up and then pulled me into his lap and hugged me tightly. "I have fallen for you so deeply and so quickly," I then whispered and he squeezed me tightly and whispered back.

"… and I you." He squeezed me tighter then carried on. "I should hope so young lady after that remarkably hot and steamy session!" he had a hint of sarcasm in his voice and so I kissed him on the cheek and stood giving him my hand to help him up.

We turned on the shower and took our last one together for now. He remarked that his legs were like jelly and his head slightly light, which made me feel quite happy that we had fulfilled each other so completely and I confirmed that my head was in the same place. We had opened ourselves up to each other in a way that I now took for granted. Ethan was so different with me from the first time we met, he was relaxed and comfortable being around me and I loved seeing him this way. More importantly to me though, I was back – me – living and enjoying life, and I've actually really missed me!

Chapter 20

By the time I had dried my hair and changed into jeans the yacht had come to a complete stop. Ethan carried my case up on deck, but before we left his room he gave me the biggest hug and kissed me tenderly. I knew that I would be seeing more of him soon, but the fact that he kept wanting to hold me made me feel extremely important to him. We met with the others on the jetty and I didn't even ask what the plan was as I knew that Josh would have it timed to perfection – I was correct. We jumped into the waiting cars and then drove to another large hotel and stopped outside. We left the suitcases in the car and entered through the main door.

Josh explained that this hotel, although not as elaborate as some others, had an amazing restaurant. It was nice to be a little more relaxed and the menu was quite extensive with a great selection. I changed my mind this evening and decided that I didn't want fish – I opted for pork with pears. We didn't go to the extreme of having starters; the meal was intended as a something to fill us before our flight or travel plans. When coffee arrived Rafael said that he would have to make a move back to the airport as his flight was an hour earlier than ours. The airport wasn't far and he insisted on getting a taxi so when he stood to say

341

his goodbyes it seemed appropriate to stand and bid him farewell properly.

He shook hands with the men first and gave Ethan a large handshake followed by a man hug with a large patting of each other's back – they obviously had a huge amount of respect for each other. Then he moved around the table and went first to Rose;

"What a pleasure it has been to meet you ladies," he started as he gave her a kiss on both cheeks followed by a large hug.

"It has been lovely meeting you too, Rafael. Let's hope we can meet another time," Rose replied as he nodded and moved on to Beth. She happily gave him a bear hug and he laughed before then kissing her too.

When he reached me he gave me a longer hug and whispered in my ear, "I've not seen him this happy in years, look after him for me!"

I looked at him and smiled then nodded and kissed both his cheeks and simply said, "I will." I noted that Ethan heard my reply and looked at me inquisitively. Then he moved to Amanda and took both of her hands in his.

"Amanda, it has been my absolute pleasure to spend time with you. You have made me laugh until my sides hurt and I have enjoyed teaching you the finer ways to relax through chess and cards. I think that I will be glad of the rest from drinking though, it has to be said." He smiled and then he kissed her on each cheek and hugged her too.

"Well, thank you, Rafael, for being my sidekick for the week – watching you fall asleep at the table while we beat you at drinking was the highlight for me." Amanda joked with him. He started laughing.

"Well, I would have to say that was very unsocial of me, but the fact that you later repaid me by trying to put your whole tongue down my throat made up for it I would say!" he mocked her. They were like old friends. She hit his arm and laughed then kissed him on the cheek again. Josh, Ethan and Hernando found it highly amusing.

"Alright. Point taken. Please don't tell your wife." Amanda then said to shut them all up. Rafael laughed, noting he wanted to retain his testicles. Josh went with him to retrieve his bag from the car and as he walked out he turned and waved to us all, then he left and it suddenly felt very sad. We were all going our separate ways.

After another coffee and as it was now eight o'clock, Ethan suggested that we should start to make our way to the airport. He had told Josh to wait with Hernando while he did the round trip and they seemed happy with that request. Amanda and I kissed both of them and thanked them numerous times for a fantastic week. Josh commented that it had been the best week that he had indulged in for years and he was really pleased that we had all met. We then realised that Beth and Rose wanted a little time together with them to say goodbye properly, and as we were sat in a quiet corner we walked with Ethan to the stairs that exited the restaurant and waited for a few minutes.

I glanced back at them, Rose was intimately kissing Josh and he squeezed her tightly afterwards and as they spoke quietly to each other and smiled – I had the strong suspicion that they would be seeing more of each other too. Beth on the other hand was simply devouring Hernando one last time. When she finished and after running her fingers through his hair messily – he looked like he had just escaped a gale force wind. Gasping for breath and dishevelled he looked a little spaced out for a moment – Beth seemed to have that effect on men. As they made their way over to us, Hernando ran over to Amanda and me and kissed us on the cheek again.

"Ladies, if you ever want to travel in style and by yacht, please do give me a call – it would be my pleasure," he offered and we all agreed that we wouldn't hesitate to call him should we need such luxury travel.

We went to the car where Josh had already made sure that all of our bags were in the boot. Ethan double checked with us before we set off and then we started the journey to the airport. My stomach was tying itself up in knots, and I must have looked anxious, because as the girls sat chatting in the back of the car, Ethan reached across and took hold of my hand. I looked at him and smiled grateful for his reassurance. He gently rubbed his thumb across my knuckles and it did ease my nerves a little, I wrapped my other hand around the top of his and rubbed his hand in return.

As the airport came into view and he parked in the car park, the girls started to exit the car. I took a deep breath and then blew it out and did the same again. Ethan looked at me; "It's going to be alright, Jenny, just think of this as a short business trip for me," he tried to convince me and I realised that I was being a little bit of a drama queen.

344

I agreed and got out of the car – the others had already taken the bags out of the boot.

They walked in front happily chatting and giving me time alone with Ethan. He had picked up my bag and dragged it while we walked with his other arm tightly around my waist. We just kept looking at each other and then the girls in front and then at each other again. When we got inside the terminal building they stopped and waited for us to catch up. Then they all came over and threw their arms around Ethan and I stepped back and laughed at him – he looked just a tad overwhelmed at their compliments and continual praising for a fantastic week at his hotel. After some time they stepped back and one by one in a more serious nature they kissed him on his cheek and said that it was the best holiday that they had experienced in a very long time and they were extremely grateful for his hospitality. Rose made a point of saying that she would love to sell holidays to his hotels as exclusive luxury and that she would be in touch with Josh to sort out finer details, which Ethan seemed happy about. They all then made their excuses and started walking toward the board that declared the check-in desks and left us alone.

"Come here," he simply said as he pulled me close to him. As I held onto his waist under his jacket he ran his fingers around my hairline and tucked it gently on both sides behind my ears, then he smiled at me and with his hands on my face he kissed me tenderly. I melted again… It was another one of those kisses that left you slightly light-headed, breathless and wanting more.

When we parted he rested his forehead against mine, and as I looked at him I couldn't help it – I let a small tear escape my right eye. He sighed and wiped it away. "Hey, don't do that. This isn't the end, it's just going to be a bit strange for a while until we can see each other again," he finished as he pressed his lips against mine taking my breath away for a moment. A good way to stop me crying!

"I know, I'm being silly – I wasn't expecting to be so pathetic," I remarked at my ridiculous reaction. He smiled at me which was not what I was anticipating.

"It's not silly – it's actually quite touching." He smiled and then I laughed as he had somehow eased the situation. So I sucked in a deep breath and then looked into his eyes.

"I have had the most amazing two weeks, and this last one has been simply out of this world. I can't believe that I have managed to meet someone like you," I told him and then carried on before I got teary again. "So you better make sure that I see you soon, because I'm getting withdrawal symptoms already!" I finished as I poked him in his chest and he laughed lightly.

"That's more like it – I want smiles not tears. This is just as hard for me, I'm pining already behind this hard exterior," he honestly replied. I rubbed his chest.

"But I like your hard exterior." I joked, so he pulled me close and hugged me tightly laughing.

"Yes, I think that we've established that this week!" he mocked me and so I laughed too. "Promise me that you will stay in touch with me daily?" he requested.

"You know that I will. I just feel like someone is going

to wake me up in a minute and tell me that this was all a dream," I truthfully told him.

"It's not a dream, honey, and I will make sure that I conclude business as soon as I can so that I can see you," he replied and I realised that he was going to miss me just as much as I him. "Anyway, for the record, I consider myself to be the lucky one for finding someone like you," he then said and I threw my arms around his neck and kissed him again.

I knew that I had to leave him and so I stepped back from our embrace and I reached into my bag and pulled out the letter. He looked at it as I ran my hand over his name written across the front; I smiled and then placed it in his inside pocket. "What's that?" he asked me with reservation. I smiled feeling glad that I had written it.

"A little bedtime reading for you tonight," I said not telling him anything more. He looked even more curiously at me. I pulled the handle up on my suitcase.

"Intriguing!" he smiled and then I pecked him on the lips and said goodbye. "Have a safe flight, and let me know when you land," He said, and as our fingers disconnected I nodded.

"I miss you already," I mumbled before I turned and walked toward the girls who were now all looking at me like doe-eyed teenagers, while embarrassingly miming gestures of sympathy. As I reached them they threw their arms around me in consolation and started to walk me toward the desk for check-in. I turned just once and he gave me a nervous smile and then waved and turned to leave.

That was it. He was gone, and I suddenly felt like I was in a bubble. All the noise around me seemed to mute as I let my head and my heart take in the fact that I was actually going home without him. When I felt someone tugging on my arm I snapped back into reality; it was Rose, asking for my passport, and as I handed it over I tried to act bravely and smiled at the others, who were now starting to complain about feeling tired with the week catching up on them.

Once checked in we sat quietly while we had coffee in a small café. As we sipped the comforting hot beverage, feeling tired and reminiscing about the last two weeks; I think that it was safe to say that we were all a little fed up that it had ended.

"Bloody hell, look at the state of us. We've just had the best two weeks in a long time and we look like we've had the worst!" Beth suddenly said. We all looked at each other and then agreed as she concluded with "God I know what it feels like to be a porn star now after those numerous sex sessions… that I've actually lost count of – my lady bits need a rest," she grimaced as she squirmed on her seat. It had us all laughing hysterically in seconds, Beth always knew how to break an uncomfortable atmosphere. She laughed too; "I don't know what you two are laughing at – you can't be far behind me!" she then pointed a finger at both Rose and me. I didn't comment and neither did Rose apart from her obvious confirmation that she too had lost count of how many times. Amanda found it highly amusing being the observer.

We sat and recalled the highlights of the holiday,

along with the spectacular scenery and injuries incurred. It really had simply been amazing. I looked at Rose who looked lost in thought;

"So when are you seeing Josh again?" I asked. She looked up quickly at me and tried to act cool.

"Who said that I'm going to see him again?" she innocently asked and we all sighed at her remark.

"Seriously – you're going to try the innocent *'I'm fine'* routine with us? We could see how you looked at him," Amanda chipped in. Beth gave her a look of confirmation that's what we all thought and then she crossed her arms.

"It's alright, Rose – we wouldn't blame you if you wanted to," I tried to reassure her and then she let it all gush out;

"I really like the guy, in fact I think I'm falling for the guy. I never do this, I don't get attached, I want to see him again, but should I? Oh God, what do I do?" she rambled and Beth just laughed more at her.

"I'd say that someone is definitely smitten and in love!" she concluded, and Amanda and I didn't say anything but nodded in agreement. She looked at us all for a minute and then continued.

"I asked Jenny this… Is that even possible after two weeks? In fact, it isn't even two weeks, is it?" she carried on flapping.

"Well that was a stupid thing to do anyway. Why are you asking Miss Loved-Up here? She's well and truly fallen for Ethan – hook, line and sinker. Think her answer is likely to be a little biased," Amanda threw in. I scowled at her.

"On a plus, they are really handsome guys, and their bodies are… well… phew, I don't blame you," Beth then added before sipping more coffee. Rose laughed at her.

"Well, I'm glad that you agree. I have no complaints there. I just love his personality and he's funny and intelligent and kind and generous…" She realised that she was sounding love-struck and so she stopped. "Oh crap, I am in love, aren't I?" she asked us all. We sat back, nodded, and then carried on drinking coffee as it sank into her head now that she had heard herself say it out loud and let herself believe it. Her expression was priceless!

"Anyway, Beth, it's not like Hernando wasn't good-looking with a good body," I added trying to point out that she had enjoyed an active couple of weeks.

"Yeah, but our age difference always meant that it was just fun. We even talked about it," she told us. I was surprised.

"And that didn't bother you? That it was only ever a holiday fling?" I queried.

"Hell no – I don't want anything serious, you know that. Anyway, he said we can hook up if I'm ever out here again, and if I can have a few like him to occupy me for a few years I'll be more than happy," she finished smiling.

"I love your honesty, Beth," Amanda said as she patted her on the arm. Rose stood and checked the board, then came back.

"I reckon we can board in twenty minutes; shall we make our way to the gate and then snooze for a little while?" she asked us, and suddenly that suggestion was very appealing. I was tired too, and really just wanted to get back home now as soon as possible.

We slowly marched to the gate found some seats and plonked ourselves down. Most nights at this time over the last week we were engaged in great conversation, eating amazing food and drinking wine. Why we were so tired I wasn't sure – most likely end of holiday blues. I sat there for a few minutes and found that I couldn't snooze like the others; there was too much noise going on around us. I reached into my bag for my book, but paused for a second when I saw that my phone was lit up. I pulled it out thinking it was probably one of my boys replying from my earlier text. It made me smile even more when I realised I had three messages – James, Mark and Ethan – the three most important men in my life right now! I read the boys' texts first which were sweet and then opened Ethan's:

'That was the longest drive ever from the airport. I don't think I'm going to sleep tonight in an empty bed. We're staying on the yacht until tomorrow late morning then we fly out to Italy. I used to like the solitude, but I'm wandering around here feeling lost without you keeping me company. Josh says I'm like a lovesick teenager – he's just as bad though. I've placed your letter on my bed, I feel nervous looking at it but I promise to read it before you land. Please keep in touch – I'm missing you immensely already. Ethan X'

I held my phone to my chest, took a deep breath and then grinned from ear to ear, feeling grateful that he had sent me a message so soon. I quickly started to reply – my excitable fingers wouldn't type fast enough:

'*Ethan – I am so close to walking out of this airport and getting a taxi back to you. I know how you feel – I feel lost without you too. The girls have said the same about me and Rose being love-struck, so rest easy; I'm getting the same torment! Don't worry about the letter – I'm hoping it will make you smile, like your text has just done for me. I'm not going to sleep on the plane either, I feel restless and I haven't even boarded yet. I will be in touch when we land and first thing tomorrow, after I have slept, I will definitely make sure I call you before you fly. I miss you immensely... Jenny X*'

I hit send and then held it for a moment forgetting about the book, which suddenly seemed insignificant and not as enticing as receiving messages from Ethan. I realised that I was squeezing the phone like it would console me if it could. It was the closest thing I had to him right now, and obviously this was my comforting response. Then it pinged again making me jump.

'*You've just made me smile. I look forward to hearing from you later – whatever the time. I just want to know that you arrived safely back so please text me, honey. I'm going to shower now – alone – have a drink with Josh and then climb into my bed – alone... This is really hard... I'm counting the days from now until I can see you. Sending you my love – Ethan X*'

I let out a small whoop of delight when I read that, then when Beth half opened her eye and looked at me, she smiled and closed them again shaking her head in acknowledgement that she realised what had delighted me.

'I will let you know, I promise… And this is hard, but it's not forever. Try to get some sleep and I will speak to you soon. Sending you my love – Jenny X – PS I love you calling me 'honey'. Pleasant dreams, handsome – night for now.'

I thought that was the last one – but he sent one more surprise and it amused me, as I never would have thought that Ethan could be so distracted from his business after the first time I had met him properly, but it seemed that he was as addicted to me as I was him:

'Night, honey! X'

As I suspected, the flight seemed long, uncomfortable and noisy. Usually the engines would lull me to sleep, but as I lay there on my side with a pillow and a blanket, I just found myself wide awake wondering what he was doing without me. Then I remembered the letter – surely he would have read it by now? What would he think? Was I a little too honest? *Give over,* I told myself, I was good at torturing myself with silly thoughts. He had after all declared that he was missing me: he would love the letter, I convinced myself. As thoughts of my week ran through my head, I found that I snoozed for a little while but for no longer than forty-five minutes. I then sat up and decided to go to the bathroom. Luckily I had sat in the aisle this time, so I was not worried about waking anyone. When I exited I stretched as there was more room. The stewardess came over to me;

"Are you alright, madam?" she asked.

"Can't sleep," I whispered back.

She in turn leant in and whispered in my ear. "Would you like a drink to help?"

I thought about that for a minute and then decided a good swig of brandy would be delightful. "Yes, please – brandy would be good." I smiled and she nodded and asked that I return to my seat.

No sooner had I refastened my seat belt when she was back at the side of me – she asked if I wanted ice, which I didn't. Then she handed me two small bottles and a glass, winked at me and then went back to where she had been sat a few moments ago. I thanked her by miming the words, poured myself the first one and then took a long sip. It was remarkably medicinal, and as the warmth of it heated my gullet I leaned back in my chair and sighed. I did doze for a little longer after the lovely soothing drink that had definitely helped me relax. The others were fast asleep with Beth snoring slightly which had amused me along with her obvious drooling.

When the pilot announced that we were descending toward the airport and the lights came on, I wasn't surprised that I was alert instantly. It wasn't like I had managed to get any really deep sleep. Beth yawned and then wiped her chin, realising that she probably hadn't looked the most refined during her sleep. I chuckled to myself and then Amanda rubbed my arm and asked if I had slept.

"Not really, couldn't switch off." I looked at my watch.

"Well it is a ridiculous hour, isn't it." she remarked as she looked at hers. I nodded in agreement.

I estimated that by the time we had taxied in and retrieved our bags it would likely be around two in the morning. I sat back into my upright chair and then rubbed my face. I just wanted to get into my bed, curl up and switch off for a couple of hours, while I got my head around being back home. Rose caught my eye and smiled at me; I can only imagine that she was feeling the same as me from leaving Josh behind. It really wasn't a very nice feeling.

The ramp tunnel to the plane that led back to the airport seemed to take forever to attach. Once the door opened though we got a quick blast of the cool morning air, which woke us all up very quickly. We were only three rows from the front and first to disembark, so we made our way quite steadily to the carousel to sit and wait for the bags to arrive. Much to my delight there was a small vending machine that had fresh orange juice and the thought of it made my mouth start to salivate after the brandy, so I offered to get us all one which seemed to help with the waiting around. I did as I had been asked once sat with orange in hand and turned my phone on to let Ethan know that we had landed. I was surprised to find three messages from him. The first at eleven thirty which read:

'Time for some sleep hopefully. I hope your flight is comfortable. I am going to read your letter now. X' I read the next one which was ten minutes later: 'It's been a long time, Jenny, since I felt almost reduced to tears! I'm touched by your honesty. It has given me a warmth in my heart that I have not experienced before. Let me tell you that your words are reciprocated – I nearly packed a bag and came after you after reading this letter, I'm so restless and want to hold you. It will stay close with me as the scent of your perfume lingers – it is comforting. I am so in love with you, Jenny – I hope that you know that? X' I was now smiling to myself. Thank goodness he had liked it. I sighed with contentment. His last one was at one thirty: 'Your letter is under my pillow, but your perfume is keeping me awake – not as comforting as I originally thought! I cannot stop thinking about you. Until I see you again I am going to be harshly tormented. I cannot wait to hear your voice again soon. X'

I happily started to text him back even though it was now two fifteen.

'My dearest Ethan, we landed safely – if it is any consolation I have not slept a wink either on the flight for thinking about you. I am glad that you liked the letter and I did mean every word. I do love you too, and I cannot wait to hear your voice as I miss you greatly after such a short time being apart. All of this hardly seems real! I will call you later this morning. I am sorry if my spritz

of perfume is torturing you, but in some ways I do like it
;-) Try to sleep well. I hope to get home and do the same.
Hope I haven't woken you again! Your Jenny X'

When the carousel sounded and the belt started turning a number of passengers let out a small cheer. It wasn't really the best place to be hanging around at this time in the morning. Once we all had our bags, (and we managed to get ours pretty quickly) we made our way outside. We all had pre-arranged taxis even though we didn't live a ridiculous way from each other, we had decided before going on holiday that landing at this time would mean we just wanted to get home ASAP. Rose had pointed out that hers was running late though after a text came through. As we exited the doors at arrivals both Amanda and Beth's drivers were waiting, so we made our way together to meet them. The drivers seemed keen to get off and so we all hugged each other. We were tired but it didn't stop us from stating that we had waited far too long to go away together and as we thanked Rose for all of her hard work organising and kissed each other on the cheek. We quickly discussed the possibility of dinner one night next week as we started to part ways. Amanda and Beth said they would call us as they started to follow their drivers, looking ready for their beds, and it made me start to look around for our ride home. I leant against Rose.

"I need my bed," I stated.

Rose looked at me and then answered, "Me too, although it's going to be very empty tonight," she sighed. I placed my arm around her shoulders and pulled her close.

"I know what you mean – mine too. You could always stay at mine and go home tomorrow, if you like?" I then suggested as I spotted someone waving a card with my name on it. I pointed him out to her.

"You know what? I will, Jen, if that's alright? Let me text this driver back – he's bloody late anyway – and I'll come with you," she replied with annoyance, and then we grabbed our bags and pulled them arm in arm as we followed our driver.

"Has he contacted you yet?" she asked me and I answered quickly.

"Three messages at various times. Think he's missing me, but he says that Josh has been just as bad since you left," I then pointed out to her. I wasn't sure whether to tell her in front of the others what Ethan had told me. She smiled at the knowledge.

"Well, that's good to know, I suppose. Yes, he's text me twice saying that he is missing me a great deal," she started. "How bloody lucky have we been meeting those two? Wouldn't it be great if we can keep them, especially with them working together? We can travel out to meet them." she grinned. I hadn't really thought about that.

"Yeah, actually that would be really nice."

We managed to stay awake during the trip home even though we were quiet. When we reached my house we abandoned the bags in the hallway and marched straight upstairs. I didn't want to be alone so I dragged her into my room and we shared my new bed. It was a nice feeling just knowing that someone was there, and drifting off became no problem at all.

Chapter 21

When I woke the next morning and rolled over to find Rose there it was both comforting and slightly strange, as it wasn't Ethan. However, the fact that she knew how I would feel this morning was consolation enough. When I looked at my watch it was already nine o'clock – I reached for my mobile on my bedside table and looked at it, happy to find another message from him:

'Morning, honey. I hope that you slept well, I did not! Getting ready to go to the airport, I wish that my destination was Manchester though. I hope to hear from you before I fly. Love Ethan X'

I smiled to myself as Rose opened her eyes and glared at me. She groaned at the fact that she obviously had not had enough sleep and it was still relatively early. I pointed my phone in her direction and mimed, "Ethan," and she smiled and then reached for hers.

After looking at the screen she then mimed back, "Josh," as she turned her phone toward me and then we both laughed at each other.

"Ah bless him," she said as she read her message. "He

wants me back in his arms, didn't feel the same waking up without me." She started texting back.

"God, I'm missing him so much already. This is ridiculous," I stated. Rose hit send and then turned to me.

"It's not ridiculous, Jenny, it's a great feeling. I've certainly not felt like this about a guy before that's for sure," she said as her phone beeped. Then she laughed. "Josh doesn't know whether to feel jealous or turned on that we slept in the same bed last night!" she said and I grimaced a bit.

"Not the latter I hope," I scowled.

"Have you replied to Ethan yet?"

"Just about to," I smiled as I started to type.

'Good morning, handsome. What a lovely message to wake up to. I slept quite well, but I missed you being here. I think having Rose sleep with me was comforting – but I only slept better than I expected due to sheer exhaustion. What time are you flying?'

I didn't have to wait long before my phone pinged to highlight that I had a new message.

'Good morning – I am glad that Rose stayed with you last night. I do wish it was me in that bed with you, though. My departure time is one thirty, so I am leaving here at around eleven to get to the airport in good time. I really hope to speak to you before I fly. Call me, Ethan X.'

I sat up, trying to wake myself properly as I didn't have long before he would be travelling they were an hour ahead of us, and I wanted to speak to him as soon as possible. I replied while Rose did the same to Josh.

'Just going to wake myself up in the shower, I will call you in twenty minutes!' X.

My phone almost pinged immediately.

'Well – thanks for that information, a little more torment for me to endure.'

I laughed softly to myself.

I threw the covers back and waltzed down the corridor to the bathroom. Somehow the warm shower spray didn't have the same effect as the blissful one at The Gessami Residence, but I closed my eyes and tried to reminisce. I realised that it wasn't just the shower itself, but the absence of Ethan sharing it that was the problem. I dried as quickly as possible, dressed and then went to get my phone. Rose was still lying in bed texting Josh and so I told her I was going to put the kettle on. When I reached my kitchen island I scrolled quickly and found his number and pressed to call. My heart was in my throat and butterflies circled in the pit of my stomach. I was so nervous, but he answered on the second ring.

"Hey, I'm so glad that you called me," he instantly said before I even spoke, and that voice of his that was like pure, smooth music to my ears stilled those nerves instantly.

"Hi, I'm glad too that I got to speak to you before you

fly. I've missed you so much already," I replied honestly. I could tell that he was smiling when he replied;

"I've missed you too. Work just seems so unsatisfying at the moment. I can't seem to motivate myself and kick my head into gear." I laughed lightly to myself loving the fact that I was on his mind.

"Hey – you're a businessman first and foremost, Ethan, and I need you to be focused so that you can get your work finalised and then speedily bring yourself back to me," I started. "I've already been trying to work out whether I could get a flight and meet you half way," I informed him.

"There will be no need to do that, Jenny. I can assure you that as soon as my business is concluded I shall be making my way back to the UK. Thank you though, for understanding and trying to fix my obsessive compulsive 'you' disorder!" he mocked himself. "I shall try to get my brain re-organised and get this work finished and out of the way."

"I'm very glad to hear that," I answered in my sexiest voice. "How's Josh? Rose is seriously missing him too," I told him. He laughed, which made me smile.

"She's not alone – he's got a very brave face, but under that façade I know that he's missing her too. I seriously do not know what type of bewitchment you two possess, but you've certainly enchanted the both of us," he said and I instantly felt like I was glowing.

"That was a sweet thing to say, but I really don't think that you are giving yourselves any credit here. We consider ourselves to be the lucky ones – we don't know quite what we did to be so fortunate finding you both, but we're certainly very grateful," I tried to convince him. He was silent for a second and then spoke softly;

"I've got to go in a minute, I need to get this flight."

"I know, will you text me when you land?"

"Try and stop me." he said. Then he coughed and changed his tone. "I hope that you have a good day," he finished; he sounded a little sad.

"It's going to be difficult with you not around for me to share it with, but I'll give it my best shot," I tried to joke, but I wasn't as successful as I hoped. Then Rose appeared at the side of me. "So, have a safe flight – I'll look forward to speaking to you soon," I finished miming to Rose that I was talking to him.

"Yes, hopefully it will be a fairly straight forward trip, but I shall look forward to being in touch soon." Then I heard Josh in the background asking if he was ready.

"Take care then, say hello to Josh for me – and try not to get into any mischief without us," I insisted in my most confident voice.

"Yeah, I'll second that – both of you behave!" Rose shouted down my phone and then I heard him laugh a couple of times.

"You both have nothing to worry about there – it's all going to be very boring and business only, I assure you," he confirmed. He paused a minute, "Saying goodbye last night was hard, but at least I could physically see you." I had to try to change the negativity as it was killing me.

"Look at it positively – you're now one day nearer to seeing me again," I tried to persuade him.

"Agreed," he confidently replied after a second or two. "So I'll catch up with you later?"

"Yes you will, we'll speak soon. Try to have a good day, Ethan."

"You too – until later then," he finished and I repeated his words.

"Until later." Then we hung up.

Even though I desperately didn't want the call to end, I was pleased that we had spoken and Rose it seemed recognised my slight disappointment. She gave me a hug.

"Look at the state of us – they've turned us into mush!" she joked. "Let's get the kettle on," she suggested as she released me, and I was suddenly so glad that she was there with me.

We sat and had breakfast with music from the radio playing in the background. We both commented that after being so severely spoilt with the food on holiday, the Special K and toast didn't really hit the spot this morning, and the coffee was not a patch on what we had become accustomed to. We both sighed, then Rose took a bite of her toast and looked at me.

"Are you back at work tomorrow?"

"Nope, Tuesday – you?"

"Tomorrow unfortunately… I knew I'd picked a good place to go, but who would have thought that I would come away not only having a great time with my girlfriends, but also possibly finding a potential boyfriend?" She looked at me for a response.

"I know, I don't think any of us came away expecting what we managed to experience. I feel more like me after this holiday than I have in years," I told her honestly.

"Isn't it great? You get to be happy with a great guy and so do I. That's if he does what he says and keeps in touch," she said pulling a worried look on her face.

"Don't think you need to worry about that – Ethan said that Josh was missing you just as much. You're in the perfect position too; you can fly out with Josh to experience places for your business. You said that Jessica had wanted to step up her role as assistant manager in your business – the perfect opportunity to leave her in charge and you travel more, I'd say," I told her. She shrugged.

"Hmm that is a possibility, I suppose. It is my business so I can do what I like. Anyway, you said that Caroline wanted to take a more active role in your shop so perhaps you can take someone else on, which you were thinking about doing, and leave them to run yours for you? Then we can both travel out together and meet them!" She clapped with a hint of delight in her voice at her plan. I nodded in agreement.

"True. This holiday's made me feel like someone has lifted a huge dark cloud from over my head, which was starting to rest on my shoulders actually. Perhaps it's time for change for both of us?" I asked questioning my own response.

"One day at a time, hun, one day at a time," she said as she patted my hand.

After chatting for a while and then finishing getting ready, I offered to drive Rose home at around eleven. I had decided that I would call in and say hello to Caroline in the shop on the way back, the least I could do after she had worked hard looking after everything for me for two weeks. Strangely enough today we had a Sunday wedding and so she was working. She was only twenty-nine and although very experienced in floristry, she also had some great ideas about changes that would be good for the shop. I had tried to state to her that I liked things just the way that they were, but I think that was just me not knowing how to change or wanting anything else to change after my grief. Thinking about it as I drove there though, I was starting to feel quite enthusiastic about the possibility of trying new things and so I couldn't wait to drop by and have a chat with her about it – "strike while the iron was hot," so to speak.

When I entered I was a little surprised to find that she had changed things around in the shop already and rearranged shelves and moved the desk that accommodated the till – more impressively she had done a fantastic display in the window. I smiled with pride that this was my shop, but when I looked at Caroline she looked a little nervous at what my response may be.

"Jenny – you're back!" she exclaimed as she walked over and gave me a quick hug. "Wow – you look amazing… and tanned." She then grimaced before saying; "I hope that you like what I've done. I know that you didn't really want to change anything, but I thought if you saw what I meant that it would be easier," she started to babble. "If you don't like it we can change it back, and I picked this colour for this wall because you love greens…" she carried on, but I held up my hand to stop her and turned to look at it all again. She waited nervously at the side of me.

"I love it!" I said and then she let out a huge sigh of relief.

"Oh thank goodness for that." she laughed holding her hand to her heart.

"It really does look great and funnily enough I stopped by today to say that I thought perhaps we should make some changes. I think that we need to sit down and have a chat about what other thoughts you have," I told her. She clapped her hands together with excitement.

"Brilliant! I'll make us a drink. I have a book in the back I've been working on." Then she stopped and looked at me curiously. "What happened while you were away?" she enquired.

"I'll tell you all about it," I smiled and then she scuttled into the back grinning from ear to ear, to make us both a cup of tea.

As Caroline had fulfilled the orders for the wedding, that were being collected in an hour and sorted tidying things in the back, we sat at the table in the shop that was set aside for brides to view books and clients to choose flowers for other occasions. She produced a very thick scrap book and started to run down her ideas for the shop; including new products and services, updating the website and much more than I had realised that she was even thinking about. I was impressed to say the least and felt slightly guilty that I had not at any point given her the chance to express any of this passion and fervour. Her energy and hunger to succeed and make the business far better than it was now was truly impressive and I made sure that I told her that, giving her the positive feedback that she was so craving.

"I think that we may have to give you some more responsibility on a permanent basis," I told her as we finished our tea.

"I'd like that," she replied before carrying on. "I can start some of these straight away if you are happy for me to do so? Of course I will not implement anything without your approval first," she then confirmed as she took another sip of tea. I felt that I had nothing to lose.

"Okay, you roll with it and I will keep a check on what you're doing."

"I like this new you – you have returned from this holiday so happy and confident and far more upbeat than when you left. What exactly did go on?" she enquired. Caroline had been one of my friends for the last six years while she worked with me, so we didn't really have any secrets. I blushed a little thinking about Ethan and then answered, trying to sound composed about the whole thing.

"A guy, actually," I grinned.

"What? A very handsome and tanned Spaniard?" she quizzed me some more. I looked at her and smiled and placed my mug on the table.

"No, a very handsome English guy. He was quite tanned though by the time we left," I smirked.

"Oh my God – get you – all coy and unassuming. You've been heating it up with a hot guy while you've been on holiday." She nudged me, and I crossed my arms across my tummy in a protective measure.

"You could say that – we all had a very lovely time being completely spoilt in absolute luxury," I added.

"How did you manage that? Sounds like you landed

a bloody dream, Jen. Tell me more… What happened, where'd you go, what did you do?" she carried on and I found myself very happy talking about him.

"We met when I fell over as I was completely inebriated," I started and she interrupted immediately.

"No surprise there then with you four!" She laughed and I scowled at her. She waved her hand in a gesture for me to carry on.

"He was an absolute gentleman and was at our hotel on business, so we bumped into each other a couple of times. He took us sailing on his yacht and then he invited us all to a charity dinner on the first Friday with his friends, one of whom was his assistant manager and Rose fell head over heels for him. Anyway… we all got on so well and it transpired he was opening a new hotel on the island – we were in Ibiza by the way – a little boutique type and he wanted us all to test run and review it before the grand opening. It was out of this world… the food, the location the luxury… and we got to do some really cool things around there too – walks, bike rides, and romantic dinners." Caroline held her hand up and stopped me.

"Okay, jealous already… but romantic dinners? You? What exactly is the name of this guy, and where can I get one?" she joked.

"Ethan – he's really quite… magnificent actually and I like him so much more than I expected to," I said as I quickly reminisced on our bedroom antics. I knew that she was staring at me and then she squinted and pulled an inquisitive face at me;

"Hmm, magnificent and like him a lot – is it more

than that? In fact before you answer that, exactly how magnificent? Have you actually let him share your bed?" she asked hopefully.

I smiled briefly and then simply answered, "Numerous times… and I think it is more than that," I answered honestly. Caroline clapped her hands in complete appreciation at my revelation.

"Oh, Jen, I'm so pleased for you. It's about time you met a nice guy and had some fun; you can't mope around forever," she replied and then asked. "When do I get to meet him?"

"Not sure yet. He had to fly to Rome to one of his other hotels to sort issues out, so he's going to be away for a while. I promise to let you meet him when he eventually gets some time off," I winked at her.

"You're on – I can't wait. He sounds perfect! Handsome, magnificent, obviously got some dosh and he travels in style on a bloody yacht. I think that you can safely say that if this works you've definitely landed on your feet," she complained sounding envious. I laughed at her.

"It's just nice to feel wanted again, and have someone want to do things for you and look after you, and make you feel so completely at ease with yourself," I tried to explain.

"Yeah and he's obviously good in the sack if you've been at it numerous times – so not fair!" she carried on complaining.

"Wait until you see him." I then added and she stopped from walking into the back of the shop and looked at me.

"He's really fit too, isn't he?" she scowled, and I simply nodded. She threw her head back and cried out. "Oh really, really not fair – think I hate you now actually, preferred it when you were on your holiday!" I laughed as she disappeared – but then she popped her head back around the door. "You know I'm only joking, right? I'm really pleased for you, honestly," she added.

"I know. You can make your own decision when you meet him. I'll stop rubbing it in now."

"Yes, please do!" she shouted back.

Caroline sent me home telling me to unpack and not worry about anything until Tuesday, so I went back to my car and hopped in then pulled out my phone and sent a quick text:

"Hey handsome. Hope your flight was enjoyable. I've just been talking about you with my assistant at work – she's very jealous that you sound so amazing and I enjoyed giving her a rundown about how incredible you are! I'm smiling at my thoughts of you but I still miss you. Be in touch soon – Love Jen X'

I hit send and then drove home, stopping to get some shopping on the way. I knew that I would speak with him soon, but not knowing when was a little frustrating. Somehow though it kept me smiling – it was just the knowing that out there somewhere, someone was missing me just as much and was thinking about me.

As the day rolled on and I finished unpacking and washing, I was happy to sit down and put my feet up by seven. I made some simple pasta and put on a very easy-watching film. I had received a short quick text from Ethan once he had landed stating that he was happy to have received my text and I was thinking about him, but he had to go straight to a meeting and so I wasn't surprised that he hadn't text back or called any more. It saddened me slightly to think that this was probably his usual routine, and the last two weeks had probably been completely out of character for him. I hoped though that he now had a different reason for getting through each day, instead of just the controlling of many hotels that seemed to have never-ending reasons for him to visit them. James called me at seven thirty to see if I had arrived home in one piece. It was lovely to hear his voice, and he had been busy with numerous projects while I had been away so hearing about them was refreshing. I really was looking forward to seeing them next weekend and I made sure that he knew. I must have dosed off on the sofa as at eight thirty my mobile started to ring and it frightened me into waking. I looked at the front screen and as I realised it was Ethan, I sat rubbed my eyes and straightened myself up – then thought, *What am I doing? He can't see me.*

"Ethan, I'm glad that you called – how are you?" I asked.

"Jenny, I'm so sorry it's taken this long to call you – meeting ended up being quite a mammoth undertaking of trying to understand the new manager's reasons for impulse spending to try new marketing. Wasn't quite what we were expecting and ended up dragging on for a couple of hours," he said sounding just a bit frustrated.

"Oh dear. I am sorry to hear about that – nothing is ever straightforward, eh?" I tried to reassure him.

"No – never. It's nice to be able to talk about it with someone other than Josh, though," he replied and I smiled. "Enough about my mundane day – what have you been up to? I'd also like to know exactly what you have been saying to your assistant," he finished, sounding a little chirpier.

"Ah yes, Caroline – she wanted to know why I was so happy and confident and more myself than before I left. So of course I had to tell her that I had met you, how handsome you are, how kind…" I started and he laughed lightly.

"Yeah, okay I get the picture." He sounded embarrassed.

"She was very jealous when I told her about The Gessami Residence, but I may have got you some new guests. She also wants to know when she can meet you," I then informed him, he fell silent for a second and then replied.

"Ah, well it looks like I have some introductions to do then along with your sons?" he asked, and it made me happy that he still wanted to.

"It's nice for me to show you off!" I said blushing a bit at my honesty.

"Well, it's great for me that you would want to do that." Then I heard what sounded like the shower being turned on.

"What are you up to right now? Sounds like you're about to get in the shower," I enquired.

"And you would be right. Josh and I haven't eaten yet and so a quick change and out for a bite to eat. Lots to discuss before tomorrow," he informed me, and even though I felt bad that they still had to work I also felt turned on knowing that he could possibly be naked.

"It's a shame that you have to still work, so make sure you eat well and get some sleep tonight, as I don't think you got much last night, did you?"

"Not really – it is catching up with me now quite rapidly."

"More importantly…" I started then paused. "Are you naked right now?" I asked and I heard him take a large intake of breath.

"Have you got that sexy, confident, and naughty head on again?" he asked in the most seductive voice. I sighed heavily into the phone.

"Maybe… my mind is certainly throwing some visual representations at me right now." I laughed lightly and then he did too.

"Well then, just for your information I'm stood here talking to you in only my boxers," he told me – and I was a little shocked at how honest and open he was being.

"I like that – that's good for me to know. I will certainly sleep well with that thought in my head. In fact no, scrub that, I'm now going to be cruelly tortured through the night having to imagine that and not have you here!" I moaned and he laughed again.

"Well – these telephone conversations could become very interesting young lady if you carry on like this," he said and I smiled at myself as I liked knowing that I could make him feel so relaxed with me. "Look, as much as I would love to keep talking to you all night,

I need to be back downstairs in fifteen minutes. Can I call you tomorrow?" he asked hopefully and I was beaming.

"Yes, I'd love you to. However, if you are rushed off your feet and don't have a minute to yourself that's fine too. I just want you to be able to get finished, so just catch me when you have a minute, alright?" I insisted. The last thing he needed was to think that I was a clingy, irritating woman needing to have him in touch with me every waking hour of the day, I was sure he would appreciate that.

"You're pretty amazing – I have told you that, haven't I?" he asked me again and I knew I had said the right thing.

"I think that you've mentioned it before," I replied feeling a little bit embarrassed. It had been a long time since any man had told me that.

"Right, honey. I'm hopping in this shower, so I will be in touch. I miss you."

"I miss you too – don't work too hard!"

"I may need to, just to finish ASAP, but I know what you mean. You have a good night."

"Oh, I have boring television and my own company this evening; trust me I'll be asleep by ten," I concluded and he laughed.

"Okay. Night, honey."

"Night," I said and then I finished the call and sat back into the sofa and sighed with a huge feeling of contentment.

Chapter 22

I was true to my word and woke on the sofa last night at nearly ten, completely shattered and needing my bed. So I dragged my tired self upstairs, sank into my lovely comfortable new bed and drifted off in no time. When I woke this morning I felt completely refreshed; the early night had done me the world of good. I reached across for my phone and quickly sat up when I saw another text from Ethan:

'Just turning in for the night, another long day and I'm having to climb into this bed alone… I need your warm body to curl up with and help send me to sleep. Still missing you X'

I had immediate intense giddiness in my stomach, like a small child riding a roller coaster for the first time. This was becoming a regular feeling when he sent me these messages, and I couldn't get enough. I sent him a reply hoping that it would arrive on his phone before he woke – it was only eight o'clock and I was certain after receiving his text after midnight he would still be asleep.

'I hope that you managed to sleep well, Ethan – I wish that I could have been there to assist you going to sleep,

376

but I suspect it would have resulted in you having even less sleep! I still miss you too – I cannot wait to hold you again and feel your hands touch my skin and your lips kiss mine. I hope you have a good day – Love Jen X'

I hit send and then stretched with a big smile on my face, put the radio on and waltzed off to the shower. As I washed my hair it felt completely unsatisfying after letting Ethan do it, but when I stepped back out I felt awake and revitalised. I dressed, combed through my wet hair and then looked back at my phone and was slightly annoyed that it would appear Ethan had replied to my text within minutes of me sending it. He was obviously woken by me or awake already. I read his reply:

"Well, my day has just got much brighter! I want those things too. Just about to start another meeting, so I will catch you later on. Have a nice day and thank you for your message – you have just put a smile on my face. X'

I was both happy at his message and sad that he was already at work; I supposed hotels didn't get a day off during the week and neither would Ethan. He must have had very little sleep to be ready to go into a meeting now. I grimaced as I felt sorry for him – this was obviously what he was used to but I certainly was not and I decided that I had to help him change that. I had to send a quick reply.

'I'm disappointed that you obviously haven't had a lot of sleep again, handsome. Don't burn yourself out or I will have to ring Josh and set some ground rules! I will speak with you later today X'

I hoped that he would see my remark was slightly tongue in cheek. I hit send and then went for breakfast, thinking that he would see my comment was humorous; he knew me well enough.

I was having lunch today with my parents. I had promised that I would see them on my return and knowing how inquisitive my mum was, I expected lots of questions. The thought of not having to cook for one today though was welcomed greatly. The drive to the pub in which we were meeting was quite enjoyable. I didn't expect to hear from Ethan until possibly later this evening and so I had no need to worry about Mum asking whom I was texting so regularly. I was going to have to let them know about him though, as at some point in the future I hoped to spend more time with him.

When I arrived, it surprised me how happy I was to physically see them. Mum was sporting a new haircut and she seemed very pleased with it: it suited her. Dad gave his usual bear hug and then we sat and chose from the menu. No sooner had the waitress taken our orders when the questions started flying. Where had I been? How was it? Was it hot? Were there any handsome men? Did we get drunk? What was the food like? I had to hold my hand up to stop any more.

"Heck, Mum. Give me chance to answer the first one, will you?" Dad just laughed at me.

"You know your mum, sweetheart. She has to know everything!" he teased her. I did a small sarcastic laugh and then decided to lay my cards on the table.

"Okay, here goes: we went to Ibiza, it was very hot but the hotel was lovely, we did get a little intoxicated, ate great food and…" I stopped a second and took a drink of my tonic water.

"And?" my mum then said, knowing that I was about to say something that she probably would be thinking already. I gave her a pleading 'don't judge me' look.

"I met a really nice businessman and he was amazing," I quickly added, before I changed my mind.

"Well, good for you, darling," Dad answered with absolute coolness as he raised his glass at me. "I wondered what that glow about you was," He winked.

"A man? Where did you meet him and how old is he, for goodness sake? You can meet some very strange men on holidays, usually only after one thing!" Mum then continued in that matter of fact motherly tone. I rolled my eyes.

"Mum, he's not like that. He's nearly forty-five, he is a private hotelier and travels a lot and he is an absolute gentleman. He even invited us all to stay at his new boutique hotel free of charge for the second week – it was out of this world – and we travelled there by yacht," I told her confidently. Her face changed.

"Yacht? Boutique hotel? And exactly who is all of you?" she then asked. I love her dearly but she did worry about me a little too much after Paul.

"The 'us' being us girls, along with Ethan as he was

the host, his assistant manager Josh and then their two friends Hernando and Rafael. We had an absolute ball, sad to come home really," I finished as I sipped another mouthful of my drink.

"Well, it sounds like a bloody cracking holiday, love," Dad said. Mum was quiet for a while and then responded;

"When do I get to meet him, this Ethan?"

"Soon, hopefully. He plans to come over here once he has concluded business in Rome," I informed her. She tutted

"Rome indeed." She lifted her glass.

Dad winked at me before saying, "Jealous, darling?"

She shot him a look of annoyance but I found it amusing. "You'd like that wouldn't you?" she said. Then she took a deep breath. "I am simply wanting to protect my girl; she's been through a lot and you know I want her to be happy." I reached across the table and took hold of her hand.

"I know, Mum – we're only teasing. You have no reason to worry about me being happy. This holiday has honestly made me feel more alive and happier than I've felt in years," I told them. Then I found myself smiling. "I know that the reason I feel like this is because of Ethan. He helped me find myself," I finished as I looked at them both. Mum squeezed my hand and looked to almost have a tear in her eye.

"That's all I want for you, Jenny, to see you smile again and be happy. I think I definitely need to meet this young man," she said.

"Well, I did say you were glowing and I meant it –

sounds like a keeper to me!" Dad chipped in. I was glad that they were happy for me.

"You know, I never thought I would find anyone after Paul and I'm not really sure that I wanted to until I went away. Ethan wasn't planned but it just happened and he was… perfect. I promise I'm not going to jump in with both feet, I just like being in the company of a man again," I tried to explain.

"Well, that sounds like puppy love if ever I heard it." My dad said as he laughed a little.

"Dad," I winced, wishing he could be serious for two minutes.

"I'm sorry," he started as he stopped laughing. "If you are happy, I'm happy, Jenny, you know that. I agree with Mum though, I think it would be nice to meet him," he then said.

"And you will." Dinner arrived on the table just then, thank goodness. It broke the constant questions for a while.

The food was comforting and welcome after a busy morning ironing and putting away my holiday clothes. I folded the new bikinis delicately as I placed them in my drawer. They were quite special to me now as I had bought them with Ethan in mind. After we had eaten and Dad waited patiently for his dessert, Mum decided to dig a little deeper.

"So did he spoil you then, this Ethan?" she asked and I knew she had obviously been toying with questions throughout eating.

"He did, Mum. Besides the yacht and beautiful hotel,

he supplied amazing food – including lobster," I said looking at Dad and knowing it was one of his favourites. He nodded in appreciation. "Then he took me to a gorgeous seafood restaurant that was out of this world actually. The chef in the hotel was faultless too. We drank champagne most of the time and fine wines. He made sure that I was well looked after and I enjoyed it immensely," I told them.

"Well, he sounds like he's doing all the right things then for my girl. Have you got a photograph of him?" Mum then enquired. I reached for my iPhone.

"I do, but I don't want any sarcastic comments!" I insisted as I opened my photo album and passed it to her. She gazed at the first picture of him and me and raised her eyebrows with surprise I think.

"This is him?" she asked as she pointed at the picture – and I knew when I nodded that she was taken aback at how handsome he was. She carried on scrolling through them. "Well, he's quite a dish isn't he?" she then said smiling and I laughed at her. "He must have made a big impression. You have a bikini on too!" she then smirked at me. I sighed at her remark as Dad snatched the phone to look himself.

"Bloody hell, Jenny – he is a handsome fella."

"Glad you approve," I smiled as I sipped my drink.

"I'm not surprised you enjoyed the holiday if that was the yacht you were on," he then said turning my phone to show me a picture I had taken while it was moored. "You still don't look half bad in a bikini either darling, I'm not surprised you caught his eye!" he then said which was a tad embarrassing if not cringeworthy.

"Yes well, I actually met him when I fell over intoxicated – you know what Beth and Amanda are like. He helped me be back to my room and was the perfect gentleman and it went from there," I explained. Dad handed me my phone back.

"Well, if he wants to still see you after going out on the lash sweetheart – and I can imagine how bad you were after going out with those three – then it says a lot for him I suppose!" Dad mocked me. I sarcastically laughed at him.

"I'm really happy that you're moving on with your life a bit, Jenny. If he makes you happy then that's great – he might remind you how to live a little," Mum finished.

"Oh he is certainly doing that – I'm missing him already," I replied. Dad raised his eyebrows at me realising I liked him so much.

"Well, I look forward to meeting him then." He squeezed my hand quickly then released it.

The whole afternoon and drive back was thoroughly enjoyable. I had told them that the boys were due back next weekend and that made me exceptionally happy. They insisted on taking us out for dinner next Sunday and I knew that the boys would love to see them and so I agreed without hesitation. When I arrived home I slumped onto the sofa and gazed around the living room while the television came on. What the hell did I used to do on my own before I went on holiday? I could always fill my time either with reading, looking online for things for work or watching television, but none of it seemed to fulfil me anymore. I felt restless and couldn't seem to focus on anything – it was highly irritating.

I looked at my phone; I found scrolling through my pictures again had me grinning from ear to ear. I reminisced briefly on where I wish I was, and then went to put the kettle on to distract my misery that I wasn't still there. For over an hour I aimlessly flicked through the channels on television wishing that I could find something to distract me further. It really wasn't working and so I put a film on to hopefully try to make me laugh. Probably not the best idea then that I decided to watch *The Proposal*, a romance, and although humorous it just emphasised that I was on my own. I was so glad when I was interrupted by my phone ringing, and even happier when the front screen revealed that it was Ethan.

"Hey, handsome. How was your meeting?"

"Hey, it's nice to finally talk to you. It was long and tiresome," he replied.

"Have you only just got back to your room?" I asked looking at my watch and realising that it was already seven o'clock here.

"Yeah well Josh and I decided that we needed to collate all of the discussions today, to try to get a head start before the main meetings tomorrow and Wednesday. Honestly, it's never-ending – I arrive to sort out one issue and a whole host of others seem to appear. Anyway, enough about my boring day – what have you been up to?" he enquired.

"Well, it's been strange really. I did all of my holiday laundry and then put it away, which made me feel miserable. Then I went for lunch with my parents and spent most of the time talking about you, which made me feel miserable. Then I came home and looked at my pictures on my phone of you and felt even more miserable, because I wished I was there with you. So trust me, my day has been pretty boring and undescriptive too." I tried to sound positive but he just laughed lightly.

"Well, that actually makes me feel better, because I've been feeling miserable being separated from you too. Not to mention that I'm finding it hard to focus on anything. I hope to get everything finished here within the week, then I will be on the first flight back to see you," he replied and instantly I felt relieved.

We chatted for about an hour. He said that both he and Josh had eaten at around five o'clock, making it a very long dinner and planning meeting. He didn't sound too bothered about joining Josh for drinks in the bar, but I tried to tell him that it was a good idea and that he should have a glass of wine for me. He told me that he would text or ring me on Tuesday as Wednesday may prove difficult. I requested that he didn't work too hard and then we said goodnight, and I was back to being miserable me, sat on my own. Roll on tomorrow and work – I needed a good constructive distraction.

When I arrived at the shop I was glad to find that I had some form of focus. It was calming to be in familiar surroundings with someone that I got on so well with. We had numerous orders to fulfil today and Caroline seemed to have everything under control so I happily worked alongside her. When lunchtime arrived I found that I was starving again. I offered to buy Caroline some lunch and wandered aimlessly to the local delicatessen that had the most fantastic sandwiches. When I arrived back at work to a nice mug of tea, I sat and slumped into a chair and realised that I couldn't really remember the walk back from buying lunch.

"Hey, are you okay? You seem really distracted today," Caroline quizzed me. I unwrapped my sandwich and looked at her.

"I've turned into a mushy wreck – I miss him… a lot! I'm not even sure where this is going, and I'm a mess just hoping that I can see him soon," I replied honestly as I picked the excess rocket leaves from my lunch. Caroline chuckled at me.

"I think it's really sweet. You look really happy – well, actually you look a bit miserable right now, but in a good way," she then said as the phone started ringing. She jumped up to answer it and so I pulled my mobile phone out to check for messages, but nothing.

I looked at my sandwich and then grinned to myself and took a picture of it, sending Ethan a quick message along with the image:

'These lunches here are just not doing the trick… Think I need another holiday – with you of course ;-) X.'

I hit send and then took a large bite while Caroline took another order. I was shocked as my lips touched my mug and my phone pinged me back so quickly. A reply that speedy was not expected:

'It could be arranged X.'

I smiled to myself and replied:

'I am having serious withdrawal symptoms... What have you done to me?'

'I'm getting my own back, because you have done the same to me!'

He replied again as quickly.

'Good answer. More importantly why aren't you working hard so that you can get back here to me?' I joked.

'I would be working hard if some sexy young woman would stop texting me!' He messaged.

I found myself laughing out loud.

'Alright, point taken. I can't seem to help myself you're very addictive,' I informed him.

'As are you. You have now just given me the perfect reason to hasten things along in this meeting. It is going nowhere fast, and I know where I would rather be,' he answered.

'That sounds like a perfect plan. Hurry up and get your arse over here to me, I'm not sure how much longer I can keep this up,' I instructed him.

'What – not seeing me or needing my arse?' he replied sarcastically.

I laughed a little more and replied, 'Both!'

'I thought so. I would love to bring my arse to you immediately and as you are my priority at the moment, I promise I will bring it willingly ASAP! Must go, but will be in touch later. Thanks for texting. X.' he finished.

I smiled, sighed and placed my phone back on the table and finished eating my sandwich just as Caroline sat back down. She noted my happy persona, but didn't quiz me anymore and just ate her lunch, chatting about the other ideas she wanted to start pursuing. As we discussed things in more depth, I found that I managed to continue the day without thinking about him too much, and I was thankful for that.

A phone call to my boys during the evening was definitely needed. They both informed me of their work, more social events they had attended, and I was pleased to hear that Mark had a new girlfriend whom he seemed smitten with. James had been dating Emma for some time now and so it was nice to hear that Mark had finally allowed a woman to be part of his life. I told him that it would be nice to meet her sometime and he agreed that if things went well he would like that. They had both decided after speaking to each other to travel home early Saturday morning. Work commitments had meant that they were not free on Friday night, but they would be staying until Monday lunchtime as they both had nothing planned for the bank holiday.

I wasn't really expecting to hear from Ethan as he sounded extremely busy and so when my phone rang at ten o'clock it both surprised and pleased me. I had just made myself a cup of cocoa and so when I sat to answer the call I turned the television volume down.

"Hey, hi. I wasn't expecting to hear from you tonight. You sounded extremely busy today," I answered.

"Hi, I had to hear your voice before I turned in for the night. It's been a long, long day and has taken me forever to sort out issues today. Quite honestly I was glad to retreat to my room," he replied.

"Oh dear, perhaps you should go for a massage – it may help you relax," I suggested hearing the annoyance of the day in his voice.

"No time, but I like the way you're thinking. It's ridiculous I'm in one of the most interesting and romantic cities in the world and I don't have the enthusiasm to venture out. Even Josh was the same today. We ate in the hotel and just mused over today's meetings," he told me.

"Sounds like work is quite demanding at the moment, Ethan, maybe because you've just taken a week off? I feel really bad that you are now having to play catch up." I sighed heavily. I did have an air of guilt that after our lovely week he was now suffering.

"Hey, there's no reason for you to feel guilty, honey. This is what it's always like. I just wish that you were here with me – it would make coming to my room at the end of the day so much more worthwhile." He made my heart melt and I know that he was smiling.

"Well, now I like your way of thinking. We could explore Rome together and I assure you that you would want to venture out – I'd want to sample that cuisine for a start." Thoughts were now running through my head of all the places we could visit, strolling along hand in hand.

"I can't fault the food, Jenny, I know that you'd love it – I think that I need to bring you here one day," he suddenly suggested. I inhaled at that remark, the fact that he still wanted to go away with me was promising. I found myself being brutally honest again;

"I'm really missing you."

"I know – I miss you too, honey," he said, and then we both went quiet for a moment. "So how was work for you today?"

389

"Quite constructive actually. Caroline has got some amazing ideas – I'm learning to let her take control a little more; she's very passionate and it's refreshing," I informed him.

"Well, sometimes you have to take a step back to see the bigger picture. I know that – I've learnt to have to do that since Josh arrived. You'll get there, sounds interesting," he replied and I was glad that he seemed enthused about what I was doing.

"So, I assume that you will have another long day tomorrow?" I asked already knowing the answer.

"Yes, well the whole trip is about the meeting tomorrow. I feel better after sorting out numerous issues today, so hopefully it should be fairly straightforward. Josh is taking control of the meeting to start with, so that's taken the pressure off a little. I may struggle to call you tomorrow as we have to take a few clients out to dinner straight from the meeting, but I'll make sure that I stay in touch somehow," he informed me and I smiled.

"You just focus on what you have to do. I'll be fine, I promise. I just want to hear the chilled and less stressed Ethan, like last week," I told him.

"That's unlikely to happen until I'm back in close proximity to you, which is a good thing," he then said.

"I'll say." I paused for a moment… "So – good luck for tomorrow, and I'll definitely speak with you soon," I finished, knowing that we would have to say goodbye now.

"You will be my first priority at my first opportunity after this meeting, I can promise you that!" he said with affection. I smiled.

"You will be on my mind as always, torturing me from afar until see you again," I laughed lightly with that line fit for a song and he laughed.

"Well, that makes me happy. Goodnight, Jenny, sleep well."

"You too, Ethan. Let me know how it all went when you get a chance," I said.

"I will… and I do miss you," he softly answered.

"I hope so," I confirmed in a tone as soft as his. Then I had to go before I started to get emotional. "Goodnight," I finished and then I hung up.

When I climbed into my bed, I pulled the covers up tight under my chin and sighed deeply. I hadn't realised how empty my bed had felt until I had left Ethan in Ibiza. Even though I hadn't spent every night with him initially, the ones that we did spend together were so intimate, comforting and fulfilling that I now missed them immensely. I tried to convince myself that things would get better as it was getting nearer to him coming to see me, but it still took me some time to get off to sleep as he was at the forefront of my mind.

Chapter 23

Wednesday was filled with flowers for a funeral, which was sad and actually reflected my mood. I managed to be as upbeat as possible and helped Caroline fulfil all of the orders. We had decided to have some new business cards made, create a new shop logo and change the sign outside. It was a little outdated and so it seemed like the right time to move things along and modernise. We managed to get quite a lot done today and I'm sure that my constructive work attitude was based on the fact that it meant I didn't have to think about Ethan. When I walked into the house at the end of the day, I sighed heavily and dropped my bag. I found the house very empty now, and could not understand why I had let myself live so isolated for so long. I wasn't even sure looking around the kitchen that this house was right for me anymore.

I made some dinner and then sat at the kitchen table and ate quietly. I checked my phone and still nothing from Ethan. I was miserable and wanted to desperately send a message to him, but I knew that he was exceptionally busy today and so I refrained. While I was putting the plates away my mobile suddenly rang and as I raced to the table to get it, hoping it was him, I managed to drop a plate, run into the open cupboard door and nearly go flying over the kitchen chair that I had left pulled out. So you can imagine my disappointment when I saw that it was Beth.

"Hi," I answered, most probably sounding like I had just sprinted from six miles away.

"Hey. How's my favourite love-struck puppy?" she asked sarcastically. I pulled a face at her sarcasm.

"She's fine, still love-struck," I replied with little enthusiasm, as I sat on the offending chair and rubbed my ankle.

"So, I was chatting to Amanda this morning and we thought that we might come around to yours tomorrow night for Chinese. Both she and I can't make Friday and Saturday this weekend – we have things on," she informed me. I hadn't even thought about our usual weekly meet-up since getting back.

"Alright – I mean I have nothing planned. I hadn't even thought about our usual meet-up to be honest, but it would be nice to see you all," I finished, meaning that the distraction of being on my own would definitely be appreciated.

"Well, we didn't want you sitting there wallowing. I was half tempted to buy you a vibrator from Ann Summers to keep you company, but then I decided if you didn't already have one, then you really were in trouble," she mocked me.

"Thanks, I am really glad that me being satisfied is obviously your main concern at present," I told her.

"Well, if I mock you, it takes my mind off the amazing sex that I was having. God, I need to find me a man; it's torture not being able to pick and choose daily whether you want it or not! Plus Hernando was bloody hot," she stated quite factually and obviously for my benefit.

"They were all really handsome. I can't believe how lucky we were finding them really," I said.

"You're damn right. You never know, maybe if I get bored I will go back over there for a week," and I knew she absolutely meant it.

"Give the poor guy chance to recover, Beth!" I joked. She laughed with me and agreed that it had been pretty intense.

"Right. I will call Rose and see if she's free – can't see why not and we will see you tomorrow, shall we say about seven?" she asked.

"Perfect. Look forward to it." Then we said our goodbyes.

I placed the phone down on the table and just looked at it, then decided I would send Ethan a text anyway:

'I can't wait any longer to say hello, and I that hope that your day has gone well? I tried to resist texting, but the reality is I'm obviously weak and have no control when it comes to you! Fingers crossed that all has gone to plan and your meal with clients is proving beneficial. Look forward to hearing from you soon. J X.'

I hit send and then placed it down like a hot potato, suddenly thinking maybe I should have left it and waited for him. What if I was coming across as a desperate woman? I frowned at myself and tried to ignore the sudden panic of wishing I hadn't sent it, when I received a message back:

'Just give me a minute, honey X.'

My heart started to race, what did that mean? Was he going to send me a long text back? I sat staring at my phone and then almost dropped it when it started to ring, it was him – I answered in a desperate rush.

"Hey hi – I wasn't expecting a phone call. I thought that you were with clients. I'm so sorry for interrupting…" I was trying to say when he interrupted me.

"Hey, I'm glad that you did." He instantly relieved my worry. "It's gone really well today, and hopefully I may have a buyer for this hotel too, which is what I wanted. It is actually all going to plan and I couldn't be happier – perhaps you're my good-luck-charm," he said with a slight laugh.

"That's really sweet… but honestly, I'm not interrupting am I?"

"No – you are not! I excused myself from the table for a minute. I told them truthfully that it was a call that I had to make." he said before continuing. "I like the fact that you are weak and have no control – it just makes me wish I was with you though. I think it would be a good excuse for some interesting requests from you on my part," he finished, and I knew he was smiling. I was blushing; I knew exactly what he meant.

"Ethan – you have a wicked mind!" I told him trying to sound serious, but knowing that I was not. He laughed. "Well, I am really glad that everything is going better than you expected. I hope it doesn't mean that you have to spend more time there though?" I asked him hopefully.

"I'm not sure exactly what day I will be leaving here just yet – paperwork and finer details to sort, but as soon as I know – I will let you know. It will be soon though I promise," he informed me, and although I had no definite date to aim toward, the fact that I knew it was going well for him was a bonus. "Look, as much as I hate to say it I am going to have to go – dinner will be served imminently so I'd better get back."

"I understand, honestly; just hearing your voice has made me exceptionally happy."

"Well that's reciprocated tenfold! I couldn't have been any happier when I received your text. I will call you tomorrow – it looks like this dinner is going to drag on into the night," he informed me, but I knew this was Ethan and how he worked and so it didn't trouble me.

"Okay, you go and enjoy yourself and be proud that you are so good at what you do. I will look forward to hearing from you soon."

"Thanks, honey. It's nice to hear that sometimes. You have a nice evening and make sure that you carry on being weak and out of control – I need you to need me." He said.

I laughed nervously; "Oh there's no need to worry about that – I am and I do!" I said and then we said goodnight and I sat back in my chair.

I looked around the kitchen and then at the pictures of Paul and I with the boys at various points in their lives. I sighed loudly as I felt the urgency of wanting to be part of something again – a relationship, a bond, security. I looked at one particular picture of Paul and found myself confessing to him:

'Paul – you know I love you and I always will, but it's time, time for me to move on and live my life. I've met someone and he is making me really happy. I need to be one half of someone again, and I think Ethan is that other half. I know that you won't be angry with me, but I am sorry that I have to stop this grieving now and let you go so that I can look toward my future.'

I had a tear roll down my cheek, but I felt good for saying it out loud. Then without hesitation I stood meaningfully, finished tidying, had a bath, and then read my book and had an early night. I woke at around 3am and went to the bathroom before sliding back into my warm bed. I don't know why, but I picked my phone up and turned on the screen just in case, as I always had it on silent at night. I rubbed my eyes twice to check that I could read 'Ethan' on the screen, so I opened the message and it simply said:

'I miss you… because I love you X.'

He had sent it at 1:30am, so I knew that he had probably just returned to his room. I quickly sent one back.

'…and I you X.'

I smiled and snuggled back down into a very deep and peaceful sleep.

Thursday already, and I had thought the night before that I should re-stock my wine if the girls were coming over. Work was fun today; we had a visit from a graphic designer who had great ideas for the new cards and shop logo. Everything seemed so much easier at the moment.

If I think back to before my holiday, I was just trudging my way through each day not feeling any great benefit – I was just simply existing. Now I felt like I had my life back and I really wanted to grab it with both hands and run with it. It was the best feeling, and Caroline commented on my positive attitude numerous times. I arrived home that evening, took a shower and threw on my jeans and a t-shirt and then quickly flicked a duster around the living room before vacuuming. I knew that the girls didn't care but it meant something to me to have the house tidy.

The doorbell rang promptly at seven and all three of them ploughed through the door chatting and kissing me on the cheek as they entered. It was actually extremely nice to see them all. As always, they went straight to the kitchen and started to help themselves to glasses. Beth always brought a bottle of wine, as did Amanda, but Rose usually joined us straight from work and apologised most times for not contributing. While Beth poured us all a glass and I started to think it looked like they were on a mission, I worried about the other four bottles that I had put in the fridge to chill. Rose and Beth had already taken a huge gulp and chinked glasses saying that they felt much better and I hadn't even picked mine up yet!

"So, gorgeous, I assume that you have heard from him. Are you still smitten?" Amanda asked me.

"Yes and yes," I simply replied and then took a sip of wine, feeling that there were more questions to come.

"Well, Josh has called me a couple of times and the more I hear from him the more I feel desperate to see him again," Rose interjected and we all looked at her.

"Oh sweetie, you are definitely in love," Beth informed her.

Rose smiled and then looked at us all and simply said, "I know."

We all stared for a minute and then raced to hug her – this was a huge revelation for Rose and the fact that she was openly confirming what we thought was a big step for her. After a couple of minutes she pushed us away telling us that was enough of the gushing sentiments. It was sweet though; I had always hoped that her career wouldn't be the only important thing in her life. Josh was a perfect match for her and I hoped that their relationship did expand to be something more permanent.

The evening was thoroughly enjoyable, good food, good wine and great conversation. We laughed about the holiday, things that had happened at work with Amanda and Beth, and they teased about me and Ethan and Rose and Josh. We were all well into being merry and laughing to the point of it becoming a little bit of a problem, when my mobile rang. I picked it up and looked at the screen, then stood and shushed them.

"It's Ethan, so behave for a minute!" I said as I made my way back to the kitchen for a bit of privacy. "Hey, good evening, handsome," I happily answered feeling elated that he had called me.

"Hey, good evening to you, honey. What are you up to?" he asked me. I grimaced a little thinking that I was back on the wine again.

"Actually, the girls are here; we've had Chinese food

and a few glasses of wine. Probably not the best idea for a Thursday night, but Amanda and Beth cannot make our usual night out on Friday or Saturday this week," I replied. He was chuckling a little to himself.

"Oh dear, I know what you girls are like with a few bottles of wine. I am slightly jealous though. I hope that you are enjoying yourself?" he asked.

"Well, I always have fun with my girlfriends, Ethan. We've laughed a lot this evening, which has been good for me because it has stopped me thinking about you continually, which doesn't make me happy at all – I'm still missing you." I honestly told him and then a whole array of slushy remarks and noises ensued from behind me.

The girls had snuck into the kitchen to listen into my conversation. I turned to them and went bright red and then heard Ethan laughing some more as they all shouted, "Hello, Ethan," and made some other gestures of undying love.

I hit them one at a time and then pushed them out of the door as he replied, "Hello ladies."

"He said hi, now go away!" I prompted them, slamming the door closed as they left. "I'm so sorry about them, they really can't help themselves," I scowled, but he was still laughing.

"Don't apologise – I love the fact that you have such good friends around you. They are highly entertaining, but do unfortunately sound like they are slightly merry." He didn't miss a thing!

"Unfortunately we all are; time for some water I think. I have to get up for work tomorrow. Speaking of which, how is everything going with you?" I enquired hoping for better news, along the lines of him travelling back anytime soon.

"It's alright, had a few issues to resolve today but on the whole it's going in the right direction. I'm not sure that I will be able to leave before the weekend though," he confirmed and I sighed.

"Oh, that's a shame, but I do understand." My voice gave away my disappointment.

"Hey, don't be sad about it – there isn't anything I can do right now to change it. You do know where I would rather be," he then said and I suddenly felt very selfish. This was business, something he and his father had taken years to build – who was I to try and make him feel guilty about doing that? I snapped myself back into reality.

"Gosh, I'm sorry, Ethan. How selfish of me to feel that way. It's business and even though I know that being together would make both of us happier, you need to do what you need to do and I am fully aware of that. Your absence will just make me even fonder of you." I was trying to sound more upbeat.

"I think that I am going to have to start a list!" he said. I was confused.

"A list for what?" I asked.

"A list of all the things you can do to show me how fond of me you actually are." he joked and I pictured him smiling from ear to ear as he said it. I smiled too.

"I may hold you to that, as long as I get to make a list too, just so that you can show me how much you've missed me," I answered as I felt my body heating up at the thought.

"Well, that's something delicious to dwell on for the rest of the evening. When we do finally meet up we can compare lists," he suggested.

"That, handsome, is a great idea."

"Okay, honey. I need to go – another business meeting tonight over drinks. I do wish I could relax during the evening sometimes. After spending a week with you doing just that I'm really missing it."

"There's plenty of time for us to do that, you just complete your deal and I will see you soon," I said confidently.

"You're on – you enjoy your night," he insisted.

We said goodbye and then I returned to the now noisy living room, but as soon as I entered they all stopped talking and just looked at me and then the ribbing started! I just sat and took it all – I really didn't care anymore. Ethan in my eyes was perfect and so they could say anything they wanted, it wouldn't change my mind. I made everyone a cup of tea before they left, just to dilute the four bottles of wine that we had easily consumed. Rose was talking about starting to do a little more travelling and leaving the shop in the hands of her staff, which was an encouraging advancement for her.

"In fact, girls, I have been invited to try out a new restaurant in the city tomorrow night. Free meal – who wants to come with me?" she asked us all.

"Don't look at me, I have something on," Amanda replied.

"Me too unfortunately, otherwise I would have been there – you will have to take our Jenny here, stop her from moping around after Mr Dreamboat!" Beth added. I did a little sarcastic laugh at her remark.

"Will you come, Jenny? I don't want to go on my own," Rose requested. I shrugged.

"I have nothing else on; the boys are coming home on Saturday late morning though so I don't want a raging hangover!" I insisted.

"Me neither – too much to do this weekend. Brilliant, I will swing by in a cab and pick you up."

"Just let me know what time and whether we are getting dressed up," I asked her.

"Definitely a dressing up session. Nice hotel restaurant, nice meal – free, which is an added bonus – and probably some nice men to look at," Beth then said.

"I'm not bothered about looking at other men," Rose added forcefully. I agreed.

"Oh that's right. I forgot for a second that you two are smitten," she laughed.

By the time they left at eleven thirty – thankfully in a taxi together just as they had arrived – I was exhausted. It was a relief, after tidying up, to change and collapse into my bed. The only downside, however, was when I woke at six, feeling like I had only had two hours' sleep, and I had a slight hangover to boot. I groaned with annoyance at myself for getting carried away during the week. Those girls never get any better with age and it can never be just one glass. I dragged myself to the bathroom and stepped into the shower: I had to stand there motionless for a while, until the water woke me up. Thankfully when I exited I did feel better – I made a mental note with myself to have an early night soon.

As I was up so early and while putting away some laundry, I stood and looked at my wardrobe. I hadn't realised how many dark coloured items I had in there, but I felt the need for an infusion of colour, particularly as I looked at the dress Ethan had bought me in Ibiza. I decided to take this afternoon off work and go shopping, it was Friday and it would be nice to get something new even though dinner with Rose was nothing special. I wanted to feel young and fresh and vibrant again, and some of these items of clothing just had to go. I instantly pulled approximately ten items off hangers and threw them into the corner, telling myself to donate them to a charity shop. Right, I resolved, I was going to have a clear out. New me, new man, new wardrobe – the perfect combination. I grinned, wondering if Beth would like to meet me for lunch this afternoon as she worked right in the centre of the city. I sent her a text while I bagged up the unwanted clothes and items and was elated when she agreed that she had an hour or two to spare. This week was turning out to be far better than I had initially thought with not having Ethan with me, but he was never far from my thoughts.

I spoke with Ethan this morning too and he told me that he would be another day or so in Italy. He then had to fly to London at the weekend and sort out some paperwork with his solicitor before there was any chance of him being able to come over and see me. He promised that very soon we would be able to physically see each other and in some small way that did make me very happy; I just wished it could have been sooner. The thought of knowing that he would be staying here with me at some point in the near future, had given me a new found inspiration to de-clutter. This morning my wardrobe, my shoes, and my underwear were sorted and rearranged. Things that had been important to Paul, but in all honesty I didn't like too much – including a painting – I decided to see if the boys wanted when they came to visit this weekend. I moved old books I'd read and magazines and went into the now tidy kitchen, feeling enthused that I had made a start on something that I had wanted to do for a long time. I decided that it was good therapy for the mind and soul to make a fresh start. I stopped on the way into work and dropped off the bags I had gathered for the charity shop before I could change my mind.

Caroline had no problem with me going shopping for the afternoon. She had everything under control, she was loving the responsibility and had a slightly quieter day than tomorrow – Saturday was always hectic. She had told me not to go in though as I was out this evening, and stated that she would be fine – saying that if she was desperate for help, she would call me. I knew this was unlikely as she was fully aware that the boys were arriving tomorrow. By the time it was eleven thirty she was almost ushering me out of the door. I happily drove into the centre and met Beth at Selfridges for lunch – it was always lovely to eat there. She came with me through the various departments picking up items that I wouldn't necessarily pick myself, but with Beth being the flamboyant one I was trying to heed her advice. I came out of there having purchased three items, so we moved on and did more shopping in an hour than I thought was possible.

I somehow managed to get a new handbag, two pairs of shoes, two dresses, a skirt, three blouses, a casual white shirt, some new jeans and a jacket. We passed a lingerie department and she dragged me into the middle of it. I had to agree that I needed some nice new 'white' underwear, not the used white versions I had at home, and so two bras and some knickers later I was exhausted. Just before she left to go back to work she stopped to replenish her favourite lip gloss.

"You should get one you know, something bright and sultry," she smiled.

"Really? I don't think I need sultry, do I?" I queried. She stopped and turned to look at me.

"Look, I know that you seem to have bagged the most handsome and very fit guy, but trust me, they still like a bit of sultry." She winked. I picked up one of the colours and then the assistant appeared at the side of me to help.

That was it, nothing else. I had only initially shopped to get something for tonight. Beth was both a good and bad influence and she was more than happy with all of my purchases. When I arrived home I hung them all up and felt instantly better that my wardrobe now had colour. New underwear took pride of place in the top of my drawer, but made me scowl at the horrible 'not white' knickers that now looked terrible against the new – I pulled them out and binned them. *Good riddance,* I thought.

A hot bath at five o'clock meant that I had plenty of time for make-up application and hair drying. It was lovely to just mooch around. I received a call from Rose at around six to inform me that she would be arriving to collect me at around seven fifteen and that we had to make the most of it by dressing up – she told me she was wearing a dress and I had to make the effort too. To start the evening Rose suggested that we should have drinks in the cocktail lounge first. I grimaced at that thought, but then realised that the worst two influences being Amanda and Beth were not with us, which was a huge relief.

I decided to wear a purchase from today: a dress, which was a very lovely shade of coral – quite deep and rich but it was lovely against my sun-kissed skin. Beth had picked it up within seconds of us going into Coast and I had to say that it was a great choice; very simple and not too fussy. I was happy when I slid into it after finishing my hair and make-up and looked in the mirror. Even though Ethan wasn't with me, I now had a new found inspiration to look my best and embrace my figure, instead of hiding it all the time. I felt young and sexy and Ethan had given that back to me. I sighed: thinking about him while looking in the mirror made me wish that he could see me tonight. Perhaps I should send him a photograph. I took one with my phone and sent it with the message, *'All dressed up, I have dinner to go to with Rose, but only you could make my night complete.'* I hit send and then placed lip gloss and money into my purse, tousled my hair and made my way downstairs. It was already seven and I knew that Rose would be arriving any time.

As I reached the bottom step my phone pinged to announce an incoming message. It was from him. *'Oh boy, that is one killer dress, honey. I am very jealous now – you are going to attract attention. I wish I was there with you.'*

I replied with a simple, *'Me too,'* along with a sad

face. No sooner had I sent it than I heard a car pull up outside. I grabbed my jacket and then picked up my keys and went to open the door. Rose bounced up to greet me with unusual energy and looked amazing in a tight fitting cream dress that accentuated all her curves beautifully.

"Wow, Jen, you look amazing! Beth rang me earlier and said you had made some amazing purchases," she informed me.

"Did she? I didn't think me buying new clothes was news enough to ring you about, but thanks you look amazing too," I replied.

"She was actually ringing to tell us to have a nice time, but your shopping extravaganza was mentioned," she joked as I locked the door. It was well known that I wasn't one for buying clothes regularly. "Right let's go – drinks to be had and food to be eaten," she finished as she dragged me down the path to the waiting taxi.

Chapter 24

The taxi ride was entertaining as we watched the many people embracing a night out on the town. Some sights were questionable, but on the whole they were just fascinating to watch. I asked Rose if she had heard from Josh and she was quick to say that she had, that she missed him and that she hoped to see him soon, but then she changed the subject and I suspect that was for my benefit as she knew I was desperately missing Ethan.

We pulled up as close as we could get to the hotel; traffic was heavy this evening and so we opted for a very short walk. The interest we received from the male species as we teetered on our heels was quite unnerving, but at the same time it was stimulating to know that our efforts had not been in vain. As we walked into the very cool and stunning interior and headed toward the lifts, Rose grinned from ear to ear.

"You seem very happy about this free meal," I noted. She did a little dance in appreciation.

"I'm so excited about it, I have always wanted to eat here," she said as the lift kept climbing.

"How many floors up are we going?" I enquired. I had never been that keen on heights, but knew that this hotel went way up into the sky!

"We're indulging tonight with a glass of champagne in the bar that overlooks the city. It's stunning up there on floor twenty-three, and classy, and our table reservation is for nine o'clock, so we have plenty of time," she then informed me and I simply agreed as she seemed to have everything planned to perfection.

I was slightly relieved when the lift doors opened and I could exit, but the view, as she promised, was stunning. Our jackets were taken for us and as I looked out of the window across the city Rose spoke quietly to a waitress asking I would assume if there was a table in the room with a view, and then came and dragged me to the bar. No sooner had we reached it, there were two glasses being placed in front of us. Rose turned to me and then smiled and chinked glasses with me.

"Tonight is going to be exceptional, unexpected and thoroughly enjoyable," she then said. I raised my eyebrows at her high expectations, but as she had invited me for free I went along with them.

"Very well, if you say so," I replied and then we took a sip just as the waitress arrived alongside us.

"Your table is ready," she smiled and Rose grinned at me and then followed along behind her as she walked us to where we would be sat, hopefully to enjoy our drinks along with the view.

As we strode across the lavish bar floor, I couldn't take my eyes off the cityscape through the windows. The sun was setting and the sky was a lovely shade of pink; the lights outside gave the impression of being in New York or some other similar city. I had barely registered that we had arrived at our table until the waitress told me to enjoy as she turned to walk past me. I turned my focus to where we were to be seated and as I did so, a figure stood in front of me in one graceful movement, and as he turned to look at me I found my heart was in my throat. Rose stood grinning from ear to ear alongside Josh, but more importantly… he was here. Ethan, my Ethan. I placed my glass on the table and probably looked like I was in shock. He stood smiling at me and said with a very smooth tone, "Surprise." There was nothing to be done other than find me throwing myself into him and into an embrace that I had missed so very much. I think it took him unawares, but he laughed lightly. He pulled away and looked into my eyes and as his hand touched my cheek he continued, "So you definitely missed me then?" he smiled and I smiled back.

"More than I can tell you," I said almost in a whisper and I suddenly felt full of emotion – happiness, excitement and love. He leaned in and kissed me and I was suddenly transported back to complete contentment.

I heard Rose say to Josh that this was the best surprise she had managed to accomplish in years, so when we stopped kissing and as I hugged him again with a tear in my eye, I looked across at her and mimed, *"Thank you."* Ethan took a step back and looked at me;

"You look amazing," he said and I know that I was blushing, but so very grateful that I had my new dress on. Then it dawned on me.

"Hey, wait a minute, was everyone in on this except me?" I asked them, suddenly thinking that Beth's shopping inspiration was probably excitement about tonight, plus the fact that both she and Amanda were miraculously busy tonight, leaving me the only one available – I suddenly felt like I had been well played by all.

Rose shrugged at me and smiled before kissing Josh on the cheek, then she let it all out. "It has been the best week organising all of this for you. On top of all the excitement I got to see Josh this afternoon too," she gushed, and I knew that she had more than likely already seen his room.

"Jenny, it really is nice to see you again – you look… revitalised," Josh then spoke as he leaned across and kissed my hand. I thanked him as I continued to hold onto Ethan.

"I thought that you two couldn't leave Italy until today or tomorrow. You're very cruel. I've been despairing that I cannot see you while Rose here has been colluding with you both and had the opportunity to see you Josh already!" I told them with a hint of both sarcasm and happiness. Ethan gestured for us to sit, which I did then he leaned into me;

"I love the fact that you've been suffering a little despair over me. Call me cruel but it is heart-warming," he grinned and then he kissed me again. Josh started laughing.

"Don't listen to a word, Jenny. He's been, I would say, at least ten times worse than you. I promise you my job has been so much harder this week – getting any useful occupation out of him has been a nightmare. So the next time we go anywhere for business, you are going to have to come along or he's going to be useless," he informed me, much to Ethan's embarrassment. I looked at him.

"So you definitely missed me then?" I confidently smiled feeling quite smug, and then we did nothing but just stare at each other for a moment. He took hold of my hand as Rose spoke.

"So… good surprise, Jenny?"

"Great surprise, Rose. I am lost for words." Josh was sat laughing at a now quiet Ethan who it seemed couldn't take his eyes off me. I changed the subject. "So Josh, did you miss Rose?" I asked, and Ethan made a sarcastic murmur before taking a sip of his drink.

"If you think I was bad he wasn't doing too well himself," he told Rose and me, then she slid her arm around his and pulled him close for a kiss.

"Yeah, I know he missed me, Ethan – he made sure he showed me how much this afternoon," she joked, and as Ethan raised his eyebrows at her honest remark and I quickly took a sip of champagne, feeling slightly heated at the thought that I may be doing the same later, Josh just grinned and looked at her.

"Not sure that she's quite convinced yet though!" he gestured and then Rose punched his arm and laughed.

We seemed to talk in our respective partnerships while we drank our drinks; we couldn't get enough of just being together again, it would seem. I found myself staring at him, but as he held my hand and the music played gently in the background I kept rubbing his knuckles with my thumb. He carried on talking to me about his week in Italy, whereas I was visually undressing him from his very beautiful Italian-looking suit and slim-fitted shirt which gave me just a touch of inspiration where it was open at the neck. I must have been either drooling or gripping his hand just a little too tightly as he suddenly laughed at me and repeated his last question before pulling me a little closer to him.

"Did you hear a word that I just said?" he whispered. I gave him that sultry, naughty look and I knew that he knew exactly what I was thinking when his heart rate changed slightly and his pupils dilated. I placed my hand on his chest and then put my lips next to his ear.

"As it would appear I'm going to have to wait until later, I have just undressed you completely with my eyes," I honestly told him. He smiled.

"Interesting… I had you down to your underwear before you even hugged me!" he remarked and then I laughed. I had all of those sexual urges back in an instant but he was, as ever, cool about the whole thing when he then whispered. "Plenty of time for that later, we need to eat first for sustenance, or you'll kill me – so behave young lady," he winked cheekily, and trying to be serious I just nodded and agreed, which made him laugh at me all the more.

I was therefore extremely glad when we were told that our table in the restaurant was ready; this meant another ride down a few floors. Ethan and I stood at the back of the car and I couldn't help but keep touching his face, arms, and his body. I had wanted him to be here so much that now he was I felt like it was possible that it could all be a dream. Rose kept chattering all the way down but in no way did she hold back from draping herself around Josh's neck, which he, in fairness, seemed to love. Ethan's hand had found its way to the lower part of my back, where he rested it in a protective manner which I had missed. As the doors opened and we walked to the waiting waitress, she happily took us to our table, which was in a perfect location away from the centre of the restaurant.

The food was exquisite, and I was far hungrier than I had first thought. Probably the adrenaline rush on arriving and then seeing Ethan had started that hunger. The wine was flowing at a steady pace and the conversation was stimulating. We laughed and talked and it was just like being back in Ibiza together: the whole evening was a moment in time that I knew I would recall with a great deal of happiness. When we had eaten dessert and the restaurant had emptied quite significantly, we realised that it was now near midnight. Ethan asked to settle the bill, and I cringed realising that Rose had no free invitation to dine, other than these two inviting us. I thanked him profusely as did Rose, but he just calmly let it pass him by.

Our jackets appeared at the table from the bar upstairs, and then Rose made the announcement as we stood, that she was staying at the hotel with Josh. I hadn't expected anything else from the moment I realised that they were here. Ethan gave me an inquisitive look, but if he thought I was leaving him alone tonight he was sadly mistaken.

"So, I'm hoping that you have a room too?" I asked him quietly as Josh and Rose were loudly discussing plans for the next day.

"Are you implying that you would like to join me?" he

enquired with such seriousness, but then grinned from ear to ear.

"If you'd rather I went home then I can, you may be tired from travelling," I sarcastically commented and then started to move away, before he had the chance to pull me closer.

"Oh, you're not using that one, Jenny Walker. You know it wasn't a question, it was more of a plea!" he smiled.

"I think I may need you grovelling a little more," I remarked and then he stopped me and pulled my body hard into his, which slightly winded me. I gasped.

"You can have me any way that you choose and I think that you know that," he said with such a sexy voice that if he wasn't turned on like I was right now then I was reading this very wrongly. I gave him that confident look that he loved.

"I need you in your room in the next five minutes, or I'm likely to explode!" I informed him and he laughed before throwing his arm around my shoulders and walking with me quickly to catch up with Rose and Ethan.

We parted ways on the twenty-second floor: I didn't expect anything less when we stopped at a suite door. On entering it was breathtaking, the lounge had floor to ceiling windows that looked across the city, champagne on ice was sat waiting and as I took in the room which was stunning, Ethan shrugged off his jacket and placed it across the back of a chair. When he turned to me I smiled before slipping off my now tight heels that were making my feet ache. I beckoned for him to come to me as I walked toward him.

"You have made me a very happy lady tonight. I think that you know how much I have missed you, but I definitely think that I need to show you how much," I told him softly as he reached me.

"Oh boy, if you're going to have that confident streak that I find so attractive and look like that at the same time I have a feeling that this could all be over far too quickly," he said looking slightly worried.

"That's probably a good thing. I think we need to get this initial heat out of our systems, then we have the rest of the night." I smiled as I let him lead me to the bedroom.

I let my dress drop to the floor feeling grateful for the new underwear purchase. He grumbled low in his chest as he started to unbutton his shirt. He pushed a switch on the wall which closed the blinds and then he walked to where I stood by the bed.

"You had no idea that I was going to be here tonight and yet you came out with sexy underwear on?" he remarked as he pulled off his shirt.

"That is actually your fault," I said. He looked confused.

"How so?"

"Well, I went shopping with Beth to buy new things knowing that you would be visiting me soon and I wore these tonight because it makes me feel closer to you, when I'm trying to look my best," I told him honestly. He seemed to like the gesture as he gently swept my hair back from my face.

"Oh, honey, that's actually quite sweet – but unfortunately

as I am here, they're going to have to come off too," he smiled as he swiftly undid my bra and tossed it to the floor.

I finished undressing him; it was like we had never been apart and as we became silent but our hearts were beating faster and our breathing became more erratic we started to kiss. I know that I devoured him with an intensity that had been raging inside me for over a week. We made love with more passion than I seemed to be able to remember from holiday – perhaps that was the fact that we had been apart and were both desperate to have each other. Whatever it was, as we lay there wrapped in the sheets afterwards I was back in that place that I found so natural and so calming. I couldn't think of myself without him now and as I thought about that and we lay there quietly he suddenly spoke.

"God, I've missed you!" he said and I looked at him.

"Missed me or my body?" I joked. He looked a little flushed at my comment.

"Both, if I'm being absolutely honest," he grinned and I laughed lightly.

"Oh good, the feeling's mutual," I replied before pecking him on the lips and wandering off to get the champagne.

He lay there in appreciation as I walked back in. That sight of him naked in bed with only a sheet between him and my imagination was such a visual tease it had me heating up again.

"God, I don't think that I will ever get used to seeing you like that," I commented as I stood there with two glasses in one hand and a bottle in the other.

"Well, if we're being open about our thoughts, could you just stand there like that a little longer – because it's really doing something for me right now?" He grinned a little more, and I then felt very naked.

I strode around to his side of the bed and sat beside him as I handed over the champagne. He leant forward and kissed me again and then opened the bottle while I held the glasses. I watched him intently as he tried to pour without spilling, but that thought suddenly gave me an idea.

"I think I'd like you to pour that down my front and then drink it from me," I said as I watched him falter and drip it all over my thigh. "Starting there!" I then remarked, and he looked intently at me before placing the bottle down on the side table and then lowering his head to where he had dripped, gently sucking it away.

I was turned on in an instant and before I could think about what I was doing I dribbled more down my left breast and let him slowly lick that away too. It seemed only right that I reciprocate, and so I put one glass down and then pushed him back onto the bed and ran some down his chest across his nipple, he groaned deeply as I made sure I caught every drop. He took the glass from me and pulled me to him for a kiss – and then I found myself straddling him and wanting more. I really didn't think that I could be this intimate and this intense in all honesty, but he made me feel so alive and I had forgotten just how much over this last week. After we made love for a second time, he suggested that we have a shower to wash all the sticky champagne from us and I agreed that would be refreshing. It was now nearly 3am and as we showered I told him about Mark and James coming home tomorrow lunchtime. I wasn't sure how he would feel, but I mentioned to him that I would like them to meet him if he was in agreement. He seemed perfectly happy to do so and suggested that he should take us all out for a meal during the evening.

As we settled down into bed, I sent them both a quick text to tell them not to rush as I had been out with Rose, and that lunchtime or after would be a perfect time for them arriving. Ethan turned out the lights and then I snuggled into his chest and sighed. I was so happy just to be able to hold him and breathe him in, he was just simply perfect. I reached up and kissed him on the lips.

"I love that you are here, thank you for coming back to me so quickly. I don't think that I could have stood the distance much longer," I told him.

"Me neither, I've never felt like this before. I love being near to you and hate being far away. Love is quite torturous at times really, isn't it?" he then asked and I smiled in the darkness.

"It can be, but it can also be absolutely amazing," I then said and he pulled me closer.

"Right, let's get some sleep – busy day for you tomorrow and I don't want you being late home for your boys, or I am not giving myself a great start with them," he then said, and it made me love him more.

"Goodnight, handsome."

"Sweet dreams, honey."

"Oh, I will definitely be having those," I laughed

lightly and he jabbed his finger into my side playfully and then shushed me.

It was the best night's sleep that I had managed since being in the same bed with Ethan in Ibiza. I was a little startled when the alarm sounded at nine o'clock, but he had as promised made sure that I was not sleeping in late and then returning home after my boys had already reached there before me. After laying there for around twenty minutes and Ethan saying good morning with an abundance of kisses that had me laughing uncontrollably, he told me that I should perhaps throw on a robe as breakfast was due to be arriving at nine thirty. As he gracefully walked into the bathroom and I watched his perfectly toned buttocks disappear, I threw myself face down onto the bed and laughed to myself. I hadn't realised that I had said it out loud but after saying, "How did I manage to get so damn lucky?" and then noticing that Ethan was now stood at the door brushing his teeth while answering me, there was no denying it.

"I don't know, honey, but I certainly feel like the luckiest man alive. Someone somewhere must have thought we deserved some luck," he said it so very matter of fact and then he returned to the bathroom, chest bare and a towel around his waist.

I reluctantly climbed out of bed and went up behind him at the mirror and hugged him tightly. It was more in confirmation of what he had just said, but also my appreciation for the fact that we had found each other. I really couldn't believe that he was here and I was so pleased that he would be meeting my boys today. Then it dawned on me that Mum and Dad were due to take us out tomorrow for lunch too. I grimaced a little – the whole family in one weekend, perhaps I was asking too much. He noted my expression and turned to face me.

"What's that look for?" he enquired.

"I've just remembered that my parents want to take me and the boys out for lunch tomorrow; they haven't seen Mark and James for a while," I told him.

"That's okay, I am sure that I have things I can work on and I am here until Friday so plenty of time for us to see each other," he said. I rubbed my hands over his chest.

"That's not what I meant, actually. My parents would love to meet you too, but I don't want to scare you half to death by insisting that you meet my whole family. I'll have you running the other way if I'm not careful," I tried to explain, but he just laughed at me and then placed his hands on my face.

"It would take a hell of a lot more than that to make me run from you. I would be honoured to meet your parents as well as your boys, if that's what you want. Why don't you speak to them and see how they feel first? I'm hoping that you'll want to keep me around for a while, so you decide when the time is right for them and you." He finished just as the doorbell on the suite rang. He kissed me on the cheek and then patted me hard on the buttocks as he reached for a robe. "Now get a robe on, it's time to eat," he dictated as he went to answer the door.

He had managed yet again in just a couple of sentences to completely ease my nerves! I watched him leave the room as I reached for the other robe, and after tying the belt I ran my fingers through my hair and brushed my teeth too. I smiled at myself in the mirror, realising that my complete recollection of him from holiday was one hundred percent accurate and more. He was everything I remembered him to be – considerate, compassionate, kind, generous, and way more handsome than I had allowed my mind to recall. Then as I thought about the sex I grinned, just as he called.

"Are you hungry, honey?" I took a deep breath, smiled and then made my way back to the lounge, where he was sat waiting for me with a cup of coffee. I sank onto the sofa beside him and indulged in a highly calorific breakfast... It was heaven.

After what can only be described as a leisurely, relaxed and enjoyable start to the day, I knew that I would have to start to get ready and get home. I leaned into him while I finished my coffee and we looked out across the city. It was a dry and fairly bright day and as he asked me where I would like to go tonight should the boys agree. I found that I didn't really know where to suggest. My mind instantly started trying to think of exclusive restaurants that I thought Ethan would like and I think he noted my indecisiveness.

"Hey, we can go anywhere you know. Somewhere that you and your boys love would be a safe bet. It could even be their favourite takeaway if that is what they would prefer. I'm aiming to ease their worries about me here, so starting with somewhere they like would be a bonus," he said, and I wrapped my arm around his waist. Ethan could eat at expensive places but he wasn't about cost or exclusivity – he just wanted tasty food in a place that we loved. My mind wandered to the Italian just a stone's throw from our house, in fact we could walk there, and the boys loved it.

"I have the perfect place – Italian, and we all love it. We can meet you there and if things go well, you can walk back and have coffee with us at our house. You can see where I live," I suggested.

"Sounds perfect. You check the boys are happy to meet me and then we can make the arrangements," he finished, and then he stood and offered his hands. I placed my cup down on the table and placed them happily in his, and he pulled me to my feet. "Do you want to take a quick shower before you leave?" he enquired – he had no need to ask, there was no way I was going to turn that down. I gave him a very heated look and he smiled. "You have a very naughty mind… but I do like it!" he noted as we started to walk toward the bedroom.

I dropped my robe onto the floor while he turned the shower on and then he turned and looked at me, dropped his robe too and pulled me close to him. "I would love to just keep you here all day looking just like that," he said. Then we kissed.

"That would be lovely. Maybe after Monday when the boys have gone back I will take you up on that," I smiled back. "I wish I had known that I would be staying here last night – I would have brought some clothes with me for today," I then said as I thought about the new tight dress I was going to have to re-wear.

"Already sorted. Rose managed to pick up some

jeans and a t-shirt for you from your place last night," he then grinned feeling very pleased that he had thought of everything.

"Oh she did, did she? How did you know that I would agree to stay with you? Are you suggesting that I'm predictable?" I asked with a cheeky tone. He squeezed me tighter.

"Actually, I did suggest that you may not wish to – but Rose was adamant that wouldn't be an issue, so I went with her gut reaction," he told me and I laughed at him.

"Okay, I'm obviously weak and have no control around you and that's plain for everyone to see. You got me – I wouldn't have said no!" I replied and then he pulled me over to the shower and under the hot spray. It was delightful.

By the time I had dressed, dried my hair and used my compact to lightly hide any blemishes, I knew that I was going to have to leave him until later and that wasn't a pleasant thought. I text Rose and told her I wasn't expecting to see her anytime soon, so I would call her later – thanking her again for the best surprise ever. Ethan walked me down to the reception, and as we walked hand in hand and I looked at his cool and casual persona in his jeans and t-shirt, I was so happy. I had him back just as I liked him – relaxed, confident and seemingly very happy just like me. When we reached the door he passed me a bag with my dress in as I looked at my shoes – these heels were a tad overdressed for jeans, but they made me the perfect height for kissing him.

I pressed my chest tight against him and placed my hand around his neck. When his forehead touched mine I kissed him tenderly but with meaning and when we parted lips we both sighed.

"I am so very glad that you are here," I told him.

"I really don't want to be anywhere else," he replied and so I kissed him again.

"Good answer," I smiled. "I will call you later when I have spoken with James and Mark, then we can make plans," I informed him. He nodded and then pulled me close for a lovely embrace.

"I look forward to hearing from you; I suspect my day is going to be very slow without you," he said and that made my insides dance around.

"Right, I best get moving and I will definitely miss you for the rest of the day," I told him.

"Likewise – don't forget to call me," he then said looking so sincere and yet vulnerable at the same time. I laughed a little at him.

"That's hardly likely to happen – I seem to be finding it harder to live without you around these days," I openly told him and then I pecked him on the cheek and started to make my way out of the hotel door.

As I walked out to get a taxi home, which the lovely doorman called for me, I turned back and looked at him just once. He was stood there looking like a lost boy staring back at me. I hoped that he too was honest at starting to find it very hard to be without me, I waved to him to try and ease his worried look and he smiled and waved back. Then I willed myself to get in the waiting taxi and go or there could be a very strong chance that I wouldn't want to. My boys suddenly sprang to mind, I knew I had to get back and so I tried to focus briefly, told the taxi driver where I wanted to go and then I sat back, turned, then smiled at him as the taxi pulled away from the pavement.

Chapter 25

I arrived home at eleven thirty; the boys had not landed back yet and so I quickly went upstairs and tidied up my appearance. I had amazing thoughts from last night and was happy knowing that I would be able to see Ethan again later tonight, hopefully. My only concern now was telling the boys and trying to predict how they may react about this whole 'me and a new man' situation. My stomach started to churn and tie in knots: this would be a big deal for them and as much as I was wrapped up in feeling better about moving on, I had to be prepared for the fact that my boys may not be. I went back to the kitchen and put the kettle on and then looked at my phone, a text from the boys and one from Ethan.

Mark and James were due to be here around twelve thirty and Ethan was just telling me that he was missing me already. I decided, knowing my boys and their appetite, that I would make a plate full of sandwiches ready for their arrival. I turned on the radio to try to take my mind off how I was going to tell them about Ethan, but it kept replaying in my mind – and badly at that, so when the doorbell rang I was glad of the distraction. I almost skipped to the door and when I opened it Mark was stood there. It was so good to see him. He was as happy to see me I think and as he stepped in the door he gave me a huge hug. It felt so great to hold my son.

"How are you, Mum?" he said as he dropped his bag in the hallway.

"I'm okay, Mark – you?" I asked in return.

"Really great, actually. Did I beat James here?"

"Yes you did, and would you feeling great have anything to do with the new girlfriend?" I asked him and he smiled, then ran his hand through his hair.

"Maybe," he simply said and I smiled at him.

"New haircut too, and look at those muscles!" I joked as I squeezed his biceps. He flexed his arm for me.

"Well, looking my best is a priority now that I have a gorgeous girl on my arm," he honestly said and it made me happy that he had met someone nice.

"Any pictures of her?" I enquired, and as he gushed about her he found a picture on his phone and then showed it to me. "Wow, Mark. She looks gorgeous," I told him. He was grinning from ear to ear.

"I know, she's pretty amazing." He said bashfully.

I put the kettle on and made him a drink and then he started quizzing me about my holiday as we sipped a cup of tea. I told him about the hotel, the heavy drinking, and the embarrassing myself, the food and then slightly reluctantly I told him about meeting Ethan and the other men. He raised his eyebrows at me.

"Hell, Mum. Have you being having a holiday fling?" he joked, but I didn't laugh. I was hoping telling Mark first would make it easier with James who was a little more protective of me.

"I really like him. He was kind and generous and an absolute gentleman," I tried to explain.

"Yeah, but Mum, it was a holiday – we all know what happens on holidays sometimes. It's hardly likely you're going to see him again," he then said as he took another bite of a sandwich.

"Actually, that's not entirely true – I had dinner with him last night," I informed him. He grinned at me.

"Bloody hell, Mum. You're a fast mover and you've been back how long? In fact hang on a minute, I thought that you said he'd gone to Rome?" he then said after my previous brief synopsis about Ethan.

"He did, but he flew in yesterday morning," I replied. Mark stopped chewing his sandwich and swallowed it.

"Just to see you?" he asked. I smiled.

"Yeah, just to see me," I told him. He shook his head and took another bite of sandwich.

"Looks like you made an impression too, then. You got a picture of this guy?" he then asked me, and with a little apprehension I showed him the pictures from my phone.

He scrolled through them, smiled a lot, nodded his head, laughed hysterically at Beth's flamboyant dress sense, but commented nonetheless at the fact that he was a handsome man. He also pointed out that I looked really happy, and I was so pleased that he could see that.

"So, you want to see more of this Ethan then?" he asked. I scowled a little knowing what my answer was going to be.

"I really would like to, but I'm also really mindful of how you and James feel about it. I'm sure it won't be easy for you two seeing me with someone else, even though Ethan is pretty amazing. He would really like to meet you both though, so that you can make any decisions about him for yourself. So he suggested dinner tonight, I thought Pappa Lorenzo's may be good?" I told him.

"Mum, you don't need our permission to see someone else. It must have been really hard on you this last three years but you're still young and I certainly don't want to think that you're going to be on your own forever. James may have something to say about it but I'm happy to meet him. I love Dad, I always will, but he's no longer with us and that's no one's fault. You look different, Mum, in a good way, so bring it on, I say!" he said considerately and I couldn't help but walk around to him and give him a huge hug.

"Thanks, darling. I really needed to hear that," I replied as he rubbed my back. Then he started laughing so I stopped and looked at him.

"What's so funny?" I enquired with a bit of confusion.

"Just that thought of my mum being a bit of a floozy; it's both funny and cringeworthy at the same time!" he joked. I hit him across the arm.

"I am not a floozy! Bloody hell, it's one guy I've opened up to, that's all, and it really wasn't like that," I tried to defend myself which made him laugh all the more.

"You better hold that bit back until last when you tell James, Mum. Not quite sure how he might handle it!" he continued, laughing.

"God, you're making me out to be some sex-crazed woman. I most certainly am not!" I kept trying to convince him.

"Well, you look pretty cosy on some of those photos. I think you've definitely got a thing for this guy – it's highly amusing at your age," he then said and I scowled at him.

"What do you mean – my age? I'm not that old. You just told me I'm still young! Yes, I am cosy with him, but honestly I tell you it was far more romantic than you're giving it credit." I finished as I walked back around to my side of the island and carried on drinking my tea. He held his hands up in defeat.

"Okay, you're defending him well, so you obviously do like him, I give up. I think I will be able to make my own mind up about how serious you are when I meet him then. He sounds quite interesting actually, with his line of work." He then said as he ate another half of sandwich.

"He's extremely interesting. It will be good if you meet him. It will make me happy, anyway," I then admitted.

"Cool," he nodded in response. Then as we carried on talking the doorbell rang again.

I smiled as I set off toward the door with Mark following. Seeing James was just as fulfilling as when Mark arrived. I hugged him as he stepped in and he hugged me back. Then both he and Mark shook hands and patted each other on the back. I loved that my boys got on so well. He pointed out that he was hungry, which was no surprise, and so with a hub of excitement from them both we moved back to the kitchen and had lunch. It was lovely to hear what they had been up to: Emma was mentioned numerous times by James and it was really nice to know that they were still in love.

As we chatted away, Mark suddenly winked at me before saying, "So – it sounds like Mum's had a great time with Beth, Amanda and Rose on holiday!" he suddenly said and my stomach tied into knots as he prompted me to tell James what had happened. James glared at me.

"Too much alcohol, Mum?" he asked. I laughed lightly and nodded. "So you said that you'd met a guy. Not like you is it really?" he then said, and his tone sounded guarded.

"Well, no. I suppose not, James, I certainly didn't go out there looking for anyone if that's what you mean," I told him.

"I'm just surprised, that's all. Sounds like you were spending a lot of time with him when we spoke while you were away," he then said.

"Don't give her a hard time, man. She was just having fun," Mark then chipped in.

"She's our mum, Mark," James then snapped.

"What, so she's not allowed to have fun?" Mark enquired sarcastically.

"Boys, please. I don't want to fall out over this. It's not going to matter 'when' I meet a new man: it's going to be hard for you no matter when that happens. He won't be your dad, but I've realised that I don't want to be alone anymore," I tried to explain. James sighed and rubbed his forehead.

"Mum, you know I don't want that. I just don't want anyone to hurt you. You've dealt with enough and yes it will be hard seeing you with someone else, but that's our problem to deal with," James then said.

"He looks fairly decent, James. He wants to meet us and let us decide for ourselves what we think," Mark then said. James looked at him then me.

"He's here?" James enquired.

"Not actually here, but in Manchester – yes," I replied.

"He flew in from Rome yesterday just to see her, man, that's pretty cool!" Mark then said.

"You said he was British, not Italian," James noted.

"He is British but he has hotels everywhere. He's just been to Rome to sort out problems with one of them. He was missing me though as I was him, so he came over to see me," I tried to explain.

"You've been apart less than a week though. I don't get it," James then said. This was not going as well as it had done with Mark.

"Smitten, I think is the word you're looking for," Mark then said quite jokily. James just stared at him.

"You're obviously finding this easy to deal with," he directed at Mark.

"Hey, I want Mum to be happy and it makes me feel better knowing that when we're away someone's looking out for her. If that doesn't make you happy then I don't know what to say," Mark then questioned. I smiled at him.

James was quiet for a minute and then he reached across and squeezed my hand. "Mum, you know this guy better than us, if he's making you happy then that's great I suppose. If he wants us to meet him, then it says a lot

434

for his character – so okay, I'll meet him. I'm not saying it will be easy, but Mark's right – I want you to be happy again," he finished and I walked around and hugged him. It wasn't going to be an easy process with James feeling like he did, but at least he was willing to take a shot at giving Ethan a chance, and that's all I could hope for.

We finished lunch, laughed about the things that they had been up to and then they went upstairs and unpacked. I sent Ethan a text to say that tonight was definitely on, and he replied instantly saying that he was very pleased that they had both agreed to let him meet them. He told me that he would make all of the arrangements and call the restaurant and then let me know what time we would be eating. We spoke for a few minutes – he had been working after I left. It would appear that Rose had only just recently vacated Josh's room, as Josh had now joined him. I felt slightly jealous that they had managed a long leisurely morning together, but I hoped that I would be able to do the same once the boys had gone back.

We decided to walk to the pub around the corner after they'd unpacked for a drink – it was actually a nice day and so sitting outside with them and talking was really special, and something that I missed. I told them about my plans for the shop and that Caroline was an inspiration at the moment. We quizzed Mark about his new girlfriend, which he was a bit coy about, but you could tell that he thought a lot about her. When it got to three thirty, we started to stroll back and shower. Ethan had suggested eating at six, partly because he didn't want to wait all evening to be able to see me, and partly because he wanted to spend as much time with Mark and James as possible.

When we set off walking to the restaurant at five thirty, casually dressed but with effort made on my part, the boys were happy to walk either side of me. Mark found it highly amusing to squeeze me and ask if I was nervous about the introduction. James told him to leave me alone, which made me smile – I assured them that there was nothing to really worry about as I was certain that they would really like Ethan. James noted that my confidence was helping his and I was grateful for that. As we approached the restaurant door, they pushed me in first and I quickly glanced to the bar to find Ethan making his way over to us in an instant. He kissed me on the cheek and then looked toward James first and reached out his hand;

"It's a real pleasure to meet you – I'm Ethan," he said with so much confidence as James took his hand and shook it happily.

"James. It's nice to meet you," he replied. Then he repeated the gesture with Mark.

"Ethan, pleasure to meet the man that's making my mum so happy!" he said with a cheeky tone, but I think that Ethan appreciated it.

"Can I get you all a drink?" he asked and the boys happily told him they would have a pint.

As we talked by the bar and waited for our table to be readied, Ethan stood with his hand resting in that perfect place at the bottom of my back. Enough for me to know that he wanted to touch me, but not so much to annoy the boys. James quizzed Ethan about his work, which he was happy to elaborate on. Mark asked about the hotels and I knew exactly what he was trying to do – anything for a free stay somewhere! Ethan told them with no hesitation that they would be welcome at any of his hotels anytime – they just needed to speak with either himself or Josh. Suddenly that seemed to ease all the tension, and by the time we sat down we were all laughing and talking like we had been some sort of makeshift family for a long time. I couldn't have anticipated anything better than the way it was going.

Ethan had arranged for a bottle of champagne to be chilling; he knew me too well already. Then he asked what the boys would prefer and they always went with red, so he requested a couple of bottles to try. We ordered, continued to talk, and laughed a lot – sometimes at me, particularly about how we met and the fact that I was intoxicated. Ethan rubbed my hand that rested on my lap and told them that he was glad that I had been, otherwise it was possible we may never have met. The food was delicious, as always, and even Ethan commented on the fact that this restaurant had the ability to make you feel like you were in a traditional Italian home eating with the family and that the staff added to the enjoyment. When the time reached nine o'clock and we had depleted the alcohol and eaten ourselves contently full. I suggested coffee back at our house and then looked to the boys for confirmation that was alright. James spoke first, and said, 'Yes, why don't you walk back with us?' I was both surprised and extremely pleased that he was being so accommodating, and Mark gave me a nod to confirm my gratitude.

Ethan insisted on paying as always and we all thanked him. He in turn insisted that it had been his pleasure to do so. We walked slowly back to the house, it wasn't the warmest of nights, but it was dry and clear. On a couple of occasions his hand found itself entwining with mine when the boys were not looking and it made me smile at him. When we reached the front door I unlocked it and we went in, I have to say that Ethan looked a little apprehensive, but Mark had noted that too and just said 'Come in, let's have another drink.' I couldn't have been happier that they both were trying to make him feel welcome.

The boys walked to the kitchen and shouted back to the hall where we stood asking what we would like. As they had pushed the door half closed I had the impression they were just giving me a minute with him alone. I didn't need any persuading, I lurched at him pressing my lips firmly on his. His hands were around my waist in seconds and it was heated briefly until we heard a cork pop. We silently laughed and then I whispered that I couldn't have imagined how well the boys were connecting with him.

"They're amazing Jen, honestly – you have two great young men there," he said and it made me peck him on the lips again.

"Thanks, I know this is hard for you – not easy either being in our house. If you are uncomfortable at any time, please let me know," I tried to reassure him.

"As long as I am close to you, I'll survive," he grinned. Then James called us.

"Are you two having a drink with us or what?" We silently laughed again as I took his hand and led him into the kitchen.

Mark opened the French doors and lit the patio heater; as the night was so clear it seemed a shame to waste it. I sat very closely to Ethan and made sure that he felt at ease, touching his knee on occasions. Both of the boys had more questions for him: I cringed a little when James asked if he had been married before but Ethan simply told him the whole situation involving that part of his life. I think that James was a little taken a back at how open he was. Mark kept asking where the hotels he owned were again and it amused me that he was plugging for a free stay... again.

"You guys have girlfriends, right?" Ethan then asked. They both nodded. "Why don't I arrange a trip for all of us?" he then said before taking a sip of wine and trying to judge their response.

"Oh man, I'm up for that – how to impress your new girl in one single step," Mark joked. Ethan smiled.

"Well I can ask Emma," James said with more subtlety than Mark.

"I can get Josh my assistant to sort the flights, nothing to worry about really just need the time to all be able to do it. Perhaps a short five-day break to start with?" he suggested. I touched his arm.

"Are you sure about this, Ethan? I mean, it will cost you a fortune – it's very generous," I tried to convey. He placed his glass down and sat up straight for a minute, taking my hand in his.

"I want you two," he said looking at James and Mark, "to understand how much I care for your mum. If it makes it easier for you to accept me by simply spending some time together, then I cannot think of a better thing to do than go away for a few days," he explained. I swallowed hard and then kissed him on the cheek. His gestures were more chivalrous than I could dream of. The boys looked at each other and then James in a slightly humorous tone surprised me when he said:

"Yeah, alright – you're not bad." Mark punched him on the arm.

"Funny," he said. "I'm all for this new adventure – where are we going?" Mark quizzed without hesitation or feeling the slightest bit bashful.

"Take your pick." Ethan smiled and a whole excitable conversation erupted between the two of them over where they should go.

I looked at Ethan and as he smiled at me I mimed the words, "Thank you," he squeezed my hand and as we laughed at them arguing and play fighting over choices based on their desired destinations over the years, we seemed to have broken the awkwardness and turned it into something special. I leaned into him;

"You know, I think they loved you anyway without you having to offer them a free trip."

"I know, I felt more relaxed with them by the end of the meal – but I want them to see how we are together and neutral ground is a good place to do that," he said. I nodded; I knew what he was trying to do and I was grateful.

The boys were now wrestling around the garden. Too much wine most likely, I gestured toward the kitchen. "Coffee?" I asked him and he stood with me to go indoors. He wondered around the dining area while I switched the kettle on and he took the time to look at our family pictures with Paul. It made my nerves flare up again.

"He was a handsome guy – understandable why those two are such good-looking lads with the two of you," he commented.

"That's sweet. You don't have to look at those, though, maybe I should think about moving them now," I said as he walked toward me.

"Please don't do that for my benefit. He was part of your life and unfortunately left it too soon. You can't switch those memories off, particularly when you look at those two." He gestured toward Mark and James still wrestling outdoors. He was now stood in front of me and took my face in his hands before kissing me tenderly. "I know it's sad that he left you, Jenny, but I wouldn't have met you if he'd still been here. Let's just honour his memory by being the best that we can be and looking after those two out there, even though it may seem a little selfish on my part," he finished.

"How do you always find the right thing to say?" I asked before kissing him again. The boys then fell back through the French doors.

"Whoa, interrupting!" Mark laughed. Ethan stepped back.

"I'll finish this coffee and then I will leave you to catch up," he said.

"We gonna see you tomorrow, Ethan?" Mark asked him meaningfully. Ethan looked at me and then Mark and James and he shrugged.

"Your grandparents want to take us out for lunch tomorrow, perhaps you wouldn't mind if Ethan joined us?" I suggested tentatively.

"Fine by me," James said first. I smiled at him.

"I'm cool. I want to find out more about the hotel choices," Mark then chipped in. I scowled at him.

"Ethan is not just a free trip, you know," I snapped at them. They both stopped joking for a second and looked at each other. Then James stepped forward.

"Your gesture is very generous and we do appreciate it," James said before offering his hand as a gesture of goodwill. I swallowed, thanking God that I had brought them up well and they knew when I was angry with them.

"Again, it's my pleasure," Ethan said as they shook hands, and then Mark jumped in.

"Yeah, really kind – so thanks," he also said shaking his hand too – he was never one for a lot of thought in his words. Mark did then push James toward the lounge saying that they would put a film on, but I knew they were disappearing for a short time to give me time alone with Ethan after their interruption.

"Lively pair, aren't they?" Ethan joked and I immediately mellowed and laughed.

"That's one way of putting it!" I remarked and then we went and sat back outdoors with our coffee.

Ethan texted Josh and asked him to send a car from the hotel for him. It still surprised me that he had this ability to command anyone, but he wasn't the least bit obnoxious with it. We snuggled in each other's arms and I managed to get a couple of mind-blowing kisses off him.

"Kiss me again like that and you're coming back with me," he whispered.

"I wish I could just let you stay here, it would finish the night off perfectly… but… " I started. However, he stopped me.

"Hey, it's too soon for them. I like your way of thinking but I can stay, if you'd like that, once they have left. This is going remarkably well and I don't want to rock the boat," he expressed and I loved him for his understanding. "Anyway, I like the thought that you'll have to wait a couple of days before you can have me all to yourself – should make it very interesting for me on Monday!" he then joked and I hit him on the arm and then laughed at him.

"Thanks – me being the sex-crazed, can't-get-enough-of-you kind of woman," I replied. He shrugged with a big grin on his face.

"Well, if the cap fits!" he then said and I hit him again. After he held my hand down and stopped laughing he then looked at me. "I love the fact that you can't get enough – makes me not look so desperate," he smiled and then we kissed again.

Once coffee was finished and we had talked for a while, he started to make an attempt to go. I really didn't want him to but as I listened to my boys in the other room, I knew I had to – it was the right thing to do. We stood and embraced for a while, kissed some more and then started to move to the front door. Ethan stopped at the lounge doorway and told James and Mark not to get up but that he was leaving and he looked forward to talking more with them soon. They held their hands up and basically said, "Later," then carried on watching television. I chuckled at the fact they were quite relaxed in treating him like an old friend. He raised his eyebrows at me in acceptance of their chilled state.

When I opened the front door a car was sat waiting. I really wasn't sure how long it had been there, but Ethan kissed me on the forehead and then gave me a huge squeeze before saying that he would be in touch very soon and I should check my phone. As I waved him off and then closed the door, I sighed feeling content with how well things had gone. Turning back down the hallway I stopped at the lounge, went in and fell into the seat beside Mark. He threw his arm around my shoulders.

"He seems really nice, Mum. Liking him a lot now we get a free trip as well. Pretty handsome guy too – you sly old thing!" he joked while nudging my arm.

"Thanks, son!" I replied sarcastically. Then I looked across at James hoping for a good review on his thoughts of Ethan. He noted my desperate waiting look.

"He's alright, seems pretty solid and reliable. Think I can learn to like him, Mum," he said. I grinned at them both.

"Have I told you two recently that I love you?" I asked feeling more than happy with their first impression of the man that I was in love with. Mark nudged me and smiled.

"Ah James, she's gone all mushy on us... She's definitely fallen for this guy," he declared, but I didn't care as he was one hundred percent correct.

Chapter 26

I excused myself after around twenty minutes while they argued about what to watch next. I offered to make some drinks, but those two had no intentions of a cup of tea or coffee, so I handed them a can of lager each while the kettle boiled. My phone was resting on the worktop; I looked to see if I had missed anything and Ethan had text me already:

> *'I cannot believe how well that went. You should be very proud of them, Jen, they are really great young men. I hope that they haven't given you a hard time after I left? Let me know about tomorrow; the more time I get to spend with you the better. I was unhappy about having to leave you, my bed will be cold and empty again tonight… but I look forward to being 'warmed up' on Monday! Stay in touch, love Ethan X.'*

I grinned at his sincerity, but his cheeky undertone had my stomach somersaulting again thinking about Monday night. I replied straight away as it would appear he sent this text as soon as he got into the car:

'Ethan, I think it is safe to say that you were a 'hit' with my boys. They both like you, although I am sorry about Mark's over keenness of a free trip! I wish that I was staying with you tonight too... but, we will have plenty of time to make up for that later. I'm going to watch some television with them now before I retire, so sleep well and I will be in touch soon – Love Jen X.'

I sent Dad a text to ask if he would mind Ethan joining us tomorrow. I know that both he and Mum were keen to meet him and, after explaining that the boys already had, I suspected that they would be happy to oblige. It took less than a minute before he answered and said: *'Of course, darling, we look forward to it. Midday at the usual place?'* I replied stating that was fine and then quickly sent one to Ethan. I suggested that he came here and went with us, as that would be easier for him and when I said that I would pick him up mid-morning, his reply was one of obvious delight.

I crashed back on the settee with Mark and we started to watch *The Avengers Assemble*. It amused me that they still loved these superhero films, but I was grateful that they had picked something light-hearted and fun. We chatted as the film played, they had another two beers before the film finished and when it came to going to bed I felt exhausted. I was sure it was the relief of getting this evening over with. It was nearly one o'clock when I hugged them both and said goodnight I realised how genuinely happy I was to have them back around the house with me. Sinking into bed, I felt like I had definitely begun a new chapter in my life and I suddenly appreciated how grateful I felt for that, I was ready.

The traffic for a Sunday morning was steady-going into Manchester. I had told Ethan I would meet him outside at ten and when I pulled up close to the hotel he almost skipped over to my car. We didn't have the chance to talk, he leaned over and kissed me full on the lips then he pulled his seatbelt across him and smiled.

"My, my – someone is happy this morning," I noted as he reached over and placed his hand on my knee. I instantly started to throb and felt the blood pulsing through my veins. It was incredible that his touch could do that to me.

"I get to spend most of the day with you. Lots to be happy about," he grinned. Before he had my legs turning to jelly I quickly pulled away trying to focus on the task of driving us back home safely.

"I like seeing you this relaxed. It suits you," I told him, after firstly looking at his face and then giving him the once over. "Plus, you look pretty hot too – I'm loving the casual look on you," I smiled back, making a point that his jeans, polo shirt and casual jacket were a hit with me. He didn't speak but simply smiled in response.

The drive back did not take long; we discussed his upcoming business and the trip with James and Mark. He did declare that he had a few nerves about meeting my Dad, but I assured him that he should be more worried about my Mum's interrogation. He laughed lightly, but the look on his face showed worry and I felt quite selfish for being so blasé – I was very lucky that he even wanted to do this. I squeezed the hand that still rested on my knee for a little reassurance. As we pulled up on the driveway, I hoped that those boys hadn't trashed the house or cooked enough bacon to feed an army, but I was pleasantly surprised to find that they had done neither. They were sat in the kitchen dressed, ready and having a coffee and they had placed extra mugs out ready for our return. The gesture was sweet, so as Ethan started a conversation with them I made us a drink too.

We sat around the table and had a conversation about many things, just the fact that we could do that was testament to the fact that everyone was willing to try to accept each other. We were getting along so well – Ethan seemed to be able to put anyone at ease and though I suspected that Mark was quite open to any relationship I had with Ethan, I had my suspicion that James was not quite one hundred percent on board yet. I needed to make sure that I was careful not to expect too much from both of them – these were, after all, early days and my boys were my priority.

The pub that we were meeting at for lunch was one of my dad's favourites, so it tended to be the regular choice. It was only twenty minutes' drive and so at eleven thirty we started to make a move. James and Mark, with no suggestion from myself, jumped into the back of the car. Ethan seemed happy to be seated with me in the front. The drive there was a medley of singing from the boys along with the radio, excitement and laughter. I had honestly forgotten how much they make me laugh – it had been over a month since I last saw them. I was starting to appreciate so many different things again and I was loving the feeling of being so involved in my own life and wellbeing.

Once we had parked, the boys walked quickly toward the pub in front of us. Ethan stopped me briefly just before we entered and said, "Thank you for letting me join you today, it means a lot to me – that you would want to introduce me to your family." I kissed him on the cheek and told him that it should be me thanking him. Then I grabbed his hand and pulled him through the door. It wasn't difficult to find them, Mark and James' voices carried whenever they were in a room – a trait from Paul, I thought to myself. Hand in hand I walked with him toward Mum and Dad and the introductions began. Mum, it had to be said, was swooning, Ethan and my dad were getting on like a house on fire. Lots of questions about the yacht and Hernando's business were asked. Dad was even happier when Ethan said that he could give him Hernando's number should he ever wish to have a sailing holiday. I did wonder whether Dad realised just how luxurious his boats were, but perhaps he had smaller versions.

Poor Ethan seemed to get interrogated about his business, his hotels, and his life. Both Mark and James were quick to intervene when the hotels were discussed telling my parents about the impending trip. Dad commented that he was a little jealous, but Ethan thankfully didn't invite them also – I'm not sure that would've been the right thing to do in the first instance. It was far more important that we build trust and respect with my boys. Overall, the afternoon was a roaring success, and after filling ourselves there was nothing more to do for the afternoon but chill and let it settle. When it came to leaving, Dad insisted that he paid. Just being able to see his grandsons brought him great pleasure, he loved to hear everything that they were up to, and this was his way of doing something for them. I think that Ethan was a little taken aback when Mum kissed him goodbye on the cheek and then hugged him rather tightly. James laughed and peeled her off him, giving him chance to rid himself of his look of shock. Dad shook his hand and then pulled him close and whispered something in Ethan's ear before patting him on the shoulder and squeezing it like a father would a son. I scowled at Dad trying to work out what he had said, but Ethan was smiling; I would ask him later.

We all left and travelled home, with more subtle music and no singing, thank goodness. I think that we were all going into a slight food coma after the amount that we had consumed. I asked Ethan if he wanted to come in for coffee, but he was, as ever, mindful at the fact that the boys were going back tomorrow morning and he wanted me to spend as much time with them as possible. So I dropped the boys off, they said their goodbyes and then I drove Ethan back into the city. Approaching the centre we passed many large stores, and after laughing at Ethan's expression with my mum squeezing the air out of him, I spotted a Sainsbury's and without any hesitation I swung the car into the car park and parked in a quiet corner.

"Are you hungry again already?" he enquired looking around as I unfastened my seatbelt and then scrambled over the gear stick to sit straddled across his lap to face him.

"Be quiet while I kiss you, because I'm very happy at how this weekend has gone," I told him before lunging at his lips.

We had a heated and passionate five minutes before we parted, breathless. "Are you trying to get us arrested?" he then asked. I laughed at the thought – but quite honestly, he was right.

"I knew if I came into the hotel, I wouldn't want to leave and if I get to your room – well, I think we both know what would happen there. I'm sorry, I just couldn't wait," I said now looking at our very intimate position at this moment in time. I climbed back to the driver's side of the car and straightened my clothing and brushed down my hair, then I felt his gaze upon me.

"You know, I like you being in control and believe me all I want to do right now is let you carry on. I love the fact that you have that naughty head on again, but I suspect if we end up in jail tonight, your boys are not going to be over enthused at our behaviour," he smiled. I knew he was right again, but every time I was with him he was like a magnet and I wanted to be permanently attached to him. He noted my disappointment, "You can show me how happy you are about this weekend tomorrow night," he then said and I nodded in agreement and started the engine.

There was an air of silence as we carried on driving,

mainly due to frustration. Then when we started talking again; Ethan was keen to ask about my dad and the fact that he had been a very good lawyer before his retirement. He commented that he may be able to run things by him sometimes, and I knew that would make my dad really happy as he always liked to feel he was still in the loop. Eventually we pulled up outside the hotel again; I had that usual feeling of regret that we had to part ways, so when he leaned across and gave me a deliciously heart warming kiss I was very happy.

"How about dinner tomorrow night in the city and then see where we fancy spending the night?" he asked hopefully.

"That sounds lovely, actually. I do understand if you find it strange to stay at my house," I tried to reassure him.

"That doesn't worry me, I'm big boy – I can deal with it. Are you working tomorrow afternoon?" he then asked. I smiled feeling happy that he hopefully wanted to spend some extra time with me.

"I don't have to," I stated, "What do you have in mind?"

"Oh I don't know – a late lunch, some shopping – whatever you would like. I just need to finish some work with Josh in the morning, but I think that he is taking Rose out tomorrow night. It would be nice to have an evening together – just us two," he said as he squeezed my hand and I couldn't think of anything better than that.

"It's a deal – how about I come here for around two o'clock after the boys have left and we can do lunch and shopping? I can bring something to change into for dinner, then we can see what takes our fancy after that," I suggested. He grinned and planted a huge kiss on my lips.

"Perfect." He climbed out of the car. Closing the door he stretched out his arms and leaned at my open window. "I need to go now before I don't want to," he smiled. "Enjoy the rest of your night with James and Mark and tell them from me that it was a pleasure meeting them. I am, however, really looking forward to seeing you tomorrow." He winked once.

"You and me both," I smiled back. "Now get yourself inside before I jump out of the car, leap across the bonnet and seduce you!" I joked. He gave me surprised look.

"That may actually be quite an interesting sight to see," he said seriously, but he had that look on his face that told me he was taunting me. I scowled at him.

"I'm going to make you wait – so back up, boy, I need to go," I answered confidently as I pressed the button to start the window up. He laughed at my response and when the window reached half way I shouted across to him, "Miss you already!"

Ethan stepped back and then tapped the roof like an order for me to move. I knew that I should, the boys were waiting for me at home. I slowly pulled away from him and he waved as he watched me leave for a few seconds before walking toward the reception doors. The clearly visible smile on his face in my rear-view mirror, was an image that I wasn't likely to forget anytime soon. The rest of the evening was a barrage of taunting me about Ethan – but in a sweet way, watching numerous television programmes and drinking a little more wine. It shocked me slightly at nine o'clock when James returned from the kitchen with cheese, crackers and other delights because as he placed them on a table he moved closer to Mark and me. It surprised me even more that my tummy growled. He then topped our glasses up and sat on the floor in front of me so that he could help himself, and when he turned and leaned his elbow on my knee I smiled at him. He smiled confidently at me and started eating and I knew in some small way this was him saying, "You're going to be alright, Mum."

Bedtime came faster than ever, and when I lay there staring at the ceiling, I wondered how long it would be before I see them again. I decided as a farewell treat that I would get up and make a full English breakfast with pancakes and the works. I smiled to myself and drifted off. After sleeping well and a hot blast in the shower, I was raring to go. It was a dry and bright morning – not really any cloud in the somewhat blue sky – and my mood lifted instantly as I looked out of the window. I crept downstairs and started cooking. The radio was playing, I was singing along… Everything to make me feel like this was going to be a really great day.

I had to go and prise those two out of bed, eventually. It was like they hadn't slept for a week. Both insisted on a quick shower first and so I kept everything warm and put the eggs on to poach while I waited for them. I had my phone and had seen Ethan's, 'Good morning,' message and so I replied with the same and a smiley face. He asked if I had enjoyed my evening and told me to make the most of this morning before they left, then he could have me all

455

to himself. I knew that he was working and so my simple reply to all this was, '*I did, I will, I can't wait!*'

After twenty minutes or so, they both appeared at the table looking like zombies. I laughed at them and poured coffee and then started to place all of the cooked food on the table for them to delve into. It was like someone had flicked a switch – they perked up and started chatting and eating faster than I care to mention. Knowing that they had large appetites I had to remind them that some of this food was for me too. They slowed themselves but carried on – I was happy thinking that whereas theirs was fuel for the journey back, mine was fuel for sustenance with Ethan. I very much doubted that he would survive my initial arrival without me having him naked in seconds.

We talked, went for a short walk to the newsagents, had more tea near lunchtime and cake that we had bought and then they started to make a move to return back.

"I want to meet Charlotte soon," I told Mark as they packed up their cars.

"You will, I promise."

They raided my cupboards taking some nibbles for the journey. As we stood in the kitchen discussing the proposed trip and when I was going to see them again – and after Ethan being briefly mentioned – James spoke.

"Mum, he seems like a really nice guy. It's good to see you so happy and he seems to really care for you. I'm okay with this – just take it slowly. I'm only worried about you getting hurt. It would be a bit too much for us if he hurt you," he truthfully said. I rubbed his arm.

"I intend on doing just that. We don't want to rush things, darling. I know he cares about how I feel and I know that he will look after me. At the moment I am happy with that," I replied.

"Okay," he nodded. Mark then leaned over and gave me a huge hug, lifting my feet from the floor.

"I think he'll prove to be a good one, Mum. Enjoy it and take it easy," he reiterated. I smiled at them.

"I'm really pleased that you agreed to see him this weekend, so thank you both for that," I told them, feeling blessed that they were so calm.

"Our pleasure, anything for good old Mum – especially when you feed us so well!" Mark cheekily said as he took a huge bite from a sandwich he had made himself. I shook my head at him.

"God help any woman either of you end up marrying, she's going to have to go shopping every day to satisfy your appetite," I scowled. They didn't bat an eye but simply agreed!

After numerous hugs and kisses, I waved them off and although I was happy that I had seen them, I was a little sad that they were leaving. I returned indoors and tidied up, just in case we came back here later tonight. By the time I had packed an overnight bag, made myself look respectable for shopping – but with underwear on that I knew was sexy – I made my way to Ethan's hotel. Once parked, I went in and up to his suite. He answered the door within seconds and had a shirt and jeans on that I immediately wanted to take off.

"Hey gorgeous – you're here," he said as he pulled me

in. "Enjoy your time with your boys?" he asked. I nodded in agreement, but I had other things on my mind and so I dropped the bags which I carried and threw my arms around his neck, kissing him without any hesitation. He kissed me back with an eagerness that reflected my own.

Before I even realised how fast we were moving I was down to my underwear and he only his jeans, there was no time to move to the bedroom, I had to have him – I dragged him to the large settee and in no time at all we had both climaxed. I laughed at our desperation, but he did too. He commented again that he had never been like this with anyone before and he loved my passion to need him, and that made me feel very special. After pulling me to my feet and us showering quickly, I touched up my make-up, unpinned my hair and re-dressed. My bags were now in his bedroom and he was ready to go.

I cannot tell you how exhilarating it felt to walk through the city hand in hand with him (particularly after what we had just done!). I caught our reflection in a couple of windows and found it hard to believe that it was me beside him – we did make a very nice couple. We shopped, Ethan insisted on buying me numerous items. He bought more casual clothing, I'd never seen someone spend so much in Harvey Nichols and Selfridges. I indulged in more underwear – which was a great shopping experience with Ethan. He kept whispering that he may need to leave the store soon as it was fast becoming embarrassing for him imagining me wearing certain items. My ego was getting the biggest boost it had seen for years!

Lunch was delightful; we shared a bottle of champagne and I found the time to ask him what my dad had whispered to him the day before after lunch and he smiled.

"He said that if I kept making you smile as much as you were at the moment, he would already consider me part of the family."

"Really? He said that? Bless him," I mumbled.

"It was a very fatherly thing say, I would like to think that I won't let him down," he then said.

"No chance of that," I smiled meaningfully and then we finished nibbling at our lunch.

Afterwards we walked and shopped some more, Ethan held my hand tightly. I couldn't stop myself glancing into the window of a jeweller's that had rings with diamonds big enough to buy an island in the Caribbean, I suspect. I'm sure that Ethan spotted me looking, but I instantly moved my hand to my neck to make sure that the necklace he had bought me was still there. When I turned to look at him he simply smiled.

Once we had done enough shopping and after realising that it was seven o'clock now as we sat at a very nice wine bar, I leant over and suggested that we go back to the hotel. Ethan looked at me curiously.

"Why?" he asked innocently. I curled my lips in nervously realising that sitting here with him looking so relaxed and remarkably hot, he had my pulse racing and I was getting those urges again. He laughed at my body language and took another sip of his wine, then leant across to me and whispered.

"If I am reading your thoughts correctly – you are needing my body right now?" he asked. Then he sat back and took another sip of wine like he was teasing me.

"I can wait..." I said trying to sound like I wasn't so desperate – it was actually slightly embarrassing how much I wanted him. I took a gulp of my wine. Ethan threw the remaining bit of his down his throat and then started to stand up.

"Well I cannot – I want you in that new underwear and in my bed ASAP!" he openly replied with confidence as he picked up all of the bags. I finished my wine and then grinned at him.

"Now I'm not feeling so desperate. I like this needy version of you," I remarked at his sudden urge to leave. He pushed me in front of him so that he could guide me to the door.

"Yes well, I'm starting to realise how deeply I'm addicted to you. If you walked away now I'd be in serious trouble," he quietly said as he walked behind me. I closed my eyes and smiled knowing that he couldn't see me. I think that was the sweetest thing that he had said to me yet. Without hesitation I stopped before we exited the door, turned to him and gave him the most sensuous quick kiss I could muster and then walked out of the door leaving him stunned for a second... Then he followed me.

Neither of us said anything, we just started walking back to the hotel, which wasn't that far. Our happy disposition was interrupted by Ethan's mobile ringing, which he apologised for but had to answer. It didn't take long to realise it was Josh. When he finished the call he told me he quickly needed to go to Josh's room and sign some documents that needed sending first thing tomorrow. Ethan must have told Josh that he didn't know where he would be in the morning and so Josh had decided to sort everything out this evening.

When we arrived in the busy reception area, Ethan handed me the bags and asked that I go to his suite while he ordered champagne and signed the necessary documents, then he promised to be with me as quickly as possible. I agreed, as I had thoughts of my own… bath, champagne, sex, get ready for dinner. The bath was running – I placed my new underwear on the bed in perfect view for when he returned, then the champagne arrived. I opened it and poured two glasses and took them to the bathroom and then went back to the lounge area and started to undress leaving him a trail of clothing to follow to where I was. Sinking into that warm bath was medicinal to my legs, which were now aching after lots of walking around. I sank my head back onto the edge of the ridiculously large bath and sighed… *bliss*.

I do think that I was almost nodding off when I heard the door to the suite close, I needed to wake myself up as he was back and so I slid completely under the bubbles hoping that the water would do just that. I held my breath for a few seconds and when I resurfaced Ethan was knelt with his arms resting on the edge waiting for me to re-appear.

"Room for two in there?" he asked as he brushed bubbles from my face. I pushed up kissing him on the lips.

"I would be very disappointed if you didn't join me," I smiled. Without hesitation he stood and took off his polo shirt, dropped his jeans to the floor and then with complete confidence dropped his boxers and climbed in behind me. I moulded myself into his chest and then passed him a glass of champagne. His other arm wrapped around my waist where he rested his hand on my stomach.

He sighed with contentment too and so I rested my other hand on his thigh which was muscular and taut. We lay there wallowing for a long time and almost finished the bottle of champagne before deciding to get out. With towels wrapped around us, I brushed through my wet hair and then turned to look at him. We didn't need words – we both had that longing look in our eye and so I dropped my towel and walked into him squeezing my chest tight against his. We moulded back into a divine embrace: the desperation we had felt earlier was no more – the frustration now gone, this was heaven itself. After expressing that I felt like I was walking on air, Ethan prompted me to get ready. Thinking ahead and obviously knowing my desire to have him so regularly, he had booked a table in the other restaurant of the hotel. So we dressed, had a drink in the bar that overlooked the city and then went to eat.

Our meal was out of this world, the wine flowing and by the time it was midnight I had no intentions of travelling home. I asked that we stay in his suite tonight, but suggested that he spend the day with me tomorrow and then stay at my house tomorrow night and he agreed without hesitation. Our evening in his room was intense and satisfying and being able to sleep with him holding me in his arms again was more fulfilling than I can say.

Monday rolled into Tuesday and I took him to meet Caroline at my shop. I had every intention of working for a while, but Caroline insisted I didn't. He was really interested in her ideas and threw in some of his own. Caroline, like everyone else, swooned in his presence and it made me proud to think that he was mine. He was never far away from either holding my hand, or placing his hand in the small of my back. We left there and had lunch at a bistro nearby, went for a walk, and then retreated back to my house at around five o'clock. I opened a bottle of wine and then we slumped onto the settee and put a film on. This was another unusual way for Ethan to spend some down time. His idea of relaxing when travelling on business was at the gym or drinks with Josh. It was lovely to snuggle up and just completely chill out.

When my small mantle clock chimed seven he asked if I would like to go out to dinner, but I was so happy with our little set up in my house that I asked if he fancied Chinese takeout instead. He nodded saying it had been a while since he had relaxed so much and enjoyed the delights of a take away and so in some small way, I felt like I had achieved another first for a long time with him. Rose had text me saying how much she was completely taken with Josh. Ethan read my text and smiled, then he commented that he was fairly certain that the feeling was mutual. The whole evening was thoroughly enjoyable for both of us so when it came to retiring, it didn't surprise me that making love twice in quick succession was anything out of the ordinary for us now.

"Do you think we will ever get tired of this?" I questioned as we lay there entwined beneath the sheets.

"That's not going to happen anytime soon for me," he replied and I gave him a little squeeze.

"Me neither," I confirmed. He rubbed my arm and then lifted my chin to look at him.

"I want to ask you something." His eyes were sparkling as he looked at me and my heart started racing a little as I had no idea what to expect.

"Anything."

"I have to leave on Friday and return to Rome – papers to sign, people to see," He explained. I felt a little sad, then he lifted my spirits. "Would you come with me?" he asked. I sat up sheet wrapped around me and faced him.

"Really? You want me to join you on a business trip?" I asked again checking that I had understood him correctly. He nodded.

"It's fine if you don't want to or you need to be here for your business. It's just, well, I cannot seem to think straight when we're not together and I would really like you to come and explore Rome with me. It's only for a week," he then started explaining as if he was trying to justify his reason for asking me. I felt a huge grin appear on my face and then I lunged at him, kissing him first before resting my head on his chest. I hugged him with a ferociousness that I think surprised him. "Is that a yes?" he asked chuckling to himself.

"I can't covey words to tell you how happy I would

be to accompany you. I just feel that I would distract you, or be too wanting, or I don't know… perhaps be just annoying?" I tried to say, but my speed talking and over excitement gave away my absolute delight at being asked. He took a hold of my face and pulled me in for another kiss.

"If you manage all of those things I will work more efficiently than I have in years – which Josh will love!" he said it with a hint of sarcasm. "So you'll come?"

"Yes, yes… I will come. I am elated that you even asked me because I hate being parted from you too. I can leave Caroline in charge," I quickly told him as I organised things in my head.

"That's good. We could talk about our trip altogether and discuss where you would like to take James and Mark and their girlfriends. It could be quite a productive trip," he then insisted.

"That's a great idea… but I am hoping that we will have spells of not talking too often!" I joked. He knew exactly what I meant and he started laughing at my passion for him.

"Right – I will let Josh know you will be joining us. You never know he may ask Rose," he then said. I gave him a look of surprise that he was relaxing into a whole new world of having others around him. "What?" he asked noting my surprised look.

"I don't want myself and Rose distracting you two from business. Likewise, I don't want Josh thinking that I am trying to have everything with you by not letting him have Rose there," I tried to explain.

"Hey, don't you worry about that. He really likes Rose – if I make the offer for her to come along and he wants her there, he will ask her," he explained. I suddenly realised how much those two knew about each other, not just in business.

I started to drift off to sleep feeling Ethan's chest rise and fall as I lay in his arms. I tried to imagine accompanying him on more regular business trips. He made me feel extremely special to him and as I imagined us visiting the Coliseum, the Vatican and so much more, I sank into a deep slumber.

Chapter 27

Friday arrived faster than I could blink. After arranging work and finding out that Rose was joining us, I was ecstatic about our trip to Rome. We went to the airport together; Josh as always had sorted all the travel arrangements and so it was fairly straightforward for Rose and me. We were travelling lightly – I wasn't taking my entire wardrobe. After talking to Beth the day before we travelled, she gave me quick tips on a capsule wardrobe to help with packing. I took her advice and felt that I had enough with me. I used to panic if I didn't try and cover all weather options – but let's face it, the shopping in Italy would be far more fun should I have forgotten something.

Even though Ethan and Josh had work commitments, we managed to spend four whole days with them, sightseeing, eating great food and drinking fine wine. It was lovely knowing that Rose and Josh were as infatuated with each other as we were. It made for a very enjoyable trip for everyone and even Ethan commented numerous times that work was so much more tolerable with me around. Josh was quick to add that Ethan had been far more productive than the previous trip without me which made me taunt him a little but I think he enjoyed it! Josh tried to make a point of insisting that no business trip was worth considering now without me accompanying them – and that thought made me very happy.

Rome did not disappoint in any way – I loved it here. Ethan's hotel was not huge in size but it had a great impact visually among the centre of all of the historical places to visit. He informed me that this one was the biggest cost to run with consistent maintenance, mainly due to its age, I assumed – but it was stunning and we had suites on the top floor. They highlighted how beautiful Rome was when looking from our balcony. He pointed out that although it was beautiful, it would be more productive for him to sell and get something that was easier to maintain.

We managed, while lying in bed one evening, to talk about where we should go with James and Mark and Ethan suggested a lovely stay on the Amalfi Coast in his hotel that was on the Cliffside. It was the perfect place to relax, with plenty to do if wanted – but he insisted that the views were spectacular. He had it sold to me in seconds and I assured him that the boys would be delighted. I was happy to be going anywhere as long as Ethan was with me. Everything seemed to be falling perfectly into place and my life seemed well and truly back on track – in fact so on track it was like I was a different person entirely. When it came to leaving, I felt sad to be going home and from the most beautiful city that I think I had ever visited. Rose agreed how stunning everything was; it had been a long time since she last came here, but… she made a promise to do it again soon.

On returning home and walking back into my house, I looked around and sighed. Maybe it was time for me to downsize a little? If I was going to be travelling with Ethan more regularly it was going to be another thing to manage. He noted my look of concern and when I ran it by him he told me that there was no need to worry about that for now. It would be something he would help me with in the future, if I would want to do that, and so I put it to the back of my mind for now. Ethan stayed with me for three days and then had to go to the stunning Cote d'Azur, where he had another fairly new hotel, it never ceased to amaze me how he just lived out of a suitcase most of the time. I had text the boys to suggest our week's trip away on the Amalfi Coast, and suggested that their next break at university was probably an appropriate time. So everything was arranged for October. They said that they would check with Emma and Charlotte but they were sure they would agree to go.

Our three days seemed to fly by. Once he had gone again it was a relief a couple of days later to see the girls on an evening out. All of our usual everyday mundane problems seemed to be apparent again, with only Rose and me feeling a little more confident with our current situation after our recent trip. Mum and Dad were well and happy for me. They said that the trip away together with the boys was a great idea. Dad congratulated Ethan on his sensitivity at trying to help his grandsons accept that my life now included him; he was so impressed with Ethan's complete dedication to their wellbeing.

The following few weeks had me seeing Ethan in small bursts when he wasn't away. He was trying to get everything arranged early so that he could have the whole week with us in Italy. I spent four days with him in London at the hotel that had started everything for his father. I think that one had a sentimental attachment for him. Josh had commented to Rose that this was the first time in all the time that he had worked for Ethan, that he had ever known him agree to take a complete 'holiday' and he said that it was a good thing as his work was demanding.

By the time October arrived and the trip away was the next day, both Ethan and I knew that we were going to be together for a long time and so this 'trip' had now become very important to both of us. Mark and James had met Ethan again when he was at our house on a visit home one weekend. They both agreed that having him staying there was not a problem. It pleased me more than ever that they had somehow accepted that we slept in the same bed, and they were okay with it. It probably helped as they had brought Emma and Charlotte with them and there was no way that I was going to try and separate them! Charlie, as she liked to be called, was great for Mark. She had an ability to calm his excitement with a simple look and I found that rather amusing.

It was good to be able to all meet before the trip: if the last time we all were together was anything to go by, then we should be in for one hell of a holiday. I had a few nerves – Rose, Beth and Amanda had managed to ease them on a night out, telling me that this was meant to be. I was glad for their support and they made it clear they wanted to hear all about it on my return.

The travelling there together was calm and easy and perfectly planned. Ethan had arranged some very nice convertible cars for us, thinking that James and Mark may want to take Emma and Charlie out, so having one each was thinking way ahead. The boys were more than happy, I can tell you!

We took walks together, visited numerous historical places and vineyards. We went to the beach, took a trip on a speedboat – which pleased the boys immensely especially as they got to steer. Ethan took us to restaurants, we played chess and relaxed… just soaking up this atmosphere together was completely fulfilling. Ethan had the boys playing cards for money with him, which was amusing for the girls to watch. He also had the opportunity to talk about business with them while he sent us girls to the spa, and was more open with them than I think that they were expecting, but I know that they appreciated it none the less.

Everything was going so smoothly and we laughed a lot together, enjoying every moment. Ethan had spared no cost; he'd thought of everything and more, and that alone showed his eagerness to please us all. I loved him so much for that. Somehow my birthday had fallen in the middle of the week while we were away and so when Ethan confirmed that we were all eating at his favourite restaurant to celebrate, I knew it was going to be an exceptional evening.

We arrived at eight after drinks and were promptly shown to our table. Charlie and Emma had commented how lovely I looked and that was flattering as they were both young and gorgeous. The meal was amazing, James, Mark and Ethan got along famously. When he told James that he could shadow him with management decisions for part of his course and that he would try to mentor him, James was both overwhelmed and over the moon. I kissed Ethan on the cheek in appreciation, my hand had rested on his thigh most of the evening and so he took it in his and squeezed it – I reciprocated, acknowledging my gratitude.

We finished our main courses and then from nowhere champagne arrived and desserts decorated with a birthday theme, along with a very lovely girl who played 'Happy Birthday' on her violin. I was sung to by all of them and I embraced the whole experience, because right there around that table the most important people in my life were sat with me. I looked at them all in turn and when they finished James raised his glass.

"To the best mum in the world, who has had to endure more than most, but who is also happier now than we can ever remember. We love you, Mum," he said and I welled up a little but managed to reply.

"Thanks, darling."

We took a sip then Mark added, "We even love you when you're ridiculously drunk!" He proceeded to start laughing, as he was hinting at the game of cocktails or nothing that they made me play with them the other night. Ethan laughed too.

"She's good at it." he added and I elbowed him in the ribs. I scowled at them all, then we all fell silent when Ethan raised his glass and said he would like to toast me. He looked into my eyes and then started;

"Jen, you are the most kind-hearted, warm and

generous woman I have ever met. You've opened my eyes to living again and I cannot imagine a day without you now. So I wish you lots of love and happiness on your birthday and I hope that this is the first of many that I get to share with you... To an amazing woman," he finished, as he raised his glass and all of the others joined him. I kissed him after taking a sip, while the others just smiled at us.

"I think that this is one of the best birthdays that I have ever had. I love you all, and I thank you for being here and making it so very special. I am one very happy woman," I told them. We all drank again and then James and Mark came around the table and kissed me on the cheek before handing a box to me that was wrapped very neatly. Before they walked away they both shook Ethan's hand and I knew with that gesture that everything was going to be just fine.

The box had two items within it. One was a very beautiful Italian picture frame that I had seen in a window when we were walking. I was shocked that they had returned to buy it. There was also a beautiful personalised cream leather journal. I wasn't expecting presents but these were beautiful. Mark looked across at me as I inspected them.

"So, Mum. We figured with the journal that it was about time that you started writing about these fantastic trips that you are going to be sharing with Ethan. The picture frame is for a new picture to start that journey – so huddle close you two, let's get one," he said, gesturing for me and Ethan to get closer together as he held up his camera.

I mimed, "Thank you," to them and as Ethan's arm found its way around my waist pulling me closer.

He whispered in my ear, *Perfect*. Mark snapped the camera a couple of times and both Charlie and Emma made little noises hinting that they found the whole thing very sweet. When he had taken around four we released each other. I went around to them both and gave them a huge hug. I was more than overwhelmed. "Be happy, Mum," they both said, returning my hug with a bigger one from themselves. When I sat back down Ethan then handed me a box, a small rectangular one – but the name on the front gave it away: 'De Beers'. I gulped. I was pretty sure it wasn't a ring – he wouldn't rush me into a decision like that – but whatever it was it was going to be expensive.

I clicked open the box and then gasped when I saw the beautiful earrings inside. They were a beautiful unusual design of diamond and white gold. Like stars that shone in the night they sparkled, and after taking in their beauty I looked at him.

"You light up my life, Jenny – I want these to make you dazzle everyone like you do to me every day." he said. I swallowed hard and tried to fight back tears of joy, but one escaped my eye and ran down my cheek.

"You light up mine too," I replied softly. "They're beautiful, thank you." I kissed him firmly on the lips. When we parted he wiped the tear from my eye and smiled at me. I laughed at the realisation that we had just experienced that moment with an audience. So I looked at them.

The girls were swooning with delight. James was grinning and then started to clap. Mark joined in and then said; "Man, you're going to have to give me some lines, Ethan. You've got all of these women eating out of the palm of your hand!" I laughed at his remark, but Ethan just blushed and shrugged like it was something that he found so natural. It seemed with me he did.

I took out the other earrings that I had worn for years and replaced them with these new beautiful ones that meant a great deal in an instant. Everyone commented that they looked amazing and I felt so very fortunate. While we had our champagne flutes refilled, a gentleman walked over to our table and whispered in Ethan's ear. He then stood and looked at us all.

"We need to move to the balcony for a moment," he stated, and with curiosity we all agreed.

Glasses in hand, Ethan prompted us to look up to the sky and within seconds of doing so a multitude of fireworks started. They resembled my earrings sparkling in the sky. I leaned into Ethan and then kissed him on the cheek.

"I love you," I told him quietly. He turned and faced me.

"I know – I love you too." And then under a sky full of bursting fireworks he kissed me delicately holding my face in his hands. When we parted he tucked my hair behind my ears and then smiled. He was looking at my earrings, and I was watching him. He kissed the tip of my nose and then turned my face back to the sky and as we all stood there and watched the biggest display we had ever seen, we were silent, stunned but so very content – my life had such new meaning.

I always knew that one day, after everything I had endured, I would start to feel differently – and now I am different and I have changed. There are constant things in our life that we are very grateful for: family, friends, partners, husbands and wives, children, our jobs, our home… our health. Then there are things that leave us feeling completely hopeless, things that are out of our control and leave us wondering how we will ever survive. But one thing that I do know is that we do survive, and good things can still happen… even late in the game. As hard as that is to believe, remarkably it's true – you just have to be willing to try. For me, life at forty-four, I can assure you, is unbelievably amazing and it's all thanks to those wonderful women in my life – my best friends – and one outrageous holiday. I couldn't ask for anything more right now, nor do I want to. I have, in a single moment standing here hand in hand with Ethan while alongside my sons, realised that I have everything I now need to be truly happy again. Ethan has given me back the confidence to believe in myself and live each day with enthusiasm and enjoyment. He's taught me that true love can happen more than once in a lifetime – and for me, that is more than enough.

Acknowledgements

I can recount so many times with the girls, where I nearly died laughing. There have been hundreds of humorous incidents that have left memories for me to cherish. We always seem to pick up where we left off, there is never any question that our friendships are lifelong. So the inspiration for this book, my second novel, is entirely from these remarkable friendships that I have with my girlfriends. I would not have been able to write so much of this if I did not have you in my life. So thank you all – you know who you are! I hope that this novel helped you to laugh a little more.

My family – who give me such encouraging support and reasons to keep writing. Thank you for continuing to support me on my new and exciting journey, it is lovely to share it with you.

Troubador my publishers – I love working with you all, you are the best team of people that I have had the pleasure to work with on both books. Again I owe you my thanks for your help, encouragement, expertise and dedication. I hope that I have the pleasure of working with you again.

I cannot end these acknowledgements without thanking so many other writers, who produce such amazing work for us all to escape into. Particularly those works which are turned into some of the most iconic films. I definitely would not be the same person if I had not had the pleasure of experiencing some of the well-loved films that we would find it hard to live without today. They have become a unique way of connecting so many people, that too is something very special.

Special acknowledgment to the following films;

"Hitch, Screenplay by Kevin Bisch"
"Pretty Woman, Screenplay by J F Lawton"
"Dirty Dancing, Screenplay by Eleanor Bergstein"

Also by the Same Author...

A Different Reflection

"The storytelling felt fresh and unique with some interesting plot devices that added plenty of twists to the narrative... I also enjoyed how the relationships in the story highlighed different aspects of Kat's personality.

· She has a warm friendship with the elderly George, who is like the father she never had. In contrast, her friendship with the fun loving Claire allows us to see Kat's wild side.

With boyfriend John, its all about her vulnerability and unwillingness to leave her comfort zone, whereas with James, she can truly be herself. Kat is a delightful protagonist and we want her to get the happy ending she deserves."

The Bookbag Review